TO
BURNI

Alan Gould was born in London in 1949 of English-Icelandic parents and lived on Armed Forces camps in England, Northern Ireland, Germany and Singapore before coming to Australia in 1966. He holds an Arts degree from the Australian National University and has had various jobs including nuclear physics technician and agricultural labourer. Since 1975 he has written poetry and fiction, augmenting his income with literary journalism and teaching. Of his five volumes of poetry, the second, *Astral Sea*, won the 1981 NSW Premier's Prize for Poetry, while his first novel, *The Man Who Stayed Below*, received the Foundation of Australian Studies Award for Best Book of the Year in 1985. His most recent books have been a collection of novellas, *The Enduring Disguises*, and volumes of poetry, *Years Found in Likeness*, *Formerlight* and *Momentum*.

TO THE
BURNING CITY

Alan Gould

Minerva

A Minerva Paperback

TO THE BURNING CITY

First published in Great Britain 1993
by Minerva
an imprint of Reed Consumer Books Ltd
Michelin House, 81 Fulham Road, London SW3 6RB
and Auckland, Melbourne, Singapore and Toronto
First published 1991
by William Heinemann Australia

Copyright © Alan Gould 1991

A CIP catalogue record for this title
is available from the British Library
ISBN 0 7493 9723 3

Printed and bound in Great Britain
by Cox & Wyman Ltd, Reading, Berks

For Marta Langridge, 1920–1990

Acknowledgements

I would like to thank various people and institutions who provided me with help in some of the research for this book: Gudrun Papak and Heidi Watson of the Goethe Institute, Brian Ridley and John White at the Australian War Memorial, Group Captain Roy Colman of the British High Commission, Max Badham, and Major Richard Gould.

I would also like to thank Anne Langridge, Philip Mead, Geoff Page and Les Murray for reading the work in manuscript and making many helpful suggestions, as well as the English Department of the Australian Defence Forces Academy for clerical assistance.

I further express my gratitude to the Literature Board of the Australia Council and the Lincolnshire and Humberside Arts Council for fellowships during part of the period in which this book was written.

Contents

PART ONE

BROTHER
HALF-BROTHER

Len 1941–44

You can remember, he thought, a place or a time being full of light, yet it can *feel* dark.

He woke and found himself staring past the white mound of his pillow toward the window. Somewhere he could hear a cuckoo. His eyes were watering, as they sometimes did when he first awoke, so he remained still, allowing a droplet to form at the corner of his eye and roll onto his cheek. Then he turned his head and allowed it to flow back floodingly into the eye. The sensation was mildly enjoyable. He was hungry, particularly so, even though he had become used to the vague sensation in his tummy that he had never eaten quite as much as he wanted. But he also had a sense of joyful anticipation, all the more delicious for not being able to remember immediately what it was that was due to happen today.

The other boys appeared to be still asleep, though the sun was streaming almost horizontally through the dormitory's one tall window, and making the crisscrossing of the stickytape shine with a yellow translucency. The stickytape, Len knew, was in case of bombs.

He had once heard the bombs. At least he thought he had. Indeed, it was about the first thing he thought he could remember and it was ages ago, an entire summer and winter, maybe more. It was before he had come to the school when he was still living with Mumma. He had woken to find her in his bedroom in the dark. She had lifted him from the bed and was hurriedly pulling a jersey over his head and telling him to be quick. She had put gumboots on him because it was quicker than tying shoes. There was a wailing which, he was told, was the siren. They went through a gap in the wicket fence to the shelter at the bottom of the next-door garden. Mumma carried him down the steps into the dark small space. He bumped his head on the corrugated iron of the roof. There was no light and a smell of Oxo, and he could hear the next-door people shuffling and talking to themselves. Someone gave Mumma a white cup with hot Oxo in it and she gave him some sips of the scalding, salty liquid. A man had said 'Hark' — the boy distinctly remembered the word — whereupon the talking and shuffling stopped as everyone listened.

Len heard another sound which was not the siren, which was above him and yet somehow also around him. It was not a groan or a whine exactly, though it contained a bit of both. He could imitate the sound if he made an uuurrrrh sound continuously. It was the bombers, which were sometimes also called the Germans. The uuurrrh seemed to grow out of the sound of the siren, get louder, though never very loud, then fade back into the siren's wail again. In the middle there was, very far off, banging and thumping, a bit like the sound of someone thwacking the carpet on a clothesline with a beater, only quieter and stronger at the same time. These were the bombs, Mumma said.

As he lay now in his bed he couldn't quite recall whether he had in fact heard them only once, or many times. Bombs, he had been told, were very dangerous: they broke houses and caused fires; they hurt people and sometimes made them dead. For this reason he was taken to the shelter and made to sit in the dark as these mysterious things thumped distantly around him. Yet there was part of him which preferred to be out in the open where he could witness for himself what these things were which fell from the sky and caused such miraculous transformations. He had seen pictures on the front of the newspaper, of course, and recently from the dormitory window he had seen a faint glow which divided the black earth from the black sky. This was Ipswich, the docks, Miss Leverton said; Ipswich was burning, and the Germans were wicked, *wicked*.

'What's "wicked" mean?' Len asked her as she stood by the window surrounded by a dozen or so boys.

'Wicked is when someone is very, very, very naughty,' she replied. 'When they are naughty on purpose,' she added.

Some of the older boys in the dormitory had also heard the bombs and the bombers, and they claimed to have heard the sound so frequently that they could tell the difference in the uuurrrrh sound between a Heinkel, a Dornier and a Junkers. Sometimes, in the evenings, Len had sat on the grass with some of these boys when they were 'plane-spotting'.

'It's a Lancaster.'

'Stirling.'

'It's a Hallybag.'

'*Lann-caster.*'

Now the boy lay, waiting for the sound of matron ringing the bell which was the signal for them all to get up. Today was Saturday. On the previous night, just after lights out, Miss Leverton had come into the dormitory and, approaching his bed, had leant down and whispered in his ear. 'I've just spoken to your father on the telephone, Leonard. He's going to come and see you tomorrow afternoon. So you must be an extra special good boy, mustn't you?' The torch she was carrying highlighted the fleshy ridges of her cheeks and the underneath of her chin, making her look ghastly, though she was really quite nice.

Or comfortable, rather. For instance, on his first day at the school just after his fourth birthday, he had come up with Mumma on the train; there was dread in the pit of his stomach the whole time because he knew what was going to happen. Mumma helped him unpack his things and put them in the locker beside his bed. Then she had a cup of tea in Miss Leverton's study. All the time the boy knew the moment was approaching. Then Mumma stood up, quickly kissed him on the cheek and went out, shutting the door behind her. He stared at the closed door. There were coats and scarves hanging on hooks, black and grey, empty and saggy. He didn't try to follow Mumma because she had told him that he shouldn't and it wouldn't do any good. So he stood there bleakly, not crying, but staring at the limp coats and scarves through his watery eyes. He knew that he had to be brave, like his dad who was in the airforce, and he was anxious lest the water in his eyes should brim over, in which case, he supposed, he would be technically crying and Miss Leverton would probably say something stern to him. If she did, he knew he would not be able to stop himself because — because it was all so hopeless, and he would feel so ashamed of himself for not being able to be brave like his dad.

But Miss Leverton rescued him from his watery eyes. She took an apple from a bowl, peeled it, dipped it in the sugar basin, and gave him the pieces. They were frosty, shockingly delicious. And when the first apple was finished, she peeled another and gave him that.

'Whatever other shortages there may be, there's plenty of yellow apples up in our roof,' she said

Len watched as she peeled the apple so that all the skin came off in one long piece. It was mesmerising.

'You could hang it on a Christmas tree, couldn't you?' she said, holding the spiral of peel up.

She was stout and her bottom seemed to stick out when she walked, but she had a round, kindly face which was divided in two horizontally by the dark frames of her glasses. The boys called her Waddle Twaddle, which aggrieved Len. Maybe she did waddle, but it was still unfair.

This would be only the second time his dad had managed to visit him in the eight months or so Len had been at the school. Mother — she was 'Mother' now, 'Mumma' had been discouraged — had come up from High Wycombe a few times, once in her WRAF uniform. Usually they went to a teashop in Ipswich, then walked up and down the Buttermarket and Tavern Street, looking into the almost empty windows of the shops. Later they would walk around the grounds of the school and out into the fields. Len told her about Lancasters and Stirlings and Halleybags.

'What's a Hallybag?' she asked.

'Handley Page Halifax,' he supplied immediately, and reeled off bits of technical information about speed and the number of machine-gun turrets.

Once he had wanted to show her where the elder boys had their dens, which he, as a four-year-old, was prohibited from entering. He was allowed to stand near them, but if the elder boys ever caught him or any of the other 'tiddlers' inside, they would stake them out and put stag beetles inside their mouths. So they had told him. Nevertheless, Mother and he set out across the fields, only to be forced to return on account of Mother's shoes.

On her last visit they had taken a bus trip to Felixstowe, and walked along the pebbly shoreline. He saw a bombed house in Felixstowe. It was queer, the way in which the houses on either side of it were intact while the bombed house was all tumbled, and so untidy, with its broken bricks and rafters. And you could look right inside; it was like a cutaway. He supposed it was rather rude to look right into a person's house just because a bomb had collapsed the front of it, but it was irresistible. You could see the smashed crockery, and a picture which still hung, skewiff on a grimy wall.

But apart from the pebbly beach and the quiet long waves on the shingle which withdrew with a drawn-out sssshhhh, Felixstowe didn't seem to be much different from Ipswich, and his legs ached from all the walking. He loved his mother being there and he wished she could stay, of course, but he always seemed to run out of things to say to her, and there were periods when they walked along in silence while he racked his brains for something new to tell her. This had never happened when they had been living together. When she eventually left on the bus, Len was filled with the sense of lost opportunity.

It was his mother who wanted him to go to the school so she could do 'war work', whatever that was. His father had come back to their home in London late one night. He entered Len's bedroom and woke the boy, and they talked to each other in excited whispers. His dad was wearing uniform and as he tucked Len back into his bed he said, 'Jiminy, we'll have some fun tomorrow,' and the boy watched as his father bowed his head beneath the doorway and creaked down the narrow stairs.

But somehow the fun was postponed. The following morning, while they were sitting at the breakfast table, Dad said to Len, 'Tell me what you would prefer, Lennie boy. Would you prefer to be evacuated, or would you prefer to go to a school?' This morning his father was wearing what he called 'mufti', open-necked shirt and short-sleeved jersey. He had finished eating the pale yellow, watery scrambled egg and was lighting a cigarette. Somehow the thin trail of smoke from the end of the cigarette emphasised the lean tallness of the man.

'The poor child hasn't a clue what being evacuated means,' his mother said.

His dad gave his mother one of his twinkling looks and then said, 'Would you prefer to go and live with another family in the country, on a farm perhaps where there will be animals, horses and chickens and cows? Or would you prefer to go to a school where there will be other boys like you?'

'I want to come with you,' Len replied.

'Ah, *mon cher*, I live in a nasty, poky barrack along with lots of other men. It's really not the place.'

'Charl, if we've decided that Len's to be evacuated anyway, he might as well be getting on with his schooling at the same time.'

'The farmyard's as good a school as any,' his dad replied, rather shortly.

'I want to be with Dad. I want to be with Dad.'

'Oh, don't I come into the picture?' his mother said, a little put out.

This made Len stop and think. 'You come too. We'll all live in Dad's barrack.'

But he had been sent to the school.

Now, in the dormitory, there were signs that some of the other boys were waking up; a conversation had started somewhere, and someone had gone into the washrooms and turned on a tap.

He would show his dad where the dens were, the boy

decided, as he heard the sound of the bell ringing from high in the roof where matron lived.

2

Miss Leverton made him polish his shoes with Dubbin, and of course he managed to get some over his fingers. He had to comb down his hair with water and put on his grey serge jacket, a tie, and the black school cap, the peak of which came down over his eyes; he had to tilt his head in order to see. Then he waited at the main entrance of the school.

Waiting was terrible. He heard the sound of the duty monitors clearing away the tables, and a clanking from the kitchens as the scullery maids did the washing up. Every time there was the sound of a car he ran out into the driveway to see if it was his dad's, but it was always something else, a delivery van or someone else's parents. He sat on the step and grownups went in and out, saying to him each time they passed, 'What, still here?' or 'Hasn't your dad turned up *yet*?' He felt like blaming his dad, only he knew he mustn't. 'We must make allowances, Len,' Matron had said last time his dad was late. 'Your father has *such* an important job, being a flier.'

The scullery maids left, the school building fell silent. He waited. Would Dad never come?

He came, driving a black car and dressed in his uniform.

'My dear old fellow. I've kept you waiting for ages. I am a beast.' He picked Len up and held him, then put him down again and appraised him. 'Jiminy, but you've grown. Let's have this cap off so we can see that noble forehead.'

'I'm supposed to wear the cap when I go out,' Len demurred

'What, and cover up that candid brow! Tell you what. I'll ditch this,' he said, taking off his forage cap, 'if you ditch yours. Then, if we're caught, we'll *both* be in the guardhouse. What do you say?'

'All right.' It felt good to be in this little act of rule-breaking together, for it had happened before, both on his dad's previous visits to the school and when the two of them had sided conspiratorially against Mother in some little act of domestic defiance. His dad had the knack of giving Len the confidence that they would get away with things, making the boy feel exhilarated and safe.

His dad ruffled his hair, then pitched both caps into the back seat. 'Hop in,' he called, and they were off.

'Borrowed the car from Leo. He's my skipper and comes from Australia, like your mum.'

Hedges, fields of green wheat or barley flashed by; white and purple flowers glimmered momentarily at the corners of Len's vision as they discussed aeroplanes.

'Are Lancasters better than Stirlings?'

'My word! The Lanc's a dream. Better top speed, better ceiling, better bomb-load.'

'Do you mean ceiling like the ceiling in a house?'

'Got it in one! Only this kind of ceiling is way way up above the clouds. As high as a plane can fly. Lancs can fly higher than Stirlings.'

'What do you fly?'

'Lancs. Re-equipped with them after Christmas. Though I'm not really the chap who flies the plane. That's Leo, our pilot.'

'What do you do?'

'Well, I sit in a little bubble in the front and see that the bomb-load falls on the right place.'

'A bubble?'

'Well, a tiny little room with a big round perspex window and various instruments. It feels like being in a bubble, because there's not much room for a chap my size. I squeeze into my bubble, lie on my tummy and look down at what's below.'

'I wish I could have a go at lying in a bubble like that.'

'Do you, old fellow?' His dad gave him a kind, momentarily sad look.

But it was grand to contemplate being in a bubble far above the earth looking down on fields and villages and towns. It would give you such . . . command over them. They stopped in a village where there was a small lake and a jetty to which a number of rowing boats were tied.

'Come on, Lanx,' called his dad. They paid a man some money and rowed out onto the lake. 'You take one of the oars. That's it. Whoops.' They spun round in circles as Len tried to manage the large pole. 'All right, together now. Heave!' In crazy and uneven spurts they rowed out to the middle of the water, then rested on their oars. His dad took a bar of chocolate from his pocket, broke it into pieces and laid it on the thwart. 'Tuck in, Old Lanxie.' Chocolate, boiled sweets, cigarettes, his dad always seemed to have plenty of these things, unlike his mother, or other parents Len had met. They shared the chocolate and his dad smoked cigarettes, and they talked about Lancs and Stirlings and Halifaxes, about airscrews and undercarriage, rudders and ailerons, hydraulics and Merlin engines.

'You've got to get those four screws so they're sounding absolutely sweet.'

'What's that mean?'

'So they sing with one voice, so you can't hear the difference between one and the other. That's the flight engineer's job.'

His dad could explain anything, *anything*. The sun fell warmly on their backs and Len watched as the wet pools on the thwarts shrank inwards quickly in the heat. They allowed the current to take the boat where it would, and they were rarely approached by other boats. Eventually they returned to the shore and found a teahouse where they had buns. 'Let's have another, come on, one of the expensive ones.' Then, in the yellowy late afternoon light they returned to the school.

'Do you want to see the dens?' asked the boy.

'Lead the way, old man.'

'We won't be able to go inside because tiddlers are forbidden.'

'I see.'

They tramped across the fields to the hedges where the dens were. To Len's disappointment some of the older boys were already there. He hung back.

'We're not supposed to go even near when the older boys are there,' he explained.

'I don't see why not. Come on.' So they approached the group and the various tunnels into the hedge that lay behind them.

'Good evening, fellows,' his dad greeted them.

'Good evening, sir,' a unison of voices rejoined.

'You don't mind if we take a peek in there, do you?'

'We'll show you, sir,' said one of them, unabashed by the strange request, and apparently unconcerned that a tiddler would be accompanying them.

They all crawled on hands and knees into the thicket. In the middle of the hedge was a cavernous space and a dry earth floor with burrows in which Len could discern various tins and boxes.

'You're a flier, aren't you sir? I can tell by the wings,' said one of the boys, pointing to the insignia on his dad's tunic.

'Indeed I am, old chap, though before I joined the RAF I used to teach fellows like you a bit of French and German.'

'*Ger*-man?' chanted a chorus of voices.

So his dad became the centre of interest, talking, as he had done throughout the afternoon, about flying and different kinds of aeroplane. He was so tall, so huge, even the ten-year-olds looked small next to him.

'Here,' he said, lighting a second cigarette and giving it to one of the ten-year-olds to pass around, 'I know what boys get up to, and I don't suppose matron will find us out in here.' The boys took tentative puffs at the cigarette then passed it on, and spoke volubly from their store of knowledge about aircraft.

'Well, boys,' his dad said at last, 'I'm glad to think that Lennie is now one of the gang and can come into the cubby when he feels like it. Am I right?' The boys murmured their assent.

Len and the airman crawled out of the den and wandered back toward the school buildings. They ambled around the gardens, not talking much, then went inside and stood by one of the windows. The light that fell on the orchard was more orange than yellow now, like clear marmalade. The leaves and the small apples glimmered and the roofs of the building had a russety glow. The cuckoo was still calling from somewhere, like the time signal on the wireless. His dad looked out of the window as though he were searching for something.

Then he said, 'Well, bless me. Look up there. No, over there. It's a vapour trail. What's the aircraft do you reckon? A Yank, I'd say. Flying Fort or Liberator? What's your guess, old man?'

Len looked. Yes there was a vapour trail, silvery and remote in the evening sky. But he didn't try to identify the plane. Instead he listened. And he heard, as he had heard before, the telltale squeak of his dad's shoes as he tiptoed away across the wooden floor. He would not look round. Not yet. He waited a long time, until he heard in the distance a car start and drive off. Then he turned. Dad had left, and once again he had not said goodbye.

3

There were boys whose fathers got killed. This didn't happen often, but when it did someone you knew, someone you had been playing with only yesterday evening, in the schoolyard or down among the ferns, would emerge from Miss Leverton's study with a face that had turned the same blotchy pink colour as the Empire countries in the atlas. Miss Leverton or Matron would help them pack an overnight bag and drive them in the school car to the station where they were put onto a train which took them to their mothers. They would be gone for a fortnight or so, and then they would reappear in the classroom one day. They would act quite normal, a bit quieter at first. But they were different somehow, it was difficult to say exactly why.

Litchey had been like this, his pudding of a face looking even more bloated than normal, and the water sponging out of his eyes as he sat at breakfast before being taken to the train. And a year or so later, it was Coutts, with his blond fringe that bobbed over his eyes, his foxy face not looking at any of the boys who were standing around watching as he climbed into the car. He had looked so . . . so *frightened*.

In theory, it could happen to anyone, Len realised.

But it didn't happen to his dad. He wouldn't let it. He didn't know about the other boys, but he obeyed Miss Leverton's last instruction to them before turning off the light each evening: 'Now say your prayers, boys.' He always did.

With the result that he had come to an arrangement with God. So long as he never forgot to pray that God would keep his dad safe from the Germans, God would do so. If ever he did forget, then he would be exposing his dad to terrible risks. This was understood between him and God. It was a big responsibility because it relied on not missing one single night. But Len did it, every night of the war, his face turned into the pillow, his eyes shut, concentrating hard on trying, first to visualise God's face — it was a long face with a neat dark beard and moustache, and brown hair to the shoulder — and then putting his plea to God to keep his dad safe.

4

Once, this was just after Len's seventh birthday in October 1944, his dad came on a visit to the school with another airforce man. The man was shorter than his dad, with a reddish face, curly red hair and a moustache which had been teased out sideways and looked as if you could pull it off. It was, Len decided, not really his kind of face.

'Lanx, this is Wilf.' Then his dad cocked his head to one side. 'Ahem, I *should* of course say Squadron *Leader* Wilfred Corballis.' The two men clearly had some sort of under-standing which Len was not privy to, and for a moment he felt excluded. 'Wilf's one of the bigwigs on my base and,' he looked down at the gingery man who was grinning with some embarrassment, 'a chum of mine.'

'Are you a flyer, sir?'

'Well, I — '

'Wilf does what are called the de-briefings.'

'What are they?'

'He waits up until we get home very, very, late at night, then he listens to what we all have to say about our trip, and writes it down in his big book.'

'Oh.' If the man wasn't a flyer, then what was there to say?

'We've got a forty-eight-hour pass. We're on our way down to see Mother at High Wycombe. Thought we'd take you out to tea on the way.'

'Can I come down to see Mum too?'

His dad's brow became furrowed, and he looked across to his companion as though for help. 'Ah, it's mid-term, old thing,' he said at length. 'We can't just drag you away like that, I'm afraid.'

Len didn't argue, but looked stolidly at the gravel around his feet.

'*Allons*, we'll get some tea.' His dad began striding toward the car. Len remained staring at his shoes.

The man called Wilf came up and put his arm around his shoulders.

'Let's get some tea, Lennie. I want to hear all about your school.' The arm around his shoulders was embarrassing, but Len allowed himself to be guided to the car, where his dad had started the engine and was bawling out a song above the din of the motor.

> *I don't want to set the world on fire,*
> *I just want to start a flame in your heart.*

The tea was all right, and they went to the cinema afterwards, sitting near the back in the steeply tiered seats. There was a newsreel showing the Allied landings in Sicily more than a year before, and also hundreds of people working in an American factory making Mitchell bombers. Len was mystified by the way that the picture came onto the screen before the second curtain had been drawn aside. He wondered about the material used for the curtain. It seemed transparent and silky at the same time, fabulous and incomprehensible.

After the newsreel and a cartoon which Len found utterly babyish, but which caused both his father and the man called Wilf to laugh uproariously, there were two films, a Yank one about a stagecoach, and another one which he had been unable to follow exactly, but which involved a group of children, two of whom, a boy and a girl, were older and were in charge of the younger ones. The older boy was spiteful to the girl and the younger children, and he was forever doing dangerous things. In the end he swam too far out to sea and started drowning. Despite all the cruel things the older boy had done to her, the girl swam out, rescued him and gave artificial respiration, lifting and pumping the boy's shoulders for a long time. It was unclear whether she had been able to revive him. It was partly her bravery that impressed Len, but also the landscape, the white wastes of sand on which the children appeared so small, and the dark, infinitely vaster wastes of the sea where you could hardly see the drowning boy at all. The wind blew the thin cotton frocks and shirts of the children so they whipped and flapped in a frenzy, and the sadness of the ending made Len feel, well, sad of course, but sad in a way that he liked, that left him with a feeling of secretness and longing.

After the dark of the cinema, it was a surprise to discover that it was still quite light outside.

'Did you like the cartoons, Len?' the man Wilf asked.

'Yes, thank you.'

They drove back to the school through the fading daylight. His dad was silent, so Wilf tried to make conversation. 'When are the hols, old chap? I bet you're looking forward to that,' and when Len didn't respond, he repeated, 'Yes, my word, I bet you are.' When they parked in the driveway, Wilf stayed in the car while his dad took him to the main door.

'Now, turn round, old Lanx.' His dad turned him around so he was facing the interior of the school hall. He took a package out of one of the pockets of his tunic. 'Here.' He put the package into one of the pockets of Len's blazer. Then Len heard the rustle of another packet and felt it being put into the other pocket of his blazer. 'Now, when I count to five, you can open them, OK, old man?'

'OK.'

He heard his dad counting slowly, and each number receding in distance. When he reached five, Len heard the car start and the crackle of gravel. He did not look round. Instead, he felt in his pockets. In one of them, predictably enough, there was a bag of 'tuck', biscuits, chocolate, boiled sweets. In the other there were cylindrical things of different sizes. Cartridges, spent cartridges of various calibres. He recognised some of them. Pistol ammunition, .303 ammunition from the turret machine guns of a Lanc, some small cannon cases, perhaps from a fighter aircraft. A treasure trove! He went up to the dormitory. The other boys were at tea, so the room was in darkness. One by one in order of size Len placed the cartridge cases on top of his locker and gazed at them.

5

A week or so after the start of the summer term, the war ended. For days they had been waiting for it, listening to the broadcasts on the wireless. The French mistress would begin her lessons by saying, 'Well, any day now.'

Finally it came. Classes were cancelled. The boys were allowed to go into the village and join the people celebrating in the High Street. In the evening there was a bonfire, right in the middle of High Street! There were some tables with the odd plate of cakes on them, though by and large the food was not plentiful. Grownups, the men in shirtsleeves and braces, the women in housecoats and scarves around their hair, were dancing with linked arms and tipping bottles of beer to their lips. The boys from the school stood around in their caps. A big woman came swirling toward Len, grabbed him by his elbow with a 'Come along, my honey,' and drew him into the welter of bodies. Len could smell her beer and her sweat, and at one point felt panicky when he was crushed against her and could smell what he thought was soil and potatoes on her housecoat. Some boys started throwing cake around, and were reported. They were sent to see Miss Leverton who gated them until mid-term.

There were still the Japs to beat, of course, and it was just possible that his dad would have to go off and fight them. It was too early to allow his agreement with God to lapse.

6

Two years elapsed.

Something had been happening at home while he was away at the school. He would arrive there for the holiday and find strange people staying in the house, people whose clothes seemed too big for them, or too old like scarecrow clothes. They would sleep in the spare room and sometimes sit at the breakfast table. Mother would bang their plates down and his dad would look at her reproachfully. Some of the men would mutter to themselves. One or two tried to talk to Len, sitting on their haunches with their arms wrapped around their knees.

'Y'ever seen a badger, son?' asked one. 'Ask y'old man if yers can come for a tramp with Reckitts. Is'll show yer badgers.'

But the men never stayed long. One morning they would be gone and his dad and his mother would be having rows all day long.

Then, one holiday, he discovered that his dad no longer lived with Mother. He visited sometimes, coming through the back door in a dark tweedy coat in the middle of the morning when other fathers were at work, sitting and having a cup of tea. Mother would always remain standing when he was in the house, or moving about the kitchen, folding things, putting things away, being busy on matters that didn't seem important. Len was often told to go and play in the garden. On those occasions when he overheard their conversation, all the things that his dad and Mother talked about seemed to concern arrangements and were said in short sentences. They never smiled. His dad always went away again before evening. Mother wanted something called a divorce and had gone to the courts to ask.

The man called Wilf used to call. He was still in the airforce, and drove down from his station. He would take Len and his mother out to tea, or to the pictures. From the pocket of his greatcoat he would pull a wad of comics — *The Beano*, *The Beezer*, *The Topper* — and hand them to Len.

'That should keep you going.'

'Thank you.'

It was difficult. He liked the comics, and read all of them from cover to cover. Because he liked them he supposed he was grateful. But he didn't *feel* grateful; in fact he felt that he would prefer not to feel grateful to the gingery man who had been getting a little plumper since the end of the war.

Once he stood at the drawing-room door and watched his mother and the gingery man together. She was twisting one of his curls around her little finger while she talked to him in a teasing, laughing voice. It was a long time since the boy could recall her in that kind of voice. She had been unhappy, Len knew, but he felt aggrieved that it should be the gingery man who had managed to get her to laugh again. He observed how she gave the curl a playful pull when she wanted to emphasise something she was saying, at which the man, Wilf, yelped with enjoyment. He went crimson when he saw Len at the door and jumped to his feet immediately.

'Hah, so there you are, old chap.'

On other occasions he would pull his moustaches out, then lurch around the room pretending to be Long John Silver with a wooden leg. It was ridiculous. What was he trying to prove?

'Do you think you would grow to like Uncle Wilf?' asked his mother.

'I suppose.' He didn't know what to say to Mother. All he knew was that she was moving in a direction he didn't want. There was that word 'uncle', for instance. It had crept into use without his having any control over the matter. How come the gingery man was suddenly an uncle? He wasn't a proper uncle. Len knew he didn't have any uncles. There was an Aunt Peg in Australia whom he had never met. And there was his dad's sister, his Aunt Eva, of course.

He spent some of his holidays with Aunt Eva, who lived in Norfolk. He could see more of his dad when he stayed with her. He gathered that his grandparents had both recently died. This didn't affect the boy much as he had hardly known them.

'You be company to your aunt, Len,' said Mother, as she saw him off on the train. 'She's a bit sad now that both Gramp and Gran have passed on.'

'Is Dad sad too?'

'I imagine he might be.'

The whistle blew and Mother waved until the train had gone round a curve and he couldn't see her any more.

After one such holiday, Len discovered that Mother had married Wilf and moved into a house he had bought.

'Now, Len,' she knelt down to his height and looked him in the eye. 'No one is going to say that Wilf is your —

your *first* father. But you must become used to the idea that he is your *second* father, and that he is going to help me look after you.'

'When will I see my real dad?'

Mother looked at the floor and didn't say anything for a moment. When she spoke, her voice sounded tired.

'I can't answer that, Len dear. It's up to him. Often, I hope.'

And after another such holiday, the boy discovered that his mother had had a baby. The birth took him unawares. He supposed he had been told that she was expecting. Wilf had picked him up from the railway station at the end of term and though he'd said nothing about babies on the car trip home, he had kept on giving sideways looks and kind of beaming. Then, as he hefted Len's trunk into the house, he turned at the kitchen door and gave him a lurid wink as if to prepare him for a surprise. When he came into the drawing room and saw his mother sitting under a standard lamp with a white, seal-shaped object on her lap, her head down in absorbed attention, Len was genuinely startled.

'You've got a lovely little brother,' exclaimed Wilf, stroking the brow of the ugly, purse-eyed, miniscule thing.

Then, not long after this, Mother and the baby went away because Wilf was posted to somewhere called Aden. Len spent the holidays with Aunt Eva. The posting was for two years. Once during that period Mother came back and for six weeks they lived in their house on the Candleware Road, sharing it with two tenants.

The baby was different. It could crawl and gurgle sounds, some of which sounded like questions and some like orders. Reluctantly, Len found himself attracted to the curly-headed thing. He spent hours playing with it on the carpet or the back lawn. He felt continually impelled to pick it up, to handle it and tickle it. He talked to it. Sometimes this was in gurgle-language which, if interrupted by Mother or one of the tenants, would embarrass him acutely. Sometimes it was a long narrative about bombers, or a story embroidered from a comic. He was allowed to take it for walks. It aroused feelings in him that were gladdening, and which took him slightly aback. Mother seemed pleased by the interest he took in the child, and when they went back to Aden, she would spend quite a large portion of her fortnightly letters telling him of the infant's progress.

Mother and the baby returned from Aden in December 1951, shortly before the Christmas holidays when Wilf was posted back to the Air Ministry. The tenants moved out of Candleware Road on the family's return. And he moved up from Miss Leverton's Preparatory School to a boarding school for senior boys.

A difference in tears 1953

1

He started to think about himself as follows ...

In the beginning there were colours. And uncolours. Sort of.

Red was momentary, the sudden splashes of red as the immense double-decker buses with their somehow horsey faces, passed backwards and forwards across the window of the drawing room. Red was focal, like the column of the pillar-box where he went with Mother or with Len to post letters to their Aunt Peg in Australia. Red was alarming, like the droplet of blood which oozed from his knee when he fell and cut it on the front doorstep. But red was also thrilling, gorgeous, like the waves of guardsmen in their bearskins, their crimson tunics, their black trousers with the red stripes which Dad had once taken Len and him to see.

Green was background, the green of the settee's back against which the visitors used to sit, the tree-line at the edge of Candleware Field, cushion upon cushion of green-ness which he could see from the window of his bedroom, like green cotton wool, unaccountably gladdening.

These two were the first real colours and the boy associated red with the front of the house and green with all that lay behind it. In front of the house were the red buses, red postboxes, red guardsmen, the dark red carpets in the big shops. And behind the house was the green countryside where the gypsies were and which began with the Candleware Field, extending, so far as he knew, forever. Guardsman red versus gypsy green: for a time, no other colours counted. They were simply not seen.

There were also grey and brown. But these were the uncolours; they were what happened to things when real colour was absent. Days were grey. Pavements were grey, as were buildings and almost everything you could see in the town. But the hall of their house was brown, and this brown-ness was to affect his recollection obscurely. Whenever he came to look back on that era of the early fifties, he would see images of burnt umber; the gravy, the double-breasted suits that men wore, suitcases, shoes, and the upholstery in cars. The brown-ness in the hallway was composed of a variety of browns, though all of them were somehow tired in their effect. The walls and ceiling were a milky cocoa, the light flex was a twist of licorice, the scorchmark on the lampshade was golden merging to char around a jagged hole where the fabric was curled and brittle; it looked like a roast potato. Then there was the banister, shoe-brown streaked with yellow from the shellac, and the surface of the big oil painting which was taken out of the box-room and hung on the hallway wall whenever Len was due to come home on holiday; it depicted the officer — not Dad but the other man — and it was sheeny umber like his mother's hat-case.

2

It began also with a name which was James Roland Corballis. The name, it seemed to him at that age, had been in place from the start; it was his and inarguable, somehow the centre, as the stone was the centre of the plum, as the packed caramel heartwood was at the centre of the tree they had cut down in the Candleware Field where they were going to build a school.

There had been other names, of course. He had been a Jimkin, a Jimballis and a Jeballis, a Roly-Poly, a Curl and an Old Draggleboots, this last because, it seems, he was sometimes dreamy. For the most part these early nicknames, and others like them, were invented by Dad on those occasions when he returned after dark from the Air Ministry.

'Where is that Curl? Where is that Slobodan Galoshes? Where's Old Gigglecracker?' Dad would exclaim as he came through the back door into the light of the kitchen. 'Where's Draggleboot Bumpkin?'

And, without bothering to take off his peaked cap and his hulking blue-grey greatcoat, or to put aside the dog-eared briefcase with his initials, W.F.C., in faded gold above the lock, he would follow Jeb's exhilarated squeals from room to room until, with a triumphant 'Ahah!', a plunging smell of pipe tobacco and a tickle of moustache, he would descend upon his hideyhole behind the green settee.

In the end, the name that seemed to stick to the boy was Jeb, plain Jeb.

3

If Dad was the inventor of names, Mother was more the disposer of adjectives. By turns the boy might be darling or naughty, clever or silly, depending on circumstances for which he was apparently responsible, but which he never seemed able wholly to control. With her dark eyebrows and dark wavy hair, gleamy like the skin of a horse-chestnut, and her trim, quick figure dressed either in the patterny housecoat or the blue serge skirt with its razor-sharp pleats which she wore in the darkening afternoons, Mother could be both ambient and sudden. During the periods of her favour, his mother was the sunshine in a spell of good weather. She was a benign, rather untouchable sovereign, made the more exotic by the fact that she came from Australia which, back then, had been at the furthest ends of the earth, remote, unimaginable. Equally she could be the swift, terrible keeper who would come marching down the Candleware Road to where the boy had strayed beyond what he knew to be his limits. Then she would administer a sharp smack across his bare legs, scoop up his tricycle in one hand, crush his fingers in the other, and return him to the safety of number sixty-six at a smart clip. It was hard to remember. Perhaps at this early age Jeb had called her 'Mumma' or 'Mum' reflexively, but by the time he was nine, she had become 'Mother'.

This was the only word which would do. But even so, it wasn't quite right. It didn't establish exactly enough that balance of proximity and distance which, by the age of seven, he associated with her.

His dad had always been 'Dad'.

By the age of three, he was aware that Corballis was something called a surname, and he had heard it described as his true name. He knew what a surname *did*. It belonged to all the members of a family. Dad was Wilfred Corballis, Group Captain Wilfred Corballis. Jeb's grandfather, who had died a number of years before the boy was born, had also been a Corballis, Roland Corballis, and so on, back and back, and back. Dad had told him this.

And he knew Mother was Elizabeth Corballis. Though with her there was some irregularity because Jeb had gathered from somewhere that she had possessed at least one other surname before he was born. How could you have more than one true name?

The real perplexity was with Len. Len was Jeb's brother, just like any brother. Yet he was called Leonard Hengelow. Jeb had heard his mother using the name once when she was having a ration card filled out by someone at the post office. The woman behind the counter seemed to take a long time to fill out the form. She asked Mother lots of questions, using the name Corballis whenever she could fit it in. 'You say you're the boy's *mother*, Mrs Corballis . . . But Mrs Corballis, he doesn't bear your surname. That's all very well, but I'm not authorised, Mrs Corballis . . .' The woman had difficulty in understanding the answers that Mother supplied. She clicked her tongue and looked disapproving, which made Mother angry. The woman behind the counter called her rude. Rude! How dare she! Jeb had felt tense and anxious on his mother's behalf, not least because of the people waiting in a queue behind them.

Mother had explained to him the difference between his surname and Len's, but to Jeb at the age of three the matter remained confusing. It was hard to fit Len into the pattern, and it raised the question in Jeb's mind, even that early, as to where Len properly belonged.

It was a perplexity which, like Jeb's own name, seemed to have been in his consciousness for as far back as he could remember, like one of the conditions of existence. Indeed the *sensation* of this perplexity was to remain in his mind long after he had reached an age where he finally understood the difference between Len's origins and his own. It persisted because it became fixed with what emerged as the contrarieties of Len's personality. And at times Jeb found it a troubling, obscure sensation, like the feeling of a question not satisfactorily answered, like the memory of having dreamt without any recollection of what the dream was about.

4

He was three or thereabouts, and sitting on the green settee with Mother. A standard lamp was behind them, illumining the chocolate pages of the photograph album. She had just pointed to a picture of a two-year-old in white rompers and a white sunhat.

'This is you when we were stationed for a year in Aden, though you probably don't remember.'

'Was Len in Aden?'

'Len was at school and with his Aunt Eva.'

She turned the page and pointed to another snapshot of a five-year-old in dark knee-length shorts and a school cap whose ridge came down over the eyes so that the boy's face was tilted upward in order to be able to see. It made him look a little gormless and somehow vulnerable.

'This is a picture of Len at his boarding school during the war. It was taken before you were even born, before you were even thought of. Think of that!'

He did think of it. For it was a case of distinguishing what he knew of his own short life from the very much vaster world before that, when there had been a war which everyone referred to as *the* War. The dividing line between these two worlds was apparently his own date of birth, and it was from the earlier of them that Len, Mother and Dad came. And to this world there seemed to belong various half-disclosed and decisive parts of their lives.

This former, this significant and irrecoverable portion of

their lives before he was 'even thought of' was to give the boy a vague sense of exclusion which, in his twenties, he was to rationalise into a desire to involve himself in that world which had affected them, particularly Len and Mother so intimately.

What had it been, he thought, this attraction to the past — curiosity, or something more morbid, a kind of manhole through which he had fallen to discover an entire otherworld of events, crumbly, obscure, misleading, but compelling and real? There would be a period in his late teens when he would plan a career as a painter for himself, but this idea shrivelled when he realised that his talent for depicting things was very ordinary. The occupation that lay in wait for him was that of historian, and he had taken up history, he later reflected, for reasons that were perhaps more personal than those of his colleagues, for reasons to do with 'that vague feeling of exclusion' which had implanted itself so early into his outlook on the world.

As for the two-year-old in rompers and sunhat, it was him all right — he could see the resemblance — but the romper suit and the rug he sat on belonged to a stranger, while Aden might as well have been Mars. The consciousness of James Roland Corballis began at sixty-six Candleware Road.

5

And it began in islands, then peninsulas of detail. There was a king called George the Sixth. And then he was dead. This seemed to happen very quickly. The death of the king was associated in Jeb's mind with a cold day when puddles lay in silvery oblongs on the pavement outside their flat-roofed, blockish house. Black cars swished down Candleware Road and the asphalt gleamed in the wet like the wings of an aeroplane. In the evening, when Jeb and Mother sat down to tea, Dad remained standing, delicately turning the knobs of the wireless until a voice came on. The voice talked about the king and, as it did so, his parents listened gravely, their eyes on the carpet. Their sadness made it seem as if the king had been one of their friends, and the boy was awed by the gravity of their feelings. Len was away at school when this happened.

Then Len was home, suddenly, on a night of frowns and high voices and shoes clomping about on the floorboards. Dad went next door to use the telephone and seemed to be gone for a long time. At breakfast the following morning Len was still dressed in his school uniform, not in the blue polo-neck sweater which Jeb knew Len habitually wore during holidays. Dad, on the other hand, was dressed in what he called his 'civvies', and when the family had finished breakfast he and Len went off together in the car. When Dad returned that evening Len was not with him.

Then he was home again and wearing the blue polo-neck because it was Easter and real holidays, and this fact made Jeb feel inexplicably cheerful. Len's presence in the household always had this effect on the younger boy at this period of his life; it made him feel somehow more complete.

There followed days when Mother committed Jeb to Len's charge and they rode on the double-decker buses, sitting, when possible, at the very front seat on the top, as high as the trees, looking down through the ribbony tracks the rain had left on the bus window upon the tides of black umbrellas which wove and interwove on the pavement. Generally these excursions had the same destination, a shop in the Pinner High Street which smelt of glue and had shelves rising to the ceiling on three of its four sides. From the ceiling, suspended by cotton, there were various balsa-wood aeroplanes. Len and the shopkeeper spent what seemed like hours in discussion, opening box after box of the wooden kits, taking out plans and parts and inspecting them closely, for the shopkeeper's enthusiasm was quite equal to Len's. Meanwhile, Jeb gazed at the large models above his head, or fingered the balsa laths and strips that lay about the counter, somewhat bored by the protracted technical conversation. Then there was the return journey, the swishing of tyres and the damp smell of gaberdine and wool in the crowded bus.

But there were also days when Len and Jeb occupied themselves out of doors. From the wooden packing cases which had contained the family's belongings on their return from

Aden, the elder boy had a flair for making what he referred to as a fuselage but which Jeb thought of as a cubby house. In his twenties, Jeb might wonder why it was that at an age when boys are usually more interested in cricket or experimenting with cigarettes Len should have found absorption in creating labyrinthine tunnels and cramped secret chambers out of wooden boxes and any other handy lumber: but these creations were something the younger boy took for granted then.

Together they crawled into the cramped interiors which smelt strongly of resin, settling themselves into the pine-straw. Then Len would tell Jeb how, while he was on one of the camps Aunt Eva arranged for him, he had swum far out to sea to rescue a boy who had been drowning, how he had dragged him to the sand and given him artificial respiration by pumping and lifting behind the shoulders. He demonstrated the technique on Jeb, pushing down on his shoulderblades until it hurt, then lifting under his arms. He told Jeb about how he had helped to catch a man who was trying to steal an aeroplane from the landing field near his boarding school, how he had tackled him and held onto him until one of the masters came up and took control. It was years before Jeb realised there was no word of truth in these stories.

There were days when the two of them sloshed through the soggy Candleware Field looking for newts, Len with a net over his shoulder while Jeb trotted a pace or two behind with a jam jar.

6

In the earliest recollections, days were like islands, grey islands, or rare blue islands, somehow unassociated with one another.

Here was one.

The boy had been, not bored exactly, but at what Mother called 'a loose end'. In this state of mind he went to stand among the coats and scarves that hung around the hatstand in the hallway. These he twisted into dark tents around himself, then peeped out. Through the mottled glass of the front door he could hear the grind of a bus working up through its gears, while, from the other end of the house through the door that led to the kitchen there came the clink of crockery and an occasional peal of laughter.

Earlier in the day Jeb had been scolded for some misdemeanour, and had bawled in his bedroom until, quite suddenly, he found himself listening to the sound of his own bawling. Whereupon he had stopped. It was one thing to weep, quite another to listen to the unrestrained racket one's grief made. The experience made the boy wonder about bawling in general. How did other people bawl, grownups in particular? The question was occupying him in a whimsical kind of way as he stood in the dark of the coats rubbing his forehead on the watery surface of Mother's silk coat-lining.

So Jeb went into the kitchen where he found her with Aunt Peg, who was visiting from Australia. They were doing the breakfast washing up, Mother shaking the suds from each plate before handing it to Aunt Peg who then dried it briskly. Both had put on their housecoats and tied up their hair with headscarves which made them look somehow barbaric, queenly and in league, though his mother, he thought, was the more beautiful of the two. The white light which fell through the kitchen window reflected off the white porcelain of the sink and crockery, illuminating the fronts of the two women. When the boy entered they had been sharing a joke, so he stood where his mother might notice him, and regarded her face for a few moments.

'How do you cry?' Jeb asked her at length.

'Pardon?'

'He's asking you how you cry, dear,' interposed Aunt Peg, who never missed a thing and who always spoke as though she were tucking in the ends of her sentences.

'Oh,' said Mother, and then, after a pause, 'Well.' She considered, and Jeb watched her face expectantly. All at once he saw it crumple inward around her eyes.

'Boo hoo, boo hoo, boo hoo!' she sobbed, while shaking the soapy water from yet another plate and handing it to Aunt Peg. But for this simple domestic action, her grief would have seemed quite real, even a little alarming.

'She should go on the stage, your mother. She's a jolly

convincing actress. Always was,' declared Aunt Peg, vigor-ously rubbing the plate and stacking it.

Jeb gazed steadily at Mother, waiting to see if any more would follow. But the actress Elizabeth Corballis smiled, first at her son, then, apologetically, at her elder sister. 'There,' she said, both pleased and a little embarrassed by her performance.

Jeb wondered if he should include Aunt Peg in his survey of family grief? She looked as if she wanted to be asked. But one glance at her decided him against it. Aunt Peg seemed too cheery ever to bawl. Besides, she lived in Australia which was a place, Jeb had been told, that was very very far away. There was no telling whether people cried in Australia. So the boy went off to look for Dad.

It was a Saturday morning, so Group Captain Wilfred Corballis was in the garage sharpening his chisels by the light of a weak and cobwebby bulb. There was an aroma of oil in the dim interior and, as Dad slid the blade of his chisel around the slimy surface of the whetstone, Jeb watched the grey oil-and-grit liquid climb slowly up the back of the tool. Every now and then Dad wiped the chisel with a disgusting old rag, then resumed his patient, circular motions on the stone.

'Hello, Old Curl,' he greeted the boy, without looking up from his task.

'How do you cry?' asked Old Curl.

The question, it seemed, was sufficiently challenging for the Group Captain to straighten from his workbench and adopt a posture of exaggerated meditation, with his hands on his hips and his bespectacled face — he wore glasses for close work, and it was his eyesight which had prevented him ever being a flier — staring intently into the shadowy rafters of the garage.

'Wah, wah, wah, wah,' he supplied, hopefully, blowing out his cheeks and narrowing his eyes. As an afterthought he licked his finger and made two tear-tracks which ran down to his chin. 'What do you think of that, eh?'

Old Curl thought it was pretty convincing, and distinct enough from the version of sorrow he had just witnessed.

But he was at an age where ideas, some ideas at least, had to be pursued doggedly to their conclusion. So now he went off in search of Len.

By the age of four, as Jeb then was, he knew this much, that Len was not his whole brother. The youngster was not able to determine the actual occasion when he had learned this; it was a fact that had crept unobtrusively into his store of knowledge between the ages of three and four. Len was something called a half-brother. Mother was Len's real mother, but Dad was not his real dad. This was the part that was unclear, because Len referred to Dad, when he had to, as 'Dad'. Sort of, anyway, in a kind of sideways voice. Why did he do this if he wasn't his real dad?

Jeb gathered that it had something to do with Len having had an earlier dad, and this was the man in the painting which leaned against a wall in the box-room.

He had sometimes gone to the box-room to look at it, though not in company with Len. Len took no interest in the picture which showed an officer staring out very intently from an umber background. He looked very unlike Jeb's own dad, even though he was wearing the blue-grey uniform of the Royal Air Force, identical to the uniforms which hung in the wardrobe of Dad's dressing room. The lean listening face looked similar to the face of King George the Sixth which Jeb had seen on a biscuit tin, only the face of the officer looked younger. He had his hands folded in his lap with a pair of brown gloves held in one of them. There were some wings and ribbons depicted on his uniform and the boy knew his name was Crispin Hengelow even though he was unable at that age to read the caption at the bottom of the scrolled and gilt frame, 'Fl/Off. C. Hengelow, 1943'. Mother had referred to him once or twice as Uncle Crispin, but he was a sort of uncle, not a real one. Jeb had heard Mother and Aunt Peg call him Charlie.

The officer wasn't dead; this much was understood. But he was somewhere else called Abroad. Why had he ceased to be Len's dad? And why did Len still have Hengelow as his true name if Dad was now also his own dad?

Len was fourteen, which is to say that he belonged to

a dimension of existence almost as far removed from Jeb's own station in life as that of Mother and Dad. Almost, but not quite. Len wasn't a parent though sometimes he was, kind of. For instance, Mother would say, 'I'm popping out for twenty minutes, Len. Look after Jeb — I'm trusting you.' So Len would leave what he was doing and entertain the youngster. He never seemed to complain. Not that he was always a particularly effective playmate at this time. When he lay on the drawing-room floor and built from a pack of cards or from Jeb's wooden blocks some intricate and teetering palace, the younger boy simply watched. As with the packing cases, Len could construct edifices which were fabulous beyond imagining, or so it seemed. But Jeb was not permitted to help, and if he tried to place a card here or a block there, his hand was brushed away, not impatiently, but firmly. Jeb did not play with Len in the same sense that he played with unpredictable June from next door who, with an abrupt sweep of the hand, was liable to flatten what the two of them might have constructed. Nor was it similar to Jeb's occasional games with Barry from further down the street, who was sometimes allowed to play in Jeb's garden and who could not be persuaded to say anything if ever bossy June was present.

No, Len was familiar in one sense, utterly remote in another.

Jeb found him in the small bedroom which they had been sharing since Aunt Peg came to stay. He was cutting out the pieces for a balsa aeroplane, hunched over a wooden board on the floor and meticulously tracing his penknife around the stencil marks on the wafery balsa sheets. There were already several struts pinned to the outline of the fuselage on the plans, and a tube of glue nearby with a drip hanging from its nozzle like the drip from a runny nose.

'How do you cry, Len?' Although Len had glanced up briefly as Jeb entered the room, he appeared not to hear the question. 'How do you cry, Len?' repeated Jeb. Again the question was ignored, though Len bent even more closely over his task and the quiff of his hair fell across his forehead. 'How ... do ... you ... cry?' Jeb asked a third time.

'I don't cry.'

'Why not?'

'I just don't. There doesn't have to be a reason.' Len allowed his voice to trail away as though he believed that by so doing he could also make the enquiry trail away.

'Everyone cries.'

'No they don't. I don't.'

'I cry. Sometimes.'

'You're only four.'

'Mumma and Dad cry, they showed me.'

Len ignored this last piece of information. His hunched figure on the carpet looked a bit like the hedgehog which Dad had called them out to see on the back lawn a week or so before.

'So how do you cry?' Jeb stood there for some while after putting the question this last time. He no longer had any conviction Len would answer it. Nor did Jeb fear a rough answer. Len would not shout that he should go away and stop being a pest, as Dad did if ever Jeb made a row during the wireless news. Len didn't get cross. Not ever. But he did go all funny at times. It was part of Len's mystery.

For a few moments Jeb looked down at his half-brother from the bedroom door, absorbed by the tension as, with infinite care, Len prised the fuselage and wing templates from the balsa, his face a few inches from the material, every now and then taking up his penknife to retrace the stencil marks where a piece proved obdurate. Then Jeb closed the door and went down the stairs, vaguely dissatisfied that his investigation into the various ways in which his family expressed sorrow should be incomplete. Outside he could hear sudden flurries of wind. A door slammed somewhere in the house and gusts of rain skittered on the window of a bedroom, as though someone were throwing handfuls of gravel at it.

7

There had been a coronation. This was why Jeb had a plastic coronation coach drawn by six plastic horses, white with red saddlery. It was a very glittery toy, but, as he sat playing with it on the small back lawn, he found it somehow dissatisfying. It didn't offer much scope.

Len was nearby, engaged in the construction of that same balsa aeroplane. A school term had intervened between the time he started it in March and now, when he was putting the finishing touches to it. Len was 'doping' the model, which involved applying a clear and pungent liquid onto the fabric of the wings and fuselage. As his brush touched the loose tissue panels, the paper tightened over the wooden frame and changed from opacity to transparency. It was magic, the way in which the slack, cloudy tissue suddenly tensed where Len applied the dope. Its effect was to make the balsa struts and templates of the model's interior become quite visible, a miniature, intricate cage in which one could see the elastic band which would drive the propeller. It exhilarated the younger boy, the thought of the model's intact but unreachable interior; it aroused in him a delicious sense of yearning, of possibility.

'Will you make me one, Len?'

His half-brother looked up from his task, the sun fully catching his upturned face. He smiled.

'They take some time.'

'No, but will you?'

'Maybe, old fellow. Some day.'

They were enough, these 'old fellows', these sunny assurances, the basis of their brotherly accord. Maybe they established that reflex, Jeb was to reflect, thirty years or so later, that over-willingness he had discovered in his character to place trust, to follow the lead, of those he took, often mistakenly, alas, to be self-possessed.

The aeroplane was finished and the dope dry by tea-time. So, in the long summer evening, Jeb, Len, and Dad took the model through the back gate of the garden into the Candleware Field. Len wound the propellor until the elastic band was taut, then ran with the plane held above his head, finally throwing it high. The model soared, then glided in a slow even flight. Glorious! Ah, glorious! It banked slightly, then drifted in a long crescent to land, gently upheld by the long grass. Dad had a turn. Then Len helped Jeb to launch the thing, then Len had his own turn, and so on. There were many flights until, after one of Dad's turns, the model nose-dived into a rut and its undercarriage was torn off. Len hurried to the spot and hunched over the broken plane, examining the detached wheels and the tear in the fabric. Jeb was unable to see Len's face, though this did not stop the youngster feeling distress on his half-brother's behalf. Things did seem to go wrong so often when Len and Dad were together, little things, not for reasons that anyone could see.

'Stick it in the hangar. Get the fitters to work on it. It'll be apples,' exclaimed Dad breezily, then added more tenderly, 'Lanx will fix it. He's such a resourceful fellow.'

'I'm Len,' the boy declared stubbornly. He took the damaged plane inside, his face bent over it to avoid having to look at Dad or Jeb. They followed him inside.

8

It must have been these same summer holidays that they had a visitor; one evening after Jeb had been put to bed he heard the doorbell ring followed by expressions of surprise from several voices in the hallway, a period of silence, then the voices again, receding into the drawing room.

Jeb lay very still and listened. Then he slipped from bed and crept down the stairs, stopping at intervals to peep through the banister rails. The voices behind the closed door of the drawing room stopped and started; he reached the bottom of the stairs and stood for a moment outside the drawing-room door wondering if he should enter. Then Mother opened the door, speaking over her shoulder as she did so.

'Well, if the boy is to go out, then he must put on a white shirt and a tie.' She started with surprise to see Jeb standing there.

'I've got a tummy-ache.' He tried to make his voice sound pathetic, but he was also sneaking a glance past Mother into the room. Mother showed no sympathy, nor did she seem inclined to introduce the visitor. She hustled him back to bed. Shortly afterwards Len came in and began rummaging in the chest of drawers which contained his clothes.

'Where are you going, Len?'

'To the pictures.'

'Who is the person who came?' But Len had already left

the room, a white shirt and a tie in his hand. He seemed in a tremendous hurry.

Perhaps Jeb slept. In any case, when next he became aware of sounds in the bedroom it was dark outside and someone had switched on the side-lamp beside Len's bed. Len was there, in pyjamas now, and there was a tall man in the room as well. This man smelt of cigarettes and he was tucking Len into his bed. It was odd. Where was Mother?

'Can we go and see a picture again?'

'Lots of pictures!' the man whispered.

'Will you stay here and still be here tomorrow morning?'

'My dear old chum, of course I will. Now, as your mother told us, it's very late, so you go to sleep.' He leaned over and kissed Len on the forehead. Usually Len recoiled when Dad or Mother tried to kiss him. It was cissy being kissed, he had once told Jeb. But now he had his arms around the man's neck and the man was finding it difficult to free himself. This he eventually succeeded in doing, and, as he straightened, Jeb saw that he was immensely tall, taller even than the wardrobe they had in the room, tall and thin. Len lay slackly on the bed now and the man bent to pat him once on the shoulder, then turned to go. In that instant Jeb saw who it was. It was the officer in the portrait; it was Len's real dad. Except that the face seemed even thinner than the face in the picture, as thin as one of Dad's chisels. Nor was the man wearing a uniform, of course, but a darkish suit and shirt. Having lived with the portrait, Jeb was unprepared for how tall and for how *shabby* Len's real dad actually looked. The man switched off the light and, bowing his head as he went, closed the door with great gentleness behind him.

Now, in the darkness, there were funny noises coming from Len's bed, snuffles and suppressed little squeals. It didn't sound much like crying, more like someone scratching their nails on a windowpane. Nonetheless, Jeb was aware that his half-brother was indeed crying, and the sound of that stifled grief made him feel utterly desolate.

But why was Len crying? His real dad had promised he was going to be there in the morning. He had promised that they would go and see the pictures again.

When Jeb awoke the following morning, the question on his mind was, where would the tall man have slept that night? With Aunt Peg in one room upstairs, their parents in another, and he and Len in the third, there was only the box-room, or downstairs on the sofa. The idea crossed the boy's mind that the tall man might have slept in the box-room, curled up on the floor beside his picture, that the box-room was somehow where the tall man in his shabby coat belonged. So, on his way down to eat his cornflakes, Jeb passed the box-room and, very quietly opening the door a fraction, he peeped inside. There was no tall man. Next, he checked the settee. There was a smell of stale cigarette smoke, and several full ashtrays, but the man was not there either. So, where would he have slept? Under a bush in the garden? In the garage? As Jeb scrunched through his breakfast cereal, he kept looking up, half expecting Len's real dad to come through the dining-room door. The boy was curious to know what he would look like in the full light of day. But he didn't appear.

'Was that Len's real dad who came last night?' he asked Mother.

'That was Len's father, yes.'

'Did he sleep in the garage?'

'Len's father didn't stay *here* last night.'

'Why not?'

'Well, he had a boat-train to catch. He was on his way back to Germany.'

So the tall man had departed last night. Then why had he promised?

Len seemed all right, though he didn't say much. At one point the grownups became engaged in one of those grownup conversations which Jeb was forbidden to interrupt. Aunt Peg said, 'Well, I still think he should give you a bit of warning when he's coming. It is very unfair on Lizzie, and on Len too.'

'You know what Charlie's life is, Peg. Here and there. It's very gypsy,' said Dad. It was Dad's word 'gypsy' that lodged in Jeb's memory particularly, because gypsies were people he had been warned against. And his impression of the tall man had certainly been one of shabbiness. Yet the man was also an officer. Or had been.

Aunt Peg was replying. She seemed more put out by the visit than Mother or Dad. Jeb was not able to make much sense of the conversation. For the most part it was a case of voices contending around him, like the remote jabber of voices between stations he had sometimes heard on Dad's wireless when, on some evenings, he fingered the knobs delicately, his ear to the brocaded fabric of the loudspeaker, jabber at the edge of comprehension, from which odd things were retrievable. 'He has duties, Wilf, *duties*,' insisted Aunt Peg. It was also a revelation to the boy that grownups could express annoyance with each other; up to that time he had thought that annoyance was a mood grownups directed exclusively to children.

At length there was a silence during which Dad and Aunt Peg simply looked at each other, warily and sternly.

Then Mother said, 'Oh Peg, how I *do* envy you going back to Australia. How I'd love to see those Monaro skies again! And that light!'

'I've told you, dear,' Aunt Peg replied, 'Wilf should leave the airforce and you should all come out. It would be a firm goodbye to dear Charlie then.'

'He's Len's father,' Mother said. She sounded tired.

Later Jeb asked his dad, 'Can officers be gypsies?'

'Not very likely, Old Curl.'

'Is Len's real dad a gypsy?'

Dad thought for a bit and then, as if unaware of having used the word during the breakfast conversation, said, 'Yes, I suppose he is a bit of a gypsy.'

'But Len's dad was an officer.'

'That's right.'

'But you said...'

9

Aunt Peg was returning to Australia. It seemed she had decided to 'accept' someone called Neville. In the very same week that she left on the boat from Tilbury, Len came into the drawing room where Jeb was playing.

'Goodbye, old fellow.'

Without waiting to register what effect his farewell would have, Len ran out. He had his polo-neck jumper wrapped around his middle. Over his shoulder he carried a leather school satchel and on his belt, Jeb noticed, he had threaded his sheath knife with the bone handle. The younger boy followed Len to the back door and was in time to see his lean figure jogging to the end of the garden, then disappearing through the gate into the Candleware Field.

'Can I go with Len?' Jeb called out to Mother. But she was upstairs making beds and didn't hear.

There was concern when Len didn't turn up for lunch, and by mid-afternoon it emerged that he had run away again. Again? Mother walked the streets, holding tightly to Jeb's hand and hurrying him along, not answering his questions. His legs ached and he whimpered, 'I don't like you when you do this. I don't like you.' But Mother appeared not to hear.

They returned home and Jeb was taken next door and given to June's mother to be looked after because Mother was going out again to search for Len. The boy sat on the edge of a chair nibbling a piece of white bread and butter while June stared at him and whispered questions at her mother. It wasn't very nice.

Dad arrived home from the office early, and he went straight out in the car to search, while Mother took Jeb back home. But it was odd. She didn't tell him to get ready for bed. Instead he hung about on the drawing-room floor, his sense of routine disoriented. Dad had come home without Len and then called the policeman. This gentleman arrived a little time later and sat on the settee with a cup of tea in one hand, a pencil in the other, and a notepad balanced on one of his huge knees. He wrote down lots of particulars and, when he rose to leave, he replaced the helmet on his head, which meant he had to bow as he went through the doorway. And still nobody bothered to get Jeb ready for bed, so in the end he simply went upstairs, undressed himself and crawled beneath the blankets, leaving the light on. Some-one must have come and turned it off because it was not on when he woke in the morning.

Len seemed to be away for ages. One lunchtime he came back through the front door in company with Dad and the same policeman. He behaved as though nothing unusual had occurred. Mother was both cross and pleased at the same time. She had tears on her cheeks and her face crumpled up every now and then in a way that was different from, but also the same as, the time when she had demonstrated to Jeb how she cried.

Dad took Len into the drawing room where both he and the policeman talked to him in low voices behind the closed door. Jeb hung about outside wanting to know where Len had been all this time. But he had to wait until later, and to hear the story from Mother, how Len, it seemed, had managed to reach a place called Dover. He had slept out under hedges and trees. When it rained he got soaked through and he spent the first sunny day hiding in undergrowth, wearing nothing but a vest and underpants while he dried his shirt, trousers and socks on branches. It remained a mystery as to whether he had eaten anything during the time he was away.

Len developed a cold as a result of his adventure, though he seemed to recover soon enough. He was 'confined to barracks' in Dad's phrase, so Mother went out and bought him a second balsa aeroplane. The model kept him occupied for the remainder of the holidays. One morning Jeb found himself alone in Len's company.

'Where were you going to go when you ran away?' Jeb asked him.

'I was going to Germany to find where my other dad lives,' he replied.

The Wold 1954

1

Then they were in another place and living in another house. Whenever Jeb came to recollect the change in later years he could not account for the actual changeover. How had they got to be there; by car, by train, by sorcery? He could recall none of the preparations for leaving Candleware Road, nor the impact that the new place, which was called RAF Gattisby, originally made on him when he saw it for the first time. Suddenly, it seemed, he was just *there*. It was one of those islands of memory, seemingly discontinuous with previous and subsequent experience. And the discontinuity was always vaguely troubling.

In contrast to the browns of Candleware Road the new house was filled with a whitish and yellowish light and this lightness may have had something to do with a new immensity in the sky above it. For the sky, from one flat horizon to the other, was suddenly so immeasurable, so unimpeded, by buildings, by overhead tramlines, by those bulking double-deckers which used to wait, throbbing, at the bus stop outside the old house. Instead there were the fields. In his first awareness of them, they were broad dark tracts, the furrows like corduroy, and the clods sheeny with the imprint of the harrow. At their extremity there would be a dyke, or a spinney of trees, blue-grey like the uniforms on the base and flat as a paper cutout against the fall of the sky. Inevitably a tractor would be dragging some instrument across this brown plain, dealing with it in a way that Jeb could not then fathom, and there came to his nostrils occasionally the delicious smell of diesel mixed with damp earth. A little later and the fields had transformed into rows of green shoots, numberless regiments of tiny spearmen; later still and they swished greenly this way and that in the breezes of June, resembling green fur.

Then there was the airfield, which the boy could see from his bedroom window, an immense expanse of grass, segmented by the runway and the taxi paths. On the far side of this stood the control tower with its green windows, some huge green sheds which Dad called hangars, and some long humpy buildings called Nissen huts. Solitary, on one boundary, the airsock fretted this way and that at the top of its pole. Sometimes, early in the morning, he watched the aircraft taking off, one after the other. Some of them had propellers and made a penetrating drone like a person clearing his throat. Sometimes it was a huge white jet which took off in a crescendo of smooth roar with a whistling undernoise.

'They're the old Lincolns,' Dad informed him, or 'That's one of the new Valiant bombers. It'll be over Germany in thirty minutes.'

Wherever this place which kept getting mentioned, Germany, was. It sounded remote

Yes, the world had suddenly grown very much broader and taller, and this seemed to coincide with a new phase in Jeb's own life, for he had started school. Each morning he was placed on a bus and driven for miles through the countryside until he didn't know where he was. On the first few mornings he felt panicky as the married quarters and the camp gates disappeared behind him; it was one thing to have wandered on his tricycle from number sixty-six Candleware Road, but he had always known how to get back.

2

But where was the Candleware Road now? Did it still exist? He gathered that their former house was far, far to the south of them. Dad pointed in a direction.

'You mean, if we had gone across the Candleware Field, and then across another field, we would have come here?'

'Well, a few more fields than that,' Dad replied, looking over the top of his newspaper.

'How many fields?'

'Well, a *good* few.' He was reading again.

'How many?'

'There's a good chap.'

So Jeb wandered outside and began walking past the houses which were stuccoed in a porridgy sort of colour, toward the main gates of the camp. How many was a good few? It couldn't be that far. Perhaps if he crossed a field or two and then climbed up a tree, he might be able to see something of their old street.

At the entrance to RAF Gattisby there was a barrier and a little house, and when Jeb approached it he was accosted by a man with a white-peaked cap, white gaiters and white belt over his airforce uniform.

'You going *far*, sonny?'

Jeb stopped, and the man squatted down on his haunches to be at the same height as the boy. His skin was brown like pastry and there were little hairs protruding from his nostrils which quivered when he spoke, and he had a curious sing-song emphasis in his speech.

'And where might *you* be orf to this Saturday *morn*-ing?'

'I'm going to look for Candleware Road,' Jeb explained.

'Where's *that*, then?'

'It's in a town called London, which is over the fields in that direction.'

'My word! Now *you're* an ambitious fellow. And what might *your* name be?'

'James Roland Corballis.' He stepped back a pace because the man's face was very close. It was odd too, because, while one of his eyes appeared to be watching Jeb, the other seemed to be looking to one side, giving an impression of there being two faces in the one.

'Well, couldn't be clearer than *that*, *could* you? Now why don't you *step* into my office for *'alf* a mo, and I'll make a *quick* phone-call on your be'alf?' And he took Jeb by the elbow and guided him into the little house, then sat him on a stool. 'Now you 'ang on *right* there.' He turned to a much younger man who was reading a newspaper on another stool. 'Thrale, *amuse* the boy. *That's* an order. And don't let 'im *move* from there.' Then the man took off his peaked cap and went into an adjoining room.

The young man had a thin face with eyes rather like those of the little deer Jeb had seen pictured in one of his books, and his moustache was little, like an accidental smear of boot polish. His hair was shiny and spiky with the Brylcreem on it and he kept smiling rather hopelessly at Jeb and then furtively going back to his newspaper. Once he pulled a very crumpled handkerchief from his pocket, unfolded it, and offered Jeb a sherbet lemon.

'Them'll fizz in yer mouth, son,' said the young man. This it seemed, was all the conversation he had.

Jeb waited on the stool, and could overhear parts of the phone conversation next door. 'Kid's name's *Cor*-ballis... belongs to the new person*nel* orffice... Was settin' orf fer *London*, if yer please... right, sarge.' Then, a few moments later, and in a different tone of voice. 'I believe we 'ave your *boy* at the front gate, ma'am... We'll send 'im back in the 'alf-tonner... ten minutes or so. *Right* you are.' The pastry-faced man returned to the room. 'Seems you're in a spot of *bother*, my son. Runnin' away! Causin' your good people loads of *grief*. That won't never *do*.'

'I wasn't running away,' Jeb stated. But the man wasn't really listening. He put his peaked cap back on his head.

'Mind the *fort*, Thrale,' he said, as he took Jeb by the arm, and led him out. Jeb felt aggrieved by the firm hold on his elbow, as though he had done something wrong which he knew he hadn't. He was *not* running away. He had told the man this. It should have been clear. If he didn't understand, then he was contemptible.

He was driven home and escorted right to the front door.

'We stopped this little adventure in good *time*, sir, ma'am,' declared his captor when both Mother and Dad answered the door.

'I wasn't running away,' Jeb repeated, reasonably.

'Going to *Lon*don, 'e said 'e was, sir. Be a bit *foot*sore by the time 'e'd 'ave *got* there, I reckon.'

As he listened, Jeb felt ashamed of his parents. They were too smiley, too talkative and they sided too automatically with the man.

'I wasn't running away. Can't you *listen*?'

'That will do!' said his mother.

'No *trouble*, sir, ma'am, better *safe* than sorry, eh?' The man got down on his haunches again and Jeb found his face once more only a few inches away. 'It's a long way to *Lon*don, old son. I'd stick to your back *gar*den for the time being if *I* was you.'

Jeb stared furiously at the one eye that was looking at him and the one that was not. The boy could have spat at them. 'I wasn't running away,' he repeated in the man's face. But the man stood up again without answering.

He was taken inside and quizzed both by Mother and by Dad.

'I was just going for a walk to the barrier.'

'The provost said you told him you were going to London.'

'No I wasn't. I was just going to see if I could see it from the next field.'

'See what?'

'Where we used to live.'

'That's two hundred miles away,' said Mother.

'Dad said it was only a few fields away.'

'A good few fields away, old chap. I did say a *good* few.' Mother gave Dad one of those looks she gave him when she was furious with him.

'You must never wander away again, Jeb. Never,' she said, and the second 'never' sounded like a hand being banged down on a table.

'I wasn't wandering away.'

On the whole he felt that his parents were more inclined to believe him now that the provost had gone. Even so, it was difficult to understand them getting upset just because he had wanted to walk a few fields and see their old house. The incident became referred to as 'the time Jeb took himself off,' and when he heard it referred to in these terms he was deeply affronted. Something that was not strictly true had been recorded as part of his past because people — the provost, his parents — had not taken enough trouble to discover exactly what he had intended. People could muck about with his past. It was alarming.

'It's on account of Len,' Dad said to him later. 'You remember how Len takes himself off sometimes. Well, our Mum worries that you might try and follow his example. You know how much you like to do what Len does, Jeb. We don't want you to go and get lost in the countryside, or fall in with any nasty old gypsies or the like. Not our own little man. So you stick around the house and the garden, there's a fellow.'

'All right.' But it felt constraining, nevertheless. Why should going for a walk always provoke all this fuss?

3

So it became a passion with him, this desire to restore the exactitude, the wholeness, the delicacy of events in the past, his own or those on the syllabus he was eventually to teach. This was why, for instance, thirty years later, he sat at a desk under an open window in an Australian house with several blank sheets of paper in front of him, attempting to place the events described above accurately in time. He was able to deduce that the family must have moved to Gattisby in the March or April of 1954, and the incident with the airforce policeman must have happened in May or June.

Outside this Australian window evening was falling and the cicadas were shrill in the long grass. He scribbled down some dates onto one of the blank pages, and felt vaguely dissatisfied. For he found the action of plotting his earliest experiences against a time chart had the odd effect of diminishing the power and colour of his recollections. It was to give them a time when part of their meaning lay in their being, not outside time exactly, but blithe of it. It was to abstract events from the trance of their remoteness, from the intimate mesh of sensuous connections. Yes, the problem *was* one of time. For he *did* want to locate the experiences of his childhood against the objective map of his century, but he wanted to do so without robbing them of their sensual integrity; he wanted to reconcile the consciousness of a particular year, a particular month, with its trance-like sensation in his memory.

Why? Well, it was because that first summer at Gattisby was to be the last occasion Jeb spent any length of time in the company of his half-brother, Len. Ever after their time together seemed snatched, curtailed. When holidays came round again, Len joined them at their home only for a few days or a week at most. The summer of 1954, therefore, became connected in Jeb's mind with an experience of the halcyon followed by an experience of loss, and from then onward Len seemed, in Jeb's recollection, to be on the move from one place to another.

4

Len came home for that summer holiday in the middle of July, having just completed something called a GCE which was obviously very important. And Jeb heard Dad asking, 'But you must have some idea how they went?' and he saw Dad was looking for Len's face in the rear-vision mirror of the car as they drove home from the railway station in Lincoln. But Len apparently had no idea how his GCE went. He shrugged his shoulders, he said that results were not due until September.

At first Len seemed different. For one thing he suddenly appeared to be taller, leggier. His face was also leaner and he wore his hair in a quiff. He was still interested in balsa-wood aeroplanes and the plastic kits which had begun to appear in the shops, but this interest had become shyer, more moody. Jeb found this out with a start. For days he had been preparing for Len's homecoming. On the floor of the playroom the boy had lined up his collection of Dinky cars, fitted together the rails of his Hornby train set, and very carefully arrayed Len's two or three balsa models. It was a great air, rail and road complex, a 'megarama-port' he called it, while Dad had referred to it as 'a work of art' when he stuck his curly gingery hair and moustache around the playroom door on the previous evening. The moment they reached home Jeb dragged Len off to see it.

'Oh yes, you must see Jeb's handiwork. It's magnificent,' said Dad.

Len was polite. 'It's very good. It really is,' he kept saying as his half-brother pointed out different features of the layout to him, but there was no emphasis in his voice, and his eyes seemed both to rest on the objects Jeb showed him and to be elsewhere at the same time; he escaped as soon as he could.

For the first few days of the holiday, Len mooched. He lay for hours in the grass just outside the fence around the airfield and watched the planes taxiing around the perimeter, the silvery twin-tail-finned Lincolns or, more rarely, a Valiant with its little bubble cockpit, its swept-back wings swaying slightly to the irregularities on the concrete perimeter track. At first Jeb used to join him, lying beside him in the tussocky grass and, in imitation of Len, chewing a stem. One morning the interminable taxiing was relieved by the spectacle of aircraft from somewhere else making low passes over the airfield in groups of three, distant black specks against the wadding of white cloud that would grow rapidly larger on a crescendo of noise then flash before their faces at a height that seemed to be lower than the green windows of the control tower, before rising once more into the cloud, their roar diminishing to an ambient after-noise. For a moment or two they could see the heads of the pilots.

'Meteors,' announced Len. And it was thrilling, this spectacle of power, of grace. Jeb could read the exhilaration in Len's eyes after each pass. But mostly they watched this routine taxiing; there was something reptilian about the planes, their gleamy low profiles and the slow inexorable progress they made around the perimeter circuit. Jeb tried to enter into the spirit of Len's absorption with the aircraft, but it was difficult. Len was not forthcoming.

'Why don't we make an aeroplane out of the boxes?'

'You make one, Jeb, I'll come over later.'

'Why don't we go and explore the woods?'

'Not right now, old fellow.'

So the younger boy would wander off, and draw pictures on his bedroom floor or play with the three-year-old boy from next door, who was not a satisfactory playmate at all. It was the company of his half-brother Jeb longed for.

Late one afternoon Dad came home with a bicycle. It was a heavily built, black contraption with three-speed Sturmey-Archer gears and a basket attached to the front handlebars. In the basket was a second bicycle seat. Dad took his purchase into the garage, and there came a sound of metal pipe being hacksawed and filed. When he emerged shortly before high tea the bicycle had its second seat fixed to the crossbar, and a footrest bolted to the frame in front of it.

'Try that for size. And there's an extra seat so that you can take Jeb along with you.' It was curious how Dad treated Len. He never seemed to use his name when he was talking to him directly, and his manner was oddly stiff.

'Thank you,' said Len.

'He'll use it to make for the Channel ports,' Mother said over her shoulder, as though casually, when she thought neither of the boys were within earshot.

'We can't coop the boy up, Beth.' And when his mother's face continued to register disapproval, Dad exclaimed, 'Oh for God's sake. I'm doing the best I can for the boy, Beth,' whereupon he stormed out of the room.

But the bicycle was a success, and on it Len, with Jeb balanced precariously on the crossbar saddle, explored the countryside around Gattisby. In particular they would go looking for the old bomber airfields, swaying out through the camp gates in the morning with some sandwiches, a couple of apples and a bottle of lime-green fizz in the basket. To be away for a whole day! Jeb was a little surprised by how much freedom Mother was prepared to let him have. In retrospect he concluded that his being entrusted for such long periods to Len's care was a strategy to deter Len from 'making for the Channel ports'.

It was pleasant sitting there watching hedgerows and ditches whizz by, occasionally glimpsing a view across miles of che-quered fields, now turning to a macaroon colour, hearing Len's laboured breathing near his ear when they had to contend with a slope, feeling the rush of wind as they descended on the other side. And, when they found one of the airfields,

Len would lift the bicycle over the fence, and they would cycle off down the runway.

'Duck your head! Here comes a Lanc!' Len would whoop, as he picked up speed along the broad airstrip. It was unexpected, hearing Len suddenly whoop.

Then they would wander over to the hangars, trying the padlocks. Once they were able to squeeze in through a gap in the corrugated-iron wall, and in the vast darkness Len made wolf howls which resounded hugely.

'I can't see you, Len. I don't like it here.'

Len didn't answer immediately and Jeb could hear nothing but the occasional wince of the iron high above him. At length Len said, 'Come on, then. Let's cut along.' So they went outside again and scuffed here and there in the earth for souvenirs. Jeb found some metal strips which Len said were from a Lancaster's airframe, though they might just as well have been from a tractor, and they once discovered lying in the grass a cache of .303 cartridge cases, which they pocketed. The two of them peered through the broken windows of Nissen huts, but could see only a floor littered with broken glass and screwed-up newspaper. There was a smell of faeces.

'My real dad used to live in a building like this. When he was an air-bomber.'

'What's an air-bomber?'

'A man who looks through a little bubble in a Lanc and sees that the bombs fall on the right place.'

Sometimes, on the journey home, Len bought icecreams, and they sat beside the road licking them, biting off the ends of the cornets and sucking the creamy vanilla through. They arrived home late in the afternoon and Jeb would be left with the feeling that they had travelled vast distances over the face of the earth.

5

In early September the exam results arrived.

'Well, there's nothing for it,' declared Dad, 'You are going to have to sit them again next summer. At the very least you must pick up English and maths. I don't understand how your reports could have described you as a fair student and you end up with this. Do you understand it?'

Len shrugged and looked sidelong. Man and boy stood facing each other and the latter now had several inches advantage in height.

'Whatever you want to make of your life depends on these exams. You talk of wanting to join the airforce. You'll not do it with only two passes.' Dad was growing red in the face as he worked himself up. He was prone to getting red in the face, either when he was pleased or angry. 'Where do you think you'll end up with a result like this?'

Len shrugged again, and continued to look sidelong over his left shoulder.

'On the scrapheap, that's where!'

There was a silence for some moments. Len's expression affected a weary disdain which provoked Dad to burst out with 'I just — I *just* can't talk to you, can I? No matter what amount of effort I put in, I'm addressing a blank wall.' Jeb had rarely seen Dad glare. On the whole his was a jolly and piratical face. But the look he was now giving Len was fierce, more, it was — unforgiving. He stormed out, and Len vanished out of the door. When he did not return at tea-time Dad and Mother had a row, with Dad declaring that he did not really care whether or not Len had run away; it was Len's business. But Len came in at about ten o'clock just as the last light was fading on the other side of the airfield. Jeb had been put to bed long before, but had remained awake, looking out of the window, waiting to see if Len would return. When he heard Mother talking to him at the bottom of the stairs, he slid beneath the covers with a feeling of immense relief.

6

So it was decided that Len would sit for his GCEs again. On an afternoon toward the end of the holiday he came up to Jeb and said, 'I'm going to look for airfields for one last time. Coming?' He caught Jeb briefly in the eye, then looked away. The invitation sounded a bit like a challenge.

'I want you back for high tea,' Mother called. 'I'm trusting you, Len.'

The morning had been hot, even sultry, and at the beginning they cycled under unblemished blue skies. Getting away from the camp seemed to improve Len's mood a little. There were people in the fields making stooks out of the mown hay and leaning them together. On their heads the men wore white handkerchiefs with knots tied at each corner, and Jeb could see the sweat running down from their foreheads. In another field he saw a line of women, all of them somehow bulky in their gumboots and aprons, moving along the furrows tossing potatoes into tin buckets. Every now and then, through intervals in the beech and chestnut trees that grew beside the road the two boys could distinguish the three towers of the cathedral, pepper-coloured in the sunlight.

They didn't find any airfields that afternoon. Instead they arrived at a broad canal.

'Hang on, I'm going for a swim.' Len threw off his shirt, shoes and socks and began picking his way down the bank.

'You'll get your trousers wet!' Jeb called, horrified at the prospect. But Len laughed at him and, with a lunge, entered the water and struck out for the middle of the stream. He thrashed this way and that, kicking with his feet and creating great fountains of water. 'I'm a paddle steamer,' he called.

Then he returned to the bank, his white shorts dripping.

'Can you swim, old fellow?'

'No.'

'I'll teach you. Come on.'

'I don't want to.' For all that the canal, sheeny-green, laced with honey-gold in the shallows beside the bank, was alluring on this warm afternoon, the prospect of wearing soggy shorts and underpants was intolerable, while to Jeb's five-year-old sensibility, the alternative of wearing nothing at all was unthinkable.

But Len persuaded him to try the unthinkable. 'You're only little. No one's going to mind if they see you in the crud.' And then, more persuasively, '*Everyone* can swim by the time they're *five*. My real dad taught me to swim when I was five.'

'What will I dry myself on?' Jeb wailed as he stumbled down the bank with nothing on toward where Len was waiting for him, knee-deep in the water. The straw of the bank prickled, and his nudity made him feel vulnerable.

But the water, cold at first, gave him a voluptuous sense of liberation as he gradually trusted himself to it, and to Len's hand, cupped under his chin. Len explained how he should kick with his legs and sweep with his arms, and as Jeb did this, the elder boy led him through the water, keeping one hand under the chin and the other behind his head. 'You're swimming! Look!' And he took his hands away for a moment, then replaced them, then took them away for a longer interval. Once Jeb went under and came up spluttering and panicky, but Len quietly took his head and restored his confidence.

They came out and lay on the bank. Len wrung out his waterlogged shorts and underpants. 'Now you can swim,' he told Jeb. Jeb didn't think this was actually true since Len's hand had been there under his chin for most of the time, but the reassurance made him glow with pleasure.

With Len pushing the bicycle, they walked along the narrow bridle-path beside the canal in the direction of Lincoln's three cathedral towers, frequently stopping to pick the blackberries which grew beside the path. Len would lean right over and pick Jeb the large ones,

'Wait until you've got a handful, then put them all in your mouth at once,' Len advised. They ate, with their cheeks bulging, the berries yielding shocks of sweetness and tanginess. It was still warm, and there seemed to be no wind, yet the sky was transforming with great rapidity above them. A vast aeroplane of cloud, the dark grey colour in camouflage, was advancing and dragging behind it an even vaster white pall.

'We'd best make for shelter, old fellow.' Len lifted him onto the crossbar seat and began to pedal. It was hair-raising, the way in which he cycled along the narrow path, with a drop on either side. Then the sun went behind the cloud. By the time they had reached the first houses of the town the wind was up and big spots of rain were falling on them. Len abruptly stopped the bicycle and, looking Jeb in the eye, he said, 'Now look, we might be in for a bit of a wetting. Whatever happens, it's important to keep your pecker up.' Then Len resumed pedalling. Jeb understood that he was not supposed to cry or make a fuss, so he hung on grimly as the bicycle bumped over pot-holed roads.

Then came the downpour. It drenched them both in a moment. The younger boy felt his shirt, shorts and underpants cling to his body uncomfortably. It plastered the hair to Len's head and the raindrops fell with such force that they hurt. Now the shops and offices looked as if he were seeing them through milk. They passed a broad stretch of water where there were some boats moored to a wharf. The surface of this was sizzling furiously in the rain. There were some swans under a bridge, and here the two of them took shelter for a while; but Len had the idea they should keep making progress toward home, so they had no sooner dismounted from the bicycle than Len was urging Jeb to clamber back on, and they wobbled off again into the rain. Len had one of those fixed looks on his face.

Then they had to climb a steep hill that seemed never to end. At first Len pushed the bicycle with Jeb sitting on it, but the narrow, cobbled alley became steeper and steeper. 'Get off, can't you,' said Len, suddenly, his chest heaving and his breath making a wheezing noise. Jeb scrambled off quickly. His face began to crumple at the abrupt unfriendliness of Len's tone, but he restrained his grief because, as Len laboured for breath, he was saying, 'Sorry. I'm sorry. Don't cry. Please, please don't go and cry.' He pushed the bicycle and Jeb toiled uphill behind him, a little whimpery, though trying to keep up whatever his pecker was. As they climbed, the younger boy saw, emerging through the white-smoking rain, the walls and towers of a castle. There were battlements and arrow-slits appearing through the trees. During their time at RAF Gattisby, Dad had not yet found opportunity to take either of them to see Lincoln Castle, so the ramparts looming above the two boys now were a startling apparition. It felt to Jeb as though he had slipped into what some of his books called 'the olden days'. The phrase had always haunted him for some reason — it was that word 'olden'. Now the high limestone walls gave Jeb an eerie sense of having been spirited utterly away, in time and in place. Despite the bicycle and the odd parked van, he felt 'olden', without being too clear about what that meant. He struggled after Len and as he did so he could not have said whether he was awake or in a dream.

They arrived at the top of the hill and found themselves in a small square with the castle gate on one side of them, and another ancient building and archway on the other. They passed through the latter and there, soaring above them, was the cathedral they had been seeing at a distance throughout the afternoon. Jeb found he was unable to stop himself shivering or his teeth chattering, though he was determined to keep his pecker upstanding.

'We'll go in here for a little. Put this on.' Len took off his short-sleeved jersey, wrung it out, and put it over his half-brother. It came down to his knees. They leaned the bicycle against the wall and went inside.

The interior of the great church was empty and all the more dark for the darkness of the storm outside. Somewhere in that cavernous interior someone was playing the organ, but the sound only emphasised the quietness now that the tumult of the storm had been shut out. They wandered here and there along the aisle, leaving wet footprints on the flagstones. Now and then someone passed them dressed in long black or pale blue skirts topped with the crisp white rim of a clerical collar. After some time they went and sat down against a wall. Jeb gazed up at the roof on which the fan-vaulting was just visible, spraying out like tree branches from either side of the clerestory. Jeb's teeth were no longer chattering, though he felt cold and soaked to the skin.

'This is like the railway station Mum and me and my real dad used to go to when my real dad had to go back to his squadron.' Len was also looking up at the lofty arches of the roof. 'I used to stand there holding onto Mum's hand and not being able to see the train through all the legs of the people and the soldiers. Then all the soldiers were in the train and I could see it moving out. And all along it there were arms waving from the windows.'

Len paused in his reminiscence, his head thrown back and gazing at the distant ceiling. Then he said, almost shyly, 'It looked like a millipede, that train. Like a huge great millipede, all those arms waving. That's one of the first things I can remember,' he finished.

'I'm hungry, Len,' Jeb said, quietly.

'Chin up, old man. We'll move on soon.'

Once a cleric came past them and stopped.

'Are you boys all right?'

'We're just keeping out of the rain for a little, sir.'

He was a large man with narrow, kindly eyes and a sharp beard, and he was wearing one of the black skirts, belted at the middle by a stout leather belt. He asked them where they were from and whether their parents knew where they were.

'Perhaps you might like to use the telephone and let them know you're safe,' he suggested.

'I telephoned them earlier, sir. We're all right. Really.'

'Well,' he seemed a little reluctant to leave them, 'they lock the doors here in half an hour.' He walked away, his skirts swishing as he moved.

'Why did you say you had telephoned?' Jeb asked.

'Throw him off the scent. Less fuss the better.' Len was silent for a few moments, then added, 'We'll make a home run, never fear.'

'Should you telephone?'

'I said, never fear,' replied Len, sharply. They sat in silence for a long time. Len was consulting the Ordinance Survey map he had been carrying in his pocket. The organ playing stopped. There was a knock and scrape of someone stacking chairs deep in the interior of the building. A little later they heard the crisp clack of shoes walking across the flagstones, and eventually they heard a jingling of keys and a shuffling of rubber soles.

'Time to move, old man.' They passed out through a massive escutcheoned door. It was still raining, though now more gently than before. 'Wait here a mo,' said Len, and disappeared back inside. He was gone for some minutes, during which time Jeb stood in the porch, fearful that either Len or he would be discovered by the man with the keys. Then Len appeared again, carrying some white clothes under his arm He stuffed them into the bicycle basket, put Jeb on his seat, and began pedalling off rapidly. When they had gone some distance, he stopped and put one of the white coat-things over Jeb's head, and the other over his own.

'It's the best I could do.'

'Did you steal them?'

'A man let me have them.'

Soaked and tired as he was, Jeb accepted what he immediately perceived to be a lie.

'Now let's not waste any more time, old thing.'

They cycled through the rain for some time. Cars swished by them with their headlights on, the surplices flapped soddenly. They passed a fish-and-chip shop with a light still showing in its window.

'Len?'

'Yes.'

'I'm hungry.'

'I haven't any money, old man.'

'All right.'

The last houses fell behind them and they cycled on past hedgerows and trees. The rain stopped, though each time they passed under the canopy of a tree Jeb felt the heavy splashes of leaf-drip upon his head and neck. The road seemed to be very straight and the amount of traffic small. Len had engaged the dynamo to the back wheel so there was a weak pool of light shed by their headlamp. He sat motionless on his seat; his bottom felt stiff and sore. He looked down and could see Len's sandals going round and round on the pedals. Round and round, round and round. And the road, so straight, gleamy after the rain. He had hunched the white coat around himself and tucked in his hands so that the garment parcelled the whole of his body except for his feet.

Did he fall asleep? He was suddenly aware that he was standing on the ground near a bush and that Len was talking to him, while getting the surplice over his head.

'Best if we ditch the parachutes, old man. Here, hups-a-daisy.'

'Parachutes?' asked Jeb, through a daze.

But Len didn't answer as he took both coats and bundled them under a bush. 'Also best if we avoid going through the front gate. Don't want a fuss, do we.' While he spoke, Len was panting.

'Are we home yet?'

'Last leg, old thing. Never fear.'

Len led Jeb to a cyclone-wire fence which was the back-garden boundary of one of the married quarters. He lay the bicycle on its side and began covering it with long grass.

'Why don't we take the bicycle?' Jeb asked.

''Cause too much notice if we try and hoik it over the fence. Best if I come back for it tomorrow. We've got to strike across country for a bit now, through people's gardens, so the bike would also make us conspicuous. Don't want to go back in the bag when we've come this far, do we.'

Jeb had no idea what Len was talking about, but he was too tired to want explanations. He found himself being lifted high in the air and dropped over the fence so that he landed with a jolt in the sopping grass. Then Len vaulted over himself, and led Jeb by the hand through various gardens onto a street, and from there down several other streets until they stood outside their home.

The lights were on and there was also a half-tonner parked beside the kerb. Len took Jeb around the side of the house and through the kitchen door. They stood blinking in the light and there, facing them, were Mother, Dad and the man who looked in two directions.

'I've brought Jeb home. I said I would do it myself, and I did,' said Len.

The commotion that followed remained confused in Jeb's recollection of it. He could recall phrases — 'They're sopping,' and 'What did you mean by...' and 'It's past midnight, for God's sake.' On several occasions he heard Len being asked why he had not telephoned them, but Len chose not to answer this question, or any other that was directed at him. He stood with his arms at his side staring with a fixed, a blazing expression like (Jeb later chose to recall) a POW resisting a histrionic interrogation. At that time the younger boy couldn't understand why Len was receiving the lion's share of the telling off, from Dad mainly, though from Mother also. It remained only for Jeb to stand in the middle of the kitchen floor, feeling over-exposed under the white strobe light, and aware of the man in the background watching the proceedings and saying nothing. He seemed able to have one eye on Len and one on Jeb at the same time, and the expression on his face was one of grave approval at this dressing down 'that Len was receiving.

At last he said, 'Well, *all's* well that *ends* well, as they say in the pictures. I'll *pop* in during the morning and get one or *two* par-*tick*-ulars for my report, sir, *ma'am*. Until then, goodnight.' On this occasion he didn't drop down on his haunches and say anything homiletic to Jeb. It may have been the presence of Len who had been listening to the blame being heaped upon his head in a mutinous silence, which made the provost refrain. After he left, there was a silence in the kitchen until they heard the half-tonner drive off outside.

Jeb was whisked away and bathed by Mother, then given a cheese sandwich and a mug of chocolate, whereupon he was put to bed. Len, meanwhile, had gone to his room and shut the door. The last thing Jeb could recall hearing before he fell asleep was Mother standing at Len's door saying, 'You must eat something.' The boy did not hear whether there was a reply.

By the time he woke the following morning, his parents were already up. The bicycle had been recovered, and Len had gone out. While Jeb sat at the dining-room table Dad, unusually still in his dressing-gown, asked him, 'Jeb, did Len tell you where he was intending to go yesterday?'

'We were looking for airfields. Then we went into the town and it poured with rain. We stayed in the big church to keep dry.' The boy decided not to say anything about the canal.

'Did Len try and persuade you to come with him anywhere? I mean, anywhere further than usual?'

'No, why should he?' Jeb saw that Mother had been listening closely to his answers. 'Why should he?' But Dad didn't answer this.

Instead he said to Mother, 'We can't be absolutely sure, you know. Not absolutely.' And Mother looked at her hands and said nothing.

Two days later Len went back to school. He was home for a few days over Christmas, and then gone.

'Where does Len go?'

'He's staying with his Aunt Eva,' Mother told him. It was the same at Easter; Len was at a camp somewhere except for a few days. And the following summer, and so on. When the exam results came through for 1955, Len had managed to acquire only one more of his GCEs.

7

In the absence of Len, Jeb played with the other children on the camp, but it was not the same. An absence entered his life and took root there. It was as simple as that. It was as complex as that. The simplicity lay in his losing a companion whose lead he had always been able to accept without question, with whom, during that summer, he was able to glimpse, but only glimpse, immense possibilities of freedom.

The complexity was more difficult to explain. It had to do with the obscure need which developed in the growing boy, then the teenager and the young man to fill that absence, and the kinds of attachment to people he formed in order to do this. It had to do with a notion of self-possession which, by his mid-teens, he yearned to be able to apply to himself but which, in all honesty, he realised he could not. He could not say that either this need, or the notion, were things that overwhelmed his life at any given time. They did not handicap his character so much as predispose it.

Reichswald 1959

1

Germany. Jermannee. Romannee Jermannee.

Romany. He had no idea what the word meant. It was just there, suddenly, when he needed it. Romany. Maybe he had seen it on the spine of a book in Dad's bookshelf. Whatever. Romannee Jermannee, he thought, as he walked through the trees and out onto the grass. The two words went together.

He was now ten years old. Sometimes it was as if his life before Germany had been intermittent. But Germany, Germany was full and continuous like a story, Germany was a crowd of sensations which he could summon back into mind in complex and epic reconstructions of his life, some of which were also true.

Like feats of swimming. It is a Saturday in late July. He is walking toward the garrison pool with a rolled-up towel under his arm and his togs on under his shorts. It is a day reserved for officers and their families and he has two of his dad's tokens jingling in his pocket, one for himself and one for Len who has come on a day's leave from Gütersloh, where he is stationed. He has just come out onto some vast playing fields where there are goalposts and a pavilion in the far distance, and he can now see the hedge around the swimming pool and the diving tower rising above it, white and lofty. Indeed the tower is almost as high as the two garrison churches, St Boniface's and St Andrew's, which stand nearby.

But he knows the pool well. He has reached the age of independent action and has been here many times during the swimming season in the company of Weasel or Smithy or Humphrey Cox. He can swim several lengths of the pool unaided, do a backward dive from the springboard, and twice he has jumped from the second highest platform. On the first occasion, a year ago, he went down, wobbling this way and that and waving his arms too much, so that he winded himself and smacked his face hard on the surface of the water — it felt as though someone had ripped the skin off his face with one instantaneous pull. But he recovered and climbed the tower again — it had become a dare because Weasel said that he was too yellow to do it again — jumping off and entering the water fast and straight like a thrown spear. Then he swam to the side and simply went up to his two companions. He said nothing and they said nothing, but he knew he had done a more gutsy thing than either Weasel or Humphrey Cox could do, so for the rest of the afternoon he let their occasional sarcasms pass magnanimously, as heroes can afford to do.

Romannee Jermannee. He can remember what has happened in long trails, starting, say, from yesterday, which was the first day of the summer holidays. With Weasel and Smithy he wandered for miles through the forests which began behind the married quarters of the garrison, wading through ferns, breaking out into open country where the wheat was higher than they were and shushed as they pushed through it.

It was a morning which felt like a month. They ran, or walked, or lay back under the bright sun, or stalked each other, fighting with sticks or bare hands, leaving great circles of flattened wheat. They prepared ambushes by the sides of the ruler-straight German roads, leaping up when a Volkswagen or Opel went past, blazing with their tommy guns, hurling pretend grenades, then dashing back into the cover of the wheat, yelling 'Stukas! Stukas!'

Then they wandered back slowly, not caring whether they were late for lunch, startling several pheasants from the undergrowth, diving for cover if ever they saw a Volkswagen of the Polizei, or an Austin Champ of the Military Police.

And as they meandered, Jeb supposed that the sense of elation, of *ownership*, he felt must be like what warrior-princes feel as they pass through their domains.

Or foxes perhaps.

Romany Germany. There had been two years of it now, of holidays and weekends, in which Jeb and his companions had come to know every cranny of the countryside for miles around the Oldenrath garrison, the woods whose paths led deeper and deeper into jagged green depths, where there were ditches and mounds which might have been trenches or tank traps left over from the war. They had discovered an old bunker outside Balkhoven which the American tanks had overlooked when they had come through in 1945, unlike the massive wrecked slabs and twisted rods of the bunkers on the road to Aachen. They had discovered the quarry behind the REME barracks, and returned there with an old tent which they used for a parachute. Again and again, with Weasel holding two corners and Jeb the other two, they leapt out into space, and plummetted with the tent billowing ineffectually above them, to land and slide on the steep mud sides of the quarry.

'Green on! Go! Go! Go!'

Sometimes a platoon of soldiers would march past in their webbing, carrying Bren guns, or the new rifle called the FN, on their way to the shooting range.

'Will you give us a go with your rifle, mate?'

'Aw, nick off boys!' they would reply, laughing.

Once they had followed at a distance behind, creeping through the undergrowth, smelling the dampness of the rotting leaves and the astringency of the ferns. They could hear the staccato of the small-arms fire from the range, and approached as closely as they dared, until they were seen and nearly caught by a small sergeant with a red face. Then they walked to the opposite end of the camp and found some more woods, where they played wars and had dying competitions.

2

Romany Germany. Yes, there was this new exuberance of the memory in his life, as if he was starting to be himself.

It was almost a physical sensation. He prided himself on how much he could remember, the 'and then, and then, and then', of his experience.

He could go right back, or start anywhere, like on the evening when Mother had told him that they were all going to Oldenrath in Germany because Dad had been appointed to the headquarters of the 2nd Tactical Air Force.

'Germany? But Germans are enemies.'

'That's all over and done with. Years ago.'

'They're on our side now, old man.'

'Who is the enemy now?'

'We-ell . . .'

He could recall how on a showery afternoon they had left RAF Gattisby in a staff car and boarded a steam train at Lincoln railway station. Houses, hedges and trees had shot away behind them in a continuous stream and he had pretended — because he was only young, like seven — that they were being gulped down by a huge mouth that was just behind them while the steam engine managed to keep them just out of reach of those invisible jaws.

Then they changed trains at Peterborough, standing for what seemed hours on the platform in a freezing wind which needled up the sleeves and down the neck of his gaberdine mac. Jeb tried to stand so that he could observe his mother without her noticing because she was wearing the coat with the grey fur collar, holding each lapel of it around her ears such that her face was buried in the fluffy spray of the fur, and this was the coat that the boy liked to see her in above all others because it was, inexplicably, more her than any of her other outfits.

(He noted, much later, that he only seemed to have these tender feelings for her on occasions, like this, when Len was far away. Mother felt more *his* at such times. He had missed Len sorely, of course, but there was this good side to Len's absence. He didn't like to, but he had to admit it.)

As he watched from the window of this second train, he saw the fields outside already dark, the sky deep blue like a horse guardsman's tunic. At length there was another station which was next to some docks, Dad hurrying slightly ahead carrying the two suitcases, distinctive in his white mackintosh, mother holding the hatbox with labels plastered all over it going back as far as Aden. With her other hand she held onto Jeb's sleeve as they half walked, half ran under huge cranes, or waited in long queues. All around them there were soldiers or airforce men, some in black berets, some in blue-grey berets, and some in khaki hats with a pompom in the middle.

'They're Kosbies,' Dad informed. 'King's Own Scottish Light Infantry.'

The Kosbies, and other soldiers, each with their regiments emblazoned in different colours on their shoulder tabs, stood in groups, smoking cigarettes which they held pinched between forefinger and thumb and sheltered by their cupped hands. They called out to him in accents he found difficult to understand, and when he answered back they would make mock-marvelling faces at each other, or guffaw loudly.

'Now Jeb, don't you be cheeky,' said Mother, who was smiling. But he continued his exchanges with the soldiers who, with their sharp faces, encouraged his cheek in a curious, partly bold, partly deferential humour, until suddenly they picked up their kitbags and marched off, their boots ringing on the concrete.

Then they were filing up the gangplank of a ship, so huge and lit up it looked like an entire town. Nevertheless their cabin was tiny and intermittently he woke up through the night, hot beneath his blankets, and heard from deep, deep below the unwavering, somehow soothing throb of the engines. In the morning he found they were tied up at a dockside. 'The Hook of Holland,' Dad announced. There were more soldiers along the dockside, and military police in white gaiters and belts, and red bonnets on top of their peaked caps.

Another train. This time they were in a compartment with a woman and a girl who spoke funny. The girl had straight hair over her ears and smiled into her shoulder. Mother touched her dress a few times, saying something like 'Shurn. Sareshurn'. They played cards and dominoes with the woman and girl throughout the morning and occasionally the woman began a conversation in her language, but it rapidly faltered into a gesturing of hands, a shrug and smiles of helplessness on both sides. Once she offered them a piece of cake, apple in jelly on top of pastry. It was the most sumptuous cake Jeb had ever tasted, more sumptuous than you would expect, perhaps, given that England had won the war. Mother prompted him to say thank you in the woman's language.

'Feelen dank.'

'Bitter,' said the woman in reply, bowing her head and smiling with pleasure. She watched Jeb's every mouthful.

In the late afternoon, after crossing the border between Holland and Germany, they came to a station called München Gladback, which sounded like the name of a knight.

Here they were met by an officer in airforce uniform who saluted Dad and drove them to the camp at Oldenrath where they were to be housed in G Mess until a married quarter became available. And, as they drove around the camp on their first arrival, there against the cold blue sky, more prominent than any other building, was the tower of the diving boards. Behind it, along the horizon, was a huge two-storey complex of buildings with many flags flying out the front.

'That's the Kremlin,' the officer told them.

'What's the Kremlin?' Jeb whispered the question to mother.

'HQ BAOR, NorthAG and 2nd TAF,' interposed the officer, somewhat unhelpfully.

So they lived in G Mess for several months until a married quarter became free. It was a low, semolina-coloured hostel with its swing doors and long corridors, surrounded by pine trees and rhododendron bushes and half hidden from Messes E and F. At the end of Trump Road was the Astra, which was the airforce cinema. Here on Saturday mornings, after they had fetched the groceries from the NAAFI and bought the weekly swatch of comics, he and Dad would go to the matinée for a Hopalong Cassidy flick, or a war film like *Imitation General* or *Reach for the Sky*.

A month or so before Christmas, and without warning, all the children were given gingerbread men. It was something to do with a St Nicholas. Then, on Christmas Eve, the officers, their wives and children, together with the German waiters and Matzi, the fat woman who was in charge of G Mess, all had a party. There was Pepsi and Sevenup, and a huge Christmas tree, lit up like a liner. But what hallowed the memory of this party was that he was allowed to stay up very late and watch the dancing, and his own mother and father were the best dancers on the floor and won three prizes, including the prize for the Scotch dancing, even though Dad was English and Mother was Australian. For all the throng of dancers on the floor, Jeb could not take his eyes off his own parents, their heads were held so high and their feet were so sure. It was as if they were two eddies of the same wind. It was as if he were looking at Dad and Mother for the first time against the floating lights and bunting on the walls, hearing the booming voice of the compere through the microphone, seeing the dance floor now suddenly cleared as Dad and Mother did a lap of triumph to the clapping and cheering of the people around the edges of the room. In his memory it was an inexplicable island of happiness, as he watched these two strangers who were also his parents, subsumed by the requirements of the dance. Finally the night came to its tumultuous conclusion when everyone joined hands in a great unwieldy ring and surged inwards and back again singing that peculiarly haunting song which he did not understand, but had heard before, he was not sure where.

We twa hae run about the braes,
And pu'd the gowans fine . . .
But seas between us braid hae roar'd
Sin auld lang syne.

This was 1957, and now it is 1959. In the intervening period Jeb has collected nine countries if you include England and Monaco, and sometimes he feels as if he stores all the world inside his head.

Now, as he walks across the playing fields, he can conjure the immense pine forests beside the autobahns, in their dense rows like soldiers on parade, the long columns of Yank army trucks with their white stars and negro soldiers looking down at the three of them in their Opel, the cannons swathed in tarpaulins, the tanks on their monstrous transporters moving south toward Karlsruhe or north toward Frankfurt. That must have been one of their winter trips because suddenly they were driving through a snowy landscape — where was that, Memmingen? Garmisch Partenkirchen? Oberammergau? — the snow shovelled off the roads so it looked like the eider-downs in hotels, and every stationary car with snow on its bonnet like a sugar bun. Or another winter journey, up the zig-zag roads to the Brenner or the St Gotthard Passes, the silent whiteness outside and the accordion music on Dad's car radio, the frontier guards stamping with the cold and breathing steam through the car window when they looked at the passports, the ski lodges in the Tyrol and Switzerland, high on their perches, the white glare of the ski slopes, the *apfel saft* in the evenings. There was the summer camping, at Jeselo near Venice where the beaches were lion-coloured and too hot to step on at midday, at Ventimiglia where they had eaten nothing but peaches, huge peaches, and at Lake Heiterwang in the Austrian Alps, the lakewater freezing and immobile, and where he had seen millions of fireflies along the walking paths in the evening. All this and much more besides. Romany Germany. Yes, it felt as if he possessed the whole world inside his head.

Len has been in Germany for almost a year now, doing his National Service as a fitter in the RAF, first at Geilen-kirchen where Jeb, Dad and Mother went to visit him on the day of the airshow and watched the Gloster Javelins taking off, one after another with their triangle wings and grey and green camouflage, taking off so quickly that it looked like they were being hauled on an invisible rope by some giant on the other side of the clouds. Later Len was at Bielefeld, and now he is at Gütersloh, where he says they have Hawker Hunters. Yes, all these things he can remember, and more, because it is as if everything that happens is like the vapour trail of a Javelin or Hunter, silvery gold and funnelling out behind to show where you've been.

But there is Len now. This is his last visit because he is due to go back to England soon and be de-mobbed. He is waiting outside the pool because, being only an aircraftsman, he cannot go inside until Jeb shows one of Dad's officer tokens. Dad and Mother will join them later in the afternoon.

As the boy approaches his half-brother he can hear the shouting and squealing from within the grounds and the ker-whoosh of boys doing bombs off the springboard.

3

'I can swim a width underwater, Len.'

'I bet you can't swim two, old man.'

'With a dive start?'

'All right.'

Jeb retreats a few paces from the edge, takes a deep breath, runs, and dives into the pool, then begins breaststroking vigorously along the bottom. He has learned how to keep his eyes open under the water and he thrusts strongly into the misty aquamarine, aware at the edge of his vision of the sun wriggling in yellowy serpents of light across the blue bottom. He touches the wall opposite and starts back, but before he has reached halfway he surfaces, gasping for breath.

'No good? Then watch this.' Len walks back from the pool, then, concentrating his features, he sprints toward the edge and launches himself in a shallow arc. Jeb can see his face as it comes through the water toward him; it is odd the way a face underwater looks somehow less lifelike, as though it is dazed, the eyes remote, the mouth pursed. Len swims past where Jeb is standing, touches the other side, then swims back, touches the side he started from, then turns once more and completes a third width underwater before surfacing next to Jeb, tossing his head violently back to shake the water from his hair and gasping noisily.

'How was that?' he pants, leaning over his half-brother, and dripping water on him. They are in the shallow end of the pool where Jeb is able to stand with his head and shoulders just above the surface, while with Len the water only reaches his middle. For Len has grown very tall, like his real dad; his face is longer and sharper than formerly; he has the same direct stare as the man in the portrait, but the directness of the gaze, in Len's case, is softened by the mouth which is set, not in apology exactly, but as though it were on the point of making some excuse. There is no doubt that Len is a real grownup now, and this fact has unsettled Jeb on each of the rare occasions he has seen Len over the past five years.

'Aw, but you're practically as big as the width of the pool. No wonder it doesn't take you so long to cover the distance,' says the younger boy. Even so, he is impressed. Three widths underwater! That is about sixty yards.

'Let's go to the diving boards.'

They swim to the diving pool, where the colour of the water changes from aquamarine to a cobalt blue.

'It's more than fifteen feet deep here, Len.'

'Let's see if you're right.'

Len hauls himself out by the stepladder, lopes over to where they left their clothes on the grass and takes something from his trouser pocket. Then he comes back and stands in the queue of people waiting to use the springboard.

'What're you going to do?'

'See how deep it is, old fellow.' As he says this, Len holds up a five-deutschmark coin in his hand. His announcement attracts the interest of the other people standing about.

'You can't. Your eardrums will burst.'

The bottom of the deep end is one of the taboos among Jeb and his friends. They have gone down, hand over hand, on the stepladder for as far as they could bear it sometimes, but never managed much more than eight feet or so before the pressure, or panic, became too much for them, and they shot up again.

'I'd be a bit careful, if I were you,' a man standing behind Len in the queue warns. But Len only makes eyes at Jeb and walks out to the end of the springboard. He tosses the coin and watches it until it disappears in the blue dark. Then, retreating to halfway down the board, he stands for some moments looking straight ahead of himself with his arms spread horizontally before him. All at once, with a sprightly bouncing step, he skips to the tip of the board, jumps once, twice, three times, gaining height each time and making the board resound with a violent boing, then, with one final bounce he rises, jacknifes in mid-air and enters the water almost

vertically. Jeb and the other watchers see Len's body diminish
to a whitish blur beneath the surface of the pool. For perhaps
half a minute it is hard to discern what is actually happening
down there. Then they see Len shooting up, his face uppermost,
like the upturned face of a white flower, and his clenched
fist out before him. Once again, when he bursts the surface
there is a great tossing of his head and panting for breath,
and he swims to the side to recover himself. As he hangs
onto the side rail he holds up the silver five-deutschmark
coin between thumb and forefinger.

'You're... right,' he says between gasps. 'It is... a deep
old... pool, isn't it.' The watchers shake their heads at the
recklessness of the escapade, or smile indulgently, then go
about their business. Len hauls himself over the rim of the
pool and sits, like Jeb, with his legs dangling in the water.

'Do you reckon you're game to have a shot at it, old man?'
he asks after they have sat in silence for a minute or so.
There is an intentness in the way Len is looking at him.

'What if I don't manage to find the coin?'

'You should start with the attitude that you will find it.'

'But what if I don't?'

'Then I'll be five marks down.'

'That's five whole weeks' pocket money for me.'

'Tell you what, if you manage to bring it back from the
bottom, you can have it.'

'Are you serious?' From being an idle suggestion, the prospect of diving to the bottom of the pool to retrieve the five-
DM coin suddenly becomes attractive.

'On my honour.'

Jeb considers. When it comes down to it, has he ever *really*
tried to reach the bottom of the deep end?

'Well, if I lose it, it's your money.' He takes the coin
and goes out onto the springboard. He doesn't want to attract
watchers so he throws the coin into the pool inconspicuously
and dives after it almost immediately. The momentum of
his dive takes him to no great depth so he kicks and claws
strongly, finding it more difficult the further he goes. The
pressure begins on his ears and temples and his first impulse
is to give up at this point and shoot up to the surface again;

but he resists, and discovers in the process that if he swallows the pressure on his ears is relieved. The further he goes down the darker the water becomes. The pain of the pressure returns a little, so he swallows again hard, pleased by the control he is able to exert. His hand touches the bottom. It is slimy and he recoils, then gropes about for a few moments, thrusting downwards constantly with his legs and arms because the impulse of his body to float back upwards is very strong. He is beginning to experience a sensation of urgency in his lower lungs. Then he panics, turns, kicks the bottom as hard as he can and begins ascending, flippering vigorously with his feet. The surface of the water glitters far above him. He feels he won't last out until the surface without taking a breath. He wants to inhale, with the force of his entire being he wants to suck in air, Oh just air, simply air. Will he never reach the top? It is ridiculous. It is terrifying, suddenly, for there to be no time left, no seconds or fractions of seconds left. For there not to be the option, simply to suck in ordinary air, it is horrible, it is intolerable.

In the event he misjudges the moment of breaking the surface slightly and so manages to suck in half air, half water. He finds himself in sunlight again amidst a chaos of sensations, of frantic inhalations which don't seem to do any good, of terrifying croaking noises which he realises are his own; he can feel his windpipe along its whole length, while at the same moment he feels himself being hauled straight out of the water and having his head thrust violently down between his legs, which makes him retch out the water he swallowed together with a great deal of mucous. He has a dull pain in his temples and ears still, and he realises the person who is gripping him by the back of the neck is Len, who is saying in a coaxing voice like that the teachers use when someone is hurt on the soccer field, 'You're all right, old man. Nothing to fear, nothing to worry about. Take it easy now, take it easy now.'

Jeb breathes stertorously. 'I couldn't find your five marks, Len. But I reached the bottom. It was all slimy,' he realises he is saying.

'Don't worry about the money. You did very well.' Len

seems to be a little too anxious to please and, as he leads Jeb over to where their clothes are, the younger boy notices that they are being watched by the man who spoke to Len earlier, and that he is shaking his head in disapproval.

'Sit tight for a bit. I'll be back in a minute.' Jeb watches Len lope back toward the deep end and dive neatly over the side. The effects of the dive and all the water he has coughed up make the afternoon already seem very long.

No, it isn't exactly that. He feels, somehow, as if he has gone far or deep into time, as though Time were a penetrable substance. And he feels disinclined, for the moment, to go back into the pool, while the pale or brown bodies which flit this way and that, jumping, diving, tussling, shouting, seem strangely remote and somehow yellowy as he watches them. Jeb is not particularly aware of having nearly drowned, but part of him has retreated to a recess of consciousness, disengaged from the hubbub around him in order to restore some inner balance that has been momentarily upset. It is odd because everything continues normally, but as though he were inside a capsule from which he can hear and see and participate in all that is going on, but at one remove.

Len seems to be gone for quite some time. Then he emerges, and goes out on the springboard and dives in again. This happens on two or three occasions, and, after emerging once, Len sits on the edge of the pool for some time, apparently recovering himself. Jeb sees the man with the disapproving expression go over and speak to Len, then walk away. Again Len dives. Eventually he comes back to where Jeb is sitting. He is breathing heavily, and water drips from his sprigs of hair and in long rivulets down his body. As he sits down he says, 'Hold out your hand, old man,' and when Jeb does so he puts the five-deutschmark coin into it. 'Buy yourself a couple of plastic kits. You deserve it for getting down to the bottom like you did. It was plucky of you.'

'Cor. Thank you.' Jeb is conscious, as he says this, of how gauche it sounds. He looks at the coin, and then at his half-brother, who had sat down beside him and is towelling his hair and face. There are many things which have changed about Len since he left his school, but one of them, Jeb perceives, is that he seems to go at things with such concentrated effort. As though whenever he does something, like dive repeatedly to search for a coin at the deep end, he is saying afterwards, 'Look, that's what I've done,' expecting someone to say back, 'That was really something,' so he can say, 'It was really nothing at all.' Only all this is never actually said, it is simply there in the silence, in the hard fact of the coin enclosed in Jeb's fist, and it makes the younger boy feel at a bit of a loss.

'What did that man come up and say?'

'Nothing you need worry about.' Then, as though to allow Jeb momentarily into a world of grownup exchanges, Len adds, 'He mumbled something about calling the attendant if I kept putting myself at risk. I told him I had done a diver's course during Nasho. That stompered him.'

'Have you? Done a diver's course?' Jeb knows Len has been on a course in the American zone recently, somewhere near the Austrian border, but the location didn't suggest a place where divers' courses were undertaken. Len merely smiles down at Jeb briefly without giving an answer.

They lie in the sun, resting back on their elbows. At length Jeb says, 'Have you been to see your real dad while you've been in Germany?'

Len looks at him for a moment, then looks off toward the diving tower. 'Why should I want to?' He is silent for a while, then adds, 'He can always come and see me if he wants to.'

'Does he know you're stationed at Gütersloh?'

'It's up to him to find out, isn't it.'

'Haven't you told him?'

'Where should I send a letter? Last I heard he was living in some cellar in Hamburg. I haven't seen him since he came to my school three years ago. Anyway, why should I want to see him? What's he done for me?'

There is nothing Jeb can say to this. It seems inarguable though in some indefinable way, not final. He sees Wilf and their mother standing near the entrance with a picnic hamper and towels. They are some fifty yards off and looking among the crowd for Len and Jeb. It is unclear whether Len is aware they have arrived when he gets to his feet and says in a throwaway tone, 'You're the only family I've got, old man.' And he lopes off and dives into the pool.

4

And so it is hard again, for he, Jeb, the one who is in between. It feels like trying to take the two ends of a broken wire and join them, with Dad coming up and dumping the hamper and asking, 'Did I see Big Len just launch himself into the pool like the submarine Nautilus?' and the smile under his moustache being big and yet, somehow having nothing to join onto . . . as he stands putting on his baggy togs the way he always does, not in the changing rooms like Mother, but in the middle of everyone with a towel wrapped around.

Mother is in her costume and swimhat already, the blue costume with the white streak across the front and the white swimhat like he had seen her once last year when the two of them had gone to the pool by themselves and she had come out in this costume, looking like a speedboat. Nor, on that occasion, had she entered the pool by the stepladder as the other mothers did. Instead, she dived off the edge in a long, unhesitating dive like a stone thrown flat to the surface, making hardly a ripple. She swam up and down the pool three or four times before skipping nimbly out and dabbing herself all over with her white towel, and Jeb said, 'I didn't know you could swim,' and she replied, 'There are quite a few things you don't know,' and later Dad told him that she used to swim in the competitions in Australia with her sister, Peg . . .

While Dad is not so much a swimmer as a wallower, a walrus with gingery hairs on its chest and freckles on its back and face. And whenever they go to the pool he always makes straight for the diving boards where he does back-dives and back-somersaults. He makes a point of jumping at least once from the very top platform of the diving tower, with Jeb watching him from below, all alone because not many dads dare to do it, then he steps back a pace and with a little skip he leaps over the edge and starts plummetting, plummetting (Jeb had always liked that word, plummetting) down with his arms going around like helicopter blades to keep himself balanced, and he hits the water with a mighty kersplosh and comes up grinning and says, 'Did you like that, Jeb Corballis?' and Jeb replies, 'Do it again,' but Dad is not to be persuaded. 'No, once is enough.'

Now, out there on the marbly-blue surface, Mother is a white blob among all the other darker blobs of heads, and Jeb can see Len's head coming over and bobbing up and down beside hers for a moment or two before he strikes out for the side and comes over, upon which Dad says in his hearty way, 'Well, hello there, Aircraftsman First Class Hengelow,' and Len says only, 'Hello,' and stares off toward the diving boards again, and Jeb wants to do something so it will all be hearty and good fun, but he doesn't know what...

So Dad asks Len whether he knows yet what he intends to take up after he is de-mobbed in a couple of months time, and Len says that he might be joining some fellows in a truck, an old Bedford, going to Africa.

'Africa's very unsettled these days,' says Dad.

'That won't stop us,' Len replies, curtly.

'It ought to make you think.'

'You had your chance of excitement in the war.'

'The war wasn't put on to give us a chance for excitement, old man.'

'It was a chance for *some*,' Len kept his gaze fixed on the diving boards. Dad looks at the grass rather sadly for some time.

'You need to be giving some thought to what career you are going to take up, Len,' he says gently. 'Something in aeronautics maybe?'

'I'm not ready to settle down yet.' So Dad changes the subject, and asks about Gütersloh, and gradually their conversation becomes less prickly.

At length Dad says, 'Let's see what we can make these diving boards do for us.'

So all three of them go over. Dad does a back-somersault off the springboard, so Len then does one where he runs along, and does a handstand on the end, then topples off into the water. Then Dad says, 'I'm for the top.' Jeb and

Len watch as he comes hurtling down through the blue sky with his baggy togs all over the place and when he comes to the surface and says 'How was that one?' Len says, 'Watch this, then,' and he climbs to the top, stands for a moment at the very back of the board, runs and dives, dives! his long body coming head first down through the sky for a few seconds. And Dad says, 'He'll give his head one almighty crack.' Although Len's body is airborne for only a short time, it seems like an age. But the dive is perfect until the very end when Len's legs come too far over and he hits the water smack, with the back of his legs. As he watches, Jeb is conscious that the whole pool must be watching. Father and son wait for Len to surface and come over, which he does, asking, 'How was that?' and Dad says, when he sees Len is all right, 'Well, I bet you hurt yourself,' whereupon Len says, 'Not at all.'

Then Jeb tries to do a backward somersault off the springboard but goes over too far and lands on his face and stomach, which winds him, so he sits with his feet dangling in the water while Len and Dad climb up to the second board and do back-somersaults from there. Only Len's is more spectacular because when he goes over he curls himself up into a ball and comes down like a bomb, a Grand Slammer, and makes a huge splash. Things are a bit happier now, because, while they are on the diving boards Len and Dad are at least talking, lost in an enthusiasm about different sorts of dives and jumps and so on.

Then the two of them go up to the third diving board and Len goes off first, doing a complicated forward roll thing — Len doesn't seem to mind how he lands in the water and whenever he ends in a bellyflop he says it doesn't hurt him, and it is all part of his airforce physical training. Dad then follows him, trying to perform the same complicated manoeuvre, only, as he rolls forward, Jeb sees him hit his head on the edge as he comes round. He hasn't pushed himself far enough out. The blow upsets his balance so that he comes down all askew, hitting the water anyhow, and when he swims up to the side his whole face is covered with watery blood, and his moustaches are ghastly and dripping crimson, and there is crimson all over his chest like the delta of a river, though he says he is all right, a bit shaken.

The attendant comes over and Dad goes away with him. When Mother is told what has happened she says, 'Oh for God's sake,' and goes immediately to the attendant's office. Eventually she returns with Dad, who has a small white plaster on his forehead where all the blood has been. He is saying, 'You see, it is only a scratch, only a scratch, injuries to the head always produce masses of blood.' Meanwhile Jeb has been feeling dread. It is like pain, it is like wanting to shrink out of the present and back into the way things were a few minutes before. For, all the while his Dad was away, he was thinking how, with all that blood, it must have been what some of his books called a 'mortal wound'. And what would they all do if Dad didn't come back? But the dread evaporates when Dad returns, with his moustaches cleaned up and the little white plaster under the line of his ginger-curly hair.

Mother says it is best if they all go now and have some tea at home instead of out of the hamper, so they take the hamper home untouched, and in the evening they go to see a 'Carry On' film at the Astra and Jeb is allowed to stay up late to see Len off on the bus to Gütersloh.

5

Not long after Len went back to England for his de-mob, Jeb returned home from school one afternoon to find Mrs Fossey busy in his mother's kitchen. 'Bossy Fossey!' he and some of his classmates had yelled from behind a hedge. When Jeb first found her in the kitchen his immediate thought was that at last he was going to get a severe telling off, but he was puzzled by the fact his mother was not also present wearing her stern face. Instead, Mrs Fossey made him sit down at the kitchen table and told him that he was not to worry too much, but his father had suddenly become rather ill.

'Heck,' was all Jeb could think to say, and then, because he thought this might have sounded as if it lacked conviction, he repeated, 'Heck.' He was more aware of being expected to register some particular emotion than of actually feeling anything.

Group Captain Corballis had been taken to the hospital at Wegberg which was not so *very* far away, Mrs Fossey continued, and Jeb's mother had gone with him, but she hoped to be back this evening. If she couldn't come back, then she was going to telephone and Jeb would go and stay with Mrs Fossey and her children. Meanwhile, Mrs Fossey said, she would get him his tea.

Jeb wandered into the playroom. He had arranged to meet Humphrey Cox and Weasel, and go up to the NAAFI to see if the new comics had come in, but he supposed, rather vaguely, that he could not decently keep the appointment now.

And when his mother did not come home that evening, it was more the strangeness of Mrs Fossey's home, and her children, one son and one daughter, neither of whom Jeb knew well, which preoccupied him. He sat in their drawing room with a book open on his knee, but not taking any of the print in, and the Fosseys were very quiet and didn't trouble him. Whenever they spoke among themselves they whispered, and the girl, who was younger, kept looking covertly in Jeb's direction. They asked him frequently if he wanted cocoa, or biscuits, and he said no thank you. He had to sleep in a made-up camp-bed which collapsed on him the first time he sat on it, and he lay in the dark for a long time, his eyes wide awake, trying to imagine the circumstances in which Dad now was. He felt the same sensation of dread as he had felt at the swimming pool all those months ago, the desire to be back at a time before this complexity entered his life, but the feeling was milder than it had been then.

Anyway, how was it possible to imagine his dad being 'rather ill'? What did that mean? He had seemed perfectly all right when he had gone off to work the previous morning with his briefcase under his arm and his pipe in his mouth. So what did it mean, 'rather ill'?

Mrs Fossey made him ready for school the next morning and said that he had better come back to their house first in the afternoon, just in case his mum was still away. The day at school was like being present in the classroom, and absent from it all at the same time. Jeb had the sense that everyone in the school had been told about his dad and that they all steered their way around him, as though he were a mine that might explode if stepped on. When he went back to Mrs Fossey's in the afternoon she told him that his mother had come home but was asleep and he could see her later. His dad's position had 'stabilised' she said. She was sure he would be all right.

When he saw his mother she looked at him for some moments as though not knowing how to act. Then she gave him a hug which seemed to last longer than was necessary, which was unusual, because, on the whole, she did not cuddle him much. She also sat him down at the kitchen table and told him that Dad had suffered something called a stroke and that he might have a bit of difficulty talking quite as clearly as he used to, or moving his right hand quite as freely. But the doctors said he had been very lucky, all things considered, and that there might be improvement with time. Jeb thought she looked somehow different. The eyes seemed to look out from deeper recesses and her skin looked rougher and paler. When she finished one cigarette she lit another one. Usually she only smoked a couple a day with her coffee.

Without quite knowing why, or even believing in his own statement particularly, Jeb said, 'You look rough, Mum.' As he was to reflect much later, it was the first occasion he had recognised his mother as a distinct and suffering being.

'I'm a bit tired, I suppose.' Elizabeth Corballis didn't cry as the two of them sat at the kitchen table; she said, 'How ever will we manage?' and, to the boy's ears, that weary question sounded far worse than any crying.

When he was allowed to see Dad a week or so later at the hospital he was horrified by the way the smile and the words came out all lop-sided from under his moustache, and by the way that when his father offered him his hand to shake he had to do it in a backwards kind of way, because it stuck out awkwardly from his side. And Dad would insist on trying to say so much; it came out slurry and the boy had to keep looking at his mother to find out what it was that was being said.

Dad came home from hospital after six weeks, and by this time arrangements had been made to repatriate him. The furnishings of their house were packed away in tea-chests by a group of soldiers who wore long leather jerkins over their battledress and belonged to the Royal Corps of Pioneers. In a day the house was bare and their belongings had been taken away in a lorry.

For their return to England, they did not take the boat-train to the Hook, but flew in a Viscount aeroplane from Dusseldorf to a place in England called Stansted, where Wilf's brother, a single man who looked after Jeb's ageing granny, met them and took them home until the tenants had had a chance to move out of Candleware Road.

There was serious talk as to whether they should go and live in Australia. This was a plan that Jeb had heard mooted on various occasions during the course of his boyhood. His mother, he knew, longed to return there, and Wilf was fond of saying that it was a land of golden opportunities and almost unlimited potential. But the move to Australia was postponed. Jeb was offered a place at a reputable boarding school which took quite large numbers of servicemen's sons. On the basis of the results of an exam he had sat shortly before they left Germany, Jeb had won a scholarship to the school which paid for half the fees. It seemed that this bursary was a real enticement. Wilf's pension could not have paid for a boarding-school education. Suddenly there was less money in the house.

School 1960–65

1

From the sluggish and troubled five years that Jeb spent at
a boarding school in the East Anglian countryside, three events
stood out. The first of these was the day of his arrival,
significant because, as it seemed in retrospect, the *character*
of his life changed on that day. Even at the time, in those
first few school terms, there were moments when he felt
immersed, overwhelmed, not by the harshness, the sporadic
bullying, the routines, but by the enclosed-ness, the totality
of the school. He had become, he realised, a part of a programme and he supposed it was doing him good — in the
long run anyway. But it had no charm, no warmth in the
imagination, as his German days had, those gypsy days he
had no wish to grow out of.

Clemstead College as the school was called, lay not far
from the preparatory school Len had attended near Ipswich.
Jeb was to be placed in one of several boarding halls, Loftus
House.

2

After turning off the main road they approached Loftus House
by a sunken lane. On one side was a windbreak of cypresses
which formed the boundary of the House grounds; on the
other, a bank of blackberry hedges beyond which were
squared-off fields, furrowed in preparation for a crop of winter

vegetables. Mother drove and Dad sat in the front, turning every now and then to utter some advice in a garble of syllables. He was making gestures with his left arm, straight stabbing motions at the windscreen, followed by an interrogatory sound; Jeb nodded in response. He knew the gist of what his father was saying. He had heard this lesson in self-defence even before Dad had suffered the stroke.

'Sure, Dad. Lead with a straight left, and keep my guard up.'

But his father kept up the demonstration for a little longer. It was unsettling, the way in which, since the stroke, Dad's behaviour seemed to be not only exaggerated and gnome-like but independent of what other people's responses were.

Jeb creaked in his new uniform, not enjoying very much the smell of newness in the corduroy trousers, the blazer and the unblemished black leather of his shoes. Innately conservative, he felt the garments had turned him out of his old self into a strange self he did not welcome. The whole morning had been spent in a department store getting him 'kitted out' for the school. Never had so much money been spent on his clothing — six sets of underwear, six pairs of socks, four grey clydella shirts, four pairs of corduroy trousers, three school ties, one school cap, one blazer, one tweed jacket, two pairs of black shoes, one dressing-gown, one raincoat, one pair of slippers, one pair of gumboots, twenty-four handkerchiefs, washbag, face flannel, toothbrush, nailbrush, hairbrush and comb, a bootpolishing set, a clothes brush, and so it went on. All these unwanted possessions made him feel encumbered, and at the same time thrust out into the cold. He was to be abandoned. That this happened to everyone at his age — everyone he knew at least — did not disguise the basic fact. The money that had been spent on him this morning was also a signal of impending severance. He felt unready.

He had felt exposed as he stood on a stool in the department store while a man whose spectacles pinched his nostrils, making him sound breathy, fussed around with a tape measure.

'If the young gentleman could just . . .'

The young gentleman. Yes, he had felt both vulnerable

and too prominent. All this attention and expense, he sensed obscurely, was improper to his status as an eleven-year-old. He was receiving the kind of attention adults enjoyed. He didn't want his own growing up to be accelerated in this way. Not that he had a say in it. With the exception of what he was wearing, all these items had been packed away into his trunk, which had then been put back into the boot of the car.

The brambles and the cypresses raced by, then they turned into the gravel driveway to Loftus House. On either side of this driveway stood tall elm trees which formed a tunnel of foliage, framing a red brick building with casement windows and steeply canted roofs. Cars of other parents were parked around the gatehouse, from which boys and their fathers were lugging trunks into the interior of Loftus House. On some waste ground to the left of the avenue of elms a group of older boys were playing soccer, shooting for goal between two dustbins.

'Put it through! Put it *through*!' The boy with the ball flicked it past his opponent then kicked it brutally at the goalmouth, where the keeper dived spectacularly and caught it.

'Aw, saved! Saved!'

It was a little daunting, the competence, the speed, the vehemence of the football game. And the way the players appeared to be so at home in this strange place.

Mother parked the car and stopped a passing boy.

'Excuse me. We're wondering where my son...'

'Noodles are in Dorm One, just through the main door on the left.'

'Noodles?'

'Noodles are first-formers,' explained the youth, a little impatient that he should have to translate so basic a word. He had an accent, Jeb noticed, like the children of the Other Ranks at Oldenrath and Gattisby.

'I see,' said Mother, though the youth had already darted off.

They walked through a courtyard, and down a corridor, their shoes clacking on the red tiles, until they found a door with 'Dormitory One' stencilled on it. It was a large E-shaped room with casement windows on two of its walls. The furniture consisted of twenty or so tubular steel upper and lower bunks and some metal lockers which had once been painted a sky blue colour but from which much of the paint had now been scratched away. As the three of them entered they encountered pandemonium as boys dashed this way and that, hurling hairbrushes or slippers at each other. It was alarming, the way in which personal property could be simply appropriated and hurled somewhere.

There were other 'noodles', easily distinguishable by the newness of their blazers or the shopfloor sheen of their grey jerseys. These sat on their beds for the most part, watching the commotion with expressions that managed to combine eagerness with bewilderment.

A hairbrush came flying through the air and Dad caught it deftly with his good arm. 'Owzat,' he called, making a motion as if to sweep the bails from the stumps. He beamed and repeated, 'Owzat.' Then he said something else, manipulating his facial muscles to manage the syllables. Jeb blushed with embarrassment. They would think he was drunk; he just knew it. The boys had in fact stopped their hurly-burly and were watching the flushed face that seemed to be pulled awry. Wilf tossed the hairbrush back to its owner, a hard straight throw which was fumbled. 'Caught you napping,' Wilf managed to say, slurrily. Why did he have to try and be like the boys in the room? Jeb kept his eyes down and busied himself looking at the labels attached to the bed-ends for the one which had his own name on it.

They found the bed. He and Mother then brought in the trunk from the car, and she gave the housemaster Jeb's pocket money for the term.

They stood by the car. Mother was going on about writing home at least once a week.

'I said I would, didn't I?' He immediately regretted sounding querulous.

Then Dad repeated his boxing motions, ducking his head from side to side, and stabbing with his left fist.

'I haven't forgotten, Dad.' The boy wished he would stop it before anyone saw. Now that it came to it, he wished they would go away. Yet part of the same wish was that he wanted them suddenly to change their minds, pack his trunk back into the car and take him home. Dad had already installed himself into the passenger seat but Mother stood offering pieces of disconnected advice. He wondered if she was going to hug him or something. He hoped not, not in front of those boys playing soccer.

'I'm sure you'll be all right.' She disappeared into the car. The boy stood hearing the gravel crackle as the car diminished down the drive. Now that it had happened, he was left with rather a neutral feeling on the whole, not bereft like the teary fellow he passed beside one car. He wandered back into the noisy dorm and sat on his bed, watching the ebb and flow of boys among the tubular frames.

There was one standing before him.

'What's your father do for a crust?'

Jeb looked up at the questioner who had short black upright hair, like a shoebrush. He also had an accent.

'He's on a pension. An invalid pension. He used to be in the Royal Air Force.'

'Why's he talk funny?'

'He had a stroke when we were in Germany. Part of his face and left arm are paralysed.' Jeb felt obscurely that he was betraying his family by revealing these details.

'He sounds as if he's drunk,' the shoebrush stated flatly, then sped away.

A boy on a neighbouring bed said. 'What rank is your father?' Jeb sensed that the question was a barbed one.

'He's retired now.'

'So-o? He's still got his rank hasn't he?'

'I suppose.' Jeb saw there were other boys listening now. 'Well?'

'He was a Group Captain, actually.'

'*Actually*!' chorussed several voices

'Gro-oup Caaaptain!' The boy on the bed rolled his eyes toward his listeners. 'Gro-oup Caaaptain,' he repeated. 'Cor!'

'What's wrong with that?'

'Does he have that scrambled egg stuff all over his cap?'

'He's retired. He doesn't have a cap,' stated Jeb reasonably.

'But *did* he, clever-dick.'

'I don't know.'

'He doesn't know! It's your father. You must know if he had scrambled egg on his,' the boy pursed his lips, 'orfficer's cap.'

'I don't see why I should tell you.'

'Ooooh!' a number of the listeners said. 'Rocky! He's rocky!' And one or two of them did some mock sparring.

'Well? What's your father?' Jeb asked the boy on the bed. The latter ignored the question. He had got up, grabbing a tennis ball from his locker, and, bouncing it hard on the floor, then catching it, he proceeded to conduct a survey around the dorm. 'Hands up anyone whose father is over the rank of a Group Captain or a Colonel?' No one put their hand up. 'Wing Commander or Lieutenant-Colonel?' Again no one. 'Squadron Leader or Major?' There were a couple of hands. The boy went down the list. Most hands seemed to go up around the warrant officer or flight sergeant mark. The boy turned to Jeb. 'Guess what, what's-your-name — what *is* your name, Rocky?'

'Jeb.'

'Your surname, stupid.'

'If you're going to be like that . . .'

'It's Cor*ballis*,' said an onlooker, reading the label on Jeb's bed.

'*Cor*-ballis,' Jeb corrected.

'Well, guess what, *Cor*-ballis, your dad is the highest rank in the dorm.'

'So?'

'So buttons, Rocky. We'll be watching out for you.' With this last warning, the boy made his way through the onlookers, bouncing the ball with great violence on the floorboards. When he reached the door he turned and, calling, 'Here, Woodsie!' he hurled it at a tallish individual with long arms and wiry hair, who took the ball easily in cupped hands and hurled it with equal force at another boy, which prompted an exodus accompanied by cries of 'Ball-tig! Ball-tig!'

The dorm suddenly became quieter. Some of the 'noodles' had joined the exodus, but here and there were others who were still unpacking. Jeb approached one of them.

'Who was that person who was asking me all the questions?'

'That's McKillop. They were all second-formers.'

'Why did he want to know all about my dad?'

The boy shrugged. He was shorter and thinner than Jeb, with black curly hair and eyes that seemed to shift about from underneath his brow, but which rarely looked Jeb in the eye. Yet somehow he seemed to talk as if he were older than a first-former should be. 'Don't worry about it. You can't predict how second-formers will react.'

Jeb felt like asking what experience this fellow 'noodle' could have already had with second-formers. Instead he said, 'My name's Jeb. What's yours?'

'Spendlove,' the boy replied. He busied himself unpacking his trunk and Jeb watched him, uncertain whether to find out more about Spendlove, or whether to start unpacking his own trunk. Then, without prompting, Spendlove said, 'My father's a full Colonel. I suppose that will get found out, but I wasn't going to tell them. So our fathers are first equal in the dorm, I guess.'

'I guess so.' Jeb wandered off and unpacked his trunk.

That first day, those first few minutes, he was to reflect much later, it was those which established the real curriculum for what was learnt, about his own times, about the post-war England he was supposed to be heir to. The Latin, the maths and modern languages, they were a gloss compared to the brutal, intricate and unflagging politics of the dormitory.

There followed four years of the same grey routine, each day beginning with a bell clanging from somewhere high up, followed by a duty monitor stomping mechanically through the dorm and stripping the beds of those who were not out of them already, the shuffle down to the chilly washrooms with their inexplicable stains on the walls, the showers that wheezingly emitted a dribble of lukewarm water, the pools on the concrete floor which never seemed to dry up, the distribution of mail, his comics and a letter from Mother arriving each Thursday like evidence of a different, sunnier planet, the walk across the fields to breakfast in one of the main school buildings. At first Jeb would walk across with Spendlove, but Spendlove began getting a hard time a few weeks into the term, so took to going about by himself. He was withdrawn from the school at Christmas.

Then there was the round of lessons, Latin, maths, and religious instruction in the Nissen huts, French and geography on the top floor of the old Georgian building, English in the prefab, science in the lab, lunch, rugger, free time, tea, prep, supper, quiet time, when some senior might take it upon himself to give an impromptu peptalk on life — or house spirit, which could be made to sound like the same poetic idea in the stillness that descended on Loftus House at this time of evening, the last daylight still lingering on the lawns, the cypresses along the boundary like gaunt helmetted pikemen from Armada times. Then lights out.

Occasionally, in his first year, there were free afternoons of wild games along the foreshores of the river, Commandos, or dam-building, but one was gradually shamed out of these enthusiasms; the adjectives 'mature' and 'immature' were the two most loaded words in dormitory vocabulary. One adopted a throwaway laconic form of speech, hands in pockets and eyes cast down. One learned to frown sceptically, to have fierce tastes in pop music, and to be cynical about almost everything else.

So, by his second year, the wild games gave way to afternoons of crushing boredom as two or three of them warmed their bottoms on a radiator, or mooched around the school grounds, perhaps with a transistor tuned to Radio Caroline or Radio London, the new pirate stations transmitting from ships moored off the coast. After lights out they would sometimes scare themselves with talk of hydrogen bombs or the eight-minute (some said four-minute) warning that would precede nuclear attack, and one long autumn evening in third form they sat in the Prep Room as the monitor, somewhat cheerfully, ticked off the minutes before the American and Russian fleets were due to encounter each other in the waters off Cuba.

Despite his inauspicious start, Jeb was not unduly bullied, as Spendlove and one or two others were. If not the most brazen of his year, he learned to hurl a tennis ball low and fast, and, as he progressed through the school, he was not above making life hard for the occasional noodle. Just as he had suffered head-raps, wrist-burns, bollock-grops in his first year, so he was part of the crowd bundling some hapless, ill-shaped fellow in the changing rooms after games. This did not occur often, but enough for him to realise, when he looked back on his schooldays, that he was not gifted with an exceptional moral sense. In the heat of a moment, he was all too prone to follow a crowd, and to hide his tracks afterwards. He was not especially disliked. Nor did he especially like his schoolfellows.

He did well at art, and from third form onwards he spent a good deal of his spare time in the art room, or, during the summer terms, with a stool and drawing board down beside the river. He would have liked to be a natural painter, like Webb or Crowdace in the year above him, producing things which made the fellows stop and whistle; but he wasn't a natural. Still, the activity absorbed him, allowed him to measure small improvements in his ability year by year, but most of all, allowed him to forget where he was for short intervals of time.

By his fourth form he was reading the nineteenth-century novelists, English, Russian, French; during a two-week bout of German measles he devoured *War and Peace*. It was also a period when he would buy the odd glossy magazine for the pin-ups. He was absorbed by the imagery of breasts and nipples, and the sight of a bikini-clad blonde or brunette lying on a fur rug, back arched, the all-important cleavage, deep and lovely, a smile directed so intimately at him alone, this filled his imagination with a delicious and unsatisfying turbulence. It was women some ten years older than himself whom he saw in his reveries, rather than girls his own age, and the doodles he drew in the margin of his 'rough book' featured pairs of swelling curves with delicate shading beneath.

'You're a sex *maniac*, Corballis.'

But he could shrug this off because the other boys were just as bad. Some of the more adventurous were coming back from the hols with stories of their adventures with girls. 'How far d'you go? Come on, how *far*?' One or two were known to be going steady.

And this is how it went, year after year, measuring one's life by the school calendar, Michaelmas term, Spring term, Summer term. By the time he reached the year of O levels he had become a dorm monitor, gave peptalks in the dark to the listening heads of the impossibly young noodles, stripped the odd bed of juniors too slow to rise, hating the surliness, the muttered comments, the disrespectful sneers that this occasioned. In the end he let the slugabeds lie, preferring to take the sarcasms of the house prefects, still unreachably above him in the upper sixth.

3

There was a winter when the snow fell on Boxing Day and lay on the ground until early March. It was like walking around on a television screen, the landscape drastically simplified into black strokes and splodges on whiteness or the greyness of the sky. The barns and tractor sheds were hunched white tumulae. On the playing fields there were epic snowball fights with hundreds per side. Boys arrived at their Nissen-hut classrooms with wet sleeves and exercise books, and sat through Latin or calculus with freezing toes. Each evening they trekked through the darkness back to Loftus House, their heads inclined against the onslaught of the wind which drove the snow in furious gusts into their eyes. It was like staggering across the Yukon. The wind, the wind; it funnelled up from the river, scouring the furrows, piling drifts against the hedges.

There were cross-country runs when, wearing nothing but white shorts and vests, they stumbled over the blade-hard ruts, or slipped and slid up and down the hills. Occasionally, on a blue day, the landscape glittered with a myriad dazzling scintilla. Momentous. It filled Jeb with a desire, not necessarily to paint it, but to do *something* with it, to take it further. In the art room on free afternoons he tried to work something up, something with acrylics, but it required a delicacy he could not manage and became a mess.

As the landscape itself did when the thaw arrived in March. From white, the fields and tracks turned brown. Everything was slushy. One's shoes became heavy and ungainly with the mud sticking to them. Little leaves began appearing on the trees.

During this thaw Jeb had a visitor. He had walked back across the fields from the main school to Loftus House after the Saturday-morning lessons. In the gravel area outside the shower block he passed a motorcycle with sidecar. In the corridor there was a tall fellow in a green windcheater and a white helmet on his head whom Jeb did not immediately recognise. He appeared to be busy studying the House notice-board but turned when he heard Jeb approach.

'Hello, old man.'

'Len. How come?'

'Thought I'd give you a surprise. Did you see my jalopy?'

'Jalopy?'

'Outside. Come on.' He led Jeb out to the motorcycle and immediately began tinkering with it, adjusting a wing mirror, polishing the petrol cap with his sleeve. 'Its a Beezer. BSA Crusader Mk 2. Not a bad old crate, is it?'

'You make it sound like a war plane. Is it new?'

'Brand spanking.'

Jeb was allowed to sit on it and get the feel of the machine, while Len explained gears, clutch, throttle, brakes, fuel cock. Jeb knew that since his de-mob Len had worked as a motor-cycle mechanic, first in Cromer, when he had boarded with his Aunt Eva, then in Nuneaton. The vehicle was certainly impressive, with its chrome flashes, its speedometer and igni-tion light. Boys were passing to and fro and soon there was an audience.

'What will it do?' one of them asked.

'On a straight road, a ton if you wind it out properly,' supplied Len. He allowed anyone who wished to sit on the pillion and fiddle with the clutch and brake levers, answering questions, relishing the attention, the knowledge he was being called upon to display. He decided that it was the opportune moment to take up a bit of slack in the chain, so took out a set of tools wrapped in a dirty rag and began loosening nuts and making adjustments, supplying more information, Jeb thought, than perhaps the questions warranted. It was the awkward business of enthusiasm again. The fellows were interested all right, but in that rather stylised low-key way with which they regarded everything. Len was being too... too high-key.

'That should do it,' he said, giving the back wheel a spin to check there was no wobble. He gave a longish dissertation about what happened if a chain was left loose. Some of the audience had drifted away.

'Coming for a spin?'

'I'll have to get permish.'

'Right-o.'

At first the housemaster was reluctant. He didn't doubt that Len actually was Corballis' elder brother but, you see, it was the delicate matter of having some, ah, authentication. Motor licence. That would do nicely. Yes, well, the name was a problem. Hengelow. Corballis.

Jeb did the explaining while Len stood with his head averted. At the first sign of difficulty his countenance became sulky, rebellious, despite Mr Elliott's rather overweening politeness and uneasy grins. Though he was by no means an ill-natured man, it was thought among the boys of his house that the Greaser, as Mr Elliott was called, tended to show his better side to the sons of colonels, wing commanders and above. Nothing was provable, though Jeb had taken some sarcasm on this account from McKillop and others. In the end the housemaster declared that perhaps the rules could be stretched 'just a little'. 'Though perhaps, Corballis, if your brother...' he looked at Len quickly, who continued to stand face averted, 'your *half*-brother could have you back in time for tea.'

With Jeb in the sidecar, Len roared off down the lanes of Suffolk. There was still some snow in ditches and under hedges.

'Nothing like '47,' Len yelled above the engine and the air-rush. He nodded at the vestigial snow. 'We had boys die from pneumonia.'

They passed a wrought-iron gate behind which Jeb glimpsed a blockish limestone-coloured building.

'That was it,' Len yelled again, pointing his thumb at it.

'What?'

'My prep school.'

'Don't you want to stop and have a look around?' Jeb yelled back.

'Never,' Len gave him a quick smile, then set his head more resolutely above the handlebars and opened the throttle.

'I wouldn't mind having a look.' But his voice was lost in the roar and in a moment the building and its grounds were behind them. They drove to Felixstowe where Len bought fish and chips, which they ate sitting on a concrete wall, watching the grey sea breaking on the brown shingle. Then they wandered around the amusement pier. There was a game in which fast-moving fighter planes appeared from left and right of the screen, whereupon you let them have it with a machine-gun button.

'Come on, Len. You've spent the equivalent of my entire term's pocket money. Let's try something else.' But the elder boy was absorbed.

He would not allow Jeb to pay for anything. 'My treat, old man.' He bought two buns which oozed artificial cream and insisted Jeb eat one. At one point in their conversation Jeb had mentioned the name of an instrumental group whose twangy guitar music he liked. They passed a music shop and before he knew what was happening, Len had gone in, and purchased an LP by the group.

'Len, I didn't mean . . .'

'Early birthday present.'

'You'll go broke.'

The half-brother waved Jeb's objections away. He had a benevolent, rather imperious smile on his face. Jeb was grateful, and a little needled. Further up the street they passed a toyshop window in which there were hanging some plastic models.

'Stay here a moment.' This time Len emerged with a box wrapped in brown paper. 'This is to go with the record — last year's birthday present if you like.'

'What is it?' The prospect of taking something bought in a toyshop back to Loftus House was not altogether welcome.

'A Lanc.'

'Oh. Umm. Thank you.'

Until a year or so ago he had occasionally bought a plastic model during the holidays and spent a contented day or two constructing and painting it on the carpet, vaguely aware that by rights he should have grown out of plastic aeroplanes. But he would never dream of doing this during term time. Now he could hear the fellows in his dorm using that word 'immature'. 'Are you sure you don't want to keep it yourself?' he asked, hopefully.

'It's yours, old fellow. I enjoy spending money. You're my family.'

They walked on for a bit.

'Have you heard anything of your father recently?' Jeb asked.

Len shrugged. 'I suppose he's around somewhere. Doing his good works.' There was a contemptuous emphasis on the word 'good'.

'Does he ever come and see you?'

'He's tried to once or twice. Came to where I lived in Cromer, came to the bike shop. I pretended to be out.'

'How come?'

'He lives like one of those homeless men, like a tramp. Deliberately. Why should I want people to think he was my father?'

'Well, he is.'

Len was silent. Then he stopped on the pavement and said, 'Look, why don't we go back to your school and make a start on the Lanc. Come on.' And before Jeb could say anything, Len was striding ahead toward where they had parked the motorbike.

With a sense of letdown, Jeb noted they were back at Loftus House before four p.m.

'Find us a hangar with a workbench, old man.'

There was, in Loftus House, a 'hobbies room', but the prospect of constructing this plastic aeroplane in front of all those scornful eyes was hair-raising. Jeb tried to think of objections which would not hurt Len's feelings, but could not.

So he led through the narrow corridors to this room, aware

of his tall half-brother behind him, and how he was somehow outsized for the confined passages with their rows of macs and duffelcoats, and the small casement windows in their dark frames. They settled down at a table and unpacked the model, cutting the plastic pieces from their spigots and commencing to glue them together. Len kept up a patter about the different variants of the aeroplane they were building, to which Jeb half listened, aware that a couple of fellows of his own form who had been playing records were giving significant looks in his direction, whispering and occasionally guffawing. McKillop and one or two other fourth-formers were also there. Drearily he realised that he would cop it after Len had gone. He looked at his half-brother, who was absorbed in fitting the two halves of the fuselage together. On the whole he would have preferred that Len had not come. At least, not this version of Len. He had longed for his half-brother's company when he was small, and still did in holiday time. But holidays were a different world. Yes, better if Len had not come. The thought made the younger boy feel ungrateful.

'I guess I had better be going over for tea, Len.' He tried to say it gently. The room had been emptying.

'Couldn't you miss tea, old man? We're just getting started.'

'Elliott did say...'

Len looked away for a moment and Jeb thought he might go into his sulks, but a moment later he smiled. 'Better not let the CO down, I suppose. I'll drop you off.' They packed up the incomplete model and put it away in a drawer. It was now dark outside. The air was freezing, though not unpleasant, as it rushed at Jeb's face. By the time Len deposited him outside the dining hall he felt as though his features were made of glass.

'Thanks for coming down, Len.' They stood, as though waiting for something else to happen. Jeb could hear the clash of dishes. They had started tea already.

'I guess it's cheerio and let's not be downhearted, eh.'

'Yes. Cheers, Len. And thanks. For the record and stuff.'

Unexpectedly Len shook him heartily by the hand, then revved once or twice, clicked into gear and was gone.

The model remained in the drawer until the end of term when Jeb, in the process of clearing out, gave it to a noodle. His mistake was to do so when McKillop was in the room.

'Is he your bum-boy, Corballis?' asked the fourth-former.

Jeb looked at McKillop. It was foolish, he knew, to say anything in reply to the insult, but he found himself saying, 'How does it feel, McKillop, to know that nobody actually likes you?' He was surprised by how mature his remark sounded. He also expected McKillop to leap across the room and lash him with his fists.

Instead, McKillop walked up to him and said, 'What makes you say that, Corballis? No, go on. What makes you say that?'

'It's just what I think, that's all.' It would come now, Jeb thought, the fist-lashing.

Instead he was given one head-rap as McKillop passed him and went out. He felt he had got off lightly. The noodle looked at him nervously, holding the aeroplane model in his hands.

4

The third event brought his boarding school days, effectively to a close. It occurred a few days into the Michaelmas term of the first-year sixth. Three months earlier he had taken his O levels, gaining eight out of the ten subjects he sat for, most of them at respectable grades.

One morning he was coming from History with a group of the fellows. A third-former ran up from behind.

'The housemaster's looking for you, Corballis. He wants to see you right away. He said to say its urgent.'

What remained in Jeb's memory about the message was how immediately, how pre-emptively, the sensation, the adrenalin, seemed to leap into all parts of his body. It was nothing to do with guilt. It was the leap of dread. It seemed to freeze-frame everything, the messenger's lingering glance, then his back as he ran off, the various quips from his fellows — 'He's found your cigarettes, Corbs' — walking down the corridor toward the chem lab, aware of the long school photos going back to the 1940s on the walls, but not looking at them, the housemaster seeing him from quite far off and immediately marching toward him, taking him by the shoulder, which was unusual to say, 'I wonder if you would just come into the office a moment,' the smell of chemicals — hydrochloric acid probably — and the dread mounting, 'I have a bit of bad news, I'm afraid...'

And then crossing from not knowing to knowing and never being able to reverse that. 'It's about your father.' Yes, it would be about his father. 'He has been taken to the hospital.' Jeb had the sense that this event had been rushing towards him ever since — ever since Oldenrath. He felt he already knew everything, even though he lacked actual information. Meanwhile the housemaster was continuing, 'I have been in touch with your mother who has asked that you be put on a train for home immediately.' There was a train just after two. He suggested that he drive Jeb back to the house immediately, that Jeb pack a few things, then have an early lunch; 'I'll arrange that. Then I will drive you to the station. All right?'

'Yes.' It was odd, after five years at the school, to be actually consulted about the housemaster's intentions, as though he, Jeb, were suddenly an adult. So he was driven to the house, where he packed an overnight bag. Mr Elliott came into the dormitory every few minutes and stood watching. Jeb noted that he did not make any comforting comments such as 'I'm sure, when you get home you'll find that everything is all right.' It was as if he had more information than Jeb while at the same time not knowing the words which could allay the fear — yes, *the fear*, which had lodged itself like a chemical reaction throughout Jeb's entire body. Jeb had no desire to ask what had actually happened to his father, as though by remaining in ignorance he could somehow annul the event. He changed from his jacket to his blazer and then, with his overnight bag, was driven back to the school for an early lunch. He sat alone in the dining room, eating the liver and mash dutifully, feeling that the two Caribbean kitchen maids who were laying the tables must know what had happened, hearing the bell announcing the end of the morning's lessons followed by the noise of shoes and voices in the corridors, the shoving, the shouts outside the swing doors of the dining room.

He was driven to the station and put on the train. The housemaster carried the overnight bag, making Jeb feel exposed rather than privileged. Mr Elliott could still think of nothing appropriate to say, so, at the carriage door, as he handed the overnight bag up, he shook hands and grinned, quickly and rather ineffectually, 'I'm sure we'll see you back soon, Corballis.'

'Thank you, sir.'

On the train trip to London, Jeb thought about his father. He assumed it was another stroke of some kind. For part of the journey he worried about how he ought to act when he encountered Mother and his stricken father. It was difficult. He felt guilty that his mind should be preoccupied with such a trivial thing in the face of the enormity (it had to be an enormity, he knew that), but he couldn't help himself. He hoped that he would act naturally, but he couldn't envisage what 'natural behaviour' might be. He hoped he wouldn't break down and make a scene.

From Kings Cross he took the Underground, standing in the crush of people and holding onto the leather thong that hung from a rail on the ceiling of the train. He was amazed that no one in the crush took any notice of him. Surely the dread that had lodged itself in his stomach and limbs must be evident in the expression of his face. It was humbling. Here he was, hurtling through the dark, a youth called away from school to be with his sick father, and all these people around him were oblivious of the fact.

Jeb found himself remembering his father in a succession of disconnected though fond recollections, the man peering over his glasses at the edge he had put on one of his chisels, the white belted mackintosh hurrying ahead of them with the two suitcases when they had taken the ship across to the Hook of Holland, the mustachioed barrel-chested man on the top diving board. The recollections seemed to come from so long ago. Jeb found that he was sniffing and that his cheeks were wet. A man on a seat opposite was looking at him. He wiped his face on the sleeve of his blazer. All at once the train broke out into daylight.

He left the train at Pinner and walked the half mile or so to their home in Candleware Road. When he came through the door of the kitchen he saw Len at the table reading a newspaper.

'Your father's in a bad way, old man.' Len's announcement was said rather calmly, Jeb thought. 'Mother rang. You've got to come with me to the hospital. I was said to ask if you had eaten any lunch.'

'Has Dad suffered another stroke?'

'On the Underground yesterday morning. He was going into the city on some business. Mum phoned Aunt Eva. I came down on the bike. Got in about an hour ago.'

'I had lunch at the school.'

'I'd better take you then.'

Jeb sat in the sidecar. Len dropped Jeb at the main doors of the hospital.

'There's someone I've got to see now. I'll come back for you. I'll meet you here.'

'Aren't you coming up to see him?'

'I'd like to but — there's this person I've got to see. I said three o'clock.' Len played with the throttle. There was a car waiting to get past him.

'He's been your dad too, no matter what you say,' shouted Jeb above the noise of the revs.

Len allowed the revs to die. He looked at the chrome cap on his petrol tank, and then briefly at Jeb. 'I'd only muck things up if I went up there, old man. When I come back, I'll hang about the carpark until you need a lift.'

'That might be ages.'

'I'll be there.' Len squeezed the clutch lever and clicked into gear.

'What'll I tell Mother?'

The half-brother shrugged and for a moment looked side-long at Jeb through his goggles. He's even more frightened than I am, Jeb realised as he listened to the noise of the motorcycle fade, he hasn't got an appointment at all. He went into the huge glassy building and asked at the desk where he might find Group Captain Corballis. The matron directed him to Intensive Care.

As he stood in the lift and walked down the corridors with their green linoleum floors, Jeb imagined that he would find his father in the same condition as after the first stroke, only worse. He would be sitting up in bed with his face horribly distorted, trying to grin and to be reassuring and cheerful. Some part of him would be paralysed. It would be horrible.

What in fact he found when he went into the room where his father was lying was, he immediately realised, both less horrible and more serious than his imaginings. The room was so clean, so orderly. Wilf lay on his left side, head on the pillow and curled like an S. The blanket had been folded back so there was only a white sheet covering him which revealed his body as a snowy ridge tapering to nothing at the feet. There was no obvious distortion of features, but it was his breathing which indicated the seriousness of his condition. He puffed and sucked, puffed and sucked, like an athlete who had run a 440. But unlike the athlete, there was no recovery of breath. The rhythm continued, suck-puff, suck-puff, the pace never slackening; the whole of Wilf's being was concentrated on this. Yes, it was all he was doing, all he *could* do. There was no movement of his body, no recognition that someone had just entered the room, no apparent awareness of the presence of Mother.

She had been reading aloud from a book when Jeb came in, but she rose on seeing him and took him out into the corridor. Her face was different, not tired, exactly, but shocked, riven. Jeb wondered if he should hug her, as he had seen people in similar circumstances do on the films. But they had long lost the habit of physical contact, not through coldness but for reasons which were obscurely connected with dignity.

They stood in the corridor glancing at each other now and then.

'Old Elliott put me on the first train.'

'Did he tell you what has happened?'

'Only that they'd taken Dad to hospital.' Both talked almost in whispers.

'The doctor has seen him. Dad has suffered a very severe stroke. They don't yet know how much damage it has done, but it is probably,' his mother paused as though to assure herself she could control her voice, 'it is probably rather massive. The main problem in his weakened condition is with secondary infection and it seems he has got pneumonia. They are trying to control this. He won't show any sign that he can recognise you, but that doesn't necessarily mean that he can't hear what is going on. So you must tell him that you have come. You can touch him too.' For all Lizzie's calmness, she would not look Jeb in the eye as she said this. 'I have been reading to him. The nurses say it is a good idea. Did you get the chance to have any lunch?'

'Yes.' Why was this domestic detail so important?

'Was Len at home when you arrived?' Jeb had been dreading the question.

'He brought me here. He said — he said he preferred to wait in the carpark.' To Jeb's relief, his mother seemed to find this fact of no interest.

'We can only hope for the best. Let's go in now and tell him you're here.'

They went back into the room and stood on either side of the bed. 'Wilf, dear.' Mother addressed her husband in a loud voice, as though he were a child who was hard of understanding. 'Wilf, Jeb is here to see you. He has come down from school.' She indicated to Jeb that he should now say something.

'Hello, Dad. I heard that you were a bit — unwell.' Jeb put his hand on his father's shoulder. It felt like a silly thing to do, and his words sounded absurd. He stumbled on. 'I'm sure you won't be long in here.' Not only absurd, but futile. This, then, was the worst part, this need to make gauche cheery utterances as though nothing really serious was amiss. 'You've got to come home to make sure your chisels stay sharp.' Gauche. Futile.

A short, stout nursing sister came in and bent over Wilf's face, examining it briefly.

'Keep talking to him. Keep trying to stimulate him. You're the son who has just come from boarding school, are you? Tell him about that. Or read to him.' The sister turned to Mother. 'And you, Mrs Corballis, I think you ought to eat something.'

'Perhaps a cup of tea.'

'I'll have one brought down.'

Jeb listened to the definite click-click of her shoes receding up the corridor. He had expected a flurry of nurses and doctors to be in attendance and was surprised how few medical staff there were given the apparent seriousness of his father's condition.

He racked his brains for something to say. The news he had seemed, in present circumstances, crass, superfluous. What could he say, that he had scored seventeen out of twenty in his Renaissance History essay, that three of his watercolours had been hung in the school assembly hall, that some fellows had been expelled for shoplifting. How could these items compare in importance with the suck-puff, suck-puff of his father's breathing.

But he told them anyway, then fell silent, looking to Mother for what to say next. Wilf showed no signs of having heard. His eyes were closed and his mouth puffed noisily. The tea came.

'Read to him. I'm going to have a cigarette outside.' Mother took her tea out into the corridor. A feeling of panic possessed Jeb at the thought of being alone with Dad. What if he died? How would he know?

There were a pile of books by the bedside, some Kipling, and Grimble's *A Pattern Of Islands*. This last was the book that Mother had been reading from when Jeb arrived, one of his dad's favourites. 'How would you like to come and help me run a South Seas Island, Old Curl?' he used to say. Jeb began reading. Mother came back after a while and sat. Nurses came and went. Mother took over the reading. The rhythm of suck-puff, suck-puff never altered. Outside the window the September evening gradually darkened.

Jeb was not conscious of keeping watch beside a deathbed.

The idea of death was simply unthinkable. He had no experience of it. And yet he could not conceive what his father's future might be like. They could deal with the pneumonia these days, he presumed, but what about the other? It was too appalling. Mother had said that the damage might be 'massive', whatever that meant. Did it mean that Dad's gestures and speech would be even more grotesque, more heart-rending than they had become after his last stroke? Or would he eventually be taken home where he would lie all day in a bed huff-puffing like this? For Jeb could not conceive the possibility of his father leaving them. His presence, both here in the room, and in the boy's recollection of him from his earliest childhood, was too vivid. Yes, the idea of death was unthinkable. Yet the alternative was too.

Mother sent him to find some supper from the canteen. He first wandered out into the carpark. A tall figure, his head bulbous under a white helmet, emerged from behind some cars.

'Len?'

'How is he?'

'I don't think he can hear anything that's being said. He lies there panting.'

'Is he going to die?'

Jeb shrugged. The directness of the question made him feel helpless. 'I don't know. Why should he?' The two half-brothers had been standing ten yards or so apart. It was Len who now approached. He stood looking down at Jeb. Jeb could smell the leather of his jacket, and the cigarettes he had been smoking.

'Why don't you go up and see him?'

'You said he doesn't hear anything. What would be the use?'

'He might. They don't know.' Jeb said desperately.

'Look, I'm better off being useful at the edge of things. I'll run you home later, then bring you back in the morning. I'd only be in the way up there. Really, old man.'

'Arh, old man! old man! why don't you quit all this "old man" stuff, Len? You're frightened to go up. That's all it is. I'm sick of all this "old man", "old chap" stuff. Why are you always trying to keep me in my place?' Jeb blazed, then seeing the hurt that crossed Len's face, he stopped.

'I thought we were friends, old man.' Len had his face averted.

'I'm not "old man",' Jeb insisted, but the conviction had left him. They were silent for some time.

'I'm not frightened,' said Len stubbornly.

'Then go up and see him. For our mother's sake.'

'I'd only be in the way.' This was almost grunted. It was the objection.

'You wouldn't,' said Jeb, fiercely, and then more gently, 'You wouldn't, Len.'

Len stood unmoving. The two said nothing to each other and after a minute, Jeb turned to go. When he was ten yards or so away he heard Len say, 'You see, old man, I can't go up there. I didn't care for him particularly. Your father. I didn't care for him.' Jeb did not stop.

He ate a fishcake and some chips in the hospital canteen, bought a bar of chocolate then returned to the sickroom. He gave his mother most of the chocolate, and together they sat, one on either side of the bed, sometimes talking to each other, sometimes reading to Wilf. Once or twice during the evening Jeb went for a walk around the corridors of the hospital, or Mother went to the dayroom for a cigarette. A little after eleven the nursing sister sent Jeb home and made up a bed for his mother in an adjoining room.

'We'll ring you if there is any change.'

Jeb went into the carpark and climbed wearily into Len's sidecar. On the latter's inquiry he said, simply, 'The same,' and hunched down under the vinyl cover. He felt older than his half-brother. Len drove him home down long badly lit streets; for all that it was getting on for midnight, the air that rushed at him in the sidecar seemed dry and stale. He went to bed without so much as saying goodnight to Len, and, for some minutes before he fell asleep he heard his half-brother clattering about downstairs preparing himself a meal. Why did he have to say those things about Dad, that he had never cared for him? Why now? Why could he not have made some effort over the years? Why could he not have pretended?

There was some light behind the curtains. Len was in the room, standing two or three yards away, saying something. He wouldn't come any closer.

'What is it?'

'Our mother is on the phone. She wants to talk to you.'

Len would not look at Jeb as he went past, but he said something hard to catch — 'Bear up?' 'Chin up?' It was something like that. The pure, ghastly sensation of fear which had taken possession of him at the school — was it only yesterday? — and which had dissipated slightly the previous evening in the ordinariness and orderliness of his dad's sick-room, now overwhelmed him again. He could hear Mother's voice on the end of the line; it was odd how her Australian accent was more pronounced on the telephone.

'Jeb, dear. Len will have told you. Dad has passed away. He went very peacefully at a little after four this morning. I was with him.' Her voice was calm, or composed at least. There was no broken sobbing, none of the stammerings of grief that he had seen on the films. And he found himself with nothing to say.

So he said, 'Right,' and wondered immediately if it was heartless.

'Darling,' his mother had not called him that since he was very small, 'it was probably best that Dad went. He had suffered awful brain damage. I think his life would have been miserable if he'd survived.'

The voice on the line stopped, then continued, 'I'll be home later this morning.'

'Right,' he said again, ineffectually. Then, as an after-thought, he added, 'Must I do anything? Like ring people up? I mean . . . ' He was thinking about the funeral but wanted to avoid the word 'undertakers'. It was too horrible a word, too black.

'No, they will do all that from here. We must let Wilf's family know. See you about eleven.' Jeb stood holding the phone for a few moments. It was the casualness, the blandness of it all that struck him, the way his mother and he, himself, acted so normally in spite of the enormity of the event.

Len was sitting at the kitchen table in his pyjamas. 'My father has died,' was the way he formulated the announcement. He might have said 'Our father' or just 'Dad' but it hadn't come out like that.

Len said nothing for a long time, then, without looking at Jeb, he declared, 'I guess that puts us in much the same boat, old man.'

Mother came home with a small parcel of Wilf's belongings. She busied herself clearing up around the house. Jeb offered to help, but she said she could manage. Sometimes, say in the middle of wiping the mantelpiece or one of the silver trophies she and Wilf had won for dancing, she would stop, sit down in an armchair and simply stare into space. There were some tears, but Jeb was surprised how few she shed, and by the fact that he didn't seem prompted to weep himself. Instead there was a sensation of weight, of burden, that had replaced the earlier dread. He made her cups of tea. Len remained out of the house for most of the time, energetically tidying the garage and garden. They ate their meals largely in silence.

On the day before the funeral Len announced that he had to return to Nuneaton because he was needed in the motorcycle workshop. Mother looked at him in the eye, held him in her gaze until Len began shifting from one foot to another. He made to leave.

Then Mother moved with extraordinary speed across the kitchen and took hold of a tuft of Len's hair that had become unwired from his quiff.

'You!' The word might have been a projectile. 'You!'

By this tuft she pulled the tall fellow to the table and forced his head down on the board. 'So you just want to *skedaddle*. And *don't* we know *who* you get that from.' She had adjusted her grip on Len's head so that she held it in both hands. It looked almost fond, but she had placed her own head very close to Len's and was spitting the words out. 'You *haven't* the charm. You just *haven't* the charm.' Each time she emphasised a word she rocked the head in her hands back and forth. 'So you will attend! You *will* attend and you will say goodbye — *properly* — to that *good* man, that *kind* man! I want you to hear what I am telling you. You *will* attend.' She released his head with a brutal backward flip and Len vanished. She looked briefly in Jeb's direction, the expression on her face still furious, unseeing, then she too went out. Jeb remained standing in the kitchen, astounded.

So Len stayed. On the day of the funeral the house filled up with Wilf's brothers and some colleagues from airforce days. The red-brick chapel was full. The three of them occupied the front pew and though he held the hymn book open in front of him, Jeb found himself unable to read the words. He felt himself to be at the centre of a nimbus of misery, dimly aware that on one side his mother's cheeks were wet under her veil, though he could not hear her sobbing, and on the other Len was blubbering helplessly. The wooden box containing his father was lifted by four men, one of whom was Jeb's uncle, and taken out to the hearse. Everyone in the chapel waited in their pews until Mother, Len and he had gone past. It was like being at the head of a medieval army. In the sunlight he found himself being patted on the back by men he hadn't met before — they all seemed to have moustaches, one or two were in uniform.

There were more words at the municipal cemetery. There was a hole already cut into the turf. It looked so neat, so small, and the stainless steel rail around it, with its rolled webbing straps to lower the coffin, so natty; it was these details that were somehow wrenching. When the words were finished a man clicked a lever with his foot and the box descended into the hole. Jeb stood, wiping his eyes every minute or so, desolate, deeply conscious that he was carrying on embarrassingly, but unable to help himself. Then people simply walked away in their different directions, as he and Mother did. He didn't know whether he should put his arm around his mother's shoulder, but she moved away and seemed to be occupied in accepting the condolences of people, so the moment passed. One of the funeral cars took them home where there was tea and some cupcakes for a few of the mourners.

Len did not return to Candleware Road that afternoon, but drove directly from the cemetery to his digs in Nuneaton. It was four years and the other side of the world before either he or Mother saw Len again.

Jeb remained at home for a fortnight, helping with papers and clothes. Once his mother stopped in the middle of their sorting and said, 'You know, I still expect him to come through the door at any moment and ask me to help him with his jacket or tell him the whereabouts of his Airforce Association tie.'

And then, the day before Jeb was due to return to school, she sat down opposite him at the breakfast table and looked at him for some moments. 'Well, it has to be faced. Dad has gone. Len has a job and no need of us. What I want to do more than anything now is return to Australia. Will you come? You could finish your schooling there.'

'If you like.'

It was as straightforward as that. He returned to Clemstead for the rest of the Michaelmas term. Meanwhile his mother wound up Wilf's affairs and their own, sold sixty-six Candleware Road, and booked a passage on a P & O liner for March of the following year. She wrote to Len offering a passage if he wanted to accompany them. A week before their departure there had still been no reply to her letter, so, on the evening Jeb arrived home from Clemstead, Mother phoned Len long-distance. It seemed he had been thinking about it, but Australia was very far away.

'From what?' Jeb sat on the stairs, listening to his mother's crisp questions. He could hear the cadence and syntax of the replies — they seemed to blare from the handpiece — but could not make out what the actual words were. '*Have* you seen him ... Pardon? ... Well, there you are ... You know what he has chosen to do with his life ... I think it unlikely ... Well, the offer remains open, Len. If at any time ... Yes, yes, I'll pass that on ... And you ... Take care. My dear.' She continued to hold the handpiece near her ear for some moments after the voice at the other end had become silent, then put it down carefully as though the moulded bakelite itself contained the voice she had just been speaking to.

'He said to say cheerio.' Mother looked at him and smiled quickly, then went upstairs to continue packing.

A week later, on an afternoon of silvery overcast, Jeb and his mother steamed southward out of Tilbury on a huge white ship with a yellow funnel.

PART TWO

LAND WITHOUT ZONES

Emergence: 1966

1

Cold light. Blue light. Gold light floodingly from astern. The shore was now passing on either side of the liner, sheer cliffs at first, then a waterfront built up with houses. The terracotta tiles of the suburbs were taking fire from the early sun. Blunt green ferries steamed past them, launches rocked in the harbour swell. The windows of a single high-rise ignited like a theatre spotlight, an aircraft carrier stood high in dry dock in the midst of a multitude of immobile cranes, the soft roar of traffic was audible from the shoreline. In the midst of a dense palisade of scaffolding, like the outline of a drawing obscured by vigorous cross-hatching, there was emerging a building with sprouting roofs the shape of two Aztec helmets. 'The new Opera House,' someone said, pointing.

Sydney. The other side of the world. It felt queer. Exhilarating too, but mostly queer. Jeb had left his watch in his cabin, but it couldn't be much past six a.m.

Now there were more people appearing on deck and making exclamatory noises, pointing to this and that.

Mother was up before him. Jeb found her standing at the rail beside an elderly Australian couple. She had tears falling down her cheeks. He felt hesitant in approaching her, but she turned and saw him.

'This is — this is marvellous. You cannot imagine . . .' she said, more to the elderly couple than to Jeb. 'Twenty-nine years.' Then, as though noticing for the first time that she had been crying, she said, 'Sorry, I didn't think it would affect me like this.'

'You cry, dear,' said the woman, touching Mother's arm. 'It's always nice to come home.'

'I feel as if I've had a lifetime away.'

'Well, my dear, I dare say you've had more than your share.' The woman patted his mother's arm again. During the four-week voyage from Tilbury, she had sometimes sat at this couple's table on bingo nights or occasions of similar entertainment. Their comfy sociability gave Jeb the horrors, so he had avoided the social functions, preferring to read Dostoievski in his cabin or pace the decks alone, wrapped in what he took to be his own and inscrutable thoughts. He was aware that Mother had told the couple a little of their circumstances and this made him feel rebellious.

Now he felt simply left out, a feeling which was not mitigated when his mother drew him over to the rail and said, 'I last saw Sydney in 1937 when I sailed away to England with your Aunt Peg. We were practically girls!' She was silent for a while, as the shores and bays of the harbour slid past. Since Wilf died, she had fallen into the habit of touching him more often than she used to, on the hand or elbow, or slipping her arm through his. He didn't mind, though it felt awkward. He suspected she was doing it more to make him feel less lonely without his father than through any need of her own.

There again, she would sometimes talk to him as though he were a child still. He was nearly seventeen. And what was 1937 to him? He tried to visualise the year and a steamer drawing away from a quay, belching black smoke. In his mind's eye he saw hundreds of people along the ship's rail waving to hundreds of people along the quay, behaving in a much more extravagant, much more abandoned way than people seemed to nowadays. He saw his mother as he had seen her in some of the photographs in their album, wearing a hat that was shaped like a conch shell. He couldn't visualise Aunt Peg as a twenty-year-old. The whole scene was, of course, in sepia.

Jeb's knowledge of what had happened to the sisters in England was sketchy. Aunt Peg, he knew, had come back to Australia after a year or so and worked as a telegraphist for many years before visiting them at Candleware Road prior to marrying Uncle Neville, a 'lands surveyor, in her mid-thirties. They lived in Canberra and had no children. Uncle Neville had been in Changi.

As for 1937, well, you couldn't look at the present, it seemed, without the past interlaying itself between, and, on the whole, he relished this; it gave him a sense of the depth, the *fissures* an experience could have. But it was frustrating too, being kept in the dark about things.

The ship passed beneath the harbour bridge. Tugboats were fussing around them, churning the water till it looked like a tangle of washing. Winches were grinding, dripping hawsers were wound in through the fairleads. Then it was done. They were attached to the new continent, tied up at an Australian wharf.

And there, beyond customs, Aunt Peg was waving; she looked summery. The beefy man dressed in a dark suit beside her was, he supposed, his Uncle Neville. Mother and son disembarked into a crowded terminus where passengers were dropping their suitcases and clasping people behind the barriers; it was like a medieval mêlée. Aunt Peg seemed to have shrunk from the woman Jeb remembered during that 1953 visit. She was stouter, more compact, and with a face like a tabby.

'And this is Neville,' she announced, drawing forward the dark-suited man and brushing what might have been a hair from his lapel. The man looked ungainly and affable. 'Your *Uncle* Neville,' she qualified, turning to Jeb. Uncle Neville stood before him, and in his black suit and white shirt he seemed to occupy Jeb's entire view. There was a large hand extended, and Jeb felt his own hand being pumped.

'Well, James,' he said, 'these two ladies *obviously* know each other from somewhere or other, and we two *obviously* don't. So that gives us something in common to be going on with. What d'you reckon?' Uncle Neville's face seemed to continue flickering even after he had finished talking. He looked as if he could have said more. His body had a backward lean, like the rake of a mast. It was difficult to pick his age, mid-fifties maybe. His complexion had a furious glow to it, and his prolonged handshake was like a challenge. But he was all right. His face seemed to be watchful, humorous.

2

Then there was the country itself. Jeb stared out of the window of the train as wide paddocks and slopes folded into each other, ashy-blonde, criss-crossed by low wire fences as though by casual pen lines; he saw sheep which were a similar colour and shape to the tussocks, the odd farm bungalow, a forlorn chimney-piece surrounded by brick litter, rusted corrugated iron sheds that seemed to lean on air, vehicles without wheels in the middle of a paddock, as if long ago their occupants had driven them across half a continent to that spot, then, having second thoughts, simply abandoned them and walked off.

The train stopped at a place called Goulburn, though few people seemed to get on or off it. There were men standing around, some in blue boiler suits, some in the same kind of ill-fitting dark suit that Uncle Neville wore. The older men wore hats. The women, Jeb noticed, tended to wear slacks rather than skirts, which was rather American, he fancied. The clothes of both the men and women appeared to lack new-ness.

The train continued, passing through the same kind of country. There were no points of focus, no church spires, water towers, silos. For a time the rails ran parallel to huge cables looping between airy pylons, but these diverged and disappeared behind a distant rise. But the eye was allowed to run on distances which, if never scenic like those parts of Austria and Bavaria he could remember from his boyhood holidays, were never tedious either. Indeed, Jeb found himself exhilarated by the spaciousness, by the immense possibilities of freedom this open landscape seemed to offer. The spaces seemed to be both more generous and more austere than the meadows and woodlands of England and Germany.

And the land was gentle too, not harsh as he had been

led to expect from the odd school geography project. Gentle, with the edge of sight bounded by an inevitable range of low hills, indigo and delicate beneath striae of whitish cloud. As he watched the low profile of the land slide by, he felt he wanted somehow to possess it, to be attached to it.

The train made another stop at a tiny station with a name that sounded like one of those Indian cities — Bangalore, Mangalore? No one got on or off. There was a mist covering a nearby hill, and he could hear birds giving off a throaty warble.

'Magpies, James. Can you hear what they're saying?' Uncle Neville put his fingers to his ear. There was something grand-fatherly about the gesture. 'Don't neglect to gargle, *don't* neglect to gargle!' He chuckled quietly to himself, adding variations as he thought of them. 'Gurgle before you burgle. Give the poodle strudel.' Jeb smiled and tried to think of a response which would not be conventional. 'Great little choristers, my word!' Uncle Neville finished by saying.

More of the same spaciousness until the train began climbing through shaly gullies, passing plantations of young pine trees. Yet another station with an even odder name — Queanbeyan — it summoned up an image of a beehive. The odd carriage door slammed, then, inexplicably, the train remained sta-tionary for a while, then there was the grunt of carriages as the train began to move once more. Minutes later, and somewhat to Jeb's surprise, they stopped at another station.

'This is it, James,' announced Uncle Neville. They had stopped at a long empty platform. On the other side was some grassy wasteland, then willows, poplars, some other kind of trees with long sleeves of bark hanging from them. Beyond them were a few wooden bungalows. 'We've arrived in the Big Smoke.'

Like the cars in the paddocks, like something in Uncle Neville's manner of addressing him that Jeb could not quite put his finger on — something throwaway, undercutting, this station was casual, off-centre. It seemed to have no sense of its own occasion. Jeb was aware that Canberra was not the biggest city in Australia, but it was the capital. He had expected the train to take him into the heart of things, into some bustling, echoing terminus with pigeons clattering high in a girder-and-glass canopy, voices booming the arrival and departure times over the loudspeakers, and hundreds of people hurrying, lugging suitcases, sidestepping each other, slamming carriage doors. Yes, it was queer, this casualness, unaccountable, but not disappointing.

3

Cold light, blue light. On the day they arrived his Australian relations took them in the Holden up to a lookout. His gaze was directed south toward a range of hills.

'The Brindabellas, James. A pretty name, eh.'

'They look like the ocean.'

Or rather, the way a painter might try to achieve an effect of the ocean's spontaneity and vitality, applying indigo or prussian blue quickly, in a thick layer at the bottom of a vast pale blue of flawless evenness. For the starkness of these hills against the sky made them look as if they might surge forward.

'I dare say they do a bit.' Uncle Neville nodded. His face suggested one who ought to have a pipe clenched between his teeth.

Facing north Jeb could see the quince-yellow of lombardy poplars where they plumed above sienna roofs and the muscatel dark of plum trees. Pale-blue gloves of mist or smoke were forming in the declivities that partly hid the suburbs. The names of the nearer mountains were pointed out to him. Unlike the futuristic city he had imagined, the parts of the town he could see from the lookout seemed to consist of a loose conglomerate of villages. Again, the discovery did not disappoint him. It was redolent of Gattisby and Oldenrath.

He was accommodated in something called a sleepout. 'Sleepouts, James. Essential part of an Australian upbringing. My word!' exclaimed Uncle Neville. Was it his uncle's deadpan face, or the pause after these brief declarations that gave the suggestion of an unstated joke, a seriousness not to be taken seriously?

The sleepout was agreeable enough. On those first mornings in the new town he would wake with mottled glass on three

sides of him and the sound of magpies quarrel-carolling outside. His Aunt Peg fussed over him, as though his father's
death had somehow made his own health delicate. She and
mother talked about Wilf sometimes, and about Len. Aunt
Peg wanted to know about Len's father and, in the course
of her daily conversations, kept making mention of him in
that clipped, tucked-away manner of talking she had. Perhaps
she raised the subject more often than was tactful. But Mother
wouldn't be drawn. She had written to Charlie, was all she
said, and informed him both of Wilf's death and of the decision
to go to Australia. There was no knowing whether Charlie
had ever received the letters. That was all there was to it.

His feelings regarding his own father were still too tender.
To avoid his Aunt Peg's probing Jeb took long walks through
the suburbs. There was a lake, puddled with the intense yellow
reflections of the willows that grew on its shores; beside
it was a large building caged in scaffolding and rusty formwork. It was to be a library, and already resembled the
Parthenon.

Within a few days of their arrival, Mother took a job as
the administrative secretary of a golf club. She acquired a
secondhand car and then, with the money from the sale of
Candleware Road, bought a house in the new suburb of Hughes.
It was a plain, white-stuccoed villa with a garage, and room
under; Jeb, with his easel and paintbox was to occupy the latter.

'You're old enough for your own garret. Do try and visit
me upstairs sometimes.'

On either side were building sites, where half-constructed
houses stood, straw-coloured timber cages with gleamy aluminium windows incongruously tacked on as though they
were temporary.

Canberra. Canberra. As he came to know it better, the
very name of the town became associated in Jeb's mind with
an idea of emergence, like something shiny emerging from
a dun-coloured carapace. Everywhere, it seemed, there was
the churning of Readymix trucks, the whine of power saws,
the g'ding of hammers. With Aunt Peg and his mother he
wandered through bright acres of lounge, dining, and bedroom
suites in the several vast home-furnishing stores that thrived

in the town. Rooms smelt of new paint and the wall-to-wall carpets had the same aroma as the acrylic paints he had used at Clemstead. Beyond suburbs of half-built houses, there were already the notional suburbs where the Streets, Crescents, Places, had been laid down, curlicues of bitumen among tussocks the colour of lionhide.

The town — it was called a city but this was a projection toward a higher and glassier skyline still a decade off — seemed to have no antecedents, no equivalents that Jeb could think of anywhere else in the world. Suburbs seemed to come into existence, suddenly, by a process like cell division. Shaly wasteland became green parkland overnight, as though a team of workers had painted it green. White concrete and glittery aluminium were reflecting the winter sunlight from hundreds of locations.

Yet the hills, magenta under their dramatic sunsets, or a brooding cobalt blue under the clarity of an autumn morning, gave a resonance, an illusion of moody antiquity that existed in counterpoint to the newness of the buildings and their contents.

The two of them moved into their house and unpacked the boxes of possessions they had brought from England. Among the items, Jeb noticed his mother take the portrait of Flying Officer Hengelow and place it in a cupboard.

'We could hang it up somewhere.'

'It would attract questions.'

'Why did we bring it with us if it's just going to sit in a cupboard?'

His mother shrugged. 'Why shouldn't I keep it?' She stood in the new bedroom with her back turned toward him. She didn't know the answer to her own question, Jeb realised. Her answer had suddenly made her seem younger in his eyes, coy almost. He had a momentary image of the woman with the fur collar turned up against the freezing wind on Peterborough Station all those years ago. She could be like this sometimes, as though she had reverted to an age when he was still too young to count for anything, or as though she could switch over into some world that had developed independently of his own.

4

He began at an all-boy school in the top form. Fellows came into the classroom, flinging ex-army rucksacks of books onto the floor beside their desks. Despite the imminence of lessons, one boy was peeling an orange, another was looking at a motorcycle magazine.

'You're a Pom, aren't you?'

From the swim of faces, a fellow had stopped by his desk and was regarding him. Jeb said that yes, he supposed he was a Pom, sort of, though his mother was Australian.

'Half-Pom. But don't worry about it. Which part of Inglan' you from?'

Born near London, he said, but they had shifted around a lot.

'Is that right? What's your father do?'

'He was in the Royal Air Force. But he died last year.'

'Jeez. That's rough. What'd he die of?'

'He had a stroke.'

'Jeez.' The fellow regarded Jeb for some moments, then said, 'I'm sorry to hear about that.'

'That's OK.'

'I'm Mark. Most people call me Rosie.'

'Um, I'm Corballis. Jeb Corballis.'

'Put it there, Jeb.' His hand was clenched, pumped once, then released. The unguardedness, the unstylishness of this introduction took Jeb somewhat aback. 'You blokes! This is Jeb. He's from Inglan'.' There was no ducking it. He was to be introduced. He heard this Rosie reel off a large number of names of which he caught some — Daly, I'Anson, Mallory, Crouch, two unrelated Robert Fords who were known as Big and Little respectively, Voe, Slattery whose real name was Italian, a New Guinean called Elli Tachmann who laughed a great deal. Some of the blokes nodded a greeting. One or two came over and shook hands. They seemed to do a lot of shaking hands in Australia.

As a new boy, he had supposed his reception would be similar to his first day at Clemstead, and it was with a sense of huge relief that he discovered there was nothing surly or stand-offish about these fellows. They reminded him of some of the characters in the Ealing Studio comedies he used to watch at Clemstead on Saturday nights with their boisterous candour — as though it were possible to ignore self-consciousness.

His acceptance among them was as straightforward as this. A few disarming questions, some handshakes and some curt nods of the head, and that was it. He had become one of them and could hardly believe his luck. The names, the faces, remained a jumble for many weeks, but he was rarely left on his own. As they went from classroom to classroom fellows would slide into the desks next to his as though they had known him all their lives. After Clemstead and its minefields of personal relationships, it filled him with a quiet elation, the ease with which he found his place among them, their interest in him and in each other, their apparent candour and sunny good nature. He found himself using their expressions, 'arvo', 'chunderous', 'the Olds', 'abortionate'. In turn they began calling him 'the Cherub', as much an elaboration of his christian name as a comment on what they took to be his English complexion.

Once or twice in those first months there were attempts to 'stir' him, quaint rather than spiteful.

'Want me to show you how these work?' enquired Little Ford in the shower-block after PE.

'Why wouldn't I know?'

'You don't have showers over in Inglan', do you? One bath per street. Dead set.' Fellows were grinning as they stepped under the wheezing nozzles.

'Who told you that?'

'It's fair dinkum.'

Or on another occasion the one called Voe. 'Do you know what Australians call you English people?'

'Poms, I suppose.'

'Nup.'

'What then?'

'Pommie *bastards*!'

'Thrills.'

The goading was easy to shrug off and it was embarrassing when one of the hulkier fellows in the class, like Rosie, rather heavy-handedly stuck up for him.

'Leave the Cherub alone, Voe, you turd.'

'It's all right. It doesn't worry me.'

For there was little that could mar the almost palpable sensation of self-possession that was coming upon him. He felt that he was emergent.

Not that he was yet able to completely manage the feelings aroused by his father's death. The sheer fact of it, so unnegotiable. This irreversibility had driven him to bouts of panicky anger during his last term at Clemstead where he used to sit sometimes in the changing rooms after the others had gone, his fists clenched, his eyes squeezing out tears, staring into the darkness. And on the ship out to Australia, he was given to standing at a rail as the bows flung off great seas, the spume smoking off across the water. The brutal momentum of the ship, the unfeeling crash of those seas confirmed him in his savage resolve not to believe in anything called 'Almighty', not when human lives could be cut off so arbitrarily. He would believe in Chaos and the Brute, the unseeing momentum of things.

He was a little surprised how delayed his reactions to Dad's death had been. If Mother or Aunt Peg brought up the subject of Wilf, he would leave the house and go for a walk. But it could be different with his newfound classmates. Talking about his father and the camps in England and Germany to Rosie, I'Anson, Couch, as they sat in the evenings at a Manuka cafe drinking frothy coffee, gave him a sense of release that he realised he enjoyed in a clandestine way.

Under the airy canopies of the candlebarks and brittlegums of Mugga Way, he cycled to the school each morning on an ancient green bicycle with drop handlebars and a basket full of textbooks, glossy Pelican histories of modern Russia, Japan, China, India, slim volumes of Gide, Molière, Ionesco, which crackled with newness when opened. He was finding that the masters, in English and History particularly, listened to what he had to say with, he thought, real attention. He entered and won an essay competition. In the half-yearly examinations he found himself top in French.

They were being initiated into the modern world and it felt good. Jeb began to change his mind about Modernity.

They studied isotopes, protons and genes, they analysed the poetry of T.S. Eliot, and bandied about terms from Freud in their essays on Hamlet. They went for their driving licences, bought their first cars, drank gallons of coffee. Though they wore the maroon school uniform, each did so with his own distinctness — some could make it look like a business executive's suit, some could make it look like a mechanic's overalls. In the lunchbreak they sat on the front steps of the school sucking icypoles and arguing about the Vietnam War. The New Life, for as such he began to see it, drew him in. It was pleasant, various, absorbing.

5

When Jeb returned home one afternoon, Mother met him at the screen door and asked him to come into the front room. He found Aunt Peg already there. A letter had come from England, she informed him, from Len's Aunt Eva.

'It seems your brother Len is in some kind of trouble. It has something to do with breaking into people's houses. He has to spend four months on a prison farm. Somewhere I haven't heard of.' She stopped and looked at Jeb, momentarily searching his face for a reaction. When he didn't say anything immediately, she added, 'Needless to say this has been a bit of a shock.'

'Bad company will be behind it, I'm absolutely positive,' declared Peg, who clearly was already privy to the news. 'Len's not a wicked boy. Not as I remember him.'

His mother seemed to stare at the empty space in front of her; occasionally she wiped the corner of her eye. When Aunt Peg had finished, Mother shook her head. The gesture expressed a kind of hopelessness, that there were no excuses, no mitigations to hide behind. 'He has been going into people's houses, sometimes while they were actually in. On his own. *Always*.' Mother looked quickly at Peg and then away again. 'His Aunt Eva has apparently visited him at this correction centre. He said very little to her but she formed the impression that he quite simply liked the thrill of it, creeping about in the dark of someone's house when they were in another room watching television, or upstairs asleep.' She stopped, then added with more animation, 'Can you imagine it?'

Jeb had watched Mother's face. She was upset. Would she break down?

'Did he resist — I mean, did he offer violence to the person who caught him?' asked Peg.

'He chatted. *Chatted!*' Mother looked from one to the other to see if either of them could understand a thing so incomprehensible. 'Quite amiably, Eva says. It's a long letter.' She patted a bulky airmail envelope that lay on the table. 'The police say that by the time they arrived the man half regretted phoning them. Anyway, they took Len back to his rooms and also the motorbike shop — there was stolen property in both places. Knick-knacks mostly. A hoard of it, but quite valueless. It seems he was, sort of — collecting it.'

His mother was silent for several moments, looking down at her hands clasped on the dining-room table. Then she said, 'I have to ask myself what more could I have done for Len.' It was said more to herself than to Aunt Peg or Jeb.

'You and Wilf did everything you could, Liz, and there's an end of it. The boy has to take responsibility for his own life.'

But his mother continued as though she hadn't heard. 'I sometimes think it's as if he never came out of me, as if he had come from outer space and I and Wilf had been picked quite arbitrarily to bear responsibility for him. There was nothing common between us I could ever latch on to.' She stopped and in the ensuing quiet, Jeb heard the hallway clock chime four o'clock. The noise of a Fokker Friendship flying over Redhill came to their ears in uneven waves. 'It was before I married Wilf. During the war I used to take him on outings from his school — the seaside, that kind of thing. We used to run out of things to say to each other even before we had stepped off the bus.'

'You are not to blame yourself, Liz. You are *not!*'

'It's not that. I'm not the guilty type. It's just I can't untangle the puzzle of it all, how things managed to slip away so.' They sat around the table, all three of them avoiding each other's eyes.

'And what do you have to say about it all?' Aunt Peg

broke the silence. There might have been some hostility in her tone.

'I don't know. What is there to think?' he replied, defensively. 'I feel — well, sorry for Len of course.'

But when he thought about his feelings later, as he lay in the sleepout, he realised it wasn't pity for Len he felt, but a sensation more akin to foreboding. It was easy to visualise Len in a cell, sitting on a metal-frame bed with his head in his hands. But two questions were fused together in his mind; what would become of Len, and what would his new-found classmates think of him, Jeb, if they found out he had a half-brother in prison? His instinct was to distance himself from both Len's trouble and his mother's sorrow. His reaction did not endear him to his aunt. In the ensuing days Aunt Peg somehow managed to make it clear that she expected Jeb to have a view and to take some kind of role. What view could he have? The thing was a fact. What role could he take?

Once a fortnight Mother wrote to Len, care of Aunt Eva. Jeb never saw what was in any of these letters. Beyond informing Uncle Neville of the facts when he returned from work that evening, Mother never discussed again the matter of Len's disgrace. She took it into herself, lodged it together with the rest of that part of her life that preceded Jeb's consciousness. Reticence? Resilience? Whichever, it was her way with emotive matters, and Jeb preferred things like this. He did not mention Len to his Australian schoolfellows and, with the exception of Mallory, whom Jeb was later to confide in, they remained unaware that he had a half-brother.

6

A day or two into the December holiday Rosie, Crouch and I'Anson called on him.

'Grab a blanket, togs, towel and your wallet, Cherub. We're going down the South Coast for a week to sleep on the beach,' Rosie instructed. It was a challenge, Jeb recognised, and had noted on earlier occasions that the degree to which his friends were able to respond spontaneously to proposals of this sort was, in the blond fellow's notion, a test of how much character they had. 'We're gunna give the Cherub a belated Australian boyhood, Mrs C.,' he explained to Mother.

'I'd like one of those myself.' 'Mrs C.' was occasionally quite flirtatious with the schoolfellows who called on Jeb. 'The charm peels off them as untidily as bark from a gum tree, but it is charm,' she had said to Aunt Peg a week before. 'Swagger,' Aunt Peg had replied, sharply.

'Come too, why don't you? Fair dinkum,' insisted Rosie.

'Have a good time, boys.'

In Crouch's station wagon they climbed the scrubby hills behind Queanbeyan, sped across paddocks which the summer had bleached to the colour of sesame seed, rattled over wooden bridges, wound slowly through the hushed State Forests of the Clyde. In Bateman's Bay they ate meat pies and chips sitting on the doorstep of a takeaway, then moved south again toward the beach I'Anson said he knew, if only he could remember the turnoff.

Until, after they'd parked among swamp-oaks and scaled some dunes, it confronted them, exploded on them almost — the empty crescent of beach with the dry seaweed and tide-wrack in neat rows, and the ocean in its flaring immensity, the crescendo of a surf so white it hurt the eye.

'You beeeyoody.' They stripped off and plunged into the avalanching foam, leaping high on the other side of a wave and sweeping their streaming hair back in the one motion.

'Bodysurfing, Cherub,' shouted Rosie, above the uproar. 'No theoretical limit to your speed.'

'Sure, Rosie.'

'I'm telling you!'

He watched the other three taking up a position, looking back over their shoulders, as the glassy blue ridges swelled, letting the little ones go, then launching themselves as a big one broke. You waited until you were inside the very jaws of the wave, it seemed, then kicked or swam furiously in the moment it greened deliciously before mashing into white.

'It's where you are and when you go, Cherub.'

'He can work that out for himself, Rosie. Jeez,' shouted I'Anson. Then to Jeb. 'Don't mind him. You'll get the hang of it.' He found both Rosie's and I'Anson's solicitude amusing, rather touching.

He missed several then caught a wave perfectly, shutting his eyes and launching himself at the moment it broke above him. All at once he felt himself being taken possession of, thrust forward with tremendous power. It was like skating, only the whole body was involved, and alive to the sensations of speed. Water was rushing beneath him like a dancefloor, a glassy runway, an ice-tunnel. And water, different water it felt like, was impelling him from behind. No theoretical limit to your speed. Wheee! That's how it felt. It was like sensing the lightning movement of fish from the fish perspective, correcting tendencies to yaw, hearing a roar as though like the firmament in his ears, until he scraped the sand and opened his eyes to a frothing brilliant lather.

'Brilliant,' he gasped. 'Bloody brilliant.'

'Told you, didn't I?' Rosie had caught the same wave and was standing, streaming rivulets, the sea around his calves.

They surfed, they lay on their towels, read their novels or automobile journals, dozed, leapt to their feet and plunged into the breakers again. Then, toward evening Rosie announced that he was going to show the Cherub how to catch pipis.

The two of them meandered along the beach, the surf rushing up the sand and over their toes, as though spreading expensive white-brocaded fabric onto a table. Every now and then Rosie would dig his heels into the sand, perform a peculiar rumba which, he avowed, was the way the shellfish were brought to the surface, then he would snatch them as they rolled down the shelf after the receding water. He reminded Jeb of Len a little, in the way he assumed a lead. They returned to their camp, adding their pipis to be boiled with the common hoard. Crouch and I'Anson had made a fire and, beside this the four of them sat, toasting white bread crudely on the ends of sticks, eating tuna straight from the tin and scooping with their tongues the salty, cartilaginous meat of the pipis from their shells. They passed the sherry flagon from hand to hand, their eyes runny with smoke, and talked about the grammar-school girls, about what lay ahead when they finished sixth form at the end of '67, University, conscription. They solved most of the Great Questions, war, justice, religions, human relationships, punctuating their talk with laconic subversions of their own seriousness. Crouch and I'Anson lit up cigarettes. Around them the evening grew purple, deep blue, then speckled black as the stars came out.

'There's more of them up there than there are grains of sand on this beach,' declared Rosie.

'Jeez he's a bullshit artist,' said Crouch.

'Fair dinks,' said Rosie, unabashed. 'I've counted them.'

'*Jeez*, but he's a bullshit artist,' from the same source.

Yes, Rosie was like Len in many ways. Or rather, he was like Len ought to have been. Without the complications.

They spent the week driving up and down the highway, staying on a different beach each night, Broulee, Meringo, Mystery Bay, Narooma, then back the way they had come and north to Durras, Bawley Point, Mollymook. They haunted the takeaway places, bought hamburgers, chiko rolls, consuming them at sticky laminex tables or in the car until it stank with the smell of stale fat. I'Anson bought the flagons because he could pass for twenty-one.

'I could live like this forever,' Jeb observed. 'Kind of de-programmed, outside time, gypsy.'

'Why don't we?'

It was not possible, of course. They returned to sixth form, Matric, Commonwealth Scholarships, aware in the back of their minds that the nation itself, with its conscription laws, its part in the jungle war to their north, had in mind its own programme for them.

But as well as this, Jeb had the sense of another constraint. He felt as if his life were being conducted in the light of Len's, as if he were examining his own experience through Len's eyes. How could it be considered the grist of experience, this round of parties beside swimming pools or in the under-the-house garages munching salted peanuts, drinking fruit punch with a daring minim of sherry or rum added, the standing round the bonnet of a car while one of them fiddled with tappets or a carby and the rest of them talked desultorily about career options. Unreal? No, it was not that exactly.

It was that whenever he visualised a conversation between himself and Len in which he was describing his life he could imagine Len's eyes losing interest, finding the subject shallow, alien. It gave Jeb the sense of being withheld, ever so little, but withheld nevertheless.

Conversation with Mallory 1967

1

He breaststroked idly and easily, and the sunlit, slappy wavelets ceased as he moved into the lee of the islet. Now the water slid away from him in green and honey plates and he glimpsed his arms pushing through the semi-transparency in brief tallowy semi-circles. Dragonflies veered and stopped and veered across the surface at his eye-height, black with tiny spatterings of peacock-blue, and once an ungainly pair of them sheered off at the last moment from his head as they were carried down a zephyr in a copulatory wreath. He could hear the occasional voice carrying across the water.

'Arh, you're a turd, Rosie. Look what you've done!'

He was a little drunk, but not as badly gone as some of the other fellows. At least he hadn't chundered. Voe had passed out and had been laid, very gently, on a bed of pebbles in three inches of water. His khaki school shirt and shorts darkened gradually as the water seeped into them; Little Ford carefully placed Voe's discarded socks over his nose and then retreated back up the beach to where the others had been watching him among the flagons of port and sherry, now sticky and half-empty after much handling.

'You rotten deadshit,' Big Ford said, grinning hugely, his face the colour of blade steak from the sun. Meanwhile Little Ford's visage was creased into such extravagant hilarity it looked as though it might never recover any semblance of seriousness. Halfway down the sand lay the school bell on its side. As they had streamed out of the school at lunchtime on this final day, Little Ford had quickly slipped the bolt holding the bell to its mounting in the belfry and, surrounded by the hullooing mob of sixth-formers, had taken it to one of their cars, whence it had come here to their end-of-school party on the peninsula. Now it lay abandoned after having been used as an enormous sherry goblet, then a spittoon, a urinal, and finally a vomit basin. There had been a rule established earlier in the afternoon that anyone needing to throw up had to do it into the bell. By this time all those with weak or middling stomachs had done so. Most had been enfeebled by the exercise, but not Little Ford, who had emptied himself while holding the heavy brass thing in his hands, then brought it, grinning, to where Big Ford was leaning against a radiata pine.

'Your turn.' Little Ford held the bell and his contribution under the nose of his hulky namesake. The latter's face was impassive whereas the former's looked as though it were on the point of exploding.

'I won't be throwing up,' said Big Ford.

'Arseholes you won't.'

So they all waited as he tipped the flagon to his mouth and drank during the hot afternoon. But they became bored when the big fellow did not oblige them, and the circle they had made broke up into a number of subdued conversations.

Now, as he swam, Jeb came upon a corridor through the willows, and he kicked more strongly against the underwater weed to reach it. The five o'clock sun was shattering through the pinnate foliage, sending spawn-green or straw-gold shafts of light down to the shallow bottom. Highlighted in these shafts were imbroglios of willow-root, carmine and crimson like the ganglia of blood-vessels in the lungs which they had all seen in a biology film. He was able to pull himself into the inlet by grasping a handful of sedge in each hand; the water was no more than knee-deep, but he was happy just to float for the moment, imagining he was a pocket battleship in its fjord, massive both above and under the surface. In

two weeks — less — the exams began; the big ones, Matric-
ulation. There were great expectations placed upon them.

'You blokes are in the top two per cent of intellectual
ability in the country,' their short physics teacher had told
them recently, during one of his pep-talks. 'You owe it to
yourselves...'

Yes, the exams would determine, so they had been told,
the nature of their employment for the rest of their lives.

So there loomed in Jeb's imagination a notion that the
exams were like a narrowing of time. Being part of the top
two per cent was all very well, but for himself, he just hoped
to 'squeeze through'. He was pitted against every other person
of his own age in the country and this thought gave him
a curious mixture of trepidation and buoyancy. They were
being impelled toward those crowded examination halls
where, for a week or so nothing would matter except the
blue or pink or fawn question papers that were placed before
them. Then they would be freed, freed, not only from the
emergency conditions of the exam, but from an entire phase
of their lives. It would be like throwing off a skin. So the
exams were not only a test, or a gauntlet rather, but a rite
which would spill them, schoolboys no more, into the wide
expanses of December and beyond, that *flaring* of time into
the multiplicity of employments and university courses which
would scatter them all over Australia.

Jeb pushed himself back and forth in the shallows and it
felt amniotic. This image somehow pleased him more than
that of pocket battleships. He rose from his little pool and
picked his way, dripping, onto the islet. Sparrows darted in
and out of the willow palisade, and the mud squeezed up
between his toes. On the other side of a grassy glade sat
Mallory, dangling his feet in the water. Jeb went over and
sat next to him.

'How come you're not with the others?'

Mallory was silent for a while, then said, 'I suppose when
it came to it, I didn't feel like making a beast of myself.'
He took a small plastic sachet from his side and, unzipping
it, took out a packet of cigarettes and offered one to Jeb.

'You came prepared,' said the latter, declining the offer,

then added, 'I didn't see you taking off.' Mallory was an odd fellow. In the classrooms and common room at school it was as if he could be present among them yet somehow he seemed not to have any actual presence. No, that wasn't quite it. One knew he was there, though he was mostly silent, watching, yet capable, sometimes, of slipping an item into the conversation that was so hilarious, or so deadly, that it took one's breath away, like when the fellows had been rubbishing Salami, their maths teacher, so-called because he was short, cylindrical and rubescent, and Mallory had said 'His wife's got leukaemia,' saying it so quietly, and in such a throwaway manner that some of the blokes missed it and went on rubbishing.

Mallory was not teased, not even in the loose, friendly way of chiacking that the fellows went on with. Little Ford and Voe both left Mallory alone. There was something too incalculable about him to risk taking the mickey or anything like that. He was part of the group clearly enough — he came to parties, almost always without a partner, and left without one too — but he was one who, in retrospect, his fellows realised they never really knew much about. He lived with his mother and his sister, his turn-out was invariably immaculate, and, out of school, he smoked a large number of cigarettes. He possessed a great deal of knowledge about German fighter aircraft of the Second World War, and would sometimes come out with it, talking at length on the subject of the various types of Focke Wulfs or Messerschmitts. His listener — there was usually only one when he embarked on one of these displays of erudition — was never quite sure whether they were in earnest, or ironic.

In any case, Mallory's knowledge of history was immense. He was top of the subject and his position there had been unassailable as far back into his school career as anyone could recall. His entire summers seemed to be spent lying on a towel with nothing on but swimmers, or shorts, and reading some work of history. Jeb, who usually came in the top four of the history class, felt that he ought to get to know Mallory better, as they both shared this passion for the past. But it was difficult. Mallory's life seemed to be so focussed, in contrast to Jeb's. Why didn't Mallory ever talk about girls, or painting, or superegos, egos and ids, and all that?

Jeb looked at Mallory and voiced something of these thoughts. 'It's odd really, you are kind of invisible in a strange sort of way. I mean, I know you're really up on history, and all that, but the rest of you is kind of —' he searched for another word, then, not finding one, said helplessly, 'invisible.'

Mallory drew on his cigarette. There was an uprightness in the way he sat on the bank, his arms and back tanned to a resinous colour after all that research in the sun. He tended to look at people out of the side of his eyes and this was how he now glanced at Jeb. When Mallory didn't answer, Jeb tried to modify his comment with a question.

'How come you like history so much, anyway?'

'Did you ever used to collect things when you were small?'

'You mean cigarette cards, things like that? Yes, a bit, why.'

'I did, all the time. Cards, plastic figures out of breakfast cereal packets, matchbox cars, plastic aeroplanes. I always wanted the complete set of everything, and I could never sit still until I had all of whatever it was I was collecting.'

'What's that got to do with history?'

'Well, I started reading books about what happened in history and the more I read, the more I wanted to read, the more *facts* I wanted to know. It's a bit like not wanting any of the facts to escape. I want to know them all, so that nothing escapes.' Mallory paused for a moment, reflectively, then continued. 'I suppose it makes my brain a bit like a large net. Besides when we were moving around, I spent lots of time on my own. So I read a good deal.'

'History's not the facts but how you see them,' said Jeb, quoting an axiom the history master had been at pains all year to instil.

'History is the facts and how you see them,' replied Mallory. 'Who said that?'

Mallory gave him a glance of surprise. 'Mallory. Who else?'

'Fair enough. Where were you moving around?

'I was conceived in England, carried across four oceans

inside my mother, and born in a fibro hut down on the south coast on a night when the telephones were out of order. At least, that's what Mum told me. Before I can remember, I had lived in India and Zanzibar, and, while my father was still around, I lived at different times on four continents. Does that make me invisible? Maybe it does. Maybe the more places you go, the more bits and pieces of yourself you scatter in your wake.'

'It makes you a well-travelled mongrel, I reckon,' replied Jeb. 'Where's your dad, anyway?'

'My dad? Oh, he comes to Mum's parties sometimes. Otherwise I don't see him much. I haven't spoken to him for a couple of years at least, since I was fifteen.'

'What, not spoken a single word?'

'Hardly a single word.'

'You must've.'

'I haven't.' Mallory gave Jeb a glance of surprise that he should find difficulty in accepting so mundane a fact.

'How come?'

Mallory's face had the same expression as when he was talking about Messerschmitts, or when he was on the edge of the group listening; it was a case of the eyes smiling in an amused and detached kind of way, as though the highly charged things he was saying did not pertain to himself, but to someone else.

'I'm not sure,' he said. 'I was in a room watching television one evening and the news came on that Winston Churchill had died. I went bursting into the neighbouring room where my parents were finishing dinner and declared, "Winnie's dead!" My father grunted once, and after that we never spoke to each other again. Don't ask me to explain it.'

'It sounds weird,' said Jeb.

'I think he may have found my enthusiasm embarrassing, or something. He's an enzymologist. He doesn't get enthusiastic. Not that it stops him paying an allowance into a bank for me each month. I ought to be grateful. I wish I was.'

They both gazed across the water to where Black Mountain confronted them, dark green in its folds, though delicately highlighted along its spurs. It looked like a broad old matriarch, shawled in heavy brocaded material. On its summit were two slender antennae from which, at intervals, red lights winked.

'Yes, but never talking to you again! Bloody odd, if you ask me.'

'It's been me not talking to him just as much as the other way round.' Mallory smoked in a reflective silence for some time. His posture and his meditative calm made him look very much older, like a person in his twenties or thirties. Then he said, 'It was indifference, I suppose, not hostility. I'd been coming to the conclusion around the age of fourteen or fifteen that I had nothing in common with my father and the television episode simply made that realisation click into place.' He took a last couple of draws on the cigarette then threw it onto the water.

'What about your mum?' Jeb had the sense of wanting to press home an advantage. He was curious. He had learnt more about Mallory in the course of the latter's smoking one cigarette than he had discovered during the whole of fifth and sixth form. But Mallory ignored the question.

'I guess we should swim back across and see who needs to be driven home.' He put his cigarettes into the plastic sachet and stuffed it into the front of his school shorts. They swam across with Mallory slightly in the lead; neither of them spoke, and following their exertions Mallory's hair still looked as if it had been freshly combed. He dried himself fastidiously on a small towel and, as Jeb watched him, he could not imagine Mallory ever looking dishevelled. The fellows on the beach appeared to be asleep. Most of the flagons were now empty, some of them broken.

'Anyone need a lift?' Mallory made the offer in his curious throwaway manner so it was doubtful that many of the sprawled bodies heard. One or two of those within earshot hauled themselves onto the back seat of his car and flopped. 'I don't suppose we can leave this here,' Mallory said, kicking the school bell. Holding it at arms length he took it to the water, dropped it in and pushed it to and fro with his foot in order to wash away its noisome contents; then he put it in the front seat of his car. He drove an old Pontiac with bench seats; the boot and bonnet had something of the expanse of the prairies and there was a magnificent chrome figurehead depicting the great Iroquois chieftain. When Mallory was sitting in the driver's seat, it made him look incongruously childlike, his neck craning to see over the broad bonnet, his legs at full stretch to reach the pedals. The size of the car meant that Mallory was sometimes roped into being the taxi for large numbers of couples on those occasions when parties or excursions were being organised by one or other of the grammar-school sets. He allowed himself to be used in this way as his one contribution to the social lives of his school-fellows. There was no evidence that he used its wide bench seats to 'pull sheilas' as the phrase went. 'Are you coming?' he asked Jeb.

'I'll wait for some of the fellows to come round. Cheers.'

'Cheers. I'll get this thing back discreetly.' And with a crackle of gravel, Mallory drove off. Jeb sat under a bush and watched the Brindabellas gradually blacken while the vivid gold-and-manganese of the sunset faded away behind their rim. After a while he was aware that Rosie had come and sat down beside him. The big blond fellow was staring out across the lake with an idiotic gaze and every now and then shaking his head and making a sound like a horse's neigh. His shirt had been discarded somewhere, though the school tie was still around his neck.

'Faahrkh!' said Rosie.

'Stick your head in the lake. It'll bring you round.' Rosie looked at Jeb uncomprehendingly for a moment, then shambled down the beach and flopped full-length in the water. He seemed to remain immobile for some time and Jeb could not see whether his head was above or below the surface. Finally Rosie stirred, and rose, like a hippo, from the water, then staggered back, and stood over Jeb, dripping.

'What happened to the bell?'

'Mallory's taken it back.'

Rosie seemed to take a while to digest this information, then he said, 'You coming, Cherub?' His speech was unslurred by the afternoon's drinking, though his eyelids were droopy.

Jeb got to his feet. 'Should we take a body or two?' They

approached Voe, who had, hours ago, rolled himself a little above the waterline; together they lifted him and put his limp body in the back seat of Rosie's car. Then they drove off.

Working with Rosie 1967–68

1

During that summer after Matric Jeb frequently found himself in the company of Rosie. In the year that had elapsed since their coastal trip, he continued to enjoy the company of this burly, sunny-faced fellow who radiated assurance, and dispelled complications. The comparison with Len remained in Jeb's mind. As Len had been once (long ago), so now was Rosie adept at initiating new possibilities, filling life with promise.

They took gardening jobs in the better suburbs; their one ad in the paper gave them enough work for weeks.

'Australia's dripping with work,' said Rosie. 'You've just got to get off your bum and find it.'

They mowed lawns and trimmed edges, harvested the early-bearing fruit trees, the loquats and apricots, weeded terraces of tendrilly tomato plants and elegant green plumes of corn. All this for two dollars an hour.

'You know what we should really be doing, Cherub,' said Rosie, stopping to lean on his hoe after a few minutes of desultory chipping.

'What's that?' enquired Jeb, who felt their employer had a right to expect exactly sixty minutes work for her two dollars, so continued scuffing the furrows with his hoe.

'We should hitch across to Western Australia and get work on the Ord or at Tom Price. You can make as much in a month in those places as the average wage in a year here.'

'Fair dinks,' he added when Jeb didn't stop work. 'Why don't we? Say tomorrow. All we'd need is a spare shirt and the money we've earned from this.'

It sounded like just the thing school-leavers should do, simply stuff a spare shirt into a canvas bag, gulp down a last mouthful of coffee and hit the road for Perth. And Rosie, Jeb had learned, could never resist offering a golden prospect. It was the form his charity took and it did not matter how extravagant or far-fetched the prospect was, he conjured it with an unabashed gaze from his very blue eyes and would suffer no cynicism or dismissiveness.

Jeb had found this out soon after starting at the school some twenty-one months previously. Despite being hopeless at all ball games, he had found himself playing football on the school oval one grey afternoon. There came a moment when Rosie had possession of the ball and Jeb, being nearby, had contrived a tackle which ended up as an ineffectual tangle around Rosie's legs. As he struggled to his feet he felt himself being patted on the head.

'You'll be in the firsts by next week. You watch,' Rosie said. Rosie was in the firsts himself.

'I'd be happy enough as linesman for the fourths,' Jeb replied, but the praise, for all that he knew it was undeserved, had filled him with elation.

'No. You're going to be in the firsts. I'm going to talk to the coach.' And then Rosie trotted off in pursuit of the ball. It came to nothing, of course, though Jeb never forgot the sheer uplift in his morale that the incident aroused.

And it had become the pattern of their relationship. Yes, Rosie had charm — or swagger — depending whose version of his character you believed. Was he calculating in the use of it? It was hard to say. Certainly he cultivated long teabreaks with their employers.

One of these was an elderly widow; the two gardeners removed their mud-caked boots and followed her through rooms dark with memorabilia. Rosie always addressed her as 'ma'am' and Jeb, taken somewhat aback by this deference from his burly partner, almost expected Rosie to pull his blond and rather pretty forelock each time he uttered the word. And, as the old lady served tea from a handpainted, chipped teapot, Rosie would point to photographs on the mantelpiece.

'Excuse I for stickybeaking, Ma'am, but is this your daughter? She's a very fine-looking woman if you don't mind me saying so. Are these your grandchildren? You can see the resemblance...' What startled Jeb was that Rosie could be so glib with these old-fashioned compliments. How would they have sounded in the sceptical dormitory atmosphere of Loftus House? They made him sound, to Jeb's ear at least, about fifteen years older than he really was. He had a knack of gaining trust, and of combining this with his own personal advantage. The teabreaks became longer as Rosie gained a greater intimacy with the old lady's absent family.

Then there was the doctor's wife who, in their teabreaks, served them with real coffee, with cream and sugar crystals. Here was proof they had arrived at an authentic sophistication.

It seemed that Rosie knew Mrs Fox slightly from before, having once done a job for her. Mrs Fox addressed him by his christian name, Mark. Perhaps this familiarity was the reason why Rosie did not remove his boots when they went in for morning tea with her; or perhaps it had more to do with creating an effect of some sort. He sat on one of her bar stools and talked about the paintings that she should consider hanging in her house, looking at her with that candid blue stare, the bristles of his first beard beginning to sprout along his glowing jowl. Beneath the kitchen bar, Jeb noticed, Rosie's knees would be jigging up and down rapidly in a display of nervous excitement; it was like the rocker gear in a motor, only the excitation was never apparent in that part of his body which could be seen above the table.

'Cherub's a painter. You'd like his pictures, they're original. He's got one that would be beaut right there above your drinks cabinet.'

Mrs Fox turned to Jeb, who looked down at his feet because he didn't think he had ever seen anyone who was as attractive as Mrs Fox, with her short dark hair falling on either side of her face and curving forward like the blades of scimitars. It made him ache. There was an exquisite bone structure in her cheeks which was visible under the tan of her skin; her brown throat emerged from the white vee of her blouse and suggested to Jeb a body that was brave and fine and athletic; indeed she had the look of one imminently about to go out for tennis or a swim.

'You must feel very fortunate to have a friend who is prepared to promote your painting so vigorously.'

'Cherub and I are like brothers, aren't we, Cherub?'

Jeb gave Rosie a glance and saw the large blue gaze fixed upon him. Rosie was a bit over the top sometimes, not that you could be sure as to whether you should be taking him seriously at any given time. 'Brothers,' he replied.

'Goodness!' said Mrs Fox. 'You must bring me some of your work to look at. Tell me, do you mind being called Cherub?'

'Of course he doesn't,' supplied Rosie. There was a tense grin on his face and his knees had accelerated. 'Do you, Cherub?'

'It doesn't worry me. It's what I was called at school.' He looked at Mrs Fox quickly and found she was smiling at him, half with amusement, half with sympathy. Mrs Fox confused him and moved him.

So Jeb sat and observed the interchanges between Rosie and Mrs Fox, deeply conscious of his own lack of charm. But also he enjoyed Rosie's apparently unabashable self-confidence. It was somehow uplifting.

Mrs Fox went out, leaving them to prune a cypress hedge. But the morning was hot and after a while they wandered into the shade of a mulberry tree and began picking the ripe berries. They were the colour of light through a glass of burgundy and tasted exquisitely acid. Jeb's and Rosie's fingers became incarnadined by the juice while the sun made diaphanous splodges of the leaves above their heads.

'She's nice, Mrs Fox, isn't she? I mean, attractive.'

'You should get into her,' said Rosie, giving Jeb a straight, if amused stare.

'Leave it out! I didn't mean anything sexual.'

'What did you mean?'

'Well, she's nice... you know. Shit, Rosie!' Jeb's fantasy

had, in fact, involved delicious scenes in which Mrs Fox seduced him with an amused and sympathetic smile. As he imagined it, she would come into a room where he was standing. She would shut the door. She would know what to do and she would guide his hands. She would have a confidence with buttons and zippers... But it was more complex, because what appealed to him, as well as these delicious scenes of sex, was the thought of simply *being* with Mrs Fox. At eighteen he had done no more than occasionally kiss some of the grammar-school girls whom he met at parties or school socials; he was liked by the girls well enough, but he had never, for instance, touched a female nipple or run his hand along the inside of a thigh, so his imaginings on this score were all the more urgent and torrid. But they were part of something larger, an exquisite anticipation of well-being — and freedom. Rosie's advice that he should 'get into her' both profaned his fantasy and stated exactly what he wanted.

'What you mean is, I want to get into her.' Rosie was grinning triumphantly.

'It's not,' said Jeb, resignedly. How could he argue? The way Rosie had interpreted his remark was obviously what was expected of him by the... the code. No, it wasn't as strict as that. By something, anyhow. He resented it, vaguely, and was frustrated that he could not articulate what he meant by saying that Mrs Fox was nice. They picked and ate quietly for a few minutes.

Then Rosie said, 'Her first name is Natalya.'

'How did you find that out?'

'She told me when I did that job for her before. And she's thirty-one or thereabouts, I'd say.' Rosie plucked thoughtfully at the little globes of juice, then added, 'And I'd say she was attracted to you.' It was one of those golden prospects, unfair, tantalising.

'Leave off, Rosie, there's not a shred of evidence for that. She's married to a rich doctor.'

'You've got no idea what goes on in the suburbs, have you? Why do you think she wants to see your paintings, you drongo. I'm telling you, she is attracted to you. I can see it. Don't underestimate yourself. You're always selling yourself short.'

Rosie was grinning still. Could he be right? Or was Rosie teasing him with his own fantasies regarding Mrs Fox?

'She's married to a doctor,' he repeated idiotically.

'So?'

'So.'

'Strewth, you won't be told, Cherub. The woman is attracted to you. Go for it.'

Jeb didn't answer this time. The sun poured through the leaves behind Rosie's head. It was hard to read his expression correctly. The two of them seemed very close together in the shade of the mulberry.

'See, your lips and your fingers are crimson with passion,' said Rosie, indicating the stains. 'Do like I say, get into her.'

'Yours are too,' observed Jeb.

2

For no reason that he could uncover, Jeb, at this period, painted pictures of the sea; it was virtually his only subject, which was surprising given that the nearest coastline was two and a half hours drive away. Moreover, his seascapes tended to have a very northern hemisphere atmosphere to them, showing volatile grey cloudscapes tinged with lemon or caramel streaks of filtered sunlight.

He had painted or drawn ships for as long as he could remember. Now, at eighteen, though he could still immerse himself in the romance of his subject matter with all its swirling, inchoate energies and brooding deep colours, the doubts he had experienced at his boarding school as to his ability and vision as a painter returned more frequently. He had moments when he saw all too clearly that painting involved an interest in forms and colours rather than ships, skies and seas. It was the matter of 'maturity' and 'immaturity' again. At such moments he knew that to develop as a painter he would have to be very much more experimental, more committed to painting as such. Rosie had once told him that his ships and seas were symbolic and that what he was coping with in his marine paintings was his father's death.

'Stop me if I'm speaking out of turn, Cherub, but look, they're bearing him away. They're unconscious symbols of loss. Fair dinks.'

It was tempting to believe his efforts had this kind of depth, 'unconscious symbolism', but Jeb knew the truth was simpler. All he really wanted to do was represent the ships and seas and skies which appeared deliciously before his mind's eye.

Dimly he suspected the desire was a childish one, as Len's interest in plastic models had been, a reflex to resist development.

Nonetheless, when Rosie dropped him off from Mrs Fox's in the middle of the afternoon, he went down to his under-the-stairs bedroom-cum-studio, took out all the bits and pieces of masonite on which his seascapes were painted and, with a fine brush, inserted his name onto the right-hand bottom corner of each. Then he went to work on the painting which was on his easel at that moment. The picture showed a schooner hard-pressed in a gale, as seen from the bows of another sailing ship which was following it. Both ships were heeling at an angle, so the painting had the effect of dis-orienting viewers, of compelling them to look at the picture askance. This was reinforced by the mountainous seas that Jeb had painted in, cobalt blue with patches of viridian; he wondered, somewhat forlornly, whether the picture's dis-orientation amounted to a technical breakthrough.

But now the painting had a new attraction for him. He was painting it for Mrs Fox. As he applied glistening dabs of colour straight from the tube, working them into the sea, striving to give a feeling of the impenetrable depths and richness of the ocean, the wild inscrutability of the deeps, he was also calculating the effect this might have on Mrs Fox. For she had become his centre, the one to whom he was prepared to be answerable, and for whom all his efforts — for the time being at least — were directed. She had become his muse.

So he worked away into the night in what he believed might be a passionate dedication to his art and muse. And as he dabbed or flicked the colours, he was able increasingly to convince himself that she would understand what he meant by the swirling wildness of his sky, the gleamy, dark, suggestive depths of his seas, the delicate grace of his two schooners leaning before the blow with the crescent shapes of their sails, the white bouquets of froth that burst on their bows. Yes, let them be symbols. She would make the connection between this and his own character, between this and *her* own character.

Of course he had no intention of violating her relationship with her doctor husband. Rosie's lewd suggestion that he should 'get into her' was improper as much for the fact that it misunderstood Jeb's sensibility, his honour. He was not seeking an *adventure* with the doctor's wife. In the exquisite notion he was forming in his mind, she would simply take her place in his life, a commanding presence, a benevolent, ever-interested companion. Would their relationship be carnal, or purely spiritual? This, despite his fantasy in the garden earlier, was vague. The understanding he would have with Mrs Fox was outside crude distinctions of this sort anyway. He was surprised at how quickly the image of Mrs Fox was able to take possession of him, as though it slid into an empty place. If Rosie was as Len ought to have been, it crossed his mind that Mrs Fox was like... No, he dropped that idea immediately, almost before he had allowed the thought to form. It was all wrong. And not altogether true anyway.

So he worked, and a little before midnight he finished. The piece of masonite smelled deliciously of that linseedy, somehow deeply stable odour of oil paint, made more pungent when he cleaned his brushes with turps. Then, perhaps because he had read in some biography or other of dedicated painters doing likewise, he threw himself onto his bed fully clothed and slept until, some time in the small hours, he woke because his feet felt uncomfortable; whereupon he kicked off his workboots and went back to sleep.

The problem as it confronted him when he awoke in the morning was how he should actually approach Mrs Fox with the painting. He wanted to give it to her; he would refuse any payment for it. Not that he could tell her, but the painting would be offered as a form of gratitude, for her beauty, for the arousing and poignant effect of that smile, balanced as it was between amusement and sympathy. He wanted nothing in return. Nothing. Absolutely. He said this to himself at the same time as he joyously anticipated her favour. What was her favour when it came down to it? Well, it was — the opportunity to be in her company, he supposed, which was problematic, not least because he knew he would be tongue-tied.

So, her favour would be her providing him with the opportunity to be near her without having the obligation to actually talk, or to be ostentatiously impressive. He would not have to *perform*, but would be given the chance to reveal what he was in himself. Mrs Fox would notice and grow to value the rich but unobtrusive qualities of his character. His conception of their relationship was, perhaps, unfortunately intricate and conditional, but it gave him exquisite pleasure to daydream about it as he lay on his bed with the sun streaming through the window above his head, and the clatter of cutlery drawers being pulled out and in as Mother got ready to go to work.

But how to go about it? He couldn't just knock on her door one evening with the piece of masonite under his arm. If he went there by himself, he would go to pieces as soon as she opened the door. He knew that. He needed Rosie's social ease, his bravura, yet he was apprehensive that Rosie would consider him ridiculous, or that he would misinterpret Jeb's offering to Mrs Fox in some lewd way.

Jeb spent the early part of the morning fiddling with the painting. Rosie called for him a little after eight-thirty, and they sat around drinking instant coffee while Rosie chatted to Elizabeth Corballis before she went to work. He seemed to be in no hurry to start. It was humid and there were storms forecast.

'Were we doing anything at Mrs Fox's today?' Jeb tried to make his question sound casual.

'Nup. Why should we?' said Rosie. His knees were jigging, and he was looking at Jeb with a knowing grin. 'We've got a heap of other jobs.'

'I thought she wanted us to clear out her shed.'

'Nup.'

'Oh. Fair enough. I just thought I remember her saying…'

'Listen to him, will you.'

'What do you mean?'

'What I mean is, you want to go and see Mrs Fox.'

'Why should I?'

'Because you're lusting after her.'

'Who says?'

'I say.'

'Bullshit, Rosie. I just said she was nice. That's all.' Rosie simply looked at Jeb knowingly and grinned at him. Jeb noted that, for all his lank, brassy blond hair, Rosie's eyebrows were dark, almost black, and bushy, and his face seemed to glow like basted meat. 'Anyway, don't you think Mrs Fox is attractive?'

'What's it got to do with me?' They were silent for a while and Rosie continued to give Jeb a stare which seemed to imply he didn't know how lucky he was.

'It's just, if we were going around there, I thought I'd show her a painting.'

'You should. Like I said, the woman is attracted to you.'

'Nah, I'll wait till next time, I guess.' They drank their mugs of coffee in silence for a while.

Then Rosie said. 'Well? What are you waiting for, Cherub. Go and get the painting.'

'What about those other jobs?'

'Bugger those other jobs.'

'So we are going to Mrs Fox's.'

'Of course we are.'

'But you said she didn't need us today.'

'Get the painting, you nong.'

Rosie took a look at the painting, liked it, and assured Jeb he would be in like Flynn. Then they drove to Mrs Fox's house in Rosie's Simca, and sat, parked outside for a few minutes.

'I'm not sure about this. Maybe I'll show her the painting as we're leaving,' said Jeb, expecting that Rosie would urge him not to be a drongo and to present the picture immediately. And Jeb had determined that if Rosie did this he would screw his courage up and make his offering.

Instead, Rosie just looked at him and said, 'All right.' It was as if he had abruptly lost patience. The mocking, goading, smiley expression had left his face in that moment. Rosie's moods could be funny.

They knocked and Mrs Fox, dressed in a white chenille bathrobe and with a towel around her head, admitted them. 'You must excuse me, boys, I've just come in from gym,' she said, leading them through. Within a few minutes the two of them were at work clearing out an old wooden shed at the bottom of the long garden.

The garden had originally been the labour of love of an elderly couple who had arrived in the capital in the early 1930s and who had planted many fruit and other trees. So the edge of the plot was a cushiony, voluptuous curtain of foliage and fruits, long branches burdened with pears and plums, figs and mulberries, apples and the still greeny-yellow persimmons. There were dark crannies of shade, ancient wooden furniture under an ash tree, a quaintly classical bird-bath, and the shed where Jeb and Rosie worked, which had been converted from a gazebo. The fantasies of courtly love that Jeb created around Mrs Fox were set against this Arcadian background.

When they began work the sunlight was falling in a dazzling puddle into the small lawn in the midst of the leafage, but within an hour or so the sky had begun to cloud over with a blue-grey, deeply swollen nimbus. They threw out encrusted paint tins, jam jars and tobacco tins left there by the elderly couple. They stacked timber, brushed away cobwebs, and swept away the dried leaves of decades from the floor.

After an hour or so, Jeb saw Mrs Fox go out to the garage. There came the sound of her trying to start a car. Some minutes later she re-emerged and came down to the shed where they were working.

'Look, boys, I'm desperate. *Could* one of you drive me down to the shops. I'm supposed to be entertaining tonight.'

'No worries,' said Rosie. 'Guard the fort, Cherub.'

Rosie and Mrs Fox left and Jeb continued working in the growing gloom. Initially the encroachment of the stormfront had been silent, a gradual invasion, high and dark and thorough, great undulating formations dragging behind them the immense white curtain of the rain. There was a period when all this was happening in the still-oppressive atmosphere, but then the wind started, clearing out the heavy, immobile air; a plastic flowerpot tumbled off a bench and rolled this way and that on the concrete path. A screen door banged open and shut. The onset of a storm always thrilled Jeb. He listened to the first spots of rain fall on the tin roof of the shed like the hesitant touch of a one-finger typist. As he continued to take the unwanted contents of the shed outside and throw them onto a trailer, he enjoyed the sensation of the cold droplets on the sleeveless ex-army shirt he wore. Then the skies opened and he watched from the eaves how the downpour seemed to hide everything behind veils of cellophane of varying thickness, the trees, the roofs of the neighbouring houses, and the almost invisible outline of Mount Ainslie.

It was lunchtime and he was beginning to feel hungry. He waited for Rosie and Mrs Fox to return, and wondered if Mrs Fox would see the painting in the back of Rosie's car. Perhaps Rosie would show it to her, and when they returned Mrs Fox would come immediately from the car with the painting in her hand to praise him for his exquisite work. Perhaps.

They must have been gone at least an hour. He hoped that Rosie would buy a couple of pies. He was beginning to run out of things to do in the shed, though it was pleasant enough in the interior. He felt cocooned within the uproar of the rain on the tin roof, and sat on his haunches, waiting. But Rosie made no appearance.

A trip to the shops could not take this long. He decided to run across to the house. The short sprint soaked him to the skin. He went through the back door and paused for a moment in the laundry while he shook the rain from his hair. He could hear Rosie's voice in the kitchen. So they had come back. Why hadn't the bugger told him? He came to the kitchen entrance with the intention of saying something indignant and, on glimpsing Rosie and Mrs Fox, immediately decided not to go in. In that momentary glance Jeb had seen that Mrs Fox was hemmed in against the sideboard, trying to put groceries away as though there were nothing unusual happening. Rosie was standing very close to her, gazing at her and talking in an insistent, low voice. He had that loosely flippant smile on his mouth and in his eyes.

'Don't you believe I'm serious?'

'Now come on. Give me some room to move here.'

'You've really touched me. I mean it. What more do you want me to say?'

'You're being silly.'

'No I'm not. You're a woman. I'm a man, and I find you — all right, I'll say it, breathtaking.'

'Mark, you are eighteen!'

'So?'

'Look, Mark. You're very sweet and I'm very flattered. But —'

'There are no buts.' There was a silence for some moments and Jeb imagined the two of them eyeing each other.

'Now come on, you big brute, you, out of my way,' said Mrs Fox at length. There was the sound of Rosie being pushed, a clunk as he conceded a step, and then Mrs Fox again. 'Out of my *way*.'

'Ouch. Who's the brute now? Ooh! Put that ladle away. Ouch! Ouch!' Rosie's exclamations of pain were accompanied by chuckles. 'Ooh, you're hurting me.'

'Good.'

'Stop it, or I'll have to defend myself.'

'Well move out of my way, then.'

'Aw.'

There was the sound of further thwacks. Then Mrs Fox said, 'Now Mark, let me go. This minute.' There was a pause. 'Mark!'

'You said I had a minute.'

'I said nothing of the sort.'

'You promise not to use that ladle.'

'Let me *go*! Mark, I won't be treated like this. Stop being ridiculous.'

This interchange had all taken place at a level of seriousness that Jeb, listening from behind the laundry door, had found hard to determine. It was as if Mrs Fox didn't particularly enjoy Rosie's fooling around, but was loath to get angry about it for fear of acknowledging that it was serious. There was no mistaking the anger in the next thing that Jeb heard her saying.

'Don't you ever do that again. Don't you *ever*.'

'It was only a little kiss.'

'I think you should leave. Right now.'

'Now you've really hurt me.'

'*Leave!*'

Jeb slipped out through the back door and went around the side of the house. A few moments later the screen door slammed as Rosie came out and went across the lawn toward the shed. The rain had eased a little.

Jeb stood in the middle of a flower-bed, leaning against the wall. It was numbness, more than anything, which he felt. He had never had any experience of being betrayed before so it did not occur to him that betrayal was exactly what had just happened to him. And yet it was absurd. Mrs Fox was lovely, but what was she to him, when it came down to it? She was a married woman. So why should Rosie's behaving in this particular way towards her make him feel so, he supposed, upset? For this was what he was beginning to feel now, injury, emergent, hard-to-explain injury; it seemed to emanate out of his initial shock like the pain of surgery out of an anaesthetic.

'Hey, Cherub.' Rosie came over to where Jeb stood. 'What're you doing here? You'll get soaked.'

'I was putting something round the front,' Jeb lied rather ineffectually. He wouldn't look Rosie in the eye. He felt he had nothing to say to him, and everything to say to him.

'Let's get lunch.'

Jeb went along and they sat in the car in a Manuka carpark eating pies.

'How come you're not saying much?'

'I don't feel like talking. That's all.'

'Come on. Something's bugging you.' Jeb remained silent, but Rosie was persistent, solicitous even. 'Come on Cherub. Spill the beans. Have I done something?'

'No. Not especially.'

'What do you mean, not especially.'

'I mean, not especially.'

'I thought we were mates.'

'So did I.'

'So. What's bugging you.'

'All right then. I come across from the shed to see if you've come back from taking Mrs Fox to the shops, and when I come into the kitchen I see you fronting her.'

'That! That was just a bit of fun!'

'You said you thought she was breathtaking.'

'Well? I thought you thought that too. She is.'

'Yes, but ...'

'So what's the problem? It was just a bit of fun. You've still got an in there.'

'No thanks.' In truth, Jeb's ardour for Mrs Fox had changed. Not that it had waned, exactly, but Mrs Fox was now somehow entangled with his sense of injury. He was heartsick, and this he found disabling. He looked gloomily out at the carpark and the pools that were forming on the tarmac, prickled by the rain. 'Besides, from what I saw this arvo she can't keep her hands off you,' he said acidly.

'Now you *have* bloody hurt me. You really have. I thought we were mates.' Jeb stole a quick glance at Rosie who was looking at him intently. And indeed there was injury registered in those large eyes and that glowing face, to the extent that it made Jeb sorry he had said what he did.

'OK. I take that back.'

They were silent for a while. Rosie rolled and smoked a cigarette.

'Let's knock off for the afternoon. It's too wet to work,' he said at length.

'What about our pay from Mrs Fox?'

'I'll pick it up this evening and bring it round.'

When Rosie dropped Jeb off, the latter took his painting from the back of the car and went down to his studio. Perhaps it was his mood, or the dismal light of the rain depression, but when he looked at the painting now, it gave him none of the exhilaration it had given him when he finished it the night before. It seemed mediocre, gauche, and the light reflected off the gleam of the oil paint anyway, making the qualities of sea, sky and ships hard to discern. He sat with it on his knees for a long time, then stood up and snapped the masonite in half across the back of a chair.

Two days later Rosie and I'Anson turned up in the Simca. The car had been fitted with a roof rack and there was a canvas water bag attached to the front bumper bar.

'We're heading for Dampier. Will you be in it?'

'When are you going?'

'In about five minutes.'

'No thanks.'

'You'll never know what you missed, Cherub. Cheers.'

'Cheers.'

As the Simca drove up the street, Jeb watched Rosie's hairy forearm waving to him until they disappeared around a corner.

Campus 1968–73

1

He woke a second time and turned over to find her earring in the bed, an opal doublet set in silver. It had been pressing into his arm and had left an indentation on the skin. He lay back, allowing the sunlight to ignite the flecks of yellow, red, green. There were depths in the little gem he could fall through, grottos of Caribbean green down there, campfires speckling the vast smoky-blue of the steppes, the harbour- and highrise-lights of American and Asian cities winking against a profound blue offing... Roma, Ronya.

He recalled that it had not been the incandescence of the stone he had noticed in the dark last night so much as the silver filigree of the setting. It had glittered on the lobe of her ear under the dark of her curls, as, intently, kindly, she had gazed at him while feeling for his dong, stroking it like a potter moulding clay, then cupping his scrotum in the warmth of her hand. Astounding, the confidence with which she had taken possession of his body.

'Didn't you see the notice saying "Private Property"?'

'Trespassers must prosecute, Cherub.'

She had been in a wrap-around skirt, black, with gold-and-red gypsy-like patterns on it and a black silk top with buttons down the front. There had been some occasion at the University — he could smell sherry on her breath — and she must have walked from there, letting herself into the house by the back door, unremarked by his housemates. It had been nearly midnight and he had just turned off the desk light. Ah! The wantonness of it. His face felt as if it had dropped open, marvelling, yearning.

2

Once or twice before she had walked over to this, his latest group house. It was usually after she had been working late on an essay.

'Give me coffee and conversation, Cherub. I've spent the last three hours locked in a life-and-death with the beastly behaviourists.'

More usually it was Jeb who went to her room in college. They talked well together, at least he had formed the idea they did. Perhaps he talked politics too much. But politics was how they had originally met.

She was unaccountable — forthright in the things she said, passive in the way she seemed to let experiences wash over her. She seemed to have no prejudices, no predispositions. He had always found her the most sympathetic, the most generous of all the people he knew, male and female, yet there were moments he glimpsed in her an oblivious self-possession. Occasionally he even wondered whether anything he had said meant anything to her.

'You remember I was saying . . .'

'*That's* right.'

Then he would be in her presence again and the warmth of her manner, the agreeable loudness of her voice — it was like a toastmaster's — would dissolve his doubts

She had come to the campus from a dairy farm near Nowra. On a hitch-hiking trip two summers ago Jeb had met her red-faced widower father who slow-marched through his house, eyes to the front, swinging his arms to the shoulders, half in pride for, half in parody of his Navy days; he referred to young girls, including his three daughters, as 'popsies'. Roma was the eldest.

And it had become clear very quickly that university for Roma was unspecific. '*Fasc*-inating!' she would answer airily, when Jeb asked her about various psychology courses she had started. '*Fasc*-inating! All that stuff about mechanisms and wired-in reflexes.' There was just this airiness about her.

'I can never pin you down,' Jeb once told her.

She was surprised by the assertion, a little embarrassed that she should be challenged to talk about herself. 'I guess I just take things as they come, Cherub. Ride the wave.' She grinned quickly.

'I want to go further than the beach,' he had replied. Then he added with a glibness that would later embarrass him, 'Except that nobody goes further than the beach.'

But Roma avoided the subject of mortality; perhaps it was her one prejudice. Instead she had simply said, 'I s'pose. My attitude is to keep going back for another ride.' She sometimes smoked marihuana of which, for obscure reasons, Jeb disapproved, and she had once shown him a tab of LSD someone had given her.

'You're not going to take it!'

'I haven't made up my mind yet. I probably will.'

She liked him, he knew, though he suspected that her liking, for all that she was younger than he, had a little of the patronising about it. He adored her, the brown vitality of her facial expressions, the way a smile seemed to animate her entire body, the alertness of her listening. Adored; and had done so ever since her first year in 1970.

He trusted her enough to tell her about Len. 'He's been sent to prison again. His third time.'

'What for?'

'The same. He keeps breaking into people's houses over there and prowling around inside them. Doesn't steal — at least, nothing of value. Doesn't molest. Just prowls. I suppose people wake up in their beds and find his head peering round the door. It would almost be comic — not for a child though.'

'He sounds very odd. He must do it for a reason.'

'The thrill? Wanting to see inside other people's private lives. I don't know. You're the one doing psych.'

And another time he had said, 'It's funny. I can visualise his cell perfectly. The iron bed and the blankets that graphite colour, the single red strip on the institutional linen, shaving brush and razor. He collects dead matches and makes things out of them — trays, a galleon. This is according to my mother who went over there in '69. It's the smells that I get most vividly. Stale stew, boiled vegetables.'

'It can't be good for you, Cherub. Living his life like that. Morbid if you ask me.'

But she was intrigued by Len's real dad. 'You should go and find him,' she had once suggested. 'I would, in your shoes. Like a shot. God! Think of the adventure!' There were days when she seemed to leap from the pages of Enid Blyton.

He made things for her, ashtrays from scallop shells inlaid with the colourful fragments of smaller shells. Or he would give her the odd drawing that he still did. Homage. Love-offerings. Egotistical, he was to realise in retrospect, realising at the same time that he himself was creating her role as a patroness. Once, back in 1971, he had persuaded her that they should begin a sexual relationship. It was unsuccessful, and afterwards they lay sweatily and uncomfortably awake all night in the narrow college bed. His own pleasure came promptly enough, but he did not know what to do about hers. He tried, she tried to guide him; he pumped away, relentlessly, but on that occasion it simply didn't work. She went to the bathroom and was away for some time. He knew, as he lay waiting for her to come back, that she had expected something and his failure to give her pleasure was going to have a decisive effect on whether they would ever live together. On her return they lay rather formally in each other's arms, and consciousness of the anticlimax had made her narrow bed all the more oppressive, so many elbows and knees, their skins sticking together like cellophane, the difficulty of breathing through her hair. In the morning she had said that she would prefer not to have sex with him again. She could be so devastatingly candid.

'Look, Cherub, I like you enormously. You're a dear boy. I just don't feel, well, that way about you. What? Yes of course we'll still be friends. I think the world of your' she smiled, '*discourse*.'

He looked glumly out of her window.

'You *know* that.'

Yes, he did, but it hadn't stopped him walking all day

and the following night along the lake foreshores and through the scrub on Black Mountain, allowing his face and clothes to get torn as he blundered about the undergrowth, persuading himself that it did not matter what became of him, that he would never be loved, and aware in another part of his mind that this was rather theatrical, rather childish. Eventually he slept on the floor of one of the common rooms for an hour or two until the cleaners evicted him. Whence he went back to the commune and ate a big breakfast. For a week he had felt his life was ruined, desolated, and he yearned to go and see her, just to explain himself, everything. But she had been away, bushwalking with the most regular of her lovers, an ample and older American called Dwight who tutored in geology. Then, a week later, she came up to him suddenly in the union — it was startling how she would be so suddenly present — and put her arm through his, saying, 'Come on, Cherub, I'll buy you a coffee.' And it had been all right again — sort of. He accepted there was no prospect of his supplanting Dwight, of her moving into the commune with him and their living together like lovers. The finality of it pained him — he had never had a lover. But she did want him in a way in her own way. It was not a case of his being fobbed off, not exactly.

'Besides,' she had said after their one sexual encounter, 'I'm not all that political. I don't think I could live with someone who's a, well, militant.'

'Oh *that*!'

3

Oh that! It had crept up on him unawares. Not that he could now renege on his commitment to the Struggle, even after Whitlam's victory. But back in first year, 1968, it was the harum-scarum of being an undergraduate that had engaged him more than activism of any kind.

He had continued to knock around with Rosie and I'Anson who had returned from the North-West Shelf just after the start of first term, flush with their oil-rig wages. Together they turned up for the disco nights in the Union, more for the beer than the dancing, then cruised the streets after closing time in the Simca, 'liberating' the odd flag from one of the many flagpoles in the national capital; this was their contribution to politics. Or they would form a threesome for a Duke of Edinburgh Scheme endurance trek through the wild country on the Naas or Gudgenby Rivers, sloshing all night through water up to their thighs, clambering over slippery boulders, jogging over paddocks, scaring sheep or horses, and seeing the dawn come up, blue-grey battlecruisers of cloud, followed by the first seams of pink above the Tinderry Mountains.

There seemed to be no great distinction between term and vacation. Time was hung on the flimsiest of structures. For there was time for all this extra curriculum, and time enough to devour the texts, English constitutional documents, the poetry of Pope and Marvell. In lectures Jeb doodled long bony faces in the margin of his pad, and in tutorials found that the mysteries of English history and English poetry were being subtly withheld from him. Sometimes he wondered what had happened to the alluring prospects that university seemed to offer. He had imagined that the subjects he studied would be a tantalising freemasonry, revelations about experience that would absorb and initiate him, as some of the Matric syllabus had done in sixth form. Instead they were called 'units' and his tutor asked such questions as 'What is the weight of such and such a word?' or 'Can you explain the tension in the poem between x and y?' He seemed more interested in keeping his pipe alight than the answer to his questions. Tension? The poetry was singularly untense.

So was life at this point. Occasionally he felt it was slipping away, from what he couldn't say exactly. A regimen? Ambition? The thought that it was possible to slip forever was sufficient to make him feel panicky, and for two or three days he would work eight hours in the library making assiduous notes on the Treaty of Utrecht or *The Essay on Man*. Then Rosie would recruit him for some 'stir', or he would wander down to the art books and gaze at reproductions of Pissarro, Sisley, Utrillo.

But harum-scarum. That was the keynote of his fresher year. Like the occasion after a dreary function at the Rowing

Club (Rosie and I'Anson were rowers), cruising in the Simca past an address in National Circuit, the three of them, plus Charmian, Jo-jo and Megan, from Girls' Grammar, all in their finery (Rosie had paid for the hire of Jeb's tuxedo). They were on their way to get a hamburger, saw the lights and parked cars, heard splashes of people diving into a backyard pool.

'Here's a stir.'

'Cocktails with the oldies, what d'you reckon?'

'I'll tell you what we're gunna do,' said Rosie. 'We're all six gunna charge in through one gate, swim a length of their pool and charge out the other.'

'Dressed like this?'

'Blood oath.'

'God, Rosie!'

'Are we all in it?'

'We're all in it.'

'Go!'

And they went. Through the first gate. Jeb found himself running beside I'Anson and Jo-jo who was holding the hem of her blue gown clear of her running feet. The gown, tucked up so that it resembled a gym-slip, was the same colour as the swimming pool which now loomed toward them. He passed several people who seemed to glance at him casually. There were one or two people in the pool. Mercifully not many. The six of them hit the water almost with the same splash. There was a second or so before the water penetrated Jeb's clothing, then it felt clammy and heavy. He breaststroked along the bottom of the pool, wondering how the girls in their gowns were managing, wondering what the people of the party were doing above. He saw a pair of legs in front of him, male, lit beautifully bluey-yellow in the pool's lighting. To his amusement the legs stepped aside. Imagine the look on the person's face! He was at the other side now, the shallow end luckily, so easy to haul himself up streaming. Jo-jo behind him, gown glued to her legs, like a duck's webbed foot. He grabbed her arm, hauled her out and began running. Ahead of him, Rosie and Charmian. Where was I'Anson, Megan? Jeez, what a stir!

'It's a prank. That's all,' a woman's voice was saying. 'They're steoodents or something,' Now through the second gate, doubling with hilarity. Rosie starting the car, into the back quick, dripping all over the vinyl. 'Where's bloody Megan and I'Anson?' 'Stopped for a beer probably.' 'Jeez.' 'Here they are. Go Rosie! Go! Go!' 'Did you see the looks on their faces?' 'Christ.' 'Jeez what a stir.'

And later, drying off in their underwear beside a fire in Weston Park, lake water lapping in the darkness, aware of the girls' breasts, aware of what might be opportunities... but their talk — ah! chaste, of cars, university courses, futures, looking modestly down at the earth between their legs, hearing the tinny decency in their voices. And the girls with Matric in front of them, Matric, what a snack, what an age ago.

In the November exams Jeb gained three bare passes. Rosie flunked and went brickies' labouring. I'Anson did well and went to Melbourne to study engineering.

'Jeez but you're a conch, I'Anson.'

'At some point, Rosie, you've got to hang on to something.'

4

It had been the pictures to some extent. Television, magazines. One was surrounded by polemical collage — the bomb payloads spilling from B-52s like boiled sweets from a sweet jar, Nasho's in their gigglehats disgorging from choppers somewhere in Vung Tau Province, running bent double, scarved in machine-gun ammunition, or sprouting aerials which flicked as they ran. Tet, Hue, Khe Sanh, Lieutenant Calley.

Or the cross-legged monk in his aureole of flame, swaying slightly, waving his fists feebly; the Viet Cong with his eyes squeezed shut in the second before the police chief shot him through the brain; the little girl leaning on her crutch, her arms swathed in bandages concealing napalm burns, her face screwed up into a grimace of atrocious agony.

'Doesn't that affect you? How can you say it can't?' someone had said vehemently, thrusting under Jeb's nose a newspaper on which this last picture was emblazoned. Of course it affected him. But there were atrocities on both sides, and there were the Dominoes — Thailand, Malaysia, New Guinea, us. Besides, the newspaper, wasn't it put out by some Commie front?

The trouble was partly that everything was affecting. The whole world came to where you were, Paris with cars turned over and burning in the streets, people in jeans and scarves who looked like oneself throwing Molotov cocktails at the riot squads huddling behind their perspex shields; water-cannon, sirens that sounded like the howl of the disco guitars, helicopters hovering above Berkeley campus showering little figures on the top of a tall building with mace gas; B-specials truncheoning a crowd in Londonderry and bleeding people with long weepy faces being interviewed; snakedancing Japanese students driving like a wedge through the ranks of the helmeted police in thrilling medieval mêlées, all of this disgorging from the screen or the pages of journals. There were so many sides one could join, there were so many acronyms one needed to know, NLF, UVF, FRELIMO, ZANU, CIA, so many names, El Fatah, Provos, Tupamaros, Weathermen, so much background information one needed to absorb, dull information about elections that failed to happen back in the 1950s, treaties that were broken.

'Nothing I say or think will affect any of that,' I'Anson had once said, quite reasonably.

'Blood oath,' Rosie had added. The two of them had been ballotted out. Jeb was due to register in the next ballot.

It was not that they were heartless, either of them, nor complacent exactly. Unless what they felt could immediately affect what they were able to do, then mere 'concern' was pointless, a little snobbish, wilful even. Concern. It smacked too much of someone else trying to police what you thought. Why should they not be allowed their nonchalance, their self-possession? He was later to apply the same defence to Roma's political stance.

Yet Jeb felt their attitude wasn't quite good enough. One *was* involved. Not that he could explain how.

One evening — it was while his mother was away in Britain visiting Len — Jeb called on Mallory. On the door of the cupboard in his bedroom Mallory had pinned two pictures. One was a colour photograph of two fighter bombers,

Skyhawks, sleek, silvery, beautiful against a flawless blue sky.
They might have been brooches of some startling modern
design. The other picture, black and white, showed an American GI holding up the charred scrags of what had once been
a Vietnamese peasant.

'A bit brutal for the room where you sleep, isn't it,'
remarked Jeb, indicating the second photo.

'I have the two of them together to remind me of cause
and effect.'

'Are you against the war?'

'Yes. For historical reasons as much as moral ones. The
Yanks should never have become involved.'

They sat for a couple of hours and argued.

'Dismiss the irrelevancies, Jim,' Mallory declared. He
refused to use any of Jeb's nicknames. 'Dominoes, Red Perils.
Look at the historical facts. From the beginning. In isolation.'
Mallory, as Jeb might have expected, knew all these facts
and expounded them methodically and comprehensively. By
the time Jeb rose to go home he had what he thought was
a grasp of the war's historical context, as well as a renewed
respect for the tidy archive that was Mallory's mind.

'You must be the only one from school who's against the
war.'

'You'd be surprised. Like the Comms, we're everywhere.'
He grinned. 'Big Ford's refusing to register for Nasho. He's
against, though very quiet about it.'

'I wouldn't have picked him as the type.'

'What type are we?'

5

Jeb joined demonstrations, standing with Mallory on the outskirts at first. Mallory invariably chose the margin of a crowd.
He had exchanged his school uniform for cavalry twill trousers, sporting tie and tweed jacket, and scorned the army surplus
styles of some of the militants. Some of these, in turn, suspected
Mallory of being Special Branch.

When brawls broke out between militants and police Jeb
was dismayed, but as well as dismay there was heady excitement as the constables waded into the crowd with badly aimed

punches, their hats flying, the shrieks. Once he saw a detective in an aluminium-coloured suit, aided by two or three uniformed men, tumbling down a grassy slope before the War Memorial in an attempt to arrest a familiar Pol Sci lecturer. The latter had come dressed for trouble in bovver boots and a tiny motorcycle helmet. Some resistance in Jeb's mind gave way as he observed this man with letters after his name being carried away to the paddywagon, writhing like a large crocodile in the hands of zookeepers.

He was outraged when passers-by accused them of being unpatriotic — while Mallory, on the other hand, would simply look at them calmly and say, 'You're quite wrong about that. Will you take a leaflet?'

Jeb began attending meetings and was elected a committee member. Along with others he was arrested for occupying offices and their names were on the local news. Mother was still away when this happened, which was just as well. Aunt Peg rang him and said he ought to be ashamed. Jeb tried to give her Mallory's line on the war but she slammed the phone down.

Then he found himself one of many speakers haranguing the Friday night shoppers from the vantage of a low parapet in Garema Place. 'Undeclared war...' he heard his voice booming through the megaphone, 'imperialist aggression... arms/Cadillac economy...' and so on. On the first few occasions the phrases felt funny, like borrowed clothes, but they assumed force the more he used them. He could reel off the tonnages of bombs dropped on North Vietnam each week, and the number of dollars the Americans were spending on the war each minute. It was as if he had suddenly woken up in the middle of someone else's life. At student meetings and rallies, after he had finished speaking, people came up to him and asked him what they could do to help end the war and smash conscription. Roma had been one of these, it was how he had met her. Indeed, as he became more engaged in politics he found himself less tongue-tied with women. For everything was political. Everything — not just the war and conscription, but all the side-alleys of significance which 'heightening of consciousness' had uncovered.

One night in Garema Place he had just stepped down from a speech against the war when a soldier burst through the crowd. He exuded a strong smell of alcohol.

'Which of youse was the person who was saying somethin' about Veetnam! Youse git back up there 'n say it again so I c'n beat the shit out of you.'

'Well, there were a number of us talking about the war,' said the ecumenical chaplain from the university.

'No. The bloke who was on just now. Which of youse was it. Let him git up there again and say what he was sayin' 'bout Veetnam.' Jeb looked at him. He was a corporal and in uniform, short and thin with a flushed face and he turned this way and that among the crowd looking for his chosen victim. There were some other fellows whom Jeb had noticed in the crowd while he was speaking, soldiers too, evidently, though they were in civvies, taller and burlier than the corporal. They now moved closer.

'Which of youse was it? Come on.'

'I was,' Jeb answered, anxious that his voice should not betray his apprehension. He recognised that this was the test — his particular test — as to the sincerity of his political stance. It was a matter of honour more than ideology.

'Youse get up and say those things about Veetnam again, and I'll skin you.'

'I'll tell you here and now what I was saying, if you like.'

'Nup. Youse git back up there and say what youse was sayin' in your speech.'

The crowd was pressing closer.

'I'll tell you here. I've had my go up there.'

'Youse git up there, you yellow bastard.'

'Perhaps we could exchange views over a cup of coffee somewhere. Will you let us buy you a coffee?' suggested the ecumenical chaplain.

'Youse git lost. *This* is my bloke.' Then turning back to Jeb. 'You're yellow. You're weak as piss.'

'I'll repeat to you anything I said in my speech. I don't understand what more you want.' The suggestion that he was a coward had stung him to the quick. Besides, it would have been ridiculous, taking the megaphone again and mouthing off to the crowd the same things he had just said. The latter had a wild look in his eye. Some act of violence was, Jeb realised, imminent.

The two burly fellows had come forward on either side of the corporal. 'You nick off, mate. Go on. Nick off quick.'

'I'm not going to run away from him. If he wants to know what...' Lead with a straight left and keep your guard up, he was thinking Dad's old advice. Not that this would avail him much against what he guessed would be the superior combat skills of the corporal. It was ridiculous, so suddenly to be so out of one's depth.

One of the big fellows took him by the shoulder. It was almost companionable. 'Look mate, no one's going to accuse you of running away. It's just better if you make off.' Jeb saw that the other soldier was now physically restraining the corporal. 'Quick, mate. As a favour, all right?' Jeb's own colleagues were also urging him to leave fast.

He did not run, he walked away. Even so, he felt little, and lessened. Later, in the Union bar, people praised his coolness. He listened unhappily. The corporal had laid down his challenge and obscurely Jeb felt the honourable thing would have been to make the speech again through the megaphone. It was a matter of honour more than ideology. Of course the whole episode was puerile. But that didn't stop there being something essential in it.

6

'Cherub?'

'Roma?'

'I remembered you were leaving for England.'

'Not for a couple of days.'

'I'm catching a lift home tomorrow, early. I won't see you.' She had sat down astride him. 'I thought because it's your last night, sort of... I know what I once said...' In the darkness he sensed rather than saw that she was smiling her collusive smile.

'But it didn't mean that I don't think you are special. And if you would like us to... you know.'

'Could I stop myself do you think?' He placed his hands

on her thighs. They were warm after her walk. He could hardly believe what was happening. Her head had come very close, her hair tickled his nose, her tongue was writing on his neck. Her right hand was searching.

'Didn't you read the notice saying "Private Property"?'

7

Mother returned from England in October 1969. She had arranged that Len should join them in Australia the following May, when he had fulfilled the conditions of his parole at the end of his second term in prison.

'He's balding, poor boy. But I can't say I found him particularly unhappy. He says the place is rather like boarding school.' Mother looked at her hands for some moments, then quickly at Jeb. 'I think that's the saddest part.'

'You always did all you could for him, Lizzie. You've no call to reproach yourself,' advised Peg, who had come over for the afternoon.

'I don't need to be *buttered*, Peg. I can work these things out for myself.'

'Well, all I'm saying is . . .'

'*Thank* you.'

Len arrived a few days before the first of the big Vietnam Moratoriums, and stayed for less than three months. The visit went wrong from the start.

Jeb saw him emerge through the barrier at Canberra Airport some moments before Len saw where he and mother were waiting. The bare forehead where the Brylcreemed quiff used to be now had no more than a wispy tuft. It was somehow shocking. The dark suit and white shirt, askew and crumpled after the long flight and connections, could not hide the leanness of his frame. He seemed, if anything, taller; Mother greeted him with a kiss he had to bend down for.

'Goodday, Len.'

'You talk like an Australian.'

'I am one these days, I guess.'

'No you're not. It's where you're born that counts.'

'If you say so.'

'It's where we're all together that counts,' Mother interposed.

She had put her hand on his elbow; the gesture was somehow tentative. 'We want you to like it here, Len. You will give it a chance, my dear, won't you?'

'Of course.'

He slept for a day or two. On the morning of the Moratorium Jeb called and offered to take him on the march.

'What march is that, old thing?' Len was reading the back of a cereal packet.

'Nationwide protest. We're demanding the troops be brought home from Vietnam and an end to National Service. There'll be thousands.' It was odd how he suddenly felt insecure about these political aims as he reeled them off for Len. 'Come and experience it, the solidarity between people.'

'What people? They're all Commies, aren't they.'

'You don't believe that!'

'It seems there's quite a mixture,' said Mother, a little to her younger son's surprise. Jeb had never been able to draw her on the question of politics. He assumed that as a serviceman's widow she would have establishment views, but she deflected attempts to probe her opinions, unlike Aunt Peg, in whom opinions sizzled.

'National Service never did me any harm.'

'You weren't made to go and fight in a dishonest little war.'

'I would have gone.' Len's face was set in a truculent gaze at the cereal packet. 'I didn't know that doing something for your country was such a bad thing.' Then he added rather smugly, 'And it was you said you were now an Australian.'

'That's mindless patriotic crap, Len. You haven't the first clue. Our involvement in the war is shonky —'

'Shonky! There's a word!'

'And the means used to fight it are grotesque. Get yourself informed.'

'That will do,' said Mother.

'If I was the Yanks, I'd go all out. I'd fight to win.'

'You would, would you? And shoot down protesters like they did at Kent State the other day.'

'I'd go all out.'

'Then you're fucking guilty along with the rest. A fascist!'

The accusation leapt out of him in a tumble with the last word curled over like a scorpion's tail, so conspicuous, unretractable. Len sat with his spoon suspended, Mother looked quickly at both of them.

Of course Jeb had heard comments like Len's many times; they came from stirrers in the crowds who had watched their protests, the ockers, motor mechanics and base-grade clerks out on their Friday-night sprees. It was sick, all of it. On behalf of those stunned peasants, those wailing little children you could not ignore any of the scurrilous 'bomb-them-back-to-the-stone-age' remarks, not even from your own family. Jeb glared at Len, unrepentant.

For his part, Len had a funny little grin Jeb had not seen on him before. There had been a boy back at Clemstead, a 'noodle', who used to provoke his seniors until they head-rapped or swiped him, then he'd draw away with a clandestine smile, as though there were satisfaction in discovering that persecution was the bedrock of human behaviour. Len's grin at that moment put Jeb in mind of it.

But Mother was berating him. 'That will *do*! I will *not* have words like that used in my house. You don't *really* know what "fascist" means. Here we are, together again, and I want it to work.'

Len went into the lounge room and turned on the television. Jeb left slamming the door, and marched from the city centre to the Parliament with the fifteen hundred or so others who turned up on that Wednesday. Freezing rain squalls blew from the Brindabellas into their calico banners and their chants rippled down the length of the procession then blew away across the parklands of the national capital. Jeb was aware that the feeling of the march was good nonetheless; he saw tweedy professors, well-groomed typists, long-haired students with knitted shoulder bags linking arms and moving forward in straggling waves, all with that strange rapt expression on their faces of people absorbed in a shared conviction, like a congregation singing a hymn. He glimpsed Roma in one of these chains and then Big Ford from school and Mallory with a wad of leaflets in his hand, and their faces seemed to have it too. It was exhilarating, this voluntary submission of oneself to a great common resolve. It was tranquil and humble and momentous, to walk with one's conscience and see the evidence all around of the inexorable, modest power of likeminded people. They would prevail. There was nothing that could stop them.

It soothed the injury with which he had come away from Len that morning. For the sake of Mother, for the sake of that old complex claim that Len had on his life, he would have to make it up to his half-brother for that intemperate accusation. He would do so when he returned in the evening.

But it wasn't as easy as that. When Jeb arrived home that evening he went straight into the lounge room where Len was sprawled on the couch watching the late news. He looked as if he hadn't moved since the morning.

'I'm sorry I sounded off at you, this morning,' Jeb said, stiffly.

'Are you, old man?' Len looked at him once, then back to the screen. Jeb stood waiting for a further reaction and wondering if he should say more. Len's gaze remained fixed on the flickering box. 'Look, they've got your lot on.' He watched the coverage which, apart from underestimating their numbers, was fair. But he had been stung by Len's reference to 'your lot' and he descended to his under-the-house room at the end of the bulletin.

On the Saturday they went to his uncle and aunt's for an evening meal. He had not quite forgiven his Aunt Peg for the phone call following his arrest the previous year. Now, by the way she banged the meat-trays in and out of the oven and beat up the batter for the Yorkshire pudding with her egg whisk it was clear to the nephew that his aunt was suppressing a powerful grievance with regard to the recent protests.

'You will have been following events in this sad country of ours, Len? These people with placards?' she said when they had all sat down at the heavy dining-room table. Uncle Neville was carving exquisitely thin wafers of meat from the joint with slow shaving motions while his wife served roast potatoes and cauliflower with a sharp clink of the spoon on each plate.

'Coms. Or as good as, Aunty Peg.'

'Two per cent of the population took to the streets yesterday,' Jeb declared. 'You reckon they're all Communists, do you?'

'And what about the ninety-eight per cent?' Aunt Peg glanced at him in that manner which suggested she thought he was simply a naughty boy but too inconveniently big to smack effectively.

'They should have been there.'

'But they *weren't*, were they?' trumped Aunt Peg.

'There's always two sides to every question,' observed Uncle Neville from the head of the table. He sat in the same way he stood, with a backward lean and the suggestion that his attention was only intermittently present.

'Not to genocide,' Jeb put in. Mother gave him a warning look.

'Indeed not, James, indeed not.' His uncle was spreading a serviette across his lap.

'I suppose you would like a Communist government here in Canberra, would you?' Aunt Peg sawed vigorously at a piece of lamb.

'It couldn't do a worse job than the one we've got.'

'It would put a stop to all your free speech, my fine young man.'

Jeb considered his aunt for a moment. He had known before he came it would come to this. Indeed he had already mentally rehearsed the action he was about to take. He pushed his plate away and rose. 'All right. For the sake of those present who are *not* all out to pour napalm jelly on the skins of Vietnamese children, I'll voluntarily give up my right to free speech at this table. It's a pity you don't have children of your own. It might make napalm and cluster-bombs so much more real for you.'

On his way to the front door he heard behind him his mother's sharp 'Jeb!' He banged the front door behind him.

As he walked quickly under the Atlas cedars of Telopea Park he thought wearily of all the trouble there would be at home either later tonight or in the morning. He would not bother with Aunt Peg any more, he decided, he would cut her off completely from his life. Her attitudes were disgraceful. Though he liked Uncle Neville, for all his complacency.

He walked to Mallory's and found him at home. 'Relatives!' he hissed, as Mallory let him in.

'You sound as if you need dousing with some plonk.'

'Look, do you have any back copies of *Time* or *Newsweek*?'

'A cupboardful. Why?'

'I'm going to cut out every picture of every bleeding and burnt child I can find, put them into an envelope and send them to my aunt.'

'Oh. What has the good lady done?'

With scorn, with bitterness, Jeb poured out the case against Aunt Peg, knowing, but not ready to admit, that all he accused her of applied equally to Len and to some extent to the uncommitted Mother and Uncle Neville; silence spells consent, as the placards had said. 'So, let her see what her politics are actually doing.' For ten minutes or so, sitting on the edge of the bed Mallory listened, feet up on his desk, his shirt sleeves rolled over neatly to the elbow, a faint smell of aftershave about him.

When Jeb had finished, he said. 'Look, drop it, Jim.'

'Why should I? She's a fascist.'

'Because it's simple cruelty, terrorism.'

'And her stance isn't?'

'It has its roots in history, just as ours does. The Cold War, show trials, you know all that.'

'That doesn't make it defensible. You don't excuse a Nazi because of the Treaty of Versailles.'

'And you don't excuse NLF terror, even though you know it's one of the means they are using to win. Or do you?'

'Probably not.' He tried to recall what had been said about VietCong terror at the various teach-ins.

'Of course you don't. Shooting humble villagers because they happen to have got lumbered with the job of headman, tax-collector or interpreter.'

'All right.'

'What about dumping offal on the heads of returning Nashos? Or subjecting their families to nuisance phone calls all through the night?'

'Strewth, Mallory, whose side are you on?'

'Yours.' He re-filled Jeb's glass. 'But when I was making up my mind as to which side to join, I found the question of terror, who does what and how much, infected what history was trying to say to me. I couldn't make a decision unless I chose to escape it. That may sound callous.'

'So moral and humanitarian considerations don't come into it, your anti-war stand?'

'If I relied on them alone I could end up on either side.'

'Why all the concern about my aunt then?'

'She doesn't sound like a fascist.'

Bloody Mallory. He always seemed to have an answer. He could be a bit preachy, a bit glib sometimes.

They talked into the small hours and Jeb slept the night on an airbed on Mallory's floor. When he arrived home the following morning Mother had already left for work. Len was in the lounge room with the curtains drawn and the television on.

'I'd say you're in a spot of bother with our mother, old man.'

At the dinner table in the evening, Mother was to the point. Jeb had behaved badly. He should apologise to Aunt Peg. What had been particularly cruel had been his reference to his uncle and aunt being childless. That was all she was prepared to say. His politics was his own affair, though he might have some consideration for the memory of his father.

The meal was eaten in an awkward silence. Mother and Len watched television in the evening. Jeb went below and worked on an essay. No. He would not apologise to Aunt Peg. The war had to be fought as much in suburban homes as in the jungles of South Vietnam. Besides, she had raised the subject of politics. But he decided he would not cut out any pictures and send them to her. Mallory might have a point there.

8

Mother found Len a temporary job on the ground staff of the golf club where she worked. It involved mowing the greens and raking the bark that the brittlegums shed untidily across the fairway. Together in the mornings they went off with their cut lunches, and returned together in the evening.

Jeb had imagined devoting considerable time to his half-brother. Len would meet Mallory, he had planned, and some of the people in the protest movement. They'd go drinking in the Union bar on Friday nights after the harangues. He had planned to borrow Mother's car for trips into the Brindabellas, taking Len up to the dams, Bendora, Corin, Talbingo, to the fire lookout on top of Mount Coree. He would show him the bush, as the song said.

But time was no longer the open-ended affair it had been in first year. When there were not lectures and tutorials there was the Cause. A second Moratorium was scheduled for September, and there were planning meetings to arrange the publicity for those draft resistors who intended going to prison.

Besides, Len's politics had put him off. At least, it was not so much the politics as the condescension. One morning, as he watched his half-brother set off with Mother for work, Jeb realised he didn't like Len much any more. The realisation aroused in him not so much sadness as fear, fear that some inner sanctum of his life had been broken into and robbed of its valuables, that no part of his past was inviolable.

Mother took him aside one evening.

'Do you know why Len has been storing food in his room?'

'Food?'

'Tins of beans and spam, bars of chocolate, raisins. I discovered them in a drawer under his socks.'

'I've no idea. You'll have to ask him.'

'I'm not sure I dare.'

There was one Saturday at the end of June when the two half-brothers took a drive into the gum forests beyond Uriarra. Parking the car at Mount Franklin chalet, they climbed to the summit from where they were able to look out across the Tidbinbilla Range towards Canberra. Here and there, delicately coating a tussock or a piece of dropped bark, there was a sugaring of snow. The sky was blue but for widely spaced tufts of cloud and on all sides the slopes folded into each other like the knees and elbows of innumerable children beneath a green counterpane.

'It's all right, isn't it?'

'You couldn't live off it, off the wild I mean.'

'If you knew what to look for you could. The Aborigines did.'

'Not like England — chestnuts, beechnuts, blackberries, eggs from hen-coops, apples and pears from orchards. You can't compare this country to England. You can belong in England. You can't belong here.'

Jeb resisted the impulse to argue. Instead he asked, 'Is that what you used to eat those times you ran away, the fruits of the forest?'

'And a pheasant once. Jumped on it, plucked it, pulled the guts out, put it in the fire. I was only about fourteen.'

'Do you think you'll stay out here for a bit?'

'Next payday I'm buying my ticket back to England. I'll have enough by then.'

'That's rough on our mother. She wants us all together.'

'She thinks she does.'

'She *does*.'

'Take it from me. I can read her. She pretends.'

'That's unkind.'

'But true.' He was looking out across the terrain, his eyes narrowed, as though assessing it. He added gently, 'I've known her longer than you.'

Again Jeb did not allow himself to be provoked. 'Anyway, I think it's best too.'

'No you don't, old man. You've got your politics to be going on with.' Len tried to make these things sound light, but his breath was short with the tension of them. He turned and descended to where the car was parked.

On the way home they were mostly silent. At one point Len said. 'Don't tell our mother yet. About me going back. I'll do it next week.'

In fact he told her three days before he left. He had booked on the first available flight after his payday, so he must have hugged the secret for a month or so.

'I don't want to stay here any more. I don't like it here.'

He made the announcement in the middle of a television programme, glancing quickly at her face and then at Jeb's. He sounded like a six-year-old.

'But your job. Have you told them?'

He shrugged.

'What will you do in England?'

'Things.'

'What things?'

'What will I do here?' His eyes were locked upon the screen and he pretended not to hear any of Mother's further questions. Jeb imagined she would like to have said, 'What about us? Our family?' But she wouldn't. There was her pride, if that is what you could call her reflex to swallow injury.

So they drove him to the airport, dressed once more in the dark suit, the white shirt and the tie loosened at the neck. He stared resolutely out of the car window. That he had taken offence in some way was obvious from the brooding set of his features as he watched the suburbs and offices pass. Had it been at Jeb's politics? Or the land itself, that didn't fulfil for the grown man some peculiarly preserved boyhood idyll of living wild in the greenwood eating pheasant, blackberries and chestnuts?

'Cheerio.'

He walked out toward the Fokker Friendship as they watched from an open balcony. He did not look back. An icy August wind from the snowfields blew at their backs and fluttered Mother's silk scarf. Her handkerchief was a tight ball in her hand though Jeb was not able to determine whether she had been crying. The skin on her face had become waxier of late, though her hair was still dark, almost as if she dyed it.

'It's as if we were uninvolved.' She said this as much to herself as to Jeb. Len had disappeared inside the aircraft, and the baggage trolleys were being towed away. 'I'll be surprised if I see Lennie again.' One of the propellors began to turn lazily. 'At times it will seem as if he never happened.' The propeller picked up momentum and the second one began to turn. Mother blew her nose. 'Come on, I'm not going to freeze out here just to see an aeroplane take off.'

In the car she said. 'Perhaps this will be the end of them, all the difficulties that the war,' she looked at him quickly, '*our* war, brought me.'

'You must recall some good things — like in the beginning with Len's Dad, or something?'

She drove, not looking at Jeb and he thought his question had been ignored. Then, slowing for a bend, she seemed to lean forward and say, 'I remember his warmth, his unquenchable, boisterous, *insidious* warmth.'

'Insidious?'

No answer.

'You mean Len's father?'

But she had said all she was going to. And it was unfair, as if she hadn't been talking to him at all. As if the little she had said was the chance spillage from a life he had arrived too late on the scene to have any rights over.

9

Though it was not alienation that made him move out of home in 1971, first into one student commune, then into a succession of others at different addresses in the northern suburbs. It was more an obscure sense of propriety. He had been receiving Army medical notices and disobeying them. Fellows were doing it all over the country. It would lead eventually to a prison term, he knew, though tactics required he make his arrest as difficult and then as publicised as possible.

It was unthinkable that he should be arrested right in front of Mother, with all the press photographers and news cameramen jostling at their suburban front door. Would she lead the policemen to his bedroom and throw open the door in a dramatic betrayal, like something from an old Merle Oberon film? Or would she cling onto him, biting and scratching the hands of his assailants? Hardly. He had a fond fantasy that this is what Roma would do. But Mother? Unthinkable.

Mallory rang him. 'Big Ford starts his thirty days for failing to register tomorrow. We're having a last drink tonight. Come and join us.' It was a surprise to Jeb the way in which Mallory had kept in touch with Big Ford in the years since school.

Voe and Little Ford, by contrast, had dropped from the scene; the latter was said to be in a rock group somewhere.

The three met in the Union bar. Big Ford was in overalls and his pudding-basin haircut made him look like a friar. Jeb learned that he had dropped out of university after second year and begun night classes in sculpture. His painting for Matric entitled 'Forest Floor' with its yellow and purple shale, the olive and pink of leaves and bark-litter knifed on until it looked like a samurai's plate-mail, had made Jeb's own Matric effort look embarrassingly immature. Without saying anything special, Big Ford could make a person feel gauche.

Jeb was all for making arrangements for the impending arrest. 'I'll get a demo together for when you turn up at the courtroom.'

'No you won't.' Big Ford gave him a level gaze.

'Rob's not planning to make an occasion out of it.'

'You'll at least make some statement for the press.'

'Nup.'

'Why not?'

'Because it's none of their business.'

'All right. I'll do one on your behalf.'

'No you won't.'

'What is this? You'll have no impact at all.'

Big Ford shrugged. 'I came here for a drink this evening.'

So they sat drinking until closing time, talking cricket for the most part — Mallory was a spin-bowler for the Old Boys. Cricket! It was ridiculous when someone was about to go to jail.

Even at school Big Ford had been peculiarly detached. Heavily built rather than fat, he moved with that gentleness and inexorableness of momentum that large fellows often have, as though he were trying to lessen the threat of his hulky presence. His size and weight had put him into the first fifteen; at scrum-downs, while some grimaced and others scowled, the expression on Big Ford's face as it bowed and locked into the scrums had been one of watchful forbearance. Odd how the image of it had stayed in Jeb's memory. He had once heard the coach of the firsts remarking loudly to watchers on the touchline, 'That Big Ford. He can shove like a bullock when he has a mind, but he's got the pugnacity of a Jersey cow.' A more acute observer on that touchline might have seen in the prop-forward's demeanour that of a person performing loosely the rituals of school behaviour, while protecting some essential inner concern, a concern too tender, too valuable to risk exposure on the playing fields or in the classrooms with their broken chairs and scribbled-on desks. Self-possession.

All very well, but there was in this reticent highmindedness something that niggled.

'You admire the way he's doing this all on his own, don't you?' he said to Mallory as the latter drove him home.

'He would be doing the same thing even if no one else was. It makes me think the word "individual" is still a term that carries value.'

'It's snobbery too though, isn't it? And bourgeois. All he does is become the Exception.'

'If everyone —'

'Everyone won't. And with those who do, oppression simply weaves a cocoon of tolerance around them and becomes all the more finely tuned for it. Groundswell is what will demolish unjust laws — *and* the unjust society. Individualism's quaint, obsolete. We live in a world of relationships, not isolated individuals.' Now he could hear himself being preachy. But he would finish. He was right this time, and he would let Mallory know. 'The really hard step, for people like us and Big Ford is recognising, deep down, that our individual effort, for all that it might be brave, is vanity if it's not part of the Common Effort.'

'You're a Narodnik,' Mallory grinned. Jeb didn't see the humour.

10

'Just lean back. You don't have to do anything. Not just yet.'

'But —'

'Relax.'

'I can't. I'm melting down.'

'Good.'

'Oh, bloody hell. Oh Roma!'
'Don't worry. We'll try again. Get a towel.'

11

The Friday-evening shoppers who stopped now no longer yelled abuse. They listened respectfully, or perhaps wearily, to the protest oratory. The war, the Americans, and the government had achieved unpopularity at last. It was becoming difficult to say things that would provoke or radicalise.

This evening they had said the usual things. Now the crowd was dispersing. In the light from a pizzeria Jeb noted that two soldiers appeared to be lingering, watching somewhat shyly for an opportunity to approach one or other of the speakers. As with the drunken corporal back in 1969, they were in uniform. One was a sergeant, the other a private. A group went over warily with leaflets.

Both accepted the leaflets, folding and putting them carefully into one of the pockets of their tunics without reading the contents.

'I just come back from there. I reckon I know what it's like.' This was the sergeant, a short, lean man. His eyes, which were not unkind, gave the impression of seeing what was before them through the filter of some other ineradicable event.

'What *is* it like?'

'I won't say straight out that you blokes are right.' The soldier spoke in staccato bursts, his silences filled with what was coming next. 'But I seen them bodies by the side of the road. That shouldn't happen to anyone, I reckon. I seen worse than that. You wouldn't want to hear the kinds of things I seen up there.'

'Quite a lot of atrocity gets into the news these days.'

'Not the things I seen.'

'What kinds of things?'

'I'm not saying. I seen awful things — things I'll remember for the rest of my life.' He looked each of them in the face as he spoke. Was he trying to impress them? It didn't come out like that. Or confess? That wasn't quite it either. There was both appeal and helplessness in his expression.

His companion hovered in the background, watchful, not contradicting. 'It shouldn't be allowed to happen. That's all.' He shrugged then backed away from them, searching each face in turn, before walking away quickly, followed by the private.

'Shell-shocked,' observed someone.

'It's his fault for volunteering to fight an imperialist war.'

'You can still sympathise with the bloke.'

'Bullshit! Sympathy's a bourgeois plot.' (You could never tell how serious some of the Movement's impromptu slogans were.) 'Anyway, spend your pity on the Viets, not blokes like him with second thoughts.'

'He's at least been there and seen it.'

'So? *You* were never in Belsen, but it doesn't stop you having an attitude about it, does it?'

Exchanges like this were not infrequent, and they caused Jeb to smoulder with a resentment that he could not wholly express or understand. Of course the war was wrong. Of course they should wage struggle on behalf of the heroic people of Vietnam etcetera. But he had been moved by the lean sergeant. That glimpse of vulnerability, that very un-sergeant-like candour, the face that had seemed to flicker momentarily, like a news item about something hideous. You can't sneer at someone's experience like that, he reflected, not when it has been laid bare. The man had allowed his guard to drop. There was still a ground where all their experiences had to meet.

He had gone to see Roma in her room afterwards. It was the night he persuaded her they should have sex. Perhaps it had been the political disquiet which the incident had awakened in him that had made the amorous adventure all wrong...

'I don't think I could live with someone who's a, well, militant.'

'Oh *that*!'

12

Now he had cleaned himself up.

'Tell me what I must do.'

She lay beside him now, looking at his face with a smile partly intimate, partly quizzical. He could try biting the lobes of her ears, she said — *softly!* — and down the side of her neck where the arteries ran. Uhuh. The inside of her arms where the blood vessels came close to the surface, he should brush them lightly with his fingertips. That's nice. Now lightly over her stomach muscles — ah! they knot up, it's lovely, lovely, Cherub. Now, stimulate the breasts — not so head-on, massage them, through the silk of the blouse first, play with the nipples, tease them, tease them, look how they begin to stand upright through the material, unbutton me now, use your mouth, uhuh, that's lovely — no, keep going, don't be in such a hurry, Cherub. All right (she was making small rhythmic pulsing motions against him, manoeuvring her mons pubis so that it rubbed hairily against his dong — he found it charming, arousing). How did he feel about using his tongue? Where? Down there of course. He supposed . . . if she liked. (He slid himself down her body and she widened her legs further. Truth to tell he had never really looked at this part of a girl's anatomy before, during the one or two rather snatched sexual adventures of the past couple of years. There was an interior more labyrinthine, more anemone-like, than he had suspected, not pretty, but not unattractive either. Without much conviction he put his tongue in and waggled it.) Wrong direction, up a bit, further, you'll find a nipple-like thing, my clit — that's it. Lost it! There! Now stroke it with your tongue. Ah! That's right. Slowly to start with . . . (At this point her advice stopped and, for all his activity he could sense the concentration of her body. It seemed to take a long time. He became aware that her breath was becoming shorter and louder, until it was being voiced — it sounded strangely like the out-of-breath bawling of a three-year-old — until there was a cry that broke from her, *broke*. He would have said it was a bit stagy if it were not that her body was convulsing along its length and that she was clutching his head with a fierce abandonment. It was extraordinary, elemental, moving, even after the climax subsided and he wiped his mouth and lay in her arms hearing her breath become normal and feeling her arms wrapping him tightly.)

When she said, 'Well, *thank* you,' it brought him up short. There had been an event. It was now over. It was as if she had placed him back at his distance.

She smoked a cigarette. He brought two glasses and a flagon of riesling from the fridge, and they drank, talking desultorily about his imminent trip. The money he had saved from builder's labouring during the past year would keep him over there for six months or so, he reckoned. He might look for work. He mentioned that he planned initially to stay with Mallory who was now doing a doctorate at Cambridge, after having taken out the 1971 University History Prize.

'I can't work him out. Is he homosexual?'

'Not so far as I know. I'd say he was a gentleman bachelor. Properly his era is late nineteenth century.'

She laughed. 'Ough! You're *incurably* Romantic, Cherub.'

'I thought I was a militant.'

'The two go together.'

When the conversation lapsed she leaned over him and began kissing him tenderly, on the lips, eyes, nipples, belly button. She handled his dong and at one point took its tip into her mouth. Then, sitting astride him again, she eased it inside her and began moving back and forth smoothly, gently until he climaxed. She seemed to be very practised. Should this thought have made him jealous? It didn't.

'I'd better use your bathroom. Are your housemates awake?'

'No.'

When she returned they turned out the light and lay enfolding each other in the dark. He said, 'I know it's not on, but I'd give up the trip if you agreed to us living together.'

She didn't answer immediately, then said, 'Dwight and I went our separate ways earlier this evening. It was mutual. He wants to go back to his wife and two kids in America.'

He was silent for a minute or so before he asked, 'Is that why you came here tonight?' He knew the answer and felt no animosity.

'Yes.' Her voice seemed to be thousands of miles away. 'But also because you're special and you're going away.'

'Would you?'

'What?'

'Agree?'

'Let's go to sleep, Cherub. My lift leaves at an ungodly hour tomorrow. I still have to pack.'

She fell asleep before he did, turning away so that her back was to him. There was a slight whistle in her breathing and he lay listening to it, full of the loveliness and the finality of what they had just done together. Joy could be exquisitely sad. Sadness could be exquisitely joyous. Which was he?

There was greyish light behind the apple trees. She was hopping about the room putting her shoes on.

'Roma?'

'My lift, Cherub. Have a *gorgeous* time over there. I do envy you.' She kissed him noisily, as an aunt might. 'Mmmmwah.' He tried to embrace her but she wriggled free.

'I'm going to miss you. Especially after this.'

'Me you, Cherub. Byee.' And she was gone. The time must have been not much after five, the light outside buttery, there were white cockatoos making a racket in the brittlegum beyond the back fence. She couldn't have had more than two hours sleep in all.

Later today, he planned, after he knocked off from the site, he would shift his things back to Mother's and stay there for the last couple of nights before catching the flight to London. He went back into a light sleep.

TO THE
BURNING CITY

Mallory's Discourse March 1973

1

Air travel. Elasticity of time. It was an aeon since the first
things he could remember, and it was an aeon since
yesterday...

   ... for how could one consider what had now come into
view as their Boeing dropped clear of the cloud cover, this
grey-blue network of meadows, villages, market towns, inte-
grated like a circuit board, silver-soldered with the myriad
glints of water from ponds, reservoirs, treatment works,
canals, and, under their flexing wings, on which even now
the flaps were grinding downwards in preparation for landing,
the broad Thames with its seepages of silvery cloudlight
in the estuary, ('it's where you were born that counts,' Len
had said three years ago), cars now visible on what must
be the motorway from London to Dover, like the shuffle
of electrons along a wire, the hump of Essex and Suffolk
disappearing in an Alka-seltzer haze to their right...

   ... yes, how could one consider all this, which once, a
lifetime ago, he might have called his homeland, (Len was
wrong, you grow out of a place — you *grow*,) to be continuous
with the hours after Sydney, that epoch ago, the olive-
splotched sesame-coloured terrain giving way to the cayenne
crinklings and smoothings of mountains and deserts — it might
have been the surface of Mars — then the short sea hop
to Singapore, and the night which lasted from Singapore to

somewhere over Italy and which had chased them around the world. It must have been during this interminable darkness, he reflected, that his time-sense became so disarrayed. Confined to a dim cylinder with the porthole so impenetrable it might have been a slab of obsidian, the roar of the aircraft's various systems so even that they might have been silence, the wailing of babies from somewhere behind, intermittent sleep broken by a steward or hostess groomed like dolls fresh from their styrofoam packaging, leaning toward him with a tray.

Once, hours back or centuries back, it didn't seem to matter which, they had come down at Dubai, seen desert sand beside the runways greenish in the arc lights, and were disgorged into a vast transit lounge lit with the same greenish tinge; it had been full of prostrate Arab bodies asleep on the vinyl benches. There was nothing upright in the entire chamber but for a bored guard with a sub-machine gun and two passengers from another flight — one of whom, a tall Indian gentleman with steely grey hair, immaculate blazer and cavalry twill trousers, a gold fountain pen in his breast pocket, had been pacing up and down the aisle, engaged in alert conversation with his smaller and scruffier companion. Imperial figment! Fantastic apparition among the creased, dingy robes of the sleeping Arabs, the shabby tee-shirts and jeans of the exhausted Australian passengers. Impossible to believe he could belong to this decade.

Further epochs in the drone darkness — what was one crossing, continents? the distance between planets? dimensions? It was the absence of a geography that created the possibility of any given place being, not continuous but consecutive with any other, separated not by time or distance but by a barrier of darkness which dissolved the meaning of both. Being between the two was like being in a coma, maybe. Or making the birth-journey. Coming from the source or going to it? Who could tell. One felt not in time, but *inside* it . . .

. . . until he became aware of the slightest blue rising behind them and strengthening — it was daylight that allowed people to know they were *in* time. And yes, they had come through, as if through stone, with the Alps below, looking miraculously just as they should, a picture from a biscuit tin or travel ad, then cloud over France and the Channel until . . .

. . . this moment, the yelp of the tyres as the plane set down at Heathrow, followed by the shuffling forward in long passport queues, the waiting beside baggage carousels as rucksacks and suitcases hatched from a tunnel and tumbled along the conveyors like eggs on a battery hen farm . . .

. . . having now set yesterday and its world at deep remove, except that Mallory, like a shade on the other side of Lethe, was there at the barrier to meet him, having acquired an expensive-looking duffelcoat and an incongruous deerstalker hat. Dapper, like a viceroy's secretary home on a spot of leave.

2

'You're going to tell me you've seen enough already and want to go home.' It was difficult to hear Mallory's voice; its pitch almost matched that of the general hubbub. His speech was even more clipped than Jeb could remember it. He had now been in England for a year.

'I've spent the last aeon in a chrysalis and I'm just coming out.'

'Don't. Butterfly weather is still months off. Do you want me to carry anything?'

Jeb gave Mallory his overnight bag and shouldered his rucksack. 'Where are you taking me?'

'Straight to my country seat. Unless you've got other plans.'

'None, let's go.'

Jeb watched out of the window of the bus as they drove through the English shires. After the elation he had felt during the descent, his immediate reaction to being on the ground was one of flatness. They passed through seemingly endless built-up areas, the saw-tooth profiles of factories, the slab office blocks with their polaroid sheen, and the terraced or semi-detached houses with their stucco the colour of school semolina pudding. Eventually there were patches of countryside, hedgerows and spinneys, dark fields newly turned by the harrow, an occasional wood hemmed in by ploughland, glimpses of what he had known as a boy.

But all of it was disappointingly smaller, and cluttered, with gigantic pylons, gleamy silos, fluorescent green or orange agricultural machinery at the edges of ploughed fields.

At intervals, rain slashed the windows of the bus, as one gale after another was tossed down from the mobile skies upon the landscape. Horses stood motionless and hairy in small paddocks, daffodils by the roadside fretted this way and that in the gusts, and the trees, leafless still, stood like the steel formwork on a building site.

Mallory had asked him a question.

'Sorry?'

'I was enquiring as to whether you intended doing the royal tour?'

'A bit of that, maybe. I'll be looking up Len, my half-brother. And I had a notion I might try and track down his father.'

'The war hero?'

'And super-tramp. My mother divorced him in '48 — about a year before I was born. I gather he knocks about Britain and northern Europe a bit like a mendicant friar. Doing good works. I've never met him, though I saw him late one night tucking Len into bed. I was about three.'

'Does he want to be found?'

'He doesn't have the choice.' Jeb gave Mallory a glance before continuing. 'It's a bit of the family history I've always felt left out of. I want to meet him, as much for himself as to give me some light on Len. And my mother. It's hard to explain. My life has always felt as if it has been in the shadow of their former existences. I never felt that with my dad when he was alive. I know you had a fairly odd relationship with yours. I didn't. Dad was all mine, if you know what I mean.'

'Your half-brother's father, he'd be what, in his sixties by now?'

'Fifty-nine.'

'What's it all in aid of, his wandering about?'

'Saving his immortal soul, my mother once said. Something happened to him, either during the war or shortly after. She's funny about her first husband. She won't allow the subject

to be raised, on the whole, which is the reason I've got to
do my own research over here. But she keeps a portrait of
him, if only up in a closet gathering dust. And she never
changed Len's name to ours after she married my father.
There's something very tangled about the whole business,
and on the one hand I want to get it clear, and on the other
I'm scared of blundering into things that she'd prefer me
not to know.'

'How does he keep body and soul together, this what's-
his-name'

'Hengelow — it's Dutch. His forebears made a fortune
draining the fens back in the seventeenth century. They've
been engineers and burghers ever since. So there's private
income of some sort.'

Mallory, Jeb noticed, had the knack of paying scrupulous
attention while appearing not to be listening. His eyes seemed
to gaze into some inner space; what gave away the fact that
he was actually listening was the slight smile on his lips.
'Sounds like an IRP.'

'IRP?'

'Irresistible Research Project.'

'Well, it's got a bit of that to it.'

'Burrow in. I envy you.'

It was now raining hard outside. The hedgerows were black
and dripping from their thorns, the houses appeared hunched,
phlegmatic under the inclement weather.

3

Mallory rented a bed-sit at the top of a narrow stair in a
terraced brick house near the Botanical Gardens. His landlord
was a bacteriologist who at one time had been a colleague
of Mallory's enzymologist father.

'The Prof knows more about spirochaetes than anyone else
in the world. He also teaches Sunday School and goes on
camping holidays with twelve-year-old boys. It's very English.
Actually, we get on very well.'

'Does he catch his bacteria from the boys?' As soon as
the question was out, Jeb wished it would go away. But
it didn't. Instead it occupied several moments of silence as

Mallory fished for his keys and fitted a Yale to the lock. When the key was in he turned and regarded Jeb steadily.

'You've no idea of how many ways innocence manifests itself in this country.' He pushed the door open, then added, 'As I say, we get on very well.' Jeb felt rebuked.

In the afternoon he watched Mallory sway off to a tutorial at his college on a cumbersome black bicycle with a basket in front, the crease in his trousers folded and held by cycle clips, a yellow plastic cape swathing his torso, and his deer-stalker giving him a slightly heron-like appearance of lofty vigilance.

'A bit of a comedown from the Pontiac.'

'Builds character,' Mallory called over his shoulder.

Jeb cooked himself some beans and then sat down in an armchair with a book intending to wait up for Mallory's return.

4

When he awoke he found himself lying on a mattress on the floor, still in his clothes, and covered over by a quilted sleeping bag. It was morning and Mallory, he saw, was already up, sitting in the light of the kitchenette, the sleeves of his white shirt rolled over once or twice as if he were still at home in Australia; despite having just lived through an English winter his forearms were a pecan-brown colour. He had not yet put on his tie and jacket and was holding a creamy Wedgwood cup in both hands.

'What happened to me?' Jeb sat upright and shook his head.

'You were dead. I took the liberty of laying you out.'

'Big of you. Is there a shower?'

'There are radio telescopes and laser surgery, jump-jets and the longest single suspension bridges in the world,' Mallory informed him. 'But there are no showers in the entire realm. None worthy of the name at least. The Prof has got a bath that stands on lions' paws which I'm allowed to use once a day — the hot water will only stretch to two baths per diem. You can have my ration for today.'

When Jeb returned he found Mallory still at the table, now smoking a cigarette, and with an atlas open before him.

Jeb came over and glanced at it, and saw it was open at north-west Europe.

'Doing some research on my behalf?'

'Whenever I look at a map I keep seeing it in four dimensions.'

'How do you mean?' Jeb took a second Wedgwood from the draining board and filled it with coffee.

'Well, it's a world of perpetual and multiple anniversaries. Take this map here. You'll be passing through some of these places, I guess, Nijmegan, Arnhem, Bastogne, or over here in the Ruhr, Essen, Duisburg, Bochum.' He paused and gave Jeb a brief glance. Mallory was about to show off, Jeb realised.

'What happens if we go back, say, twenty-eight years?' Mallory now placed his fingers on the map. 'What are we now, March, right March '45 let's begin with... say the afternoon of the 6th. Just about now tanks of the American ninth armoured division are rolling into Meckenheim, here,' and he pointed to a little village just south of Bonn.

His fingers jumped this way and that each time he mentioned a place. They were like a virtuoso pianist's. Jeb was astounded that anyone could know a map so intimately, to say nothing of the facts and figures that attended them. Mallory's voice, in contrast to the quickness of his fingers, and the violence of the events he described, was oddly gentle.

'March 7th, General Hoges' combat command B divides into two, half crossing the River Ahr here at Sinzig, the other half, with astounding good fortune, capturing intact the Ludendorff Bridge over the Rhine here at Remagen. Over this the US First Army's third corps now moves, fanning out into a bridgehead on the other side. In the days that follow, frogmen, and long-range artillery of the German Fifteenth Army together with attacks by the new Arado 234 jet aircraft, make repeated attempts to destroy this bridge.

'Meanwhile, up here, after a devastating attack by British Bomber Command on Cologne, the tanks of First Army's seventh corps have entered the city on March 5th, thirteenth corps having already taken München Gladbach on the 1st, while Neuss has fallen to Ninth Army's nineteenth corps on the 2nd —'

'I used to live near München Gladbach.'

Mallory made no indication that he had heard the interjection.

'Between March 6th and 8th, the Canadians are clearing German paratroops from what is known as the Xanten Pocket, round here. By March 10th the British and Canadian twenty-first army group, and the American twelfth and sixth army groups are standing on a front along the River Rhine from,' he drew a line down the map, 'Emmerich in the north, to just above Strasbourg down here.

'On March 10, Lancasters from bomber command's 3 group, attacking through ten-tenths cloud, are devastating the synthetic oil plant at — here, look, it's tiny, Scholven Buer. Dortmund, here, is being bombed by eleven hundred aircraft on March 12th and here at Bielefeld, 617 squadron together with de Havilland Mosquitoes from 627 squadron destroy the railway viaduct in the late afternoon of the 14th. And so it goes on.

'Think of it! Think of the millions of gallons of fuel, of oil, of glycol, the hundreds of miles of belt ammunition, the bombs on their trolleys and the rockets on their shackles, miles-long convoys of trucks all moving either westward to the front or eastward from it. Think of the noise, all of north-west Europe resounding with the crescendo of propellers. Day and night! Think how *busy* everyone was.' Jeb wondered whether this last comment was ironic or in earnest.

'OK. It is the night of March 22nd, and Patton is pushing elements of his Third Army across the Rhine at, where is it, ah here, at Oppenheim.' Mallory went on, his speech quickening just a fraction. Jeb let the tide of names and manoeuvres wash over him. As he listened Jeb looked at the map with its lines and colours, the blue-green of the Nether-lands and the Niedersachsen flatlands, the gentle white-and-shade as the terrain became hillier to the south crazing into deep fissures as one approached the Alps, the spidery oranges and reds of the autobahns and other main roads and the irregular cellular growths of cities and towns at the inter-sections of these.

In his mind's eye he was also seeing scenes from various

photographs or film histories which he had looked at during his boyhood and teens, four-engined bombers, somehow so tiny against the vast backdrop under them, passing over blurry maps of alternating darkness and bursts of light which, like a photograph of a galaxy or the behaviour of electrons, both suggested and defied some complex ordering. Bombs tumbling from bomb bays as though they were on an invisible conveyor belt, the momentary concentric shock waves of explosions. Artillery pieces leaping backwards like huge lizards in defensive posture, jeeps and Sherman tanks covered with riding infantry, soldiers squint-grinning at the camera with their thumbs pointing upward as they stood about in what were once cities but which had become delicate coralline structures surrounded by piles of white-looking rubble. He had been steeped in this imagery, as had his entire generation.

'... And so on into April, when the American Third Army will liberate the concentration camp at Ohrdruf on the 4th, and the camps at Nordhausen and Buchenwald on the 11th, while the British eighth corps will reach Belsen on the 12th. The American Ninth Army is going to reach the Elbe on April 11th, by April 21st the Russians will be in the outskirts of Berlin, and on the 25th April Americans and Russians will link up on the Elbe. It will all come to an end on May 8th.'

'Strewth,' said Jeb.

Mallory looked suddenly a little sheepish. 'Sorry, did I go over the top?'

'You went all the way to Berlin!'

'Ar. It's just that D Day to VE Day, north-west sector, is my field. One of them.' He kept his fingers on the map. The smile on his lips had changed subtly to one of self-consciousness, as though he had been caught out.

'I thought you were part of the peace movement.'

'I was, and am.'

'How come this attraction then? With World War Two, I mean?'

Mallory was silent for a while before he said, 'I guess I have to admit I find it immensely, well, *moving* to contemplate. Think of it, millions and millions of human beings in danger and in movement, soldiers, airmen, civilians. To have been alive then would have been to have felt so swept up. The massive dislocation. The tremendous, *tremendous*, simultaneity of all that human experience. Much of it was horrendous and ghastly —'

'I'm glad you concede that.'

'Of course. Thirty-five million civilian and fifteen million military casualties. But it *is* history, it *has* happened, and so it lives in us, and it can't be uprooted from our consciousness. It possesses me. I find it so utterly *awesome*.'

But the thought had crossed Jeb's mind: Yes, but why so particularly with you, with Simon Mallory?

His friend's fingers were now still, spread across the map from the Heligoland Bight to Bavaria.

'I still don't get it exactly. It's not the only event in the past to have a bearing on our present. How come it grabs you so particularly?'

'It's the Troy of our times, the grand poem.' Mallory said.

'How do you mean?'

'Well, one of the things about wars, particularly big ones, is that they are talked about long after they have finished, not only by the war generation but by the generation born afterwards, who had no direct experience of it either as children or adults, but for whom "The War",' Mallory emphasised the two words, 'forms a kind of dark mental horizon. War not only has a tide, but a backwash. Exclusion can be as powerful a tonic to the passions and imagination as participation. With regard to the last war, we are the excluded generation. In some of us, not everyone, that results in a reflex to try and recreate what we were excluded from.'

'You're going to tell me that some future Homer — one of the excluded ones — is going to come along and write an epic poem about World War Two.'

'Maybe we're fermenting that poem now — or, to be more accurate, proto-poem. It has no one author. It's the work of everyone who continues to talk about it, imagine it, recover or recreate it. It's Troy before Homer got to it. Sometimes I've thought it's as if History with a capital H generates epochs of enormous centripetal force, epochs that polarise the consciousnesses of people, that root themselves deeply into the pathology of the individuals who live through them. The generation that comes afterward, the excluded ones, can't cope with it either because they can't rid themselves of the sense of having *not* been there, having *not* been *measured* by events.'

'We-ell...'

'So it becomes vicarious in their lives, in their play, and their language. Notice how often our generation argue about how the war was won, notice the heat of such arguments. Then there's the protest movement. Not being provided with Jerries and Japs, we found the Fuzz, and, instead of grenades, hurled cobblestones and abuse.'

'Hang on...'

'Maybe what epic poetry and the writing of history share,' continued Mallory in his headlong way, 'is an attempt to process — no, to manage social trauma, to accommodate it in the general consciousness as being within the *flow* of events, to disentangle what was truly immense and awesome in the experience from the apocalyptic dreads and demoralisations that went along with it at the time. Preserving the immensity, removing the enormity.'

He stopped for a moment, then as an afterthought, said, 'I suppose that makes historians the psycho-therapists of society.'

'You're joking.'

'Maybe.' He swirled the dregs in his cup, then drank them. 'Actually it is the *welter* of old WW2 that possesses me. The welter of it all.'

Now that he had come to an end, Mallory remained, peculiarly upright in his posture, his hands resting across the map and his eyes fixed on a point in front of him. His reflex after these long 'raves' was usually to undercut himself with some throwaway or debunking comment, but on this occasion he remained in sober contemplation for a few moments while his listener watched. It struck Jeb that Mallory had come as close to stating a religious conviction as he was likely to.

'I take it your thesis is something to do with Allied strategic policies of that period.'

'Hell no. I'm writing about the history of recreation. Cricket, skittles, that sort of thing.'

Aunt Eva March 1973

1

The line blipped and crackled once or twice and then a woman's voice said, 'Hello.'

How much was it possible to infer from two clipped syllables? A guardedness? An authoritative manner? A woman in her early sixties from what once might have been called a background of 'good breeding'? Intelligent? The telephone receiver would neither confirm or deny these conjectures. Instead it produced a second, slightly more interrogative 'Hello.'

'Miss Eva Hengelow?'

'Speaking.'

'Look, my name's James Corballis. Len is my half-brother.' There was a silence on the other end of the line, so Jeb supplied, 'I gather you're Len's aunt.' Still a silence. 'Leonard Hengelow,' Jeb added.

'Yes, yes. Of course.'

Jeb continued. 'I'm over from Australia for a few weeks. I wanted —'

'How extraordinary,' the voice interrupted.

'Pardon?'

'You're Lizzie's boy?'

'Yes.' There was another silence.

'You've taken me very much by surprise.' Was it an accusation?

'I'm sorry. I didn't mean —'

'My understanding has been that your mother did not want any contact with our family other than that which has been absolutely essential for Leonard's welfare.'

'I didn't know — your brother, I mean, Len's father, came to see us once or twice.'

'I've no doubt Crispin did. What I'm saying is that we were always very sorry that your mother never applied to us for help.' There was a pause before Miss Eva Hengelow added, 'Financial help.' Another pause. 'We liked her. We were extremely sorry about how things turned out.' Jeb was a bit taken aback by how rapidly the intimate subject of money had been introduced into their dialogue. And who was 'we'?

'Well, she married my father and we were posted all over the place.'

'Yes, we used to know your father a little, during the war, and after. As you probably know, he was an intelligence officer at Crispin's base.'

'As a matter of fact I didn't.'

'No. Well, you see there is a trust account. It's money sitting in the bank to which your mother has always been entitled. She must have been told. Surely Len would have mentioned it. Crispin insisted that Lizzie and Len be amply provided for.'

'Look, I'm sorry. I don't know anything about all that. I'm ringing for two reasons. I want to look up Len, obviously, but I'm unclear as to where he actually is at present...'

'So am I.'

'Oh.'

'He's not in prison.'

'And you've no idea.'

'None. In England probably. I'll hear something, sooner rather than later. He has his room here.'

'The other thing is, I'm quite interested in making contact while I'm over here.'

'Does your mother know you are doing this?'

'No, as it happens.' He wondered if he should feel guilty for going behind Mother's back. 'It's my choice. I'd like to meet,' he searched for the right word 'your branch of the family.' He paused before asking, 'Would it be all right if I visited you?'

There was a silence on the line before Eva Hengelow said, 'I suppose that's possible.' Was that a 'no' or a 'maybe'?

'What I'd also like to do is make contact with Len's father. I was wondering if you had an address for him.'

'He's practically a tinker. Addresses are difficult.'

'Yes. Do you know whereabouts —'

'Well, he is a most *negligent* correspondent.'

'If you knew even just the city —'

'And his visits to this country are very random.'

'If it were just the city where you last heard from him. I gather he's hard to trace.'

'There are a couple of addresses in Hamburg, but the most recent is two years old. Do you have enough coins to hold the line a minute?' Jeb listened to the shuffling of papers at the other end. It was odd how the sound coming out of a telephone receiver managed to convey both a sense of distance from and intimacy with another location. Jeb could hear a faint babble of voices on other lines, and yet he could also hear the parping of the traffic outside the house of Eva Hengelow. He imagined her standing in a vestibule with dark wood panelling, holding a telephone of 1940s pattern, the bakelite worn to a matt black, a braided cord.

The most recent address was in the Altona district of Hamburg. There was an earlier address for the Hammerbrook district of the same city, and a third address in Cologne which went back to the 1950s.

'Altona is probably your best bet. He calls this one of his "safe houses", but really, that could mean anything, so I should warn you, this is not very helpful. Crispin doesn't answer letters much. Most negligent.' She used the word again and, in the light of it, the prospect of visiting Len's aunt became more forbidding.

'Thank you. It's a start. I'll use my wits.'

'I'm quite sure you will.'

The two of them ran out of things to say to each other at this point, yet it seemed to Jeb he should say more, he somehow owed more, and there was more he wanted to know. But too many incalculables had arisen. The telephone started beeping for more coins, and Jeb scrabbled among his loose change.

'When is your visit likely to be?' he heard the crisp voice saying. He pushed some silver into the slot.

'Um —'

'May I suggest this weekend?' It was not so much an invitation as a declaration of his one option.

'Um, fine, thank you.'

'I'll expect you for lunch on Saturday. You can then suit yourself if you wish to stay the night. If you do, I go to church on Sunday morning.'

'I see. Thank you. Yes. If you hear from Len, you will . . . Good, Saturday then.'

'I shall expect you. You have the address? Goodbye.'

2

Three days later and a little nervous that he would be late for his lunch appointment, Jeb took the first bus of the morning to the outskirts of Cambridge, then began hitch-hiking up the A10. His route took him through the fen country around Ely, those strange white-wet levels half-dissolving their church towers, their barns and windbreaks in a mist so ambient that it seemed to be an extension of the earth. It was cold and as he waited beside the road his breath steamed. But his lifts were good; he was passing through King's Lynn by ten, and by eleven had reached Wollstanton where Len's aunt had a house with a view of the Wash. To arrive early at the house of Miss Eva Hengelow, he reasoned, might be as unpardonable as arriving late, so when he had ascertained where the house was he wandered around the little seaside town for an hour or so, lingering outside the amusement parlours and shops which, even in this cold season, were festooned with gaily coloured requisites for the seaside, plastic buckets and spades, floats, paper flags.

Aunt Eva's house was massive enough, though ordinary, three-storeyed, semi-detached, with a bay window on each floor — the top one would have a view of the Wash, he saw. In the front was a microscopic garden with a privet hedge, and a tiled front porch. It was identical with all the other houses on that side of the street, unassuming, bourgeois he might have said. Certainly he had expected a dwelling of more character, given what he had heard about the manorial background of the Hengelows.

The front door opened before he had time to knock, and he found himself initially looking at a large amber brooch set in a silver filigree. When he raised his eyes to the wearer he saw he was being inspected by a tall woman with straight hair tied behind in a bun. She wore a dress on which there was a leafy pattern in scarlet, lilac, and aureolin-orange. It made her look both patrician and like a large pre-Raphaelite vase.

'You have your mother's face and build. I can't see a trace of your poor father at all. You had better come inside.'

He was served lunch while being quizzed methodically and incisively by Miss Eva Hengelow on what had happened to his family during the course of twenty-seven years.

She knew the salient details from Leonard, of course, Gattisby, Germany, Australia, but she wanted minutiae. The old lady's curiosity was inexhaustible. Every now and then Jeb would say, 'But I'd like to find out something about your family,' only to be answered curtly with 'There will be plenty of time for that. I haven't finished yet.' So, through a first course of chops and mash, a dessert of stewed apples, accompanied by plain water, then coffee and a single chocolate, he disgorged both family information and the facts and figures of Australia.

'And Leonard's visit?'

'It was all wrong somehow. He took a set against the country. He and I quarrelled about politics. It was all very tense somehow.'

'Poor Lizzie.'

'Can I ask how you get on with him when he stays here?'

'As a boy he loved it here. And he always returns here. He has his room upstairs.' Then she directed her questions back to Jeb. 'Tell me what you did your degree in?'

'History mostly.'

'What period of history did you study?'

'Lots of Modern. Imperialism — British, French, Belgian, American, and the liberation movements in the Third World.' Jeb hesitated, then added, 'I guess I was a bit involved in the anti-imperialist struggle myself, so far as the peace movement in Australia was concerned.'

'I have gathered that.'

'We all were. It has been a very political time in Australia, these last seven years or so. Hence my fights with Len. We were henchmen in Vietnam, there was conscription. Racism, neo-colonialism, all that stuff.'

'I'm well aware. Of course it is fashionable to decry imperialism these days, but it was also a form of love, an opportunity to discover and express love.'

'You're joking.'

'I most certainly am not.'

'Imperialism is exploitation of vulnerable people. How can that be love?'

'So now you are going to quarrel about politics with me?' She looked at him sidelong. Was there a hint of amusement in her eye?

'No. Well. But —'

'When a colonial official has strong feelings of affection, loyalty and commitment to the people in his charge, that is one of the forms of human love. When those people have strong feelings of affection, loyalty and commitment toward the official and his family, that also is one of the forms of human love. And such relationships existed throughout what used to be the British Empire, India, Africa, the islands of the Pacific. Not just the British Empire either. It is disgraceful the way in which fashion has attempted to make people of different races shame-faced about these relationships. And the way we have become shame-faced about our past. I think we live in a very derisory time. People seem to turn to derision as reflexively today as an earlier age turned to sentiment.'

'There were lots of hate-filled relationships too.'

'I have no doubt, and lots of exploitation of vulnerable peoples, as you say. When I left Girton College in 1934 I spent three years as a teacher in what was then called

Nyasaland. I was appalled, of course, at the instances of cruelty and ignorance that I saw — more ignorance than cruelty, I remember. Equally, I was moved by the evidence of love. Yes, love. Pure and real and mutual, that existed between some individuals and the communities they were attached to.'

'Individuals,' Jeb seized on the word. 'But that doesn't tackle what imperialism is *fundamentally*.'

'The highest stage of capitalism, do you think?' Aunt Eva was rolling up her serviette and pushing it through a silver ring. 'That's what Crispin once tried to persuade me of in a letter.'

'Well, yes.'

'I think,' she paused, and began collecting the plates, 'I think it is not for us to know what imperialism, or anything else, for that matter, is *fundamentally*, because we are unable to stand at a distance from what involves us. We can only try and describe things by being as honest as possible about what those things *include*. Imperialism includes exploitation, racial prejudice, ignorance. But it also includes love, love that flowed both ways. As I observed it, anyway.'

'If we can't stand at a sufficient distance to judge what is fundamental and what is not, what can?'

'Well! Of course what *I* would say is the Almighty. You may not find that a satisfactory answer.' She then looked Jeb in the eye and smiled. 'If you don't, then you may need to consider that fundamentals don't exist apart from what one fashion or other chooses to call fundamental.'

'But you've got to have some notion of the fundamental in order to have grounds to take action. What you've just said disables action.'

'There's a little too much action in the world at present. For my taste, at least. And I'm bound to say that I think this includes your own anti-war generation which is a rather bellicose one — more so than I remember my own being, and heaven knows we went off to war readily enough.

'But, to return to my point, I have no trouble finding a ground for taking action. I accept the Christian principle of "Love Thy Neighbour As Thyself." If one were looking for a dynamic outside that, well, I don't know — perhaps it would be a matter of persuading oneself that something is a fact when, at another level, one suspects it is no more than the emphasis a particular time puts onto a reality which is complex, and irreducible from its contradictory parts. Now I'm starting to sound like some of those people who took my education in hand forty-odd years ago.' She laughed at herself with an odd girl-like giggle. Jeb found it startling after the earnest way in which she had pursued her argument.

Despite her swipe at his generation, Jeb found himself rather impressed. Not that he was converted suddenly; but he warmed to the way that Aunt Eva was prepared to tackle things head-on, waiving the niceties of hospitality, the fear of giving offence. He found himself rather liking this tall, somewhat imperial lady, with her crisp views on things, her readiness to make her position clear, her acknowledgement of other points of view.

3

They washed up the dishes between them, then she suggested they go for a walk. She took him out onto Wollstanton Sands, a beach unlike any Jeb had seen in Australia with miles and miles of flat wet sand which merged imperceptibly with the water.

'Not the seashore I've grown used to, but this is very attractive in its way.'

'I wouldn't call it attractive,' said Miss Hengelow, 'but it has a large sky which is conducive to being able to think clearly. And the tide comes in very quickly, which is good for one's presence of mind. I have been coming here ever since Crispin and I were children and we used to holiday here with our parents. Now, what is it you would like to know about us?'

The weekend, it seemed, was to proceed methodically.

'I gather you haven't always lived here?' Jeb had to raise his voice because they were walking in the teeth of a strong wind.

No, said Eva Hengelow, they hadn't. The family had owned somewhere called Litcham Elms which was south and inland on Massingham Heath. Their parents had been, she supposed, well-to-do. The name was originally Dutch, of course, and they were descended from a van Hengelouw family which had come over in the sixteenth century, Elizabeth's time. Part of a plan to drain the fens. There was a town, Hengelo in Holland near the German border of course.

Of course.

Crispin was two years younger. No, she said, looking at Jeb sharply for a moment, she did not think their upbringing had been particularly strict, though she thought they had been taught to think for themselves, particularly in matters of right and wrong. And there had been the Church, though Crispin had lapsed, at least from the sacramental part. It might have stood him in good stead particularly at the time he became determined to leave Lizzie and Leonard. They walked on in silence for some moments, bending slightly forward to oppose the force of the wind. Eva Hengelow stopped and tied her headscarf more firmly around her chin.

'Why did he do that? Leave my mother, I mean.'

'It seems Crispin was — *exposed* to some experience at the end of the war. It was never made clear to me what this was. I suppose, when we were children, I tended to take the moral lead somewhat. This kind of influence has its effect, you see. By the time Crispin married your mother in 1937, he had, as he put it, 'tossed out all the bunk', which meant the Church. I think he was on the edge of the Communist Party at one point; many people of our generation were. I don't blame Lizzie in the slightest. But it meant that, ten years later, when she and Crispin went through the divorce, he had become shy of confiding in me in the way he did as a child.

'I managed to help him in a practical way, however. During the war, and afterwards, I was a hospital administrator, and, when he came out of the airforce in 1946, I helped to find him a position with the British administration in post-war Germany. He rather let me down over that. I shan't say why. I had expected him to take Lizzie and Len over to Germany with him. Instead he left them.

'And Lizzie remarried. It was Crispin who introduced Lizzie

to poor Wilf. I have sometimes wondered whether, after the war was over, Crispin was not encouraging their friendship. Very cynical if he was. And I can't reconcile what I know of Crispin with cynicism.'

'How often do you see him?'

'He turns up once every couple of years, dropped off by some lorry, or motorist. Sometimes he stays a week, more often a night or two. I make a point of buying him socks. Several pairs of strong, warm socks.'

'Why?'

'The walking!'

'Does he see Len on these occasions?'

'Naturally they have bumped into each other.'

'How do they get on?'

'Leonard has been very unforgiving. He generally makes himself scarce when Crispin is staying here. It is very difficult.'

'Does Len's father see anyone else that you know of?'

'There are members of his squadron. They have reunions every ten years or so. Crispin attends them.'

Jeb expressed surprise. 'I thought he had turned his back on his airforce days.'

'Not at all. Crispin has spent twenty-six years trying to atone for what he believes he did in the past, but he has never *rejected* the past. That would be quite a different thing.'

'Do you have the name of anyone in particular?'

'I'll furnish you with something.'

They returned to the house where Jeb was given afternoon tea.

'I don't know how much I should say. I was very sorry to hear of your father's death ten years ago. Leonard, of course, told me about it. He was a very *good* man, a very *kind* man, your father. I know he and Leonard had a very strained relationship. I could tell that from the occasions Leonard stayed with me during holidays and after his national service. But he never spoke *against* Wilf. I'd like you to know that.

'When Lizzie married Crispin in 1937, they were very smitten with each other. I suppose that goes without saying.' (*His warmth, his unquenchable, boisterous, insidious warmth*, Jeb remembered.) 'Crispin had finished at London University the year before — he didn't quite make Cambridge. I had just come back from Africa, and would stay with them at the school. I gathered it had been quite a sudden marriage, but my feeling was that they were well suited. They had a very similar sense of justice, and they derived such enormous fun from each other's company. They used to talk about going off to Borneo or China and starting a school between them — very disinterested, though never long-faced about it. I accompanied them on a walking trip from the school in Kent across to Land's End one summer holiday, just after they were married and I had come home from Nyasaland. Spur-of-the-moment decision. How we tramped! And Lizzie! She was so game, keeping up with us two long-legged Hengelows day after day. She could swim like a fish too.'

'Still does.'

'She seemed to have such an enormous appetite for experience. I took it to be an Australian trait. But it was England itself. Lizzie was enchanted by this country. At that time, anyway.

'When the war came along, Crispin resigned from the school and tried to enlist. His knowledge of languages meant that, initially he was put into a reserve occupation, reading the German and Vichy newspapers for the Ministry of Information. Apart from being bored stiff, he felt that it was too privileged a position. He said he needed to be part of the common predicament, to be endangered. Len was two years old by this time. They had moved to London and kept Len with them, reckoning him too young to be evacuated. Eventually Crispin managed to gain selection for aircrew, trained in Canada under the Empire Scheme, then returned and joined a squadron. Len was sent off to a boarding school soon after he turned four. I think it was that which first made me wonder whether all was well with the marriage. Despite the emergencies of the time, I thought he was far too young to be sent away from home. Lizzie wanted to be involved in war work too, whether as a way of coping with Crispin's perils and long absences or whatever, I don't know. Perhaps, like Crispin, she also wanted to reject privilege and safety. I think there was conflict about this, but who knows what goes on inside a marriage. I'm certainly not one to know. It is water under the bridge, I suppose. But I was sorry not to have had any further contact with your mother after 1948. I remember her as a splendid girl. Yes, I *did* hear from Len that she was in England in 1969 — I was saddened when I did not hear from her. Lizzie was enormous fun to be with. I wish she had availed herself of the trust fund set up for Len and her. That would have been some contact, at least.'

'She has never talked about that time to me, or anyone, so far as I know. I've learnt more today about it than during the rest of my life.'

'That is also very sad, I think. I have often thought of Lizzie and Leonard. The situation distresses me, and always has done.' She looked into the bars of the electric heater, her face reddened by their glow. Her hands were clasped and slack upon her lap, her long face reposed in a meditative sadness. It was growing dark outside and the two vermilion strips were the only light in the room. Perhaps two minutes went by with only the occasional car going past outside. Then Eva Hengelow straightened.

'You haven't said whether or not you are intending to stay the night. I shall make up a bed if that is the case.'

'If it's OK.'

'I'll put you in Crispin's room.'

The room was small and bare — notably, for there was no shortage of pictures, family photographs and the like decorating the other rooms of the house. He helped her make it ready and when they had finished, she announced, 'I always like to read for an hour or two at this time. I'm sure you won't mind. There is the television,' she said, pointing to a small black-and-white set. 'I keep it for the occasional thriller. You may find something to watch. I shall be in the study.'

He tried the channels, found nothing to arouse his interest, so decided to go out. On the way he looked through the door of the study where Aunt Eva was sitting beneath a standard lamp, wearing horn-rimmed spectacles and reading a Pelican book on the troubles in Northern Ireland.

'I thought I'd take a stroll.'

'I generally retire to bed at nine. If you could lock the front door . . .'

Jeb indicated the paperback. 'What *is* going on over there?'

'I'm very much hoping to learn.' She regarded him for a moment, then turned all her concentration on the book.

4

Beneath the lamps on their huge stalks, the streets and pavements of the town had a greasy orange gleam. The colourful seaside merchandise he had seen in the morning had vanished behind closed doors while the traffic had diminished to an occasional car or motorbike roaring off several blocks away. He ambled among the guest-houses which were mostly dark, save for one or two from which a chink of cosy light or the flickering of a television could be distinguished behind heavy curtains.

Had it been among any of these houses that Len had acquired his vicarious habit of entering and prowling about people's homes? The offences he had been arrested for, Jeb knew, had been committed elsewhere, in Nuneaton and Leicester. But they must have had their origins back in teenage days when he spent holidays with his aunt.

As a boy he always loved it here, she had said. Of course. And it was unkind, Jeb knew, to lay any responsibility for Len's odd behaviour at Aunt Eva's door. She had provided him with a regular home. Regular. But something wild in his half-brother's character had been unappeased by the crispness, the clarity, the highmindedness of his aunt, by the cosiness of the seaside town, and indeed by those vast flat sands, and gradual sea sliding in and out surreptitiously, leaving or swallowing its pools.

He walked back to Aunt Eva's tall, narrow house, a fine rain coating his face, and locked the front door behind him.

5

When he awoke next morning he could smell meat cooking. He went downstairs and found Aunt Eva preparing the midday meal.

'I am going off to church directly. You are very welcome to come too.'

'I guess I'm not much of a churchgoer.' He felt the obscure need to offer an explanation. 'It never seemed to have much effect on me.'

'Of course. That is entirely your affair.'

He made himself some toast and coffee, read for a little, then began to wander around the empty house. In the study an entire wall was taken up with books; volumes of Kant and Berkeley were wedged beside Dorothy Sayers paperbacks, devotional works were side by side with pamphlets on Suez, Cyprus and decolonisation in Africa. He wondered which was Len's room and climbed the stairs in search of it. On the dressing-table in Aunt Eva's room, among the other photographs there was a wedding shot which, Jeb realised with a shock, showed his mother and Crispin Hengelow. The latter, with his chest puffed out like a cartoon figure from *Punch*, looked ridiculous in his cocky pride — how decisively a gesture could date a person. But Mother — well, she was not Mother. It was something to do with the gaiety in her facial expression, the whole face lifted in some hilarity of thirty-five years ago. She was the dark-haired young woman from the 'time before he was even thought of'. Impossible to imagine she could be connected to him. It was the only photograph of her first marriage Jeb could recall seeing — she must have destroyed or hidden her own records of the event. Looking at the picture was like looking at something through a reverse telescope, seeing it smaller, utterly clear in its delineation and utterly remote.

He put the picture down and went out. The stairs to the third storey were narrower and the landing admitted no natural light. He climbed and came to a small landing where there were three doors, one to a tiny toilet, one to a box-room, and the third to a room which was in darkness, made all the more dense by black curtains. Jeb found the light switch and turned it on.

The sight that greeted him took him a little aback. The room occupied most of the entire third storey of the house. It was large and high and in its centre, pointing toward the bay window, was a structure which stood perhaps nine feet high in the high-ceilinged room, measured some seven feet across and twenty feet long. It occupied perhaps half the available floor space and stood on what appeared to be light builder's scaffolding. Jeb recognised it immediately as a Lancaster bomber's front end, from the astrodome and cockpit to the air bomber's perspex blister forward. There was as yet no front turret surmounting this blister, but from the pieces of shaped perspex and strips of metal lying around on a bench at the rear of the bedroom it was clear this was in the process of being created. Wires, tools, diagrams, and strips of metal lay about the floor.

Jeb walked around the outside of the structure, then mounted the steps at the rear, entering the fuselage which was olive drab in colour and composed of light vertical formers every eighteen inches or so, strengthened by stringers running its entire length, onto which the metal fabric of the skin was attached. He clambered over a substantial girder which, he imagined, represented the main spar of the aircraft's wings, and found himself in the confined area of the flight deck. On a raised platform was what he took to be the pilot's seat, while on the right of this and lower there was a second seat which folded against the fuselage to allow access to a bulkhead with a narrow entrance and a yellow rail leading into the bomb-aimer's compartment.

Was it the real thing, painstakingly disassembled from somewhere, brought back to Wollstanton and up the stairs of Aunt Eva's house? The compactness, the colours and sheeny patches of duralumin where the paint had flaked away, the press of instruments, suggested a scrupulous authenticity, though Jeb noted one or two of the formers were actually constructed from ½″ plywood. He climbed carefully into the pilot's seat and looked out to his side. A panel of the cockpit could be slid open. Before him there were the control column, throttle levers, pedals, at least one compass, and a dazzling array of dials and switches. On his right and slightly behind him there was another panel of gauges, oil, glycol and fuel in ranks of four, various fuel cocks, switches, sockets. Again it was unclear whether the dials were genuine aircraft parts or perhaps bits and pieces salvaged from a motorcycle repair shop, but various tags rivetted to the panels and saying HYDRAULIC GEAR EMERGENCY ACTUATION and CENTRE AND INNER PULSOMETER PUMPS MUST BE ON FOR TAKEOFF AND LANDING seemed to be authentic.

Jeb squeezed through the bomb-aimer's hole and found himself looking down through the cupola at a white screen set at an angle to the bedroom floor. This part of the Lancaster was not as finished as the upper cockpit, though on his left there was a box with dials, indicators, and various leads issuing from it, while on his right were an array of switches and what appeared to be some kind of timing device. He lay down on the two vinyl-covered cushions with his head close to what he assumed was a bombsight, a rather beautiful instrument with a small glass plate that rotated from side to side, and what appeared to be a periscopic device above it. He looked down through the perspex directly upon a small slide screen and, on turning his head he grazed it on an automatic slide projector which was held in a metal bracket and pointed at this stark white screen. Jeb took a slide from the magazine and held it to the light. It was an aerial picture of a city, Kassel he noted from the neat handwritten inscription. He wondered if it was authentic, or just any old street plan. He took out another; it depicted the red, then yellow converging lights of a runway.

The thing was extraordinary. Meticulous, ingenious, thoroughly odd.

He climbed back onto the flight deck and sat once more in the pilot's seat, fingering the controls. The control column had a 'heavy' feel to it, as though it were, in reality, attached to all the cables which manipulated a large aeroplane in flight. The throttle levers also had this greased heavy feel, as did a bank of levers immediately beneath. Yes, extraordinary! If he looked out to his left he could see a sheaf of cables bound with yellow insulation tape leading off to a cupboard. Presumably there were some working parts which required electrical current. He flicked two switches on the right of the instrument panel. The sputter that suddenly erupted made him switch them off again quickly in fright, then experimentally try them again. It seemed that the two switches activated a recorded engine noise from some hidden tape recorder. He flicked the two other switches in the same bank and a further sputtering followed by a determined roar came from speakers which, he discovered, had been cunningly tucked away behind the panel on the left and right of the aircraft. Jeb recognised the throaty racket from the old Lincolns at Gattisby. He flicked all four switches off, fearing that Aunt Eva would hear the noise and discover him snooping.

He climbed out and inspected the cupboard where the wires led. There was not one tape recorder, but four of varying sizes, together with sets of headphones hanging from hooks. The cupboard also contained various items of clothing, a leather airman's helmet with an intercom/oxygen mask attached to it, white webbing harness, sheepskin-lined boots, a mae west. He shut the doors on all this and walked around to the other side of the fuselage where he found a projector standing on a table and pointing at the white wall. The bench at the back of the room, illumined by a strong neon light, had, in addition to the bits and pieces of perspex, various pieces of tubing which it appeared were being fashioned into machine guns, for the front turret presumably.

And he always returns here. He has his room upstairs. So Aunt Eva had said. And this, at least in part, was the meaning of it. He must have been at it for years. Perhaps ever since he left the RAF. Jeb leaned against the access ladder, peering under the flight deck floor at the wires, bicycle chain, pipes and shafts which led this way and that. Astonishing, the loving aeronautical knowledge with which it had obviously been put together, the great incongruous bulk of it in the middle of a bedroom.

But what it meant, what it gave away — that was something different. Len was thirty-six. Most people were married with kids by that age. And why had Aunt Eva made no mention of how singular the function of Len's room upstairs actually was? Why had Len not told him about his creation when he was in Australia three years ago? It was hard to say why, but the thing was furtive somehow.

The room contained little furniture that did not serve this

consuming passion. There was a bed, the plastic model of a Lancaster bomber hanging from a hook in the ceiling, a chest of drawers with a stack of war comics on top, and a bookshelf with various aeronautical books showing photographs and cutaway plans of various celebrated bombers, and paperback copies of Guy Gibson's *Enemy Coast Ahead*, Paul Brickhill's *The Dambusters*, and other air-war titles.

Jeb opened the curtains, then went and sat down in the pilot's seat again and took the control column in his hands. From the height of the cockpit he could look out across the roofs of Wollstanton toward the waters of the Wash, indistinguishable at their horizon from the grey sky. He allowed himself to imagine what it might have been like to fly, each night, on raids over the Ruhr or Berlin, the ground below prickled with the fires of incendiary bombs, a searchlight leaping back and forth, like the huge pale blue needle on a black dial, streams of slow tracer rising bok-bok-bok toward them. How vivid it was, how easy to slip back into this kind of phantasmagoria. He got up quickly, drew the curtains carefully, and went out, shutting the door to Len's room behind him.

6

Over lunch he said to Aunt Eva, 'Look, I have to confess I took a wander through the house while you were out. I ended up in what I guess is Len's room.'

'Ah. Well that makes me just a little cross. You know Leonard's room is really private to him.'

'Yes, I'm sorry. I was curious to know how he lived. As kids we often shared a room. It's quite a set-up he has there.'

'Yes. A Mark III Avro Lancaster's cockpit. I know a little more than I need to about four-engined bombers of a certain period.'

'It's a bit bizarre.'

'Oh, I don't know. I think it's a very impressive construction. He brings new bits and pieces to add to it when he returns to stay here.'

'But the fact of it — isn't it, well, regressive or something?'

'Surely you don't expect me to inform on Leonard, do you?'

'No, I — I just want to get an idea of what's going on. In Len's mind.'

'He leads a vivid imaginary life, aided by a very authentic stage set.'

'But that's evading the issue, isn't it?'

'You're trying to grasp at fundamentals again.'

'Yes.'

'Then you must come to your own conclusions. My job is to look after Leonard's needs when he comes here.' She paused, then regarded Jeb steadily, 'And not to inform on him.'

'No. Of course. I'm sorry.'

They ate in awkward silence for some minutes. Jeb wanted to heal the breach he sensed had opened between them. In the end it was Eva Hengelow who spoke.

'It is quite natural you should want to understand Leonard. He is a puzzle. And of course I do have views on the matter. But I am not the one to help you in this. You see,' she stopped and looked at her plate, and then at Jeb, 'for reasons that I am sure you can deduce, it is imperative that Leonard should be able to rely on my loyalty to him. *Imperative*.'

7

They made their farewells. 'If you do find Crispin, you must give him my love,' she said.

'I'll telephone you if I find him and give you the news.'

'That would be most considerate.' Then she added, 'You may come and see me again if you wish.'

'I would very much like to. And if Len turns up . . .'

'I have your postal address in Cambridge.'

They shook hands on the front doorstep. Aunt Eva hesitated, looking at Jeb in a manner that suggested she owed him something more by way of explanation. At length, what she said came out in a rush. 'Crispin has an enormous gift for making other people feel he values them. It is his charm and it is quite innocent, I think. It means that he creates in other people a very strong desire to be in his company. His enthusiasms are a form of enchantment. Perhaps you can see the consequences of this when he — when his spirit moves on. People — Lizzie — they must feel let down. But he means no harm. He means no harm.' She went inside and shut the door.

8

He was back in Mallory's rooms by nine in the evening. Over a bottle of wine he discussed with his friend all he had learned at Aunt Eva's. When he described the cockpit in the bedroom Mallory looked thoughtful.

'Sounds like monomania. Nothing wrong with that. His imaginative life, which he appears to pursue with considerable vigour, is spent doing what his father did in the war. Sure, to us it sounds like reversion to childhood, but look at it from his point of view. Flying aeroplanes is what adults, heroic father-figure adults did. Your half-brother's imaginary Lancaster represents a simulacrum of the most desirable, the most worthwhile job a fellow can do. The rest of the time, all that schoolboy running away you told me about, his long absences from his aunt's home, well, that sounds like another example of the way his behaviour imitates that of his supertramp father. If what you say is right, he claims to have rejected his father, yet he is locked into re-enacting his behaviour.'

'But how can Len shut the rest of reality out?'

'That part of the mechanism I don't understand. Does he have many friends?'

'I doubt it — his fellow motorbike mechanics maybe; I've never thought about it. He spent a lot of time with me as a kid.'

'And then you went away to Australia.'

'Where he came too.'

'Ah, but by then you had already left for the Land of Politics.'

'What if he hasn't? Got any friends I mean.'

'Then the life of his imagination will replace them. After all, reality is what we need to be reminded of by others.'

'Maybe.' He saw Mallory looking at him with a slight smile playing at the corner of his mouth. 'Jeez, but you're a smart-arse, Mallory.'

'Not at all,' he said suavely.

Aiming Point March 1973

1

In the middle of the week there was a cold blue day.

'I'll take you up to the Old Roman Road,' Mallory suggested. 'The Prof's away. You can borrow his bike.'

They pedalled out of town and began to ascend the high ground on the road to Fulbourn, passing broad open fields and a beech forest on their right. They came out on level ground and picked up a rough but very straight track.

'This is it. The old road from Cambrigiensis to Camolodunum, as Colchester used to be called. Come on, let's walk.' They locked the bicycles together under a hedge and set off. There was a belt of woodland on one side of them and intermittent hedgerows on the other. The sky fell away, white and immense, toward Holland.

'The place is studded with tumulae and remains of one sort or another.' Mallory pointed to their right. 'Just over there is Wandlebury Camp, an earth fort from the Iron Age, taken over by the Romans. The golf course you can see there is on the GogMagog Hills, named after the legendary giant who was hurled into the sea by Corineus when Brutus brought the remnants of the Trojans to Britain. That's according to Geoffrey of Monmouth, at least. Doubtful history, but people believed it once. That makes it intimate. All facts are, I suppose, that's the appeal of studying history — to me at least. As if one were peering at night through windows into the intimacy of past lives, astounded by their differences, their similarities...'

'I knew it. You're a voyeur!'

Through what was unspoken was the élan each felt in the company of the other. It was unclear how much social life Mallory had enjoyed in the time he had been in England. Not much, Jeb guessed. The way he carried on he sounded like someone released from solitary confinement.

'Did you know that humans have been moving across this terrain for a quarter of a million years?' Mallory continued, ignoring Jeb's flippancy. 'That's how long ago they think the first paleolithic peoples came to the British Isles. Makes the Aborigines seem young, doesn't it? Those first Stone Age people used to follow the animals over the land bridges, then retreat back across them when sea levels rose.

'It's fantastic, isn't it? Nothing in the animal world has even a notion of grandparents, and yet we humans trace ourselves back three million years to the Rift Valley. And with such extraordinary detail, in places, anyway. Take the people they dug out of the Danish bogs — we're able to actually see what individuals looked like, how they dressed and did their hair, what their last meals on this earth were before catastrophe hit them.'

Jeb listened as Mallory expounded, marvelling at the purity of his friend's love of the past. It made him seem remarkably old-fashioned.

'I guess this was what I was trying to get at the other day when you asked me about the war,' he continued. 'It's not just the fact of the war, though like I said, I do find that it obsesses me. But it is the human past, the planetary past, when seen as an entirety, that is so overwhelming as an idea, the thought of what it means to be conscious of such an immensity. It is as if we, in the present, are on the crest of a — of a huge wave, yes, a wave of immense momentum, with all that human energy behind us, or beneath us, not just the European past, but the past of every continent, Africa, Australia, Asia.'

Mallory walked beside Jeb, staring straight ahead as he spoke and conveying something of the intensity of his conviction, not by the pitch of his voice, it was never raised, but by the very straightness of his bearing, by the fact that he did not once turn in Jeb's direction.

Suddenly he grinned brilliantly and said, 'We're time-surfies. Let's find a pub.'

In the pub at Fulbourn Mallory asked, 'When are you thinking of heading off to Germany?'

'In a day or two, probably.'

His companion thought for a bit, then said, 'I don't suppose you'd want some company over there, would you?'

'You want to come?'

'It's an IRP. Yes, I wouldn't mind.' Mallory looked Jeb steadily in the eye. 'I'm a bit of a mole when it comes to IRPs.'

'What about Cambridge, and the history of cricket?'

'Season of disaffection. A couple of weeks off might do me good. Besides, you've made me more interested in this Hengelow bloke than I am in the history of organised games at present. I reckon we could find him in a month, then, who knows, we could make a side trip or two to, say, look at the ANZAC battlefields in Flanders, or search for Nazi gold in the Alps. I've got the funds.'

'All right. Settled.'

'It'll be my first actual trip to northern Europe.'

'You're joking.' Mallory shook his head. 'But you gave me the impression you knew north-west Europe like the back of your hand.'

'I do. Theoretically.'

'I assumed you'd either tramped or driven through all that country.'

'Nup,' said Mallory. Then he smiled at Jeb and savoured what he was about to say for a moment or two. 'I've only ever seen that country in black and white.' There was shyness and some self-deprecation in the smile.

'To a successful IRP then. Cheers.'

2

They set off three mornings later, taking the train to London, then straight through to Canterbury where they stayed, spending the afternoon wandering about the flint-walled streets and the cathedral.

As they stood in the nave looking upward, Mallory provided his own version of a tourist guide's commentary. 'Those windows used to be stained glass. Cromwell found the stained glass offensive; it got in the way of man's relationship with God. So he turned his cannons on them, and they have been clear glass ever since. Think about it. As those cannons opened fire, metaphor went out, analysis came in.' He reflected a moment, then smiled, 'It's the birth of Scientific Method.'

'That's a bit cavalier, isn't it?' Their laughter attracted the looks of other sightseers.

Next morning they continued their journey to Dover by coach. The Downs of Kent were shrouded in a rainy mist which allowed the gaze to penetrate for a few yards on either side, and for perhaps a hundred yards along the road ahead. Headlights like the eyes of deep ocean fish came toward them on the westbound carriageway in an unbroken stream, while the Dover traffic swished past, tail-lights diminishing to inconsiderable specks, then vanishing.

At Dover they found a rail strike was delaying all ferries, so they spent several hours wandering around the castle with its various displays of spiky weapons, pikes, halberds, sabres, bayonets, poniards, stilettos, all oiled and gleaming.

'I used to love swords and suchlike, but I find this lot rather grisly, don't you?'

'They're a bit intimate. You can hear the slice and grunt.'

By the time they had passed through the terminus and boarded the ferry, the mist had dispersed and the sky was smeary and mobile with low cloud. The Channel slapped and crimpled around the huge wharf piles, then grew dark and sheeny as the ship moved out into deeper water. A great rabble of seagulls followed in their wake, descending in noisy frenzy whenever trash was thrown over the side. Gusts of rain blew in their faces from the direction of France while the crests on the whitecaps looked soiled with sewage or industrial dyes. There were ships crowding all their horizons.

They passed the time exchanging laconic comments about fellow passengers or in contemplative silence watching the prodigious sea traffic. They went down to the cafeteria and queued for an unconscionably long time before buying limp sandwiches and black coffee that tasted like charcoal and dishwater, while the table they eventually found was smeared with tomato sauce, littered with crumpled serviettes and empty sugar sachets. The refectory was crammed with people and they found they had to keep moving their chairs to let them pass.

'And they call this the off-season.'

'Everything seems so over-used.'

The coast of France, when they saw it, oozed columns of smoke and steam from factory chimneys, fairy-floss or urine-yellow in colour. They disembarked and immediately boarded a coach for Liège in which they sped down broad Euro-routes, skirting Lille, Namur, passing under necklaces of orange lights, seeing the lights of towns pass below where the road was upheld by immense concrete pylons. In Liège they immediately boarded a second coach for Aachen, and arrived in Charlemagne's city a little after eleven.

'So when did the Allies get here?' asked Jeb, as they went off looking for a hostel.

'I have a distaste for examinations,' replied his companion curtly.

'I didn't mean —'

'And to being caricatured.'

'I take my question back,' said Jeb, a little put out by Mallory's sensitivity.

'Fine.'

They walked on in silence. After some searching, they found a hotel room with one double bed. Somewhat self-consciously, they arranged to sleep, one under the covers, one on top in his sleeping bag.

Some five minutes after they turned the lights out Mallory said, 'The answer to your question is that the Aachen garrison surrendered to the American First Army on October 21st 1944.'

'Oh.'

'Goodnight.'

'Goodnight.'

3

At breakfast the following morning Jeb suggested they trust to their luck and hitch rides to Hamburg rather than take an inter-city train, or a coach.

'I'd like to have a squint at Oldenrath, where we used to live. It's actually quite close. We could hitch there, and still get into Hamburg tonight if we wanted to.' He was a little taken aback by his companion's adamant rejection of the idea.

'Why introduce needless risk?' Mallory looked resolutely at his plate as he pulled a white roll apart and folded a piece of salami on top of it.

'It's a more intimate way of seeing the country.'

'I'd prefer to know I was going to arrive.'

'No worries. We'll get there.'

'I dislike uncertainty, and I dislike being beholden.' He popped the piece of roll and salami into his mouth and chewed methodically. His gaze, Jeb noticed, was now directed out of the window. It was a gaze that seemed to listen rather than see, and suggested that the subject of hitch-hiking was touchy ground, for reasons that Jeb could not fathom.

'It's an *adventure*,' he persisted.

Mallory looked him in the eye for a moment and said, 'I'll pay for your coach ticket, if you like.' Then he looked out of the window again.

'It's not *that*.'

In the end they bussed.

Using local buses they reached Oldenrath in an hour, and began to wander around the garrison. Jeb kept up a non-stop description of his boyhood years on the base, though, truth to tell, the woods, the diving boards, the distances between different parts of the camp were all smaller than he recollected. Not that this prevented him wanting to convey to Mallory the very spirit of that delicious freedom he attached to his boyhood years.

'You sound like someone who's in love with his childhood,' observed the latter.

Jeb looked quickly at Mallory. 'D'you think?' The idea was new to him. He didn't like it much, and was afraid it might be true. They wandered rather aimlessly for a few minutes, then Jeb stopped and said, 'All right then, let's go.'

'I didn't mean to blight Memory Lane.'

'It's not that. I'm finding childhood to be a more haunting place in the memory than it is on the ground.'

They bussed into München Gladbach in time to take the midday Hamburg coach which drove them through an afternoon of wide horizontals and slender perpendiculars. From behind the tinted windows they gazed as northern Germany went by, the neat farms with their broad roofs the colour of mercury oxide, the newly ploughed, squared-off fields with a solitary black-and-white windmill, or a bristle of woods at their horizon, canals and irrigation ditches with their angular reflections, chrome and jet black. Quite abruptly the skyline would become industrial, the huge domes and beakers of a nuclear power plant, chimneys like long battleship gun-barrels marking brown-coal *Kraftwerke*, the intricate girdering of pylons, aerials, cranes, silvery high-rises, their reflective windows like monstrous insect eyes, compounding the overcast day's stainless steel light into a myriad not-quite-identical scintilla.

They crossed the Rhine near Düsseldorf, skirted the Ruhr cities of Witten and Dortmund, switching from autobahn to autobahn, bypassing Münster and Osnabrück, being overhauled once by an inter-city train, a slab-faced, wine-red serpent, growing close as road and rail converged, then curving into the immensity of the Niedersachsen sky. Horizontal and perpendicular, but scored by the parallel curves of power lines, suspension bridges, the intersections of autobahns. It was not, Jeb supposed, a specifically German landscape so much as a north-west European one. Everywhere it bore the imprint of recent human effort, colossal, beautiful, terrifying.

'It's like travelling across an engineer's blueprint.'

'I know what you mean. I feel as if my importance is deserting me.'

Late in the afternoon they changed coaches in Bremen. During their wait in the terminal they were approached by a bearded man of about their own age, his long body swathed in what had once been a gaily coloured Mexican blanket.

'*Bitte, Können Sie mir Geld geben. Heute habe ich nichts gegessen.*'

Mallory looked him steadily in the eye for some moments, assessing him. '*Nein.* No money! No money!' He then averted his face.

The beggar turned to Jeb who gave him a handful of marks and pfennigs. Instead of the expected '*Danke,*' the man cast an eye up and down Mallory's neat getup, then turned conspiratorially to Jeb, '*Ihr Freund ist ein fetten Kapitalist, denkst du?*' And to emphasise his point he spat on the highly polished lino floor of the terminal, then shuffled off with an apparent limp. His phlegm glistened at Mallory's feet.

'What a bunch of charm he was.' They watched him as he approached other people.

'You were pretty definite about charity back there. How come?'

'He was degrading himself and degrading me by asking.'

'Does that mean you think I degraded myself by giving him something?'

Mallory shrugged. 'It's your affair, Jim. I'm not your person.' Jeb was a little stung by the reply. They looked at the gob of spittle near Mallory's shoe.

'Let's move seats,' he suggested.

They reached Hamburg in the evening and took the U-bahn to Landungsbrücke, travelling for a while beside the Elbe and keeping pace with a liner which was moving downriver, outlined by the lights of its portholes. From the station they walked out into Altona, asking their way, and within half an hour they had located the flats Aunt Eva had mentioned.

Hengelow's 'safe house' was in one of several blocks of flats, each of them a red-brick monolith set on massive concrete claws, and arranged close to the other blocks so that they formed deep canyons down which a wind from off the Heligoland Bight funnelled coldly. There were, perhaps, thirty blocks, each one with a hundred or so flats.

The lifts were not working so they toiled up the stairs, gaining at each level a more commanding view over the dock area. The flat they were looking for was on the second highest floor. Here they knocked and waited. After some moments they could see a figure behind the mottled glass, then the door opened to reveal a woman, perhaps in her mid-thirties, with straight, rather thin hair, clear skin and thick glasses. She had a child on her hip.

'Um, *Guten Abend.*'

'*N'Abend.*'

'*Wir suchen einen Mann, er heisst Herr Crispin Hengelow.*'

'Iss all right. You may speak Englisch.'

'Oh. Right.' Jeb introduced himself and Mallory. 'We're looking for a Herr Hengelow. I was told that he sometimes stays here when he is living in Hamburg. I would have phoned, but...'

'You are friends of Charlie?'

'Charlie? Oh, right. Um, he's got a son called Len. Long time ago my mother was wife of Herr Hengelow. That is no more. *Schluß*,' said Jeb, not really knowing why he was simplifying his English for the woman. 'I am Len's, um, *Halbbruder.*'

'*So, Stief-bruder. Bitte, Komm. Komm.* Now iss Charlie not here. Comes soon, for his *Abendessen.* You wait here.'

'He is living here now?

'Of course. *Komm.*'

'Hey! Bullseye in one. Um. *Danke schön.*'

They followed her down a corridor, dumping their rucksacks where she indicated.

'I am Ronya. This is my mother's apartment. You will meet her.'

They passed into a small sitting room where a colour television flickered. The first view that Jeb had of another person in the room was a fluff of red hair visible above a chair back, and lit by the light of the television. The woman made no effort to turn around and greet the newcomers, so it was not until he had been ushered well into the room that Jeb caught sight of her face. He was unprepared for what he saw.

It was puffy, shapeless, pale, the whiteness of the skin accentuating the redness and thickness of the hair and making it look synthetic, doll-like almost. Black puffy holes marked where the eyes should have been, whether seeing or blind he was not immediately certain. There was no discernible nose so much as two small airholes above a mouth which seemed to pull and wrench at words in reply to his reflexive *Guten Abend*, while smiling, kindly, hideously, the head nodding in gentle reassurance, as a grandmother might to her grandchildren. The sound reminded him of his father's efforts at speech, the indecipherable gurgles in the early days after his first stroke. Only Dad's face had been twisted into the trenches of a half-smile, half-frown by his misfortune; it had been made somehow more emphatically human, more individual. Its deep lines had been a record of struggle, humour, good will. This woman's face looked as if it had been rendered back to some basic original, like a lump of white clay, experimented with, then rolled into a blob and discarded.

It might have been piteous, but it was also repulsive. For all that, as a boy, Jeb had learned to live with the violent rearrangement of his dad's features, he could not bear to look at the woman. It was the most fearful distortion of the human visage he could remember having seen. Yet he knew that, for the sake of decency, he must look at her as though nothing were amiss. He was afraid his repulsion must be evident in his manner.

The visitors were ushered to seats by the younger woman, and given coffee. The two-year-old was placed among some luminescent building blocks, but instead of playing with them he stared solemnly at the newcomers. No effort was made to turn off the television, so its flickering and babble made conversation a distracting business. Jeb wanted to demonstrate that he was unshocked by asking the red-haired woman a question or two; something banal, anything.

'*Können Sie*, um, *den Hafen von hier gut sehen?*' he tried. The sentence felt grammatically wrong. The blob appeared to grin and nod vigorously, and her hands were moving on her lap in some indecipherable expressive gesture. There were sounds coming from her.

'She is saying that you can see for yourself. Please, here is the window.' Jeb got up and pulled aside the curtain. The view consisted largely of the brick wall of the neighbouring block. There was a thin margin of sky in which an aerial with a winking red light could be seen. He turned to find the two women seemed to be enjoying the hugeness of the joke. In the cackle that came from the elder, Jeb thought he caught the words, '*So, shöne Hafenaussicht.*'

'She says, Do you enjoy our beautiful harbour view?' Jeb nodded and tried to join in the spirit of the mirth, but to no avail. It was clear their humour required him to be sheepish, but for all that it seemed a bit immoderate, their amusement was not, he recognised, unkind. It was just that they were going to make the most of it. Indeed, he was to find that his innocent question was liable to set them off throughout the evening.

Mallory asked if he could smoke, and offered around his packet. Both women accepted a cigarette.

When Ronya discovered Jeb and Mallory were from Australia she pursued the topic with a relentless, deadpan questioning, and Jeb found himself offering the facts and figures of summer and winter temperatures in different parts of Australia, the ratio of sheep to humans, the distances between major cities, and so on. As he did so he was aware of the white clay and red hair being turned attentively toward him. But he prattled on, exhausting each topic as it came up, while Mallory smoked and listened, his eye on the flickering television, not making much effort to help out with conversation.

'*Jeb ist ein gutes Handbuch, glaubst du?*' he leaned back and said to the red-haired woman at one point, which occasioned another bubbling of amusement.

'Iss good for my mother to have visitors. She is from her flat very little.'

They had been there perhaps an hour when they heard footsteps stop outside the door and a key scrape in the lock.

'So, Charlie is come back already.' Ronya went out and they could hear her voice speaking in lowered tones in the corridor. She came back in, followed by a tall figure.

4

Jeb recognised immediately the gaunt, shabby man who had been in his bedroom over twenty years before. There was a look of inquiry on Hengelow's face when he entered the room, but he took one glance at Jeb and the inquiry vanished.

'My dear fellow,' he burst out, 'Why, you're the image of your mother. Elli!' He strode over to the couch where the red-haired woman sat and, taking her by the shoulders, put his head behind hers and guided her gaze onto Jeb. '*Elli, hier ist der andere Sohn von Lizzie, Stief-bruder zu Len.*' The clay and red furze nodded with enthusiasm. Hengelow stood up again, shaking his head with the fortuity of it all. 'Jiminy,' he kept repeating, and 'Bless me.'

For it was extraordinary. *Erstaunlich, Elli*! That Lizzie's boy should be here. Last seen him as a tiny little fellow with a sunhat. How did he find the place? What on earth prompted him to come? No, never mind that. Let's have a look at you. There was no doubting the warmth of his manner.

Except that his face clouded for a moment, and, coming up to Jeb and wringing his hand, he said in a tone of grave concern, 'My *dear* fellow, it's unforgivable of me, but do you know I've quite forgotten what you were called?'

'Jeb,' said Jeb, looking away in some embarrassment, for Hengelow was looking him unabashedly, searchingly in the eye. 'Officially it was James, but they seemed to settle on Jeb. I was called Cherub by the fellows at school.'

Hengelow hit his forehead with the palm of his hand as soon as the syllable 'Jeb' had escaped, and this was followed by a twinkle of charmed amusement at the 'Cherub'. The immediacy with which his face registered reactions had something of the amateur theatricals about it. Not that he seemed insincere so much as extrovert. The initial impression that Jeb gained was of a type — headmasterly perhaps, or like some bluff colonial official organising hundreds of people onto trains in, say, Hyderabad, or Bulawayo. He gazed at Jeb, holding him at arms length for a few moments, then turned to Mallory. 'Do forgive me. And you are —?' he asked. Mallory had stood up and was hovering in the background.

'Simon Mallory. I'm one of those schoolfellows.'

'Bless me, and you've just got off the plane from Australia?'

No, Jeb explained, they had come from Britain. He'd seen Aunt Eva. Had been given two or three not very reliable addresses. 'She sends you her love.'

'Bless her. So you struck gold in one!'

. . . Had wanted to piece together a bit of the family history. So was in Europe for as long as the money held out. And so on. Hengelow's warmth ('insidious warmth'? It wasn't remotely possible), his charm, and the attentiveness with which he listened and questioned, prompted Jeb to be voluble, made him feel instantly — what was it — valued, yes, *valued*. He was reminded of the effect Rosie had had on him at the beginning. Perhaps he should be on his guard. No. It was impossible. Because as they sat down and he began to relate family matters, he recognised that Hengelow, like Rosie, was one of those characters to whom one succumbed.

Ronya prepared them a dinner, small sausages and beans from a tin, toast and beer. It was welcome, if rudimentary. Hengelow, Jeb noticed, cut Elli's toast into small segments, and she appeared to use only her right hand when eating.

'I wanted to ask you — that is — no one I've talked to seems too clear as to what you actually do over here,' Jeb began.

'Not too clear myself.'

'Charlie iss — *was heisst es*? — *der gute Samariter*?'

'Good Samaritan?'

'Nonsense, Roni.'

'He helps the poor men and the poor women.'

'How do you mean?'

'Roni!'

'He goes out, perhaps in Altona, or San Pauli, perhaps in Hammerbrook, finds someone in trouble, alcoholic, *Gastarbeiter*, *Dirne*, addict, brings home perhaps one, perhaps two. Then, spends the next day sorting out their problems.'

'Here? To your home?' Jeb had in mind the beggar at the bus terminus in Bremen.

Ronya looked Jeb in the eye for a moment. 'When Charlie is with us here in Hamburg, we are with him,' she stated simply. 'We share with his work.'

'Dear fellow, this is all nonsense. I lead a very *privileged* life among these people, and the little we are able to do here is quite outweighed by what our friends share with us from their own lives.' He had sat with his knees crossed looking down his long face, and he appeared to be genuinely embarrassed by Ronya's description of his charitable works.

'And you travel about?'

'Inveterate gypsy. I do a bit of work in Darmstadt, Cologne, one or two of the Ruhr towns.'

'Charlie has *Sicherherbergen* — shelters — in these places. Like our apartment here.'

'But how do you live? Money-wise?'

'Ha!' His eye twinkled but he was unforthcoming. Jeb wondered if the question had been indiscreet. Hengelow turned to Ronya. '*Roni, Heute abend werde ich Tobias seine Bad geben*, OK?'

'OK.'

They cleared away. Mallory helped Ronya at the sink, Elli became absorbed by a programme on the television, turning every now and then to grin encouragingly at Jeb who hovered, trying to be useful. Hearing the sounds of Hengelow and the infant in the bathroom, he wandered into the tiny cubicle. There he witnessed the plump, soapy child gurgling with hilarity in his three inches of water as the huge man, resting like a penitent on his knees, ducked his head beneath the rim of the bath, then popped up suddenly with a *kuckuck*! The face of Hengelow was equally creased with good humour — when he laughed his countenance seemed suddenly to wrinkle more radically than it was possible to guess from seeing the face in repose.

'Yours?' Jeb felt free to ask.

'Tobias? Mine? Bless me, the very thought.' Hengelow looked at the child as it splashed about in the water. Its father, he declared, had been a poor addict Roni had known; decamped. He took a plastic boat that was floating in the suds and drove it around and around the infant, to the latter's squealing delight, and in the midst of this game he revealed, 'I've only ever had one child — and one wife.' He smiled at Jeb, sheepishly the latter thought.

5

When Jeb suggested it was about time he and Mallory went looking for a cheap hostel, Hengelow and Ronya wouldn't hear of it. There were campbeds, there were cushions. 'Why

are you not being our guests here when there is no problem?'
Ronya looked at them almost reproachfully, then gave a
nervous laugh.

'Won't we be in the way?'

'You might hear a bit of stamping about in the small hours.
But young fellows like you . . .'

Some time after nine a youngish man wearing a windcheater
and scarf called for Hengelow. His name was Sig, he smiled
a great deal and looked at his feet, shifting from one to another.
The two of them went out. Jeb heard doors slam, and a
van drive off.

When she had provided them with their lilos, pillows and
towels, Ronya retired to bed. 'Our work here means I am
awake in the night sometimes.' Jeb, following her example,
set up his airbed under the window, crawled into his sleeping
bag and lay there listening to the gabble of the television
and the intermittent conversation in broken German that was
taking place between Mallory and Elli. From where he was
lying he could see Elli's face and red hair lit by the flickering
picture. She was smiling that strangely encouraging smile
as she struggled to make intelligible sounds. Mallory, it
seemed, had asked her how she had come by her disfigure-
ments. A bit tactless of him, wasn't it! Or ruthless. But Elli
didn't seem to mind. Her right hand was floating above her
lap. '*Die Tommies,*' Jeb concentrated hard to catch the intelligible sounds. '*Die Tommies . . . mit Ihren Phosphor Bomben . . .
Im Krieg . . . Mein Haus war in Hammerbrook . . . Feuersturm. Neun-
zehnhundert drei und vierzig.*' She made a gurgling with phlegm
against her tongue to imitate the roar of the fires, then nodded
her head again in that distinctive smile. It was a fixture.
It seemed ebullient almost, yet so at odds with what she
had been actually saying. As though her injuries had been
no more than a vicissitude, like spraining an ankle or getting
soaked on a hike. Mallory's head was turned away from Jeb's
view. He was asking further questions in that quiet voice
of his, and offering cigarettes. But it was difficult to catch
all of it.

Jeb woke and looked at his watch. It was a little before
four a.m. The television was now off and Mallory appeared

to be asleep on his lilo on the other side of the room. There were voices in the corridor and the sound of people bumping into things. A foldup bed had been set up on the floor. Ronya was moving about in a dressing gown, preparing something in the kitchenette. Hengelow and the man, Sig, came into view, supporting a drunk. They placed him on the foldup where the top part of his body lolled, never quite losing its balance. Subdued conversation came from the kitchenette and a mug of coffee was given to the newcomer who, since his arrival, had been keeping up a cheerful monologue. He slurped noisily at the beverage, then seemed to become aware that there were sleepers in the room. So, placing the coffee with enormous care on the carpet, he crawled on all fours, first over to where Mallory lay asleep, then to Jeb. The latter saw a face grow toward him — gold-rimmed spectacles with one of the lenses cracked, black hair, moustache and beard, coarse skin. There was the smell of liquor — something strong, Kirsch, perhaps. He looked Oriental, but hulkier. Seeing Jeb was awake, the man grinned at him. '*Ich bin Bob Dylan*,' he nodded waggishly.

'*Wirklich.*'

'*Ich bin Offizier von den Dunkel.*' His face could have been no more than a handspan away from Jeb's.

'*Komm, komm, Lass ihn schlafen.*'

'*Ich bin der Todengel. Bist du Jesus? Bist du Buddha?*' he asked, grinning broadly, as he allowed Ronya and Hengelow to lead him back to the kitchenette.

'Can I help?'

'Go back to sleep, old man,' Hengelow whispered. 'We'll put this fellow into my room so he won't disturb you.'

'Who is he?'

'*Gastarbeiter.* Name's Aco. From Yugoslavia. High as a lord. Been robbed and locked out of his digs. He'll be right as rain after a sleep and some breakfast.'

The commotion died down. Jeb woke several hours later to find Hengelow on the foldup lying under a couple of coats, his legs curled so that the short bed could accommodate his length. He looked vulnerable.

Later, having breakfasted with Ronya and Tobias, Jeb sat

238

lingering over his coffee as the man, Aco, his face yellow, had his breakfast cooked by Hengelow. The Slav's account of himself was somewhat sorrier than it had been during the night.

'*Ich habe meine Stellung verloren. Du verstehst!*'

'Poor fellow's been given the sack. We'll run him down to the *Arbeitsamt* and see what we can wangle.'

'*Meine Ausweis auch.* Someone steals them. *Residenzpermit. Geld, Alles verloren.*' He was unstoppable. '*Aufnahme meiner Freundin, Aufnahme meiner Eltern . . . alles verloren.*'

'We'll straighten you out, old man. *Wir machen alles gut.*' He put his arm around the dejected *Gastarbeiter* and gave him an affectionate shake.

6

Jeb and Mallory spent the day wandering about the centre of Hamburg, under the copper-green spires of St Petri, St Nikolai, the Rathaus, or beneath the colonnades that flanked the waters of the Binnenalster. But there was an aimlessness about their sightseeing. They had come to the city in the spirit of a quest and had found the object of this quest almost immediately. Not that the city itself was unattractive, with its arcades where the pigeons scattered like fragmenting metal, the glittery canals with their high old warehouses and slow-gliding swans, or, where they walked in the later afternoon, the cranes leaning above the ships, as if they were huge stick insects feeding from equally enormous larvae.

In one renovated warehouse they saw an exhibition of pictures advertised — EXPLOSION, HAMBURG 1943, HANOI 1973. They went in.

At first glance the exhibition seemed to consist of perhaps a dozen photographs of devastated buildings, helmetted firemen peering out from doorways, peasants crouching in man-holes, all magnified to enormous size so that the images were scarcely recognisable. Beside each blow-up was a tatty cutting from a magazine depicting in miniature the same subject.

'I don't get it,' said Jeb.

Mallory was scrutinising the magnified surface of one of the blow-ups.

'*Verstehen sie nicht?*' A man in black skivvy and jeans had approached them. 'It is very simple,' he explained, on finding out they were from Australia. 'I have taken some press photographs and analysed, how shall I say — their atomic structure. See,' he directed Mallory to look very closely at the magazine cutting. 'It is the behaviour of the dots when the tone changes. The molecular bonds. You understand? So. I reconstitute the image by cutting out tens of thousands of these molecules and sticking them down. I anatomise the image. My anatomy is a comment on what the image is saying. Forgive me. I must help these other people.' He retreated to where another couple stood before a picture and Jeb saw him commence his explanation again..

'A bit heartless, isn't it?'

'Yes, but effective. Look at the way that all these molecular dots give the impression of disintegration; not just the buildings, but people's faces, this fire-cart, the profile of this woman. It's as if their atoms are drifting off them, turning into soot or flares. That's saturation bombing for you.'

'I think he's using his technique to latch onto other people's experience and exploit it. There's something cynical going on.' Jeb began to move on. There was something in what Mallory had said, he supposed, but he found the exhibition cold, disengaged, and likewise their rather patronising creator hovering with his explanations in several languages.

'Certainly they're not sunsets and sailing ships,' Mallory responded, still scrutinising.

Jeb was unprepared for the hostility of the remark. 'That's a bit below the belt.'

His companion glanced at him briefly. There was a cruelty, Jeb thought, in the urbane smile. Feeling injured, Jeb wandered out of the gallery and stood leaning on the rail overlooking a canal until his friend emerged.

As dark fell, talking little, they made their way back from the docks through St Pauli and found themselves on the Reeperbahn amidst its brilliant angularities of light. At street level were the illuminated signs of the bars and theatre restaurants, Aladdin's, Tempe's, Palais d'Amour. Above these, emblazoned on the sky, were the neons of the wristwatch advertisements — ROLEX in green and yellow, OMEGA in orange. ZILLERTAL BLEIBT ZILLERTAL read one huge hoarding to their left, picked out in white and azurite; it appeared to advertise holidays. In a window Jeb glimpsed a huge poster showing a woman holding a stockwhip; she might have been some Aryan goddess with her swept-back, luxuriant blonde hair, dark arched eyebrows and black eyelashes, the disdainful mouth and large pale breasts tumbling from her inadequate leather bodice. In another window a girl, nude but for black stockings, was kneeling on a rug of synthetic fur stroking her mons pubis, leaning toward the one or two onlookers who had stopped; it was a moment before Jeb realised this girl was real and not in a picture. Mallory walked on, his eyes to the front, his carriage somehow rigid, repelling the carnal possibilities around them.

'I wonder what she would have cost?' Jeb indicated the girl in the window they had just past.

'Don't let me stop you.'

It had begun to rain. The traffic swished and the fine drizzle made a mélange of the lights on the further side of the road. As they passed a theatre-restaurant a girl in denims walked out toward them; abundant red-gold hair to her shoulders, such a direct, candid gaze, her hands were tucked into her jeans, her tongue slightly protruding, only one button fastening her shirt where the breasts bulged. So casual, so natural. She might just have got off a horse — Jeb was reminded of Roma. Adorable. Ah, if he had the nerve, the money, he thought, if Mallory hadn't been there. They walked quickly on, boarded the S-Bahn, and were back at the safe house by seven in the evening.

7

Aco the *Gastarbeiter* was sitting opposite Elli tackling a plate of dumplings and gravy. The lens of his glasses had been mended. In the course of the day, Ronya informed them, he had been dealt with — new job, new papers, and a room with a family; he was to be dropped off when Sig called later with the Kombi.

'Worst part of this kind of work. Hanging about actually

waiting to talk to someone about a problem. Eh, Aco!' Hengelow clapped his back boisterously, and the *Gastarbeiter* nodded
happily as though he had understood the English.

'*Dein Onkel hat goldenes Vortrag.*'

'He thinks I'm your uncle and that I'm a bit of a talker.'

'Are you? A bit of a talker?'

'Discovered the knack of wangling things back in RAF
days, I suppose.' He winked at the infant in his high chair,
and popped a spoonful of mush into its mouth. Then he said,
'I've arranged for you fellows to come out with us this
evening,' he turned from the task of spoon-feeding, 'if you
would like to volunteer, of course.' There didn't appear to
be much room for negotiation.

'By all means.'

Sig called at nine and by ten they had collected Aco's
belongings from his former lodging and taken him out to
what Jeb guessed was one of the northern suburbs. Hengelow
was known by the family and greeted effusively. As Jeb
watched through the window of the van he saw heads thrown
back in laughter. Aco embraced him and it was with some
difficulty that his benefactor extricated himself and returned
to the front seat of the Kombi.

'The dear fellow's beside himself with gratitude. Quite
out of proportion. *Er weinte, Sig. Arme Herr.* Let's hope he
stays off the schnapps for a bit.'

They drove back towards the Elbe and parked beside it.
On the further bank the dim profile of an oil refinery was
brilliantly escutcheoned by hundreds of floodlights; a flame
licked and lolled hypnotically against the blue of the night;
a BP sign seemed to hang on nothing, yellow letters inside
the green outline of a shield.

'We're going to patrol a couple of these riverside parks.'

They spread out and began their search, investigating spinneys, thickets, shelters. Jeb wondered what Mother would
say if she heard he was helping her ex-husband look for drunks
in a Hamburg park. He half feared he would stumble on
someone. It was disconcerting how, at night, a strip of plastic
wrapping immediately suggested itself as a pair of legs half
hidden beneath a bush, or a piece of broken styrofoam leapt

242

from beside a toolshed in the form of a white shirt. There were catcalls down near the riverbank, though quite far off. Then he could hear Sig calling.

'*Charlie! Ich habe hier jemand gefunden.*'

By the time he arrived Mallory was already there. Their 'find' was lying on his stomach and in response to Sig's questions, he emitted groans. Hengelow came up.

'*Betrunken?*'

'*Glaube ich.*'

'There's blood,' said Mallory. 'I've got it on my hands.'

'Can you see where it's coming from?'

He peeled back various clothes. 'Not immediately.' Then he said, 'Here.' Hengelow knelt beside him and examined. '*Gebrochenes Flasche...*' then he addressed the man. '*Sie müssen sofort ins Krankenhaus.*'

'*Nein, nein. Verschwinde!*' The body writhed and attempted to crawl away.

'*Keine Frage.* You fellows, turn him over gently now, hup! Steady.' The man emitted an agonised cry.

They lifted together, Hengelow and Sig in front, Mallory and Jeb at the feet. The latter was still unclear as to what was wrong with the man.

'He's got a broken bottle rammed up his arse,' Mallory told him.

They hefted their burden to the road, then Sig brought the Kombi and they lifted the afflicted man into the back. Jeb caught a glimpse of fair hair and a lupine face, eyes shut and teeth locked in a grimace. As they drove to the hospital in Altona Hengelow kept up a non-stop patter of soothing noises. They were not words so much as drawn-out animal vowels and as Jeb watched him bending low over the man he was struck by how heedless, how focussed, Hengelow's manner was. Ridiculous too, were it not for the authority of it. They passed a sign saying *Allgemeines Krankenhaus, Altona*. Outside Jeb could see the hospital, immense monoliths of striated light.

Hengelow was greeted as a familiar by the immaculate sister at the casualty desk and the wardsmen in their starched tunics. That he was a frequent visitor there was evident in the way he would place his hand familiarly on a shoulder, or lean forward to catch what someone was saying. Their 'find' was taken away on a chrome trolley. The tall man came over to where Jeb was standing.

'Look, there's something I'd like you to do for me. When they've picked the glass out of that poor fellow, I want him to find that he's fallen among friends. Sig and I are back to the job — we'll take Simon with us — you stick around here and show your countenance to our friend as soon as practicable. Some friendly words. I've squared it with Sister. A fellow from the *Polizei* might drop by, but I've given all the particulars. We'll pick you up in a couple of hours or so. OK?'

'Fine, I suppose.'

Hengelow squeezed his elbow and the three of them left. It was a little before midnight. Jeb settled himself into a vinyl chair and waited. The sister busied herself with paperwork; wardsmen went past, pushing stretchers on which people lay. Occasionally he heard moaning, occasionally he saw a hand holding a sopping red gauze pad in place, as the victims of road accidents or bashings were wheeled back and forth. But it was curiously undramatic.

He had an inkling now of what Mother had meant. Insidious warmth? He was a lovely fellow, Hengelow, of course, but the man did have a knack of thrusting one into situations. What on earth was he going to say to the bloke they had brought in? *Ich bin ein Freund. Schade daß du ein wenig krank bist.* The fellow would simply stare back out of his pain and humiliation and wish him to hell. It was as clear as daylight. And there was just the suspicion in Jeb's mind that he was being tested, that Hengelow had contrived this trial of the spirit, to find the measure of his charity.

'You may see your friend now.' The sister was standing before him. It seemed she spoke good English.

'He's not — I don't even know his name.' But she was leading the way past mobile screens to where the fellow lay face down on a stretcher. There was no blood that Jeb could see. The man's clothes had been removed, revealing a tanned back. A white sheet covered the area of his injury.

'Uh,' he felt so ridiculous, '*Sie sind mit Freunde. Ich heiße ...*'
Ridiculous.

'*Verschwinde.*' The man turned his face the other way.

'Um ... *Hoffentlich sind Sie bald gesund.*'

'*Hau ab! Du Arschloch!*' Jeb heard angry sobs coming from
the blond head. He looked at the sister who indicated he
should leave.

'I've never seen him before tonight. We found him in a
park,' Jeb protested as he followed the sister back to the
foyer.

He was not asked to see the man again. To kill time, he
wandered around the foyer and grounds of the hospital, found
a cafeteria and sat for a while, then returned to his vinyl
chair at casualty, where eventually he fell asleep. He woke
to find Hengelow standing over him shaking him gently by
the shoulder. 'Let's get you back to base, old man.'

'I tried to talk to the bloke.'

'You gave it your best shot.' The man's face was creased
with sympathy.

8

Sundays were inviolable, Hengelow told them. The Day of
Rest. They would all take an outing on the harbour. A lunch
was packed, Tobias was pushed into boots and nylon parka.
But when it came time to leave, Elli sat down and shook
her head. She would not come. The smile had changed subtly.
It was now somehow fraught. 'Always this trouble,' Ronya
told Jeb.

But the tall man would not hear of leaving Elli behind.
She would walk out with Simon on one arm and himself
on the other. She must show off her two sweethearts —
ihren Liebsten. He tucked his arm through hers, lifted her to
her feet and patted her hand. Mallory was quick with his
cue and slipped his arm into place on Elli's other side. The
poor woman was grin-weeping. Jeb found that the toddler
had been placed on his shoulders.

'*Jetzt promenaden wir!*' exclaimed Hengelow.

So they took the S-Bahn to the St Pauli jetty and boarded
a cruise launch. Mallory and Hengelow were as attentive

as any sweethearts, helping Elli on and off the tram, taking her hand up the gangplank of the launch, leaning and saying something confidential in her ear which made the elderly woman's face collapse, in part with mirth, in part with an apologetic expression which seemed to say, Really! what have I done to deserve such indulgence. Jeb was surprised that Mallory's German was proficient enough to manage wit.

Ronya said, 'Simon is very — *ach, Charlie, was heisst wohltätig auf Englisch?*'

'Charitable,' Hengelow called back.

'So, Simon is very charitable, I think.'

'He probably wouldn't thank you to hear that. He doesn't believe in giving money to beggars. Thinks it's degrading.' Jeb had not yet learned from Mallory how he reconciled assisting Hengelow in his good works with his attitude to the Bremen beggar. Had he also simply succumbed to the force of the older man's character?

'*Er ist wohltätig.* Charitable. Yes, I think so.'

They sat together on a bench at the stern of the launch, throwing pieces of bread into the churning wake and watching the seagulls diving for it in screaming flurries. Perhaps an hour went by as they made down the Elbe toward Blankenese passing beside the slab ships with their high orange or black hulls and their white superstructures and derricks, each like the icing and candles on a wedding cake. Jeb was busy holding onto the squirmy Tobias whose ambition seemed to be to vault the rail and join the squabbling seagulls in the wake. Jeb heard Mallory talking to Hengelow about the war. Words like 'momentum', 'welter', 'millions of human beings in danger and in movement', floated across to him. Still the war. Mallory was giving Hengelow the same 'rave' as he had given Jeb in his Cambridge kitchen a week or so ago. Hengelow was listening impassively. There was a relentlessness to Mallory's discourse which suggested to Jeb a vulnerability in his friend, as if he was looking for Hengelow's approval. Jeb shifted down the bench so he could hear better.

'The thing is, we're still too near to events, both those who took part and those who were, well, excluded. History has yet to cope with the shock to humanity which that war brought in its train...' Mallory faltered, unsure, finally, of Hengelow's interest. Characteristically, he tried to undercut himself. 'That's the theory, at least.'

'And that's what you think, Simon. Well, I daresay; but I'm reminded of a fellow I know. He helps us out occasionally, gives us the use of a couple of rooms in his apartment, drives the minibus when Sig takes a night off. During the war he was in the *Fliegerabwehr* — that was their ack-ack mob, down in the south.

'Well, the Yanks pulled our friend out of a Nazi jail where he had been languishing because he was once overheard wishing us bomber boys — "*Hals und Beinbruch*" — that's "Good Luck!" as we flew over. A month or so later he was able to get out of the American zone and return here, to Hamburg, what was left of it. You'll know the city took a pasting. He got a room in a boarding-house. Anyway, the story is that one evening an English soldier turned up in a jeep. Wanted a room, a front room, he said, so he could keep an eye on his jeep. The good *Hauswirtin* gave him what he asked for, together with towels, linen, all beautifully fresh and clean in the best tradition of Hamburger *Gastfreundschaft*, and the fellow retired to his room.

'In the morning he'd gone and the dear lady was livid. Unappeasable! *Unglaublich*, she hissed. *Abscheulich. Skandalos. Wie ein Mensch so schlecht sein kann.* Apparently she'd found one of her *Handtücher*, screwed into a ball and with black smears all over it, on the roadside where the jeep had been parked. He'd used the towel to clean his shoes.

'What amused our returned soldier was that the good lady and her establishment had come unscathed through all the calamities of world war, including the most catastrophic bombardment and firestorms in human history, to find the very pit of human baseness in a soldier's cavalier use of one of her towels to polish his boots!

'So you see, Simon, I guess not everyone was "swept up", as you put it.'

Mallory looked at Hengelow steadily for some moments before saying. 'I accept the homily. But I don't need to be patronised.'

'My dear fellow, I didn't mean...'

Later, as they stepped off the launch at Landungsbrücken, Hengelow leaned across to Jeb. 'Keen on the war is he, your pal?'

'He thinks we're all under its spell, the generation who took part, and those who came after.'

'It was our affair, my generation's. He should think himself lucky to have been born afterwards.'

They ate together in a restaurant and, as if to mollify Mallory, Hengelow talked with charm and humour about airfield life, the peculiarities of the fellows who shared his Nissen hut, the pubs in the nearby Lincolnshire villages, the technicalities of the various aircraft he had flown. Neutral stuff. He avoided mention of their target cities.

At one point in the meal he mentioned casually that he had to go to Darmstadt. The announcement appeared to take Ronya by surprise, for she looked up sharply from her plate, though she said nothing.

'We'll escort you. We were due to head south ourselves,' Jeb suggested, looking uneasily at Ronya.

'I usually try to catch a lorry.' But Mallory and Jeb between them persuaded him to come with them on the train. 'It'll be a chance for a good yatter, I guess. What's taking you fellows south?'

'We were going to look for Nazi gold in the Alps,' Jeb answered immediately. Then he flushed, and turned to Ronya, 'Look, I'm sorry, I suppose you must get sick of every foreigner talking about Nazis.'

'Why should it be a problem? It is no problem. I am only a small child at the end of the war. What do I care? I hope you find the gold of the Nazis. I hope you both will be rich.' She was annoyed, Jeb saw, but not about Nazis. He glanced at Elli at the other end of the table, Elli with her pale lump-of-clay face. She was looking directly back at him, the inscrutable smile-fixture levelled at him, with its suggestion both of kindly exhortation and utter indifference.

Later that night, after they had returned to the apartment, there was a stifled little row between Hengelow and Ronya, which ended with the man affecting to read the newspaper

as though nothing untoward had happened, and Ronya busying
herself in the kitchen, her shoulders hunched against the other
occupants of her mother's apartment. The quarrel, Jeb
gathered, had something to do with Darmstadt.

9

Even as he came up out of his dream, Jeb found himself
trying to soften its effect by accounting for its sources. At
university he had read up a little on the physiology of dreams
and he had found this practical method worked when dealing
with his not-infrequent nightmares.

So, as he analysed, what had been a quite chemical terror
began to subside. He could feel the sinews of his body gradually
relax. It would be all right.

He stared out of the window, at the margin of night sky,
faintly luminous, graphite in colour, but green-tinged, like
a solution in a laboratory flask. In the top right-hand corner
of the frame the red light on a mast, something to do with
the docks, winked on-off, on-off; hypnotic, relentless. He
was sweaty and could feel the mesh of the campbed springs
under him and hear the roar of the traffic on Stresemann
Strasse and Elbechaussee. There had been the exhibition he
and Mallory had looked at the other day, and one of the
films they had used for consciousness-raising in the anti-war
movement — a black-and-white documentary style piece
about a nuclear attack on Canterbury — that had contributed;
and Elli's face.

In the nightmare he had been with Mother, Len and Hengelow in a confined, concrete place. At the beginning Ronya
— or Roma? — had been there too, but then she had gone,
or merged into Mother, it was unclear. Dad had not been
present. There were no light bulbs, yet there was, from some
undisclosed source, a thin pallor of light in the gloom which
allowed him to see that the walls of this chamber, or whatever
it was, were very high, and massive. All around them there
was uproar, concussion after concussion, so that the ground
and the walls, for all their massiveness, were continually
trembling. But the concussions were only lesser or greater
climaxes in the more ambient, the more inexorable drone

of aircraft. They could hear them passing overhead, what sounded like hundreds, no, thousands, of large aeroplanes, four-engined jobs at least, Lancasters, Stirlings, Halifaxes, and his understanding in the dream was that the planes had been passing over for several weeks and might do so forever.

Yes, the earth trembled. It did not quake. It trembled. It was not an obviously violent motion, and yet it was deeply violent, because it conveyed the sense that nothing anywhere was still or stable, not on the other side of the world, not at the centre of the world. Nothing could be still. In the dream this had planted in Jeb a terror which he seemed to feel with his entire body. It huddled in him and took the exact shape he was. It was a feeling of radical insecurity, that nothing, not the earth nor anything on it, could be relied upon to hold firm under the seemingly endless onslaught. It was a terrifying exposure to one of the fundamental and simple facts of the universe, that everything can disappear, that nothing can be trusted. This, he realised, both in the dream, and as he came out of it, was the meaning of aerial bombardment, this trembling of the earth, this reverberation of the skies.

And the dust! A rain of thin dust falling on everyone and everything, shaken from shelves, cornices, rafters, from all the unreachable crevices of human habitations, where it might have been lying for hundreds of years, now coating their hair and shoulders. Mother's chestnut-gleamy hair (she looked younger than she had ever been in Jeb's life) was dull and powdery. Dust was in their mouths. He could grind it between his teeth. He could see it on Len's eyelashes.

In the dream he had realised that they were somehow in the city during the notorious firestorm raids of 1943; this was the eerie part of it, to be caught up in an event, the horrendous outcome of which, the historical significance of which, he already knew at the very time that it was thundering and crashing outside the shelter, if shelter it was, as though it were a matter of course that one could simply enter the historical stream at any point, charged with a knowledge of the outcome.

Then Len had risen to his feet and said, 'I am going to

take Dad out of all this.' And he lifted his father, lightly, as though the latter's long figure were no more weight than a shop mannequin and, stumbling over the legs and bodies of hundreds of huddled people, he made for a door. Jeb and Mother followed, protesting that it was not safe. Together they emerged onto a street. There were bits of fire like confetti, flying through the air in one direction. They walked in the face of the fierce, hot wind that was driving the sparks, and which stung their eyes. He saw items of clothing or pieces of newspaper hurled downwind, igniting and shrivelling to nothing as they went, as though by sorcery. He was very young in the dream, he realised, and he had the idea that Len was in fact his father rather than his half-brother. Mother seemed to accept the direction in which Len was leading them. There was a ship, Len was saying, there was a ship waiting for them at the docks, which would enable them to get away. Sometimes they met people who were being compelled downwind, their backs arched like sails as they struggled against the invisible force; they shouted to Jeb and his family to return to the shelter. Jeb found it quite natural that they all spoke English, and quite natural that Mother, Len and he should prevail against the strength of the hot, dry blast while these other people could not. They passed what looked as if it had once been an ornamental lake and saw it was full of people's heads. Some of these heads called to them. At one point they had to move onto the pavement because the road had melted. There were people stuck in the asphalt, on their hands and knees, trying to pull out their limbs from the searing, sticky substance. Their mouths were opening and shutting as though they were calling out, but Jeb could hear nothing, and the burns on their faces had melted down their features so that they seemed crude and puppet-like. Then the four of them were passing lump-like things on the road which Len forbade both Mother and him to look at, but Jeb could not help but glance. They had been people, he realised. They lay with their faces to the pavement and their arms over their heads, as though protectively. There was one which consisted of a head and body with charred stumps where the legs and hands had been. Its clothes had been scorched off for the most part. Unlike the other lump-things, the face was turned towards him; there was no hair or eyebrows, and the eyes were slits of black coal, half closed, like a person assessing the quality of something. A little further there was a group of bodies, very pale, apparently unscathed by the fires but for the fact that their clothing had been burnt off them. They were still wearing their shoes.

All the while Len trudged, slightly ahead of them, calling back advice over his shoulder, leaning forward to balance the long, dangling body of Hengelow. 'Keep your pecker up! Shan't be long now,' he called, and from these cheery exhortations and the phlegmatic way in which he hefted his burden, it seemed he was little affected by the danger and devastation around them.

Their march through the streets of the burning city, attended always by the mighty roar of the aircraft high above them, had all the confusion of duration that characterises dreams — it was years, it was seconds. Until, disconnectedly, they were at the waterside where there was a ship and a long queue of people holding pieces of white paper which two men near a gangplank were inspecting, and Jeb was filled with panic because he knew they did not possess the piece of white paper. Len assured them that this did not matter and, directing Mother and him to follow his lead, he marched with his burden straight past the two officials who simply nodded their heads when they saw it was Len and waved him past onto the ship. Once on board they stood on the foredeck. Len placed his father on a seat of wooden slats. Jeb was puzzled by Hengelow and looked at his face. His eyes were open and staring downward as though he were quite unaware of all that was going on around him. There was no sign that he was alive and yet Jeb had the understanding that he was. It was while the boy stood staring at his long, bony face, the red glow of the incendiary-bomb fires flickering on one of his cheeks, that he woke up to find himself regarding the winking red light outside the window. A block or two away he could hear the thunder of traffic on the main thoroughfares.

He rummaged in his pack for a pen and notebook and

began writing down the details of the dream as he could remember them, accounting for the images as he went along. By the time he had it all on paper he could see its mythological parallel. He had never actually read the story of Aeneas carrying his father Anchises from burning Troy, though he was familiar with it from somewhere. The parallel both pleased him with its fortuity, and troubled him. He wondered if he should tell Mallory about it, but decided against it. Things were changing between him and Mallory. It was difficult to say how. Mallory would have an interpretation that would be too ready, too clever. Or he would be subtly dismissive. Maybe their differences would clear up once they were on the move again.

Train Conversation

1

In the morning Mallory went by himself into town and returned with three inter-city tickets. 'My treat,' he told his two fellow travellers.

'Inter-city! Dear boy, they must have cost a fortune!'

'I've never yet been out of pocket. It's one of my problems. Accept the ticket in return for the hospitality of,' he put his hand on Elli's shoulder, '*meine besondere Freunde.*' Hengelow watched the gesture with approval. Jeb wasn't so sure. Again, rather uncharitably, he suspected Mallory was trying to please.

In the early evening they made their farewells. Hengelow hugged Ronya and Elli in turn, embraces which, Jeb thought, were not so much formal as a bit stagy. A bit overdone. Their Charlie was only going away for a week or so, wasn't he? The big man stood clasping the red-haired mother with his face set on one side and a rather stylised expression of affection and sorrow on it. Jeb had no right, he realised, to question the sincerity of the man's feelings, but the embrace looked as if it had been learned.

Learned. Certainly in comparison to the spontaneous way which Elli buried her face in the shabby fawn raincoat, or the impatient way Ronya released herself quickly from his clasp, then, in affectionate, slightly pained afterthought, straightened his collar and fastened the buttons. With Jeb and Mallory, Ronya shook hands formally, though when she came to inviting them to come and stay with her again, it was Mallory she looked at. Jeb shook Elli's hand and mouthed off some conventional things as she grin-nodded at him. Mallory had hugged her and made a joke about *ihren Liebsten*.

As the three of them walked out into the blue evening, Hengelow turned to Mallory.

'Dear old Elli. She's over sixty, you know. Hard to tell, isn't it? She told you what happened? Her burns? I think you'll always be welcome there, Simon.'

'I like them.' They walked on toward the U-Bahn in silence for some minutes before Mallory said, 'I guessed they weren't just saying goodbye to you for a couple of days.'

Hengelow didn't respond immediately. Then he said, 'Hard to tell, old man. In all the places where I have tried to set up the kind of thing you have seen in the last week, I discover the great kindness of people. I will see Ronya and Elli again, of course. In the fullness of time.'

'You're leaving them for good?'

'Hardly for good, Jeb.'

But for some time, obviously. So why had there been no warning of this until in the restaurant last night? Why so sudden?

'What happens about the safe house — all your work?'

'Sig is quite ready to take over. He and some of the others will keep up the good work. Elli's apartment, I imagine, will still be available. There are other Hamburg safe houses. A couple in Eimsbüttel, a couple in Hammerbrook.'

'But how come you can just leave it like that?'

'Darmstadt calls, old man,' Hengelow said, airily.

Jeb fell back and walked a pace or two behind as they went down into the Underground. The explanation was not good enough. He wondered whether it was simply a case that Hengelow had grown weary of Roni and Elli, of the Altona apartment. Insidious warmth? They boarded a train. Was it charity that compelled this journey to Darmstadt, he wondered as he listened to the whine of the U-Bahn, the pouff! of the automatic doors, or restlessness? He put the thought out of mind as unworthy. Had he not seen how people worshipped Hengelow — Charlie — how he dedicated himself so completely to helping the unfortunate. You can't criticise people who have committed their entire lives to good works. There was something unassailable about them. But what had Mother meant?

2

As though propelled on a cushion of air, the three were rushed by the Inter-city southward, across the vast Lüneberger Heide, for the most part in an unwaveringly straight line, but occasionally leaning into a long, shallow curve. There were none of the sounds one associates with trains, the clickety-clack of the wheels over the rail-jointures, or the ticca-ticca-ticca as the carriages went over points. It was more like travelling in a private jet. One sank into the green upholstery and watched through the aquarium-size windows as the seven o'clock after-sun gave the newly furrowed fields a last orange tinge and the odd lake a last dazzling burnish. Mallory, relaxing into the plush seats, looked at home. Hengelow, in his creased raincoat, looked incongruous.

'You know,' Mallory began, 'this whole part of Europe; it's like an exercise in clear thinking. The ruled-off look, the clear-cut edges to things. The sense of there being no waste. Every tiny parcel of land made productive. You can't believe in inefficiency in this landscape. Or respite. Hard-edged,' his eyes twinkled as he emphasised these two words, 'and you get the feeling that the whole machine, agriculture, industry, offices, is working at maximum capacity. It's startling and impressive. But there's the sense of no reserves, and that makes it, well, sad, as well, in comparison to what I grew up with, at least.' He stared out of the window for a few moments, then added, 'It makes me feel homesick for Australia.'

'Won't be long before that fills up too. Bit of a surfeit of the human resource in the world,' Hengelow observed. 'But then, beyond swallowing pills or wearing rubber things, not much one can do about it. How does one cull individuals, I wonder.'

Jeb listened and looked out into the gloom, remembering the immense spaces, the forests and wheatfields, the long journeys south on the camping trips of his boyhood. He had discovered new possibilities of freedom and space during his childhood in Oldenrath. But he knew there was truth in what Mallory and Hengelow were saying, so he remained silent. The recent visit to Oldenrath garrison had been deflating, and his experience generally, of both Britain and those parts of Europe they had crossed so far, was at variance with what he thought had been the boundlessness of his childhood at Gattisby and Oldenrath.

'I think if I lived here, I would always feel programmed,' Mallory ended by saying.

'Oh crikey, it was a mess when I first saw it,' observed Hengelow.

They passed through Hannover, where the train stopped for five minutes. Then they were hurtled southward again. Sometime after ten Jeb saw Mallory with his eyes shut and his features in repose, his forehead rocking slightly against the glass. He assumed he was asleep. Hengelow was sitting upright, smoking, taking little interest in what was outside the window. All at once he began.

'You came here for an explanation, old man. As to why I walked out on your mother.' The abruptness with which the subject was broached took Jeb a little aback. Yes, it was exactly what he had wanted to discover.

'I wanted to fill in a bit of the family history. That was all really.'

'I'm not sure history, family or otherwise, offers itself up for explanation. I once had a dream in which I was being given some vital documents to safeguard. The documents consisted of powdery lettering on perspex tablets, and almost in the same moment I was handed them my sleeve had brushed over the lettering, making it illegible. Always remembered that dream. Vivid. I sometimes think the past is like that — spoiled handwriting. Illegible. Because the present from which it is made, is too delicate, too intricate, too ephemeral to be transferred. It's as if the micro-organisms were dead before they got to the microscope. Still, we know some things, don't we?'

'Eva told me a bit. Mother didn't ever talk about you.

Not that it was an explicit taboo, just a feeling we had around the house. We had a painting which ended up in a cupboard . . .'

'That painting! So Lizzie hung onto it. It was quite a good likeness, if I recall. Done by a squadron pal of mine, Albert Chesney; got the chop on one of our Mannheim runs, poor fellow.' Hengelow smoked in silence for some moments before resuming.

'You'd be surprised how good a qualification modern languages turned out to be when I qualified as a bomb-aimer in the air force. I came through the war unscathed, you see. Enlisted early '42, and joined my squadron early '43. Well, I completed two operational tours and not once did we cop a packet. Once or twice the odd night fighter came snooping, but our rear-gunner was a genius of alertness — ended up a hopeless drunk after the war, poor fellow. Lots of flak, of course. You could watch it, slow, like water from a hose, and hear it sometimes — pok-pok-pok-pok. But we were never damaged by anything worse than ice. We led a charmed existence.

'This was fairly rare. Fellows I knew, like Albie, were disappearing all the time, killed for the most part, that was the way of it — bomber command losses were the worst in the war. Of course we saw a few poor devils going down. Yet our crew flew out and back sixty-odd times. But for the target, we might have been a taxi run.

'I had a belief, a superstition if you like. I thought, if I do as little thinking about the business as possible, if I just do the job, reflexively, setting the fuses, sighting up over the target, guiding the skipper in, left a little, right a little, steady, spot on, bombs away in their sequence, check for hang-ups, settle back for the return trip, sometimes taking my turn at the flare chute to chuck out leaflets, or the little metallised strips we used to jam the Jerry radar, then I'd come through all right. It was like saying to one's consciousness, Look, just wait outside for a bit, OK? It was immediate, but out of consideration, if you see what I mean. Sly mental gymnastics.

'So I thought, if we got the chop, then that's the way the event might happen, a background that would steal up unawares and snuff me before I knew what had happened. No use thinking about it. I put a bit of time into the technicalities, what was called the Mark 14 bomb-sight, its computer and so on. I was reckoned to be moderately effective. Old Spot-on, they called me, because that's what I used to say all the time. Spot on, Leo, spot on, old man. Leo was our pilot, an Australian, as it happens.' Hengelow stopped, shook out another cigarette from his packet, and lit it. Then he resumed.

'I hated saying goodbyes. Part of the superstition, I suppose. But I felt that I had to pretend there were no — discontinuities. I could explain this to Lizzie when I saw her, but it would have been a bit hard on Lennie. He was five in '43. How do you tell a five-year-old that an adult finds wishing him goodbye an unbearable thing to do? God knows how he interpreted it.' He dragged on the cigarette.

'We weren't naive. We knew what it was we were being asked to do . . .'

'Which was?' Jeb interposed.

'Bring cities to a halt. Put down such a burden of devastation and fire that life became impossible for the people in whichever target city was chosen. This wasn't the object of every raid. Far from it. But it was the strategy of the Hamburg raids of '43, and those on Düren, Darmstadt, Saarbrücken, Cologne, the Berlin raids, and the Dresden operation in February '45. It was called area bombing.

'What I'm getting around to saying is that when, at the end of the war, I flew over some of those cities in daylight, the extent of the catastrophe came as a shock. You'd think I would have had a good vantage to observe it, lying on my belly looking down through my little bubble at the front of the aeroplane. Well, it was night, and all one really saw was fireworks and a shadowy grid of streets. There were the photographs we took, or those taken by aerial reconnaissance the day after, but they didn't disclose anything particularly human. Besides I was looking at them professionally, rigorously so. It was part of the mechanism of not taking a wider interest, of putting certain things out of consideration. Of course I saw the bombs going off, and the fires, but at twenty thousand feet — well, to tell the truth, it all looked rather beautiful, the green and red marker flares, the thousands of incendiaries, the concentric shocks of the high-explosive stuff. I knew, as a casual abstract fact, that I was looking at havoc, devastation, misery. But what I saw in all that pyrotechnics was beauty. Stunning, momentary loveliness. What an appalling admission to have to make.'

Jeb heard Mallory emit a grunt. Was it approbation? sympathy? Impossible to tell.

'As I say, came through unscathed. Or perhaps not. Your mother thought not. She said I got a delayed action wound. Like our rear-gunner, only with me it wasn't drink but this habit of putting things out of consideration. Not that it worked for everything, as you'll see. Still, maybe Lizzie was right. She was very bitter when I decamped. Rightly, of course.

'At the very end, from about March or April '45, many of us were employed in food drops over Holland and ferrying home all the prisoners of war, twenty-three bods per load. We flew over by day, so this was the period I started to see our handiwork a little. We were flying into Brussels at first — not much to see there, but later it was Bremen and some of the German towns after the armies had been through them. Then the war stopped. There was a day, not of anarchy exactly, this was service life, but a day when fellows seemed to be jumping into aeroplanes and going for junkets over some of the target towns. It was to give the ground crews a look at what we had been up to all those years. My skipper chose to have a look at Hamburg — we'd been there twice in '43 and again in early '45. As well as our groundcrew, he took me, the navigator and the flight engineer.

'It was a fairly cheerful trip out, I recall. Our groundcrew was a decent set of fellows. Perhaps the decency was what struck them dumb, struck us *all* dumb, as we circled around the centre of what had been Hamburg. You're lucky. You were born afterwards, old chap. You cannot conceive the calamity of that destruction. What we saw were hundreds of five-storey residential buildings gutted by fire. Not blown apart. There was the odd gap where a high-explosive bomb had gone off, but mostly what struck one was how eerily intact they were. They stood like elaborate houses of cards. As we flew over, you could see right down into them, no roofs or floors, just high fragile-looking walls. Shells. Not a sign of life. Nor a sign that there had been life — and we came down to a couple of thousand feet at one point. It was like looking at some intricate colony which insects had built and abandoned long ago.

'It was fascinating. Yes, I mean that word, *fascinating*. And beautiful too, in its dreadful way, until one began to wonder what had happened to the people who had been through all that fire.' Hengelow's voice was even, but Jeb thought he saw the corner of one of his eyes glistening. As he spoke he stared fixedly at the cigarette pack on the laminex table before him.

'As I did. Not that I tried. But those intricate, vacant inner suburbs stuck in my mind. It was as if, after that trip, my life, which had been freewheeling along, was put onto rails and given a push in a particular direction. I wanted to look at that destruction again. No, that's not quite right. It wanted to see me again. That's how it felt. It wanted to see me.

'I was in luck, you might say. Our squadron got the job of ferrying officials across to Germany at the time they were setting up the civil administration. I was waiting on my de-mob, so came along once or twice for the ride — officially a sort of flight attendant, my own expertise not being needed now that peace had broken out. We flew into the ex-night-fighter field at Stade. This would have been a month or so after the war ended.

'We landed about mid-morning, and had a wait. The fellows went to the airfield's canteen, but, without any strong incli-nations, I cadged a ride with an RASC chap in a jeep who was going into Hamburg, which was some twenty miles down the road.

'How did it feel, being on those rails, pushed toward an event? People don't sense their fates hanging above their heads. I think I felt curiosity, maybe, and a desire to provide congenial company for my driver. He drove me into that centre and we cruised about under the shells of those buildings I had seen from the air a month or so before.

'You must understand that the bombing I had seen else-where, in London, in Hull, gave the impression of being haphazard, local, capricious almost. A house or a row of houses here, a factory there. The effect was spread, diffuse. But this was methodical, efficient, comprehensive. "You lads sure knocked this place about," my driver kept saying to me. Knocked about? It was impossible to conceive how life could have survived such intense incendiarism. High explosive doesn't leave very much behind, a hole and some rubble — but you get the sense of being able to start again. But incendiaries, they leave a husk where a city was, as if the life had been sucked out with the smoke.

'A little life had survived. There were groups of women here and there, mostly in black, forming long lines and passing buckets filled with rubble. It was women who began the task of reconstruction — the menfolk were either dead or still prisoners. I left my jeep and took a wander. Again, I can't say there was much by way of purpose in my mind. But I was on those rails all right, which was how I came to meet her, the woman, I mean.

'Oh, I know you can't talk about things being predestined like that, but do you think one just strikes up a conversation with people at random? Or for deeply veiled unconscious motives? Bother the unconscious motives. Predestination is how it seemed on this occasion.

'She was in one of the gangs. They had stopped work and were sitting around drinking water; they may have had the odd scrap to eat, I can't recall. She had gingery hair, not as fiery red as Elli's, rather dusty, and cut in that severe wedge shape that was fashionable before the war and after. I can fix her image vividly in my mind's eye now, even though it's been thirty years. I'd say she was in her late twenties, maybe older, modest, and a way of tilting her head when listening that suggested she was intelligent and perhaps whimsical. I watched her for a bit. One of the women, a big lady, was making the rest of them laugh — can you imagine it, they were sitting on the wreckage of their city throwing back their heads in laughter! But my girl — she *seemed* young, though worn, emptied out almost — tended more to smile and look at her feet, as if she wasn't sure she'd been given permission to lose herself in jollity.

'Our orders were not to fraternise, but few people were taking much notice of that. I started talking to her. She was not unfriendly. I asked her questions. She had a husband, but he was away still, in the south, a prisoner of the Americans, she hoped. She hadn't heard that he was dead, at least.

'"*Haben Sie Kinder?*" I asked. What an unbelievably complacent question that was.

'"*Keine Kinder*," she answered, and looked down at the rubble around her feet. The action gave her away, I suppose, though what possessed me to utter my next question, I don't know.

'"*Nimmer?*" I persisted. What a deadly little question it was, yet I think I asked it as though I were asking her whether she had ever owned a fur coat or a pair of silk stockings. What was I hoping to find out? I can only plead that I had been left in a bit of a daze by the ruins all around me. I got what I asked for.

'"*Keine Kinder mehr*," she informed me.

'Only now did my instinct tell me to change the subject. But too late. She was going to tell me now. "*Zwei Mädchen, einen Junge; neun Jahre, sieben Jahre, vier Jahre alt. Neunzehnhundertdreiundvierzig im Feuer verbrannt . . . Mit ihren Großeltern.*" Then she glanced at me quickly before lowering her eyes to the rubble at her feet again. The other women were no longer taking any interest in our little confab.

'What she said next was not in what I would call an accusatory voice. It was stated matter-of-fact, as though she were saying I was tall, or had curly hair. But she looked me straight in the eyes and considered me. "*Es ist eure . . . nein, es ist Ihre Schuld*," she informed me.' Hengelow looked up at Jeb. The gleam in the corner of his eye seemed to have disappeared.

'Bowled me over, that did. Do you see what I mean when I say modern languages is as good a qualification as any to go bombing with. "*Es ist eure . . . nein, es ist Ihre Schuld.*" How good is your German, old man? Do you see what she was saying? She had begun by declaring that we were all collectively

guilty, then she had changed her mind and told me that I,
in particular, was to blame. Perhaps she thought my persistence
in asking about whether she had children was prying, or
gloating, and she would give me a little emotional shock for
my troubles. She did that. Yes, she had stated, simply and
inarguably that I, as an individual, was answerable for the
death by fire of her three children. And I recognised the moral
logic. Despite all the excuses and pretexts of the time, I had
put myself in the way of dropping bombs on her city, and
I was answerable. The fact that thousands of other chaps from
both sides, swept up in the same spirit, all did the same thing,
did not alter my answerability one iota.

'I think I muttered a "*Ja*," and "*Es tut mir leid*," something
to fill in the silence after her flat statement? And then I
simply wandered off, stunned by the havoc, the unimaginable
human misery I'd bumped into, so casually, as it were. I
suppose the length of time she looked directly into my eyes
was about ten seconds. Incredible, isn't it, what a hold on
you ten seconds can have.'

Hengelow stared down at his long fingers. On his right
hand they were orange with nicotine. It seemed he had come
to the end of his story.

After a silence of perhaps a minute, Jeb cleared his throat
and asked, 'But what about the German atrocities? The camps,
the mobile gas chambers? What about their devastation of
Rotterdam, Coventry, Belgrade? Surely you —'

'Dear boy, there are all those terrible things. But it has
never seemed to me that it is my job to reckon up the balance
of atrocities. They are not what I was confronted with. I
was confronted with a mother whose three children together
with their grandparents had been burnt to death in the 1943
bombing of Hamburg and who held me responsible.' He drew
on his cigarette and looked out of the window for some
moments, then resumed. 'As it happens, I had been on those
firestorm raids. But that fact made little difference. I would
have felt compelled by her simple statement even if I hadn't.
She could have been a woman from Düren, or Wesel, or
Saarbrücken. I flew against those places too.'

He stopped and the three of them were silent for a time,

then Hengelow took up his meditation again. 'You see, the problem was this. I had been a man of war, a particularly effective one. And a lucky one. And I had to make myself into a man of peace. So that it *meant* something. That's what I was kept alive for. And as I considered what it did mean, I realised what an awesome gulf it was, between the two, man of war and man of peace.

'Sadly, it became clear to me in the years after the war that I could not do that satisfactorily if I remained with Lizzie and Len. You'd be amazed how much personal freedom an expiation requires.' He gave a little laugh.

'But what makes you such a special individual that it is your reaction that matters so much?' Jeb wondered if his question had been too brutal. Since meeting Hengelow five days ago, Jeb had found he harboured contradictory feelings toward this man his mother had once been married to; a tender regard for a person he did not wish to hurt, with odd moments of antagonism he could neither quell nor account for.

But if Hengelow was stung by the question, it didn't register. He looked out of the train window for a few moments. The smile never seemed to leave his face, yet in the short space of their acquaintance, Jeb had already seen it mean so many different things; welcome, various kinds of amusement, embarrassment, or, as now, the cover for an ironic and exquisite vulnerability. The train was hurtling through the darkness, though there was nothing beyond their own reflections that Jeb could see in the glass. Mallory, Jeb noticed, had his eyes open.

At length Hengelow said, 'I thought that was what we were fighting for, old man — the fact that an individual's position in the world matters.' He regarded Jeb and his smile now looked apologetic, as though he were sorry he had to remind a young, educated man of so elementary a fact.

3

For maybe ten minutes, Hengelow was silent, his body swaying slightly with the smooth rhythm of the train, his hands clasped loosely on his lap, his eyes staring straight ahead. He might have been praying. Jeb watched his reflection in the window. Apart from the odd neon lights of a hamlet, or the sudden flood of light as they flashed past a service station, there was nothing to break the illusion that the reflection in the window was the real world and there was nothing outside. So deeply immersed in his own contemplation did Jeb become that he didn't immediately hear when Hengelow had begun talking again.

'. . . so it didn't dawn on me for a few years that Lizzie and I needed to go our separate ways. I started collecting all the information I could, numbers of casualties, of homeless, all that sort of thing. I saturated myself in the statistics, all the things I had carefully ignored while flying. It was obsessive and futile, of course. You can't get an idea of human misery from the figures. But it was a stage I had to go through. This was pretty trying for Lizzie, particularly since, for a period in '46, I was around the house all day. I wasn't looking for work then, and using up savings. I suppose I became rather tiresome. I'd bring people back to the house, tramps and suchlike, offer them a meal, or a bed for a night or two. Sometimes they were reluctant to move on.

'Yes, I must have been a trial. Not that Lizzie wasn't good about it at first. She put up with all manner of unsavoury things. What a sanguine soul your mother was in those days — still is, I'm sure. But she had taken hold of the idea that I was, well, going against myself with this kind of Samaritanism. We were very young when we married, barely into our twenties. We'd talked about setting something up together, a college or something in Bechuanaland or Papua, building from scratch, all our own ideas. Lizzie had thrown herself into the life of the school. She was popular. Then, when I went away, she was adamant she had to do something significant for the war effort too. But Len had come along by then. Of course she had the hard job of worrying about my safety, not seeing me for months. Inactivity is a damn sight harder to bear than danger, don't you think? Perhaps she was right to feel cheated by the fact that I had a proper activity and she did not.

'Oh, it all became somehow messy and confusing. I couldn't

understand how something so good could turn in on itself, as our marriage did. Do you mind me carrying on like this, old man? I haven't really put it all into words before. I tried once or twice to explain it to Evie. As a kid she was my confidante. But things change, don't they. I miss being a kid sometimes. Don't you?' He didn't wait for Jeb to reply.

'Well, then my parents both died within about a year of each other — this was '46 and '47. Evie and I came into a bit of property.

'Well, that did it. I had been one of the few who were spared, and then I had been handed a small family fortune. For what? I couldn't evade *that* question, you see. Why did it trouble me so? I'd been brought up religious, but I'd tossed religion before the war, and the war did nothing to rekindle it. I'd been on the edge of the Communists at one stage just after I started teaching, but I'd chucked that too.'

'Yes, Eva said . . .'

'I applied for a job with the civil administration in Germany in November '47. Evie helped with that — she'd been administrator of a hospital and had some well-placed acquaintances. I suppose the arrangement with Lizzie was that I would nip back across every three months or so and see her and Len. But things between the two of us were pretty shaky by then. And I knew, deep down, what I was going to do once I went over.

'I wanted to deal face to face with my people, those I came across in the random process of conducting everyday affairs. "Love thy neighbour as thyself." I hadn't forgotten all my religion.'

Jeb recalled his conversation with Eva a fortnight or so before. 'I have no trouble in finding a ground for action,' she had said.

'But who was my neighbour?' Hengelow continued. 'I've heard clergymen argue it is all of mankind. The Socialist polemic that all men are brothers runs on the same line. It's wrong. Christ used the word "neighbour". That's the fellow alongside you. But in the parable the man who gives succour is a foreigner and a traveller. That affected me too.

'You see, it was delicate. That woman and her three dead

kids. What an *awesome* loss.' Jeb noted the stress Hengelow placed on that word 'awesome'. It was the word Mallory had used.

'I couldn't abide the misery I saw around me at the end of the war — can't abide misery, full stop. I suppose Lizzie was right, it was a kind of neurosis. But I owed my neighbour a life, and I knew it was my job to seek my neighbour out and offer such charity as I could, but it had to be charity as between one human being and another. It was *my* life I owed. And *my* life I intended to give. Furthermore, having dropped bombs on people I *couldn't* see, I was at least going to try and atone for that by helping people I *could* see. So the agencies were out. Besides, at a national level, the Germans were pretty keen on repairing the damage to both their country and their society themselves. I soon found that out. The postwar miracle, as it was called. The word hides a colossal human effort.

'No, what I felt compelled, yes, compelled, to do didn't have anything to do with rebuilding a nation. I felt I had to burrow in among the people until I could see their individual faces. I wanted to put myself at the disposal of this one and that one and I became attracted to those mendicant religious orders of the Middle Ages.

'From the early fifties I've wandered around Germany, Holland, England, on foot for a lot of it, or getting rides on lorries, being with people who don't have all that much, buying them a meal or a bed for the night, or a couple of bottles of Heineken. Then, from the late sixties I started to set up these safe houses in different places, using up my share of the Hengelow estate, and making good friends, like Elli and Ronya.'

Suddenly he sat upright in his seat and slapped his knee. 'Jiminy, but look how you've prompted me to become conceited about the whole thing. Or perhaps I needed no prompting.' He laughed, and stubbed out his cigarette in the ashtray, then almost immediately shook out another and lit it.

For ten minutes or so they did not speak and Jeb stared out of the window. At length he turned to Hengelow.

'Do you mind if I ask you something?'

'Fire away, dear fellow.'

'Do you think you'll ever be reconciled with Len again?'

Hengelow's long face seemed to grow grave. 'I don't see why not. Depends on Lennie a bit, doesn't it? I've tried, you know. Looking him up when he's at Evie's, or once or twice at his digs in Cromer or Nuneaton and elsewhere. I usually remember to post him a cheque at birthdays. It's him who avoids me, not the other way round.'

'Look, it may be none of my business...' Jeb began.

Hengelow looked at him steadily. 'You can say what you like, Jeb.'

'Well, it's just that, I know Len says he has no family...'

'He has his aunt.'

'... but I think it would do an enormous amount of good if — well — if things between you could be repaired.'

'Don't think I haven't tried.'

'What I'm saying is, I don't think his hostility, both towards our mother and towards you, is designed to repel either of you. I think — I'm not sure about this, but I think he wants to be rescued.'

'Do you?'

'It's like a child, say, who swims further and further out. The further he swims the more he wants Big Dad or someone to put the effort into swimming out and fetching him back. And, well,' Jeb faltered, then said, 'it's a matter of how much time there is. You're pushing sixty.'

Hengelow was shaking another cigarette from the packet. He had compressed his lips slightly and his eyes remained on the activity of his hands. Jeb sensed he had said something which had slipped under the older man's guard. At length Hengelow said, 'It's not much fun, you know, when one's son crosses the street to avoid meeting.'

'All right, I'm talking in the dark a bit because all of this happened before I was born. I can only remember Len from when I was a boy in England and at the camp in Oldenrath. When he came to Australia once, we didn't hit it off. But look at it this way, you've spent three decades facing up to what the war made you do —'

'And now I should face up to the family I deserted when

I ran off to appease my conscience. Did you really come all the way from Australia to tell me that?' There was just a hint of pique in Hengelow's voice.

'I wasn't going to put it like that.'

'It has crossed my mind over the past few days, you know, that you might be an accuser Lizzie has sent. As I say, she was bitter.'

'I'm not. I'm here on my own behalf.'

'So you think I'm to blame for causing Lizzie a lot of bitterness? I admit it, but it was thirty or so years ago. And she did re-marry. For screwing Lennie up. All right, he had an unsettled boyhood. I'll take the can for that. But he's a grownup fellow now.' The irritation had grown more obvious during this speech, but Hengelow's tone moderated when he said, 'People are more resilient than you think, old man.'

'I'm not talking about blame. It's just that all I know of Len adds up to a picture of someone who is incredibly — unconsoled.'

'Another war victim, you think?'

'Yes, in a way.'

'Like Elli?'

'No, of course not!'

'Let's drop the subject then.'

'I think there has to be peace,' Jeb found himself saying, 'between you and Len and you and my mother. And it's you have to make the peace. By contriving to see Len and by writing to my mother.' He was surprised to find that this was what he wanted, but it answered the case exactly. It would dissolve the perplexities that had lingered obstinately in the background of his own life since childhood, the heartache of contemplating his half-brother's resentment, his powerlessness on those occasions he had glimpsed Mother's bitterness, her stony silence on the subject of this part of her past, kept alive by the surname her eldest son continued to bear and a portrait at the back of a cupboard.

Hengelow looked at Jeb steadily for a few moments, then rose to his feet. 'I think you are indeed trespassing, old man.

I'm going to find a cup of tea from somewhere. Shall I bring you one?'

'No thanks.'

4

They had passed through Göttingen and Fulda. Now Jeb stared out at the middleground blackness which whipped past his own reflection in the window with enormous speed. Had he offended Hengelow? He found himself not caring very much, and the reaction startled him; for the story about the woman and her children was shocking, moving. Hengelow was impressive, of course. Jeb liked him, he supposed. So what had slightly soured this liking? The suspicion that all that warmth and charm was fake? It wasn't, not exactly. Yet the man did seem to walk out on people rather easily — Ronya and Elli, Mother, Len, others probably. Why shouldn't he? Because he had inspired their love, their devotion. Jeb wondered if indeed he had begun to regard Hengelow through the filter of some of Mother's grievance, if he was an accuser on her behalf. But it was all before he was born, before he 'was even thought of'.

He found Mallory looking at him. 'We arrive in about twenty minutes. I think Charlie plans to go straight on to Darmstadt.' Mallory paused, then added, 'You may want to say goodbye on good terms.'

'You were listening?'

'I couldn't very well not.'

Jeb went looking for Hengelow and found him in the corridor holding a cigarette and a styrofoam cup of black tea.

'I was very sorry to hear of your dad's death.' Hengelow remained looking out of the window, swaying slightly. 'Wilf was a good man. A kind man.'

'That's what everyone keeps saying.'

'Don't you think it's true?'

'He was my father.'

They swayed in silence for a little. The train passed through Offenbach without stopping.

'Did they get on well together, Lizzie and Wilf? In your view.'

'I suppose so. I never had to think about it. They danced well together. Why do you want to know?'

'I only ever wanted Lizzie to be happy.' He paused, then added, 'That's very much the kind of thing my generation was in the habit of saying about their wives. As though happiness was a pool you could simply plop someone into and watch them swimming about in for the rest of their lives.'

'Did you encourage my father's courtship with my mother?'

'I was trying to be practical. And I turned out to be right, didn't I?' The train had slowed and was moving quietly past suburban streets. '*Jetzt kommen wir in den Frankfurter Hauptbahnhof,*' he observed. They were engulfed by a vast neon-lit pavilion of glass and girdered steel. There was a voice booming on the station loudspeaker. Jeb realised Hengelow had taken him by the shoulder and was talking to him rapidly. 'You've hit home with one or two of the things you've said to me old man — that business of Lennie swimming out and wanting to be rescued. Maybe I've caused a deal of unhappiness that it's time I did something about. I'll go and see Lennie when I'm next in Britain. And I'll try and write to Lizzie. Odd to think that if there hadn't been a war, I might well have been your father. Now, I'll go quickly and get my things, and say an *Auf Wiedersehen* to Simon. He's an astute fellow, but he should forget the war. It's not his business.'

Jeb watched Hengelow walk away, then he called out, 'That woman was wrong. It was not your fault alone. You put yourself too much at the centre.'

Hengelow stopped and turned. He looked at Jeb quickly, and then at the floor of the carriage. There was a quizzical smile on his face. 'Ah, if I am guilty of putting myself too much at the centre, then the woman was right, wasn't she?' He disappeared into the compartment, leaving Jeb perplexed by the statement. The train had come to a stop beside the platform and there were people coming along the passage manoeuvring their suitcases past each other. Jeb could hear doors slamming along the length of the train. He began to return to the compartment and was passed by Hengelow coming the other way with the plastic bag that contained his few possessions. 'I've taken my leave of Simon. It has been splendid, your turning up like this, I can't tell you... Take care, old man.' He continued along the corridor and through the carriage door, inclining his head so as not to bump it. Jeb saw him merging with the passengers who were streaming toward the gate, a head and shoulders carried along by the tide.

5

It was midnight or thereabouts; no cheap hostel accommodation available at that hour, said the grey, balding man at the *Informationsbüro*. Mallory was for finding a hotel, no matter how expensive, but this was out too, said the cheerless informant, closing the glass.

'Let's find a park and doss down under a bush,' Jeb suggested.

'I'm not sleeping in a park. You've seen what goes on in parks.'

'There's two of us.'

'I prefer a roof over my head and an electric light.'

'There are no roofs. We've just been told that.'

'Then I'm staying here.'

'Sleeping out worries you?' Mallory made no answer to this, but sat down on a vinyl bench in the huge foyer of the Hauptbahnhof. 'Well I'm going to find a park.' Jeb began to walk away. Suddenly it had become unreasonable that he should have to cater to Mallory. He had covered fifty yards or so before he heard his companion behind him.

'All right. You don't need to leave me on my own.' It was the first time Jeb had seen him at all flustered.

They crossed the river and walked for some time until they came to a stadium on their right and an area of forest on their left. 'This is stupid,' Mallory muttered as they entered the trees. But he followed Jeb and when the latter crawled into the middle of a copse and spread out his sleeping bag on the bare ground, Mallory crawled in likewise; the sight of his dapper friend on all fours made Jeb want to burst out laughing.

The night was clear and moist and they were able to look at stars through the branches above their heads and hear the roar of the three a.m. traffic on all sides of them. Mallory seemed to have accepted the makeshift accommodation and, after tossing and turning in the effort to find a comfortable position, he lay still for some time.

'Are you still awake?' he asked at length.

'Why?'

'I was going to ask you what you made of Charlie?'

Jeb didn't reply for some moments. He was hesitant to use the word that had come immediately to mind. Then he decided to say it. 'I think he's an egotist.'

'Why?' asked his companion, quietly.

'All that business about destiny and his life being pushed along the rails. Oh, everything. Everything. It's the way he arouses expectations. Look how he was taking on the fathering of Roni's little boy, bathing him, all that stuff. Look at the effect he could have on Elli's morale. Now, with no warning, he effectively leaves them.' As he spoke, Jeb found he was convincing himself.

'How are Elli and Ronya to know whether or not it was simply a case that Uncle Charlie had grown tired of them all? What I ask myself is, Does he move from one place to another because he's needed in those locations, or simply because he gets restless? My mother might have wondered that when he left her after the war. I realise now that the more I was getting to know him, the more I found myself looking at him through my mother's eyes. Actually he hinted that that was what was happening.

'I can't work him out. He's percipient and insensitive at the same time. Maybe I'm being unfair to him. But thousands of blokes must have been affected by the war. I think he puts himself too much at the centre. I told him that.' They lay in silence for a minute or two looking up at the sky with its stars, like flecked bitumen. 'Anyway, what did you make of him?'

'I got what I came for.'

'Is that all?'

'Listening to what the war did to him, I feel now I've put in an important little bit in one of those 5000-piece jigsaws. He's a sannyasin. The war made him into a sannyasin.'

'A sann-what?'

'Sannyasin. They're Hindu holy men who wander around the countryside seeking the purification of their spirit, doing good works. The Christian church had some equivalent of this back in the Middle Ages. I admire him. I also think he's a case study.'

'That's a bit patronising.'

'Maybe.'

'He said you should forget about the war, that it was his business.'

'He's wrong. I live in the historical process.'

Again they were silent for a little. Jeb turned over and announced that he was now going to sleep. A siren was wailing over in the direction of the Hauptbahnhof. Perhaps five minutes went by.

'Jim?'

'What?'

'I'm returning to England tomorrow. I bought the ticket in Hamburg. I can't see the point of further travel. Not for myself. I prefer books on the whole.'

Jeb lay, curled on his side in the sleeping bag. He felt betrayed. 'How come you couldn't have let me know about your plans?'

'I didn't want them to influence yours.'

'Thanks a bunch.'

'You'll be better off on your own. If the truth be known, I don't think I'm very good company over long stretches. Perhaps I lack any real human involvement.'

'You sound like the man we left at the station.'

Jeb could hear the tension in Mallory's breathing even though the latter's reply was not immediately forthcoming. 'You are being unjust to an extraordinarily good man. I hope that fact will return to hurt you. Good night.'

Romannee Jermannee

1

He awoke from a dream involving Oldenrath and Len as
a boy. The canopy over his head was sprinkling sunlight on
the forest floor, highlighting here a patch of almost luminously
green grass, here a rust-gold fretwork of pine needles. He
could hear the roar of traffic, more urgent now than it had
been when he had finally fallen asleep in the small hours.
To his nostrils there came smells of resin, leaf mould, the
lanolin waterproofing of his sleeping bag, a trace of car
exhaust. Grey squirrels were scampering around the base of
trees, birds were rustling in the undergrowth. Romannee
Jermannee.

Mallory and all his gear had vanished, and Jeb had a reflex
to pack up and go home himself. There was something infectious in Mallory's observation about further travel being pointless. If Jeb was honest with himself, he realised it was an
obscure sense of duty rather than curiosity which beckoned
him to the museums, galleries, palaces and historical sites
of Treasurehouse Europe. So, beyond finding Hengelow, a
discovery accomplished more rapidly than he could have
expected, why had he come over here?

Romannee Jermannee. As he lay listening to the feral noises
in the undergrowth the phrase came back from his childhood.
Yes, his being here had been partly to do with discovering
Hengelow. But that, he told himself, was only half of it.

There had been at the back of his mind, scarcely articulate, another and related recovery he hankered to make. It was to do with a notion, a fragile, elusive idyll which he ascribed to his childhood, perhaps to all childhoods, that one could lose oneself in a time freed from the clock and calendar, wander across countries which were simply Country, where distances were irrelevant, that one could journey, not only far, but deep, deep into a kind of enchantment of terrain, a suspension of time's passing, where the actual and the imagined were one. One could become almost like a random particle fired across space, nameless, unattached, characterised only by one's movement.

For, as it seemed to him at that moment, this kind of life had always offered itself to him as one of the poles of existence, an opposite to the entanglement with people and their affairs. It was what he associated with Len on those occasions in the distant past when Len had run away from home or school. It was the childish idea he had formed of Hengelow's life at that same time. And, with Mallory gone, Hengelow and his concerns behind him, this idyll offered itself to Jeb now.

Perhaps, as Mallory had suggested, he did worship his childhood. But if the mysterious sensations and experiences which he thought he could recall from that time were what fascinated and puzzled him, then so be it. He would pursue the idyll by being simply 'on the road', by wandering, not especially in the direction of the cultural shrines, though he would take them in where he came across them, but toward whatever horizon lay in front of him. If this was romantic, then he welcomed it because romance was the only way of recovering the truth of so delicate and elusive a thing as he recalled this childhood idyll to have been. And maybe not just his childhood. There was Len and his wanderings, and Hengelow's restiveness. Was there not, in their *Wanderlust*, something to do with trying to recover those same delicious, remote sensations? Jeb focussed on this idea. It allayed the discouragement caused by Mallory's abrupt departure. He would not be a tourist, he would be a wanderer.

While the money held out.

On crawling out of the copse Jeb found himself being watched by a man in the uniform of a park warden. '*Camping verboten*,' the attendant told him, amicably, offering him the bottle of Coca-cola from which he had been drinking. The two stood, taking it in turns to swig, companionable for all that their conversation consisted of repeating their original '*Camping verboten*' and '*Es tut mir leid*,' several times. Slight as the encounter was, its cordiality, Jeb decided, was auspicious. People were well-disposed. He would not pack up and go home. Not yet.

He walked into the city centre, bought breakfast at a stand-up café, wrote a postcard to Aunt Eva saying he had made contact with Hengelow, then took a series of buses to the outskirts of Frankfurt, and began hitch-hiking south-eastward.

As with the trip across northern Germany a week before, he found it disconcerting how quickly the distances could be covered. By early afternoon he had skirted Würzburg and was in Nuremburg, wandering around the narrow streets of the *Alte Stadt*, under the walls of Barbarossa's fortress, through the low rooms of Dürer's house, charmed and vaguely oppressed by the picturesqueness of the red-brick, orange-tiled jumble of old buildings. He tried to imagine the monstrous banners, the blond men and women waving from the overhead windows as they had done in the Nazi Rallies of the 1930s, but it was not possible to see past the evidence of affluence, the gleaming duco of the sports cars, the tourists disgorging from their high plush coaches, the bright-coloured nylon rucksacks of American, Canadian and Australian hitch-hikers emblazoned with their various national emblems. Jeb quitted the city as it was getting dark and hitched south toward Ulm and the Alps.

In the three months that followed, he roamed across Europe, hitching rides, occasionally taking buses and trains, occasionally leaving the main routes to walk into the hinterland of villages and farms, never stopping anywhere for more than three days. He lived on bread rolls, cheese and salami, peanut or muesli bars, the occasional plate of soup or goulash, fruit, coffee, Coca-cola. He dossed down wherever he could find shelter, under hedges or bridges, in youth hostels, on building sites, once or twice, on nights of downpour, braving the barking of dogs to crawl into outlying barns, piling the hay high under himself then sleeping, blissfully, leaving before he might be found in the iron-grey light of daybreak.

High in the cabs of juggernaut trucks he would sit and shout conversations to the German, Dutch, Scandinavian, or Scots drivers above the engine-roar. '*Wohin fahren Sie?*' '*Nach Ankara... nach Tehran...* All the sodding way to Damascus, laddie!' The rides could be alarming, like with the driver who, when he stopped, announced that he had driven non-stop from Düsseldorf. '*Sage etwas. Sage etwas. Ich kann nicht halten. Ich muß nicht schlafen,*' he had kept requesting Jeb, between sticking his head out of the window to revive himself.

Near Klagenfurt the south-easterly trend of his wanderings was reversed when he was picked up by an American and his Berliner girlfriend in their campervan. With them he drove westward for a day along the valley of the Gail River, crossed into Italy, and camped that first night near Cortina beside a fast-flowing silt-coloured river under a mountain that fell, a breathtaking rock face, down to the opposite river bank.

'Stick around, John. We'll travel some.' For an unknown reason the American, whose own name appeared to be Doc, insisted on misprising Jeb's name.

'You will be our friend. I will like that very much,' the girlfriend, Dagmar, told him. Doc 'n Dagmar. They might have been in their early thirties. He was dark-bearded and wore an Afghan jacket. She was tall and wore flowing skirts and a blouse with mirror-fragments sewn onto it.

Jeb found the invitation disarming. 'Sounds beaut.'

Inside the Kombi, around the blue flame of a primus, the three of them huddled, passing a bottle of cheap red wine from hand to hand and drinking from it, talking, listening to the roar of the river outside. Jeb found himself babbling on about his background, Len, the RAF camps, Australia. Doc, it seemed, had hitch-hiked or Kombied around the world, through Peru, India, the Sudan. This was his third tour of Europe.

'I guess if people ask me what my occupation is, I have to say bird of passage.'

'What's the attraction?'

'Doc likes to grow. Travel is good for this. You think so too?' There was something a little startling about Dagmar. With luxuriant auburn hair which flowed down to the small of her back, her long face and nose, her upright carriage, she had the aspect of a gypsy matriarch. Her conversation, on the other hand, was like that of a secretary quoting from a language primer.

'Some people travel to extend themselves. Some people to console themselves. Which are you, John?'

'Consolation probably.' Jeb had meant the tone of his reply to be throwaway, but Dagmar placed a hand over his.

'This is very sad, I think.'

'I'm not unhappy.'

'It is perhaps because you don't know you are unhappy,' Dagmar informed him. Sometimes she sounded like something out of D.H. Lawrence. He regretted mentioning his Dad and Len in the conversation earlier. It had given them a false impression. He feared vaguely that they would slot him into the scheme of their sympathies.

They insisted he occupy the top bunk under their extendable roof. As he lay listening to the river's commotion outside he became aware of nearer sounds. Their sleeping bags appeared to rustle for far longer than might have been necessary to get comfortable. There came stifled grunts and squeals. Then Jeb became aware that the campervan was squeaking at its joints gently. The two beneath him were making love, he realised, apparently unconcerned by his presence just above them. What should he do? Get up and go for a walk? He couldn't, not without treading on them. Cough to remind them he was there? How could they have forgotten? The squeaking became more urgent, there was a grunt from Doc like that of a man clearing his throat before making an after-dinner speech, then silence for a period until the process began again. Only this time the squeaking of the Kombi's parts became more feverish, added to by the panting of Doc's breathing. He was like a runner on the last leg of a cross-country. Jeb found himself rigid with suspense. At last it began to arrive. Dagmar's own breathing became quicker and louder until she commenced to sing. Sing! No words, but a tune, or semi-tune, that sighed and mounted, sighed, rose, moderated in little variations, as if the voice itself were the control and not the expression of what was taking place in her body, now mounted with more urgency, subsided, then mounted in one last *sforzando*, as though freeing itself from the singer, leaving diminishing echoes of itself until there was no other sound but the river's uproar outside the van's windows. Jeb didn't dare move, fearing that if he did they would remember he was there and resent his involuntary voyeurism. But what if they had calculated on his being there? It crossed his mind that they might have wanted a witness. And had all that singing been real, or a piece of primal theatre put on for his benefit? He had nothing to compare it to except the one occasion of Roma's orgasm.

'You are lonely up here.' Dagmar's face was near his in the darkness. She had voiced a statement, not a question. For a wild instant Jeb imagined she was now going to start making love to him in his cramped alcove. But her interest was more purely therapeutic. 'You come and lie with us.' She had begun to haul him down.

'No, I'm right. Really.' This was awful. And it was impossible to hold onto anything, his hands being trapped inside the sleeping bag.

'You are lonely, I think,' she insisted. Down onto their bed he came with a crash, and found himself between them. There was a momentary glimpse of large pale thighs and a dark delta of pubic hair as Dagmar climbed back under the covers and put her arms around him. Doc had his face to the wall, apparently uninterested. 'People must tell their feelings, I think. There must be no shame. We are all like one another. Now you are our friend, John. You must give yourself more. You see. I can feel the tension in you.' She had partly unzipped his sleeping bag and, feeling inside his shirt, had placed her hand on his belly; he wondered if he was expected to put his hand on the corresponding part of her anatomy. 'Here, your stomach, the resistance. It is saying "No" to life; this is not good, I think.' Jeb tried to relax. He found his head pressed into her nightshirt; it smelt of sweat and perfume. He wondered uneasily what had happened to all Doc's sperm. 'We will go to sleep now, John. It is good to sleep in the arms of friends.' As he struggled to adjust his position so that he could breathe, he marvelled that Dagmar's pronouncements could sound as though they had come directly from some cult paperback. Soon both she and Doc were snoring and he lay rigidly between them, trying not to touch the indiscreet parts of their bodies, convinced that sleep had forsaken him forever.

But he must have slept, or dozed for an hour or two. In the morning he found Doc boiling frankfurters and Dagmar knee-deep in the swollen, glacial river, her Indian cotton skirt knotted around her thighs; she was washing her hair, sweeping the dripping rope of it back in a superbly primitive, if self-regarding gesture.

They wound their way down through the Dolomites and entered Venice.

'I think I'll cut out on my own again,' Jeb informed them.

'Sure, John. If that's what you want.'

'Thanks for the ride.' But they were not interested in his gratitude. He had the sense that he was an experiment that had failed. So he strolled around the sights, milling with the crowds in San Marco, unmoved by the huge, ill-lit Titians in the freezing halls of the Doge's Palace, soured by the multitude of young travellers just like himself. Venice, Italy, Europe, was being 'done', consumed, and he couldn't escape the feeling that he was just another tourist. Tourism was the degradation affluence had made of travel. It depressed him, not least because he recognised how glib his formulation of it was. He longed to be able to perceive himself as a wanderer, hived with rich human experience gathered from the far reaches of the globe, not like Doc whose travelling appeared only to have produced a tendency to pontificate or patronise, but like — well, like his boyhood perception of Len, or Hengelow. Then he realised he was being as self-regarding about travel as Dagmar was about washing in glacial streams.

He wandered down some of the back streets, became lost, and once, passing some children in a small piazza, was surprised to see stones rattling across the cobbles after him. When he turned to face them, the children didn't flee, but stood scowling and casting about for more ammunition. He found his way back to San Marco and spied Doc and Dagmar standing together spooning yoghurt from a common plastic cup. Thinking they had seen him, he waved, but Doc turned the other way and Dagmar stared through him as though he were part of the crowd. So he left Venice and hitched south to Ancona, reaching the port a little after dusk, where he boarded a ferry for Zadar in Yugoslavia. In less than six hours he had crossed the Adriatic and by midnight was gliding toward a shoreline tiaraed with points of light.

Walking through the empty streets of Zadar, with their white flagstones still gleaming from the nightly hose-down, was like walking through an opulent 1930s film-set. He slept in a park, in the morning breakfasted on greasy burek, then bussed to Dubrovnik down the spectacular Dalmatian coastline with its bouldery mountains plunging straight into the blue Adriatic. Now he had left the main tourist haunts, Jeb found himself moved by the austere beauty of the landscape, the coralline intricacy and picturesqueness of the coastal towns, the candid warmth of people he met on the buses, the men tieless in white shirts and ill-fitting suits, the women in shapeless black dresses and headscarves.

But Mallory's phrase would not leave him alone. 'I can't see the point of further travelling,' he had said. Indeed, what was the gain, beyond a head full of images, mostly ephemeral, though some which haunted his imagination deliciously. But it was the passivity of travelling, the suspicion it was not a preparation for anything. He was an observer. But in aid of what? And what gave him the right to such disengagement?

Certainly it had not become the enchanted state of being he had hoped, the journey far and deep into significant experience he had imagined for himself. One was too present, too beset by the immediate. He had not found the immense spaces he ascribed to his childhood. The distances between places in modern Europe were too shrunken, the world was too well signposted, too crowded with tourists and other would-be gypsies. So he looked down into the unimaginably blue lagoons and grottos of Dubrovnik with heartache and disenchantment.

And continued his journey, through the mountains of Montenegro and Macedonia. In Thessaloniki he was half-heartedly mugged by two youths flexing coshes while their mini-skirted girlfriends stood some distance off and watched; they relieved him of his drachmas, but did not bother with his passport or travellers' cheques.

In Istanbul he stayed for three days in a fleapit near the covered market while he took in the sights, the soaring, dowdy, interior of Aya Sofia, the twilit cavernous spaces of the Blue Mosque, the treasures of Topkapi which included a fabulously bejewelled dagger with a tiny clock suspended below it, like a quarter-moon and planet, and what was reputed to be John the Baptist's forearm, cast in gold with a section removed to reveal the mouldering ulna and radius. He sat in the sunlight watching the bear-handlers leading their dusty animals among the crowd, prodding them to rear on their hind legs for the cameras. Several times he was approached by Turkish or American hash dealers. In the evenings he strolled across the Galata Bridge or under the city walls, watching the small craft in the Golden Horn or the larger ships making up and down the Bosphorus, their bulks dimly suggested against the smoky blue sky and sea by their navigation and bridge lights.

For all the exotic imagery that the city paraded before him, Jeb found himself disaffected and lonely. He thought of Hengelow and was sorry he had judged him so harshly that night in Frankfurt. He thought of Mallory and regretted they had parted on awkward terms. There was something self-sufficient about Hengelow, Mallory, Aunt Eva. They seemed unconcerned about the attention of other people. It was a self-sufficiency he recognised he lacked.

Take this business about wayfaring over the face of the earth, for instance, himself as the perennial wanderer. What he was really doing, surely, was trying to construct a romanticised self which others might find attractive? He thought of Roma. Yes, it was a case of wanting his life to be witnessed. He wasn't being quite fair to the notion he had formed in Frankfurt of recovering those haunting sensations of space and time he was sure had been a periodic feature of his childhood. He *had* wanted to do that. But he realised, as the smoky light on the Sea of Marmara darkened, that his quest was corrupted with self-regard. He wanted to be witnessed. He wanted his inner life to be judged real.

He thought of Hengelow and Mother. They had once lain in one another's arms and been as familiar with each other as his own Dad and Mother had presumably been. It didn't seem very likely. He felt he had learnt from Hengelow and Aunt Eva some of their story but not those details which would make their ten years of marriage seem possible. He wanted to know these details, believing, now more than ever, that the story was needful to complete his sense of himself. He would have to broach the subject with Mother, his nearest and least approachable primary source. He walked back toward his dormitory in the darkness. Here and there in the old city walls, where a part of the masonry had come away, fires were burning and there came the smell of cooked meat and onions. There were families up there, Jeb realised, eking shelter in those meagre crannies. Families.

He took a coach to Athens. For a day and a night, as a loudspeaker blared interminable Turkish pop music, he stared out at the treeless landscape, the yellow rapeweed and blood-red poppies growing among the wheatfields of northern Turkey and Greece. He dozed intermittently, got out of the coach briefly in Thessaloniki where he glimpsed in doorways the prostitutes in their leather mini-skirts. Then he slept, aware the elderly Greek matron beside him was asleep on his shoulder; he woke in the dawn to find they were among tawny mountains splodged darkly here and there by pine plantations. He kept perfectly still, fearing to wake the matron whose mouth and jowls had fallen open and who was breathing stertorously.

He stayed two days in the Greek capital, accommodated on a few square feet of balcony in a hostel off Patission packed with Americans and Canadians, spending the daylight hours sightseeing among the museums and ruins. He stood under the columns of the Parthenon and, to his relief, found the great cultural ikon did indeed take his breath away. It emerged from all his preconceptions, from the biscuit-tin lids, the postcards and calendars on which he had seen it represented, more massive, more dynamic, more thrilling than he could have anticipated, like a shockwave of creative genius running through the centuries, its columns bulging deviously in order to preserve the illusion of straightness, austere, untouchable above the city's fumes and uproar, above the camera-slung crowds toiling toward it through the alleys of the Plaka.

From Piraeus he took an overnight ferry to Crete and for a fortnight roamed the island. In retrospect he thought it was the most intense experience of travelling that he had in the three months, and left him with a jumble of haunting images and sensations: police, coming at dawn to move him, not unkindly, on from where he was sleeping on the beach of a tourist-brochure town; a seasnake gliding past a headland at Nikolaos, gold head and silver length shimmering like electricity on the sea's turquoise; a great dolphin leaping from the palace wall at Knossos; the statuette of a Minoan goddess holding a snake in either hand above her head in the museum at Iraklion, and another of an athlete diving through space. At Myrtos, he saw men in leather leggings and tasselled caps drinking thimbles of coffee, and had nights of mosquitoes and dysentery in the hostel outside Ierapetra where in a dream he cried not for Mother or Len, but for Dad to bring his 'Old Curl' home, waking fitfully to hear a man jingling keys and turning on lights in the small hours. At Rethimnon he had himself shorn and doused with kerosene to rid himself of teeming headlice. On a mountain ledge beyond the deserted village of Samaria, he passed a gaunt old woman all in black, chasing goats, nimble as her quarry and uttering vile-sounding curses after them. The next image was of making toward Hora Sfakion on a small boat, the sea an aniline blue and the hippies living in the caves along the coast, waving, fluttering in their sarongs and dhotis. Kriti! Yes, if in retrospect he achieved that state of enchantment where the images of times and places seemed to merge and shed their precise ordering, it was during his time on Crete. But by the end he realised he was tired, tired of being on the move, tired of the ephemeral company of hostels, buses, car-rides.

So, when he reached Piraeus at five in the morning, he bussed to Syntagma Square where he booked a seat on a coach going through to Rotterdam. By midday he had begun his return journey across Europe, aware that the true traveller would have turned his back on the prospect of home and continued, crossed the Bosphorus into Asia, or found in Chania harbour a trading smack that would have taken him to Port Said and Africa.

For most of the two-day journey he slept, waking inter-mittently, headachey and light-headed, to find himself on an autostrada near Belgrade, in undulating forest country between Zagreb and Graz, or speeding under the huge blue and white signs of the German Autobahns. Incredibly, fifty hours after leaving Athens, he had crossed Europe diagonally and was waiting for a train at Rotterdam station to take him to the Hook of Holland. That evening he landed at Harwich and hitched to Cambridge through the light of a late June evening. He knocked at Mallory's door.

A man in shirtsleeves, wearing hiker's shorts and boots, answered. Mallory had gone back to Australia, six weeks ago at least, he informed Jeb. Given up his doctorate! Why? No idea. 'Mistake if you ask me. First class mind. But touchy. Know his father. Colleague.' Exhausted as he was, Jeb listened to the staccato of the man's speech as though from a great distance. This was presumably the Prof Mallory had mentioned back in March. Jeb asked if there was any mail for him.

'Sent it on. An address in Norfolk somewhere.'

Did he know anywhere Jeb might stay for tonight?

'Difficult. Peak of the tourist season, of course.'

Any chance he could doss down here? He had been counting on Mallory a bit.

'Ah!' He eyed Jeb's cropped hair. 'Bad moment, unfor-tunately.' Just got back from camp himself. House not really fit for visitors. 'Try the youth hostels people.' The door closed on him.

It was now dark. As Jeb walked through the town, people were spilling from the curry houses and stepping into sports cars. He had looked forward to perhaps sharing a bottle with Mallory, certain that their coolness to one another in Frankfurt would by now have been forgotten. Mallory's departure was inconvenient. No, it was more than that, it was upsetting. He turned left at what he remembered from his March visit to be the Catholic church, then walked until he found the Cam and followed the river downstream until he found a quiet place of willows. Here he spread his sleeping bag and lay, listening to the nocturnal sounds and weeping quietly. He had depended, unreasonably perhaps, on Mallory's room being journey's end. The peremptory fellow in the shorts had made him feel like a beggar. Yet why should he shed tears, why now? This, after all, was the condition of wayfarers when all else was stripped away, to be pitilessly alone under the stars, with, on one side of him, the restive allegro of a river, on the other the remote monotone of traffic. One should be grateful, he reflected, to be brought face to face with the ground-rules of existence. He turned over. The tears fell across his nose onto the hood of his sleeping bag. He sniffed. It was ridiculous.

In the morning he rang Aunt Eva.

'The fact is, I've lost my base and I need somewhere to sort myself out for a week or two.' He hated himself for sounding plaintive. The Prof had made him wary of asking for hospitality, even from someone he thought he knew.

'You are family. Of course you are welcome. I shall expect you this afternoon.'

'Thanks, I wasn't sure.'

'You will be very welcome. I enjoyed your card and am looking forward to hearing your news. Besides, Len is here at present. He will be glad to see you again, I'm sure.'

End of a Tour

With the onset of the Northern Hemisphere summer holidays, Jeb discovered eastern England was swarming with hitch-hikers, English, French, Germans, Americans, dishevelled figures, often overdressed for the warm July weather in leather jackets or cutaway ex-army greatcoats. They stood at ten-yard intervals on the exit ramps of service stations, raising their arms to the passing motorists in gestures which were both supplicant and disdainful. It took Jeb nine hours to cover the distance which in March he had covered in one and a half. When he arrived at Wollstanton, Len had gone out. There were letters from Mother and a postcard from Roma. Gratefully he fell under Eva's direction. She made him a supper, cocoa, and sent him off to bed.

To be released from the responsibility for himself! One could fall forever into that warm abyss. As he drifted off to sleep he fancied childhood was a state of being which called out to you all through life, tempting you back. He slept late into the following morning.

Now he and Len sat in Aunt Eva's front room, tentatively trying to establish some ground between themselves. Len had taken a job as a petrol-pump attendant at a local garage. He had the morning off, and leaned forward in his overalls, smoothing back the puff of hair on his otherwise bald forehead. His face seemed bonier and whiter than Jeb could remember it from Australia.

'Are you still wrapped up in all that politics, old man?'
Jeb recognised the challenge in the question.

'Not much opportunity,' he deflected. But even as he fell
into the old pattern with Len, part placatory, part needing
to assert that he too was present and counted for something,
Jeb was nettled by this pressure Len always brought to bear
on him, pressure to account for himself, to accept his status
as an amiable second fiddle. Why did there always have to
be this sense of a wrangle going on, of having to resist being
absorbed into whatever it was that Len wished to demonstrate?
And why his own reflex always to seek peace? He recalled
how, by the end of the Australian visit, he had disliked Len,
aware too that embroiled in the same recollection was the
fact he had idolised him as the tense, accomplished mentor
of his childhood.

'In the last few months I've been down to Istanbul and
Crete,' he continued. He thought it wise to delay telling
Len that he had also stayed with Hengelow in Hamburg.

'What did you go there for?'

'Just travelling. Isn't that what you do when you're away
from here? Tramp the country, meet life head-on?'

'Nope. I'm always out looking for things.'

'What things?'

'I'll show you if you like.'

He followed Len up the stairs, pretending not to know
what he was in for.

'What do you think?' the overalled man asked when he
had opened the door on the Lancaster's cockpit.

'My God.' Jeb tried to sound surprised, admiring.

'All my own work. From scratch. Keen, eh? Climb in.'

Len took a couple of pairs of earphones from his cupboard
and clambered after Jeb.

'Park yourself in the pilot's seat. I'll give you the gen.'
For twenty minutes or so the elder leaned over the younger,
explaining, enthusing. Jeb heard a multitude of technical terms
reeled off and described with flamboyant authority, ignition
switches, boost gauges, rpm indicators, booster coil switch,
feathering buttons, starboard and port master engine cocks,
flaps position indicator, throttle levers, propeller speed control

levers, boost control cutout, altimeter, airspeed indicator, direct-reading compass switches, and so on. Jeb found himself overwhelmed by the force of Len's technical expertise so that for a moment he was persuaded it had indeed been absurd, frivolous, *aimless*, to have wandered down to Istanbul and Crete. For here was a focus of interest that burned white-hot, an environment concentrated intensely around bringing off the one effect, absurd once you could put a distance between it and yourself, but not here, with Len leaning over his shoulder and the power of the illusion so present.

'I run the acoustics off four tape recorders in that cupboard you can see. One for the two port engines, one for the two starboard, one for intercom and one for combat noises. They're hooked up to these controls so that when I throw this set of switches here . . .' he flicked two from a set of four switches to the right of the ignition switches and there came (as Jeb had inadvertently discovered before) first a labouring splutter, like a car being started, then a roar from an amplifier on the left side of the fuselage. Len searched Jeb's face for a reaction. Jeb wished he had not taken a preview.

His half-brother then flicked the other two switches in the set and there was a splutter, then roar from the right-hand side of the aircraft. 'I've wired up the volume control to the throttle levers, so,' he pushed the four throttle levers forward gently and the roar mounted to a crescendo. 'Neat, eh!' he grinned at Jeb. 'The tone control on the recorder is wired up to these propeller speed levers, so they sound as if I'm altering pitch. You've got to get them running sweet,' Len shouted at him above the roar, adjusting the four levers he had indicated. His adjustments gave the illusion at least of harmonising the discordancy between the two recorders. He glanced at Jeb, looking rather pleased with himself.

'Put your earphones on, I'm going to switch on and syn-chronise the intercom tape.' The third recording device was switched on from the instrument panel and Jeb heard bursts of static interspersed with the measured telephonic tones of a man going through a take-off routine. It was like a Lin-guaphone record with gaps left for a listener to contribute his end of the crosstalk. Len picked up a leather airman's helmet and put the mask with its microphone to his face, making the appropriate technical responses to the crackling litany while casting his eye over the panels in front of him, reading dials, turning knobs.

Switch off booster-coil, Jeb heard Len instruct. *Booster-coil off*, the earphones replied. *Ground/flight switch to Flight. They can take away the ground battery . . . Check . . . I'm opening all engines to 1200 revs.* A pause in which only the static and the uurrh of the four engines could be heard, then *All engines at 1200 . . .*

'Who is the other voice?' Jeb shouted, lifting one earphone and pointing to it. It had the sing-song rhythm of 1940s film English, soothing, with its suggestion of hearty professional competence.

Len grinned and pointed to himself.

'It doesn't sound like you one bit.'

The intercom continued to crackle with crosstalk, temperatures, pressures, fuel crossfeeds. Jeb heard the words 'boost' and 'supercharger', 'magneto', 'master cocks'.

'What about combat noises?'

Len flicked a switch on the flight engineer's panel and, after a few seconds there came a tremendous clattering, like someone banging a hammer inside a large iron tank. 'That's the rear-gunner dealing with a night fighter. I can synchronise the combat sounds to the intercom so that I, as pilot, can respond to what my gunners are telling me to do.'

Jeb took his earphones off and requested with his hands that Len shut the system down.

'What do you think, old man?' Len asked, when the cockpit again became quiet.

He was at a loss for words. 'How long have you been making it?'

'Seven years. Since you went off to Australia. Though I've been collecting bits and pieces for much longer.'

'And you mean to tell me all your travels about the country are to find bits and pieces for this?'

'Yes.'

'How much of it is off a genuine Lancaster?'

'Some bits. I've got a genuine Mk 14 bombsight. Some of these instruments are from an old Avro Lincoln, which was really the same aeroplane as the Lanc. But I can copy. I make replicas of things where I have to. Fadge where I can't. Aunty won't allow liquids — too leaky. So I have to fadge those gauges, fuel, glycol, oil, hydraulics. I had to fit a three-phase power outlet to the house to cope with all the electrics.'

'But where do you get all the information?'

'I just know it,' he answered, a little defensively. Though he was prepared to add, 'Books I suppose, plans. If I hear there's a set of plans in a records office up north somewhere, or down in Devon, I go there. I went to Avro up near Manchester. I used to scrounge around the places where I heard Lancs had been scrapped, like Wroughton and up near Lossiemouth. Sleep rough if I have to. I learnt quite a bit about aircraft during Nasho. I go to see some of the fitters I knew. When I was a motorbike mechanic I picked up a lot of useful things.'

'It sounds as if your whole life revolves around this.'

Len did not reply immediately. Then, 'Why shouldn't it?'

'No reason.'

'Are you thinking I shouldn't be mucking about like this at my age?'

'Of course not!' In part it was exactly what Jeb was thinking. But he was also remarking the difference between Len's voice as it had been on the intercom tape, so self-possessed, so authoritative, and the voice now, touchy, looking for approval. It was as if his interest was a magic cave that could transform personality. He decided to appease. 'This is magnificent, Len. I've never seen anything like it before. The metalwork, the engineering, the electrics. You must have access to a well-equipped workshop.'

'Electric drill, pop-rivetter, screwdriver and some spanners. I can mould the perspex on Aunty's stove. If I need anything done I go and see a fellow in Norwich who I know from Nasho days. He's got a lathe and mill.'

'What's in these boxes?' Jeb indicated two boxes near the ladder.

Len opened them. One contained tapes, the other reels of film and carousels of slides. He pointed to the reels of film. 'They were a find! Picked them up at an auction. Genuine aerial film of different ops. No sound on them. I supply that with these intercom tapes. Each tape gives the different route bearings, Berlin, Essen, Hamburg. Karlsruhe, Dresden, different weather, different TI details.'

'TI?'

'Target Indicators. They're the flares that the Pathfinder fellows drop so the rest of us know where to aim our load. Red, yellow, green.' Len took a film and fed it into the projector Jeb had noticed in March. 'I can control this from the cockpit.' He climbed back in and flicked a switch, whereupon a black-and-white film was thrown onto the wall. Clearly it was a propaganda film from the war, depicting aircrew relaxing or kitting up, aircraft being serviced, men in forage caps riding bicycles, 'I don't use any of that stuff,' Len informed him. It was a five-minute sequence of aerial views of some city being bombed which interested him, a panorama of flickering points of light, some widespread, some in dense clusters. Every now and then it was as if the ground underneath had a spasm, for there would be a pulse of light and movement as a bomb went off. The eerie feature of the film was the lack of sound — there was only the grind of the reels on their arms and the celluloid going through the sprockets of the projector. He turned it off. 'When I get round to it, I'll probably ditch the rest of the film and just keep the bombing shots.'

'You can't just cut up a film like this! It's historically valuable!'

'It's mine. I can do what I like with it.' Again Len looked defensive. Jeb shrugged.

Len continued his exposition. 'The slides are for the bomb-aimer. I've got aerial shots of the centres of all those German towns I mentioned — Berlin, Hamburg, Essen. I had slides made from wartime reconnaissance photographs.'

'So you, well, fly all over Europe.'

'Some targets in France.'

'Why France? I thought they were friendly.'

Len regarded him for a moment before replying. 'Preparation for the invasion.'

'Which invasion?'

'Normandy.'

Half conscious of the betrayal of trust involved, Jeb smiled, 'I thought it had already happened.'

'You think it's stupid, I can see.'

'I don't, Len. I was just being mischievous. I think it's — incredible. Really.'

'You're laughing. Up your sleeve you're laughing.' Why could he not take even the lightest ribbing?

'I'm not. Not really'

But he was not believed. Len fiddled with a screwdriver, adjusting some mechanism in the still-incomplete front-turret. Jeb watched him as he became absorbed in the technical task, that resilient puff of hair on his forehead falling forward and being brushed back. No, he was not laughing that a full-grown man should have made in his bedroom this monstrous facsimile of a World War Two bomber's front end. Rather, he was marvelling that a life could have such intense focus. He didn't quite dare ask whether his half-brother was still getting into trouble for prowling around people's houses but he gathered indirectly that this was a phase now over.

'How do you afford the materials for all this?' Jeb asked.

'I get different jobs, like the one I've got at the garage.'

'There wouldn't be much left of that after living expenses come out of it, would there?'

'What living expenses?'

'Well, you'd be paying Eva some board, wouldn't you?'

'No.' The 'No' sounded as surprised as if a ten-year-old had been asked whether he paid a weekly consideration to his parents for his upkeep.

So Eva looked after Len's material needs entirely. That would give him a fair disposable income for his — hobby, if that was the right word. And the bill for all the electricity that flowed through his three-phase socket? Presumably. Her tolerance must have been considerable, to have all that building going on in her roof, the procession of materials through the house. She must have had a word to say about the noise levels at different times.

As to its being a historically accurate replica, Jeb supposed the question of authenticity didn't matter that much, not as much as the simple act of faith which could transform a bedroom into the aerodromes and night skies of thirty years ago. Though how 'simple' that act of faith was, Jeb was not sure. Upon it rested a fantasy life which was impressively self-sufficient, and drawn out. *Best if we ditch the parachutes, old man*, the teenager had said in the teeming night outside Gattisby. That was nearly twenty years ago! And Len on his visit to Clemstead, the unwanted plastic model — *Find us a hangar with a workbench*. There had been other odd things over the years — the hoard of tinned food and chocolate in his drawer during his visit to Australia. (No wonder he had disliked Australia, it had been keeping him away from this all-consuming project.) Yes, there had been glimpses into this fantasy life, fleeting, baffling. But this elaborate facsimile — it revealed how extraordinarily consistent, dogged almost, how focussed and durable Len's parallel life was. From this third-storey room in a seaside villa, and by a simple act of faith, the air war over Europe was being protracted, unflagging in its intensity and showing no promise of respite.

However, one of Jeb's illusions about Len had dissolved. He was no gypsy. For all the talk of eating berries and plucking pheasant, it was clear that when he was absent from home these days Len was on business, relentlessly. It was a little predatory even, the way he evidently roamed the country for useful bits and pieces. Manchester, Lossiemouth. And he had that remorseless outlook of the monomaniac — only it was more naked than that of the odd enthusiast Jeb had encountered back in Australia, those affable, tedious, non-political folk for whom an Armstrong-Siddeley motor car or a collection of medals were the nearest imaginable thing to the godhead.

There was, Jeb was well aware, a pathology bound up here. It was as if the huge, intricate structure in his bedroom effectively consumed, but did not resolve the grudge, the unhappiness which Len's life seemed to have been founded upon ever since Jeb could first remember.

2

They went walking on Wollstanton Sands. 'I've seen your father, Len. I stayed with him in Hamburg,' Jeb decided to say, and wondered how much of the encounter he should divulge. Len was not encouraging. He listened, hands thrust into his overall pockets, head bent, making no reply. 'I went over with a friend of mine from Australia. We stayed with him. He runs a charity house for people down on their luck. He's pretty popular over there.'

'When I was a kid — at the school — I used to pray every night that God wouldn't let the Germans get him. I didn't miss a night all through the war. I kept him alive, I reckon.'

'If he came here, would you see him?' Len didn't answer. 'Look, you may think it's none of my business, but I'd be happier knowing both of you got on.' Again, Len gave no response. 'So I think I managed to persuade him to look you up. He said he was going to be in England over the summer some time. I guess he'll look Eva up. If he does, you won't cold-shoulder him, Len? Whatever happened, it was decades ago. He means well. Give him a chance.'

Len walked beside Jeb and continued to stare at the ground for a time, then he looked up suddenly and said, 'If you say so, old man.'

'You'll see him?'

'I'll be ready.'

3

In the evening he sat with Aunt Eva on the terrace overlooking her small back garden. Len was on shift at the petrol station. The old lady asked Jeb about her brother and Hamburg. Jeb related what he and Mallory had seen.

'Thank you,' she said, when he had finished. 'Crispin *will* treat my inquiries rather airily. Now tell me, how did the two of you get on?'

The directness of the question took Jeb a little aback. 'Pretty well, I suppose.' But he was loath to be evasive with Aunt Eva. Of the three Hengelows, it was she who inspired in him the greatest trust. 'He's loved by the people over there.

I could see why. He's so vivid. But I found myself becoming wary.'

'Wary of what?'

'Of being — taken over. Put into situations I hadn't had time to think out.'

'Yes. I think dear Lizzie might have felt that at times. Crispin can be so very *headlong*.'

'Mallory had a word for him. He called him a sannyasin.'

Eva looked at her hands. There was an orange light on her face from the last of the sunshine which had been broken into dazzling fragments by the climbing plants on a trellis at the border of her garden. It was some time before she answered, and when she did she would not look at him. 'Sadly, your friend is not quite correct. It is necessary for a sannyasin to have discharged his worldly responsibilities before he goes off to seek the purification of his spirit. Crispin did not do that.' She stood up and went inside.

4

Hengelow turned up one morning when Jeb was reading a book in Eva's study. Jeb sensed rather than saw a person flicker across the window then, a few seconds later, heard the kitchen door being opened. They met in the corridor and Hengelow wrung Jeb's hand.

'You here! Dear *fellow*! And Evie?' It was as if suddenly his presence filled the house.

'She's out shopping. Have you come from Darmstadt?'

'Roundabout. The local milk lorry dropped me off in the High Street. Lennie here?'

'Upstairs.'

'I'll surprise him.'

'Should you?'

'Why not? Bang on the kettle, will you.'

'It's the room at the top.'

Hengelow had already begun to climb the stairs with a springy tiptoe movement, as a father might who had come to put presents beside the beds of his sleeping children. Jeb filled the kettle, lit a gas ring, then, curious to witness the meeting between father and son, he mounted the stairs.

Hengelow was standing in the doorway and there was the roar of the recorded Merlin engines filling the interior. 'Lanx?' he shouted. There was no answer from within. 'I can't see you, old man.' Then, coaxingly, 'Let's have a light.' He groped for the switch and tried it but nothing happened.

The father advanced into the blackness of the room as Jeb came up behind. He could make out Hengelow looking a little helpless as he tried to discern his son in the darkness.

'What is this?' Hengelow shouted at Jeb.

'He's been building the front end of a Lancaster bomber. It's incredible!' Jeb shouted back.

Hengelow groped his way around to the side of the structure where he could see Len above, faintly lit in the glow from a small light on the instrument panel. He was absorbed making various checks, his eyes scanning back and forth. He had on his head the old-fashioned leather airman's helmet and the intercom mouthpiece hung by a strap which every now and then he would lift to his lips in order to give a direction.

'Lanxie!' Hengelow waved, then smacked the metal of the fuselage a few times. Len looked out to his left and saw his father. He had fastened the mouthpiece so that now only his eyes and the bridge of his nose were visible. He looked down at his parent for some moments, then opened the flap of window and twiddled some knob inside which lessened the volume of noise.

'Lanx?' his father shouted, 'It's been years. Too long.' He reached up, offering to shake hands awkwardly through the small window, but Len did not respond. 'I've dropped by to see how you were getting on. Thought we might go out and take in a flick. How about it?' then, after a pause, 'Is there a light?'

No answer.

These, Jeb realised, were the crucial seconds, and he was uncertain what to expect. Anything. Len had said he would be ready to meet his father, whatever being 'ready' meant. But he was quite likely to stalk out, dropping his gear petulantly on the floor as he left, angry to have been cornered by this parent he had been avoiding for so many years. Or he might shut off the various sound systems and simply sit, sullen, disabled, a grown man made suddenly conscious that he had been caught out in childish role-playing. Just as easily Jeb imagined father and son embracing each other in the kind of reconciliation that occurred on afternoon television serials. Hengelow was certainly demonstrative enough to do this. Each of these scenarios assumed for the father an emotional advantage. But none of these things happened.

'Been expecting you, old man. Climb in,' Len had lifted his mask slightly and shouted this down, then for a few moments he became absorbed in his instruments before giving the man standing beneath him his attention again. 'It's another of the boss's "maximum efforts".'

That voice! The cheery authority of it. It was Len and not Len.

'Lennie! What's going on?'

'Maximum effort, old man.' He closed the window flap and hunched once more over his instruments. Len and not Len.

Hengelow turned to Jeb for an explanation. Jeb shrugged, then shouted, 'Maximum effort. He's being friendly. The best thing might be to play along.'

Jeb was to regret this piece of advice, but at the time he was rather pleased with himself. It sounded like adventurous therapy, like something out of a paperback on new psychiatry, fostering trust between hostile parties by getting them to take active roles in their fantasies. Jeb glanced at Hengelow and, for a moment in the darkness, thought he saw a mirror of the mutinous resentment he had seen at different times in Len. Then, raising his eyes to the ceiling and muttering 'This is ridiculous! I thought I was done with these things,' Hengelow went to the ladder, climbed up, banged his head while negotiating his way over the main spar, and shuffled toward the front. Jeb followed him up.

'Duck down into your burrow, old man,' Len told him when Hengelow came abreast of the pilot's elevated seat. Normally tall and slender, Len looked hulking in the harness, mae west and flying boots that he was wearing. This fact, Jeb was to surmise later, together with the slightly elevated position of his pilot's seat might have been one of the reasons Len was able to control the events that followed. But more decisively, perhaps, it was the ineluctable engine-roar, the way it heightened tension, allowed no reflective calm. It seemed to obliterate self-consciousness.

'Lanx, I'm too old to go crawling about this contraption. Look, let's give all this a miss, go downstairs and have a yatter.'

'There's a chap. Last op of the tour.' It was uncanny how Len could simply ignore, not the fact that this was his father he was addressing in this breezy way, but all which that relationship had always entailed. Throughout the rigmarole which was about to ensue, Jeb was aware of a suspense as to whether Len's nerve would fail, whether his 'play-acting' would crumble and he would become Len again, sullen, mutinous, inconsolable.

Len handed his father a pair of headphones attached to a lead and pointed toward the hatchway into the bomb-aimer's compartment. Hengelow stood holding them, uncertain.

'Lennie, this is grotesque!' Again he looked to Jeb for advice, but Jeb, who had placed a second pair of headphones over his ears, shrugged again and silently shaped the words 'Maximum effort'. It seemed to work. Hengelow stepped through the narrow entrance into the domed front of the plane and even went so far as to put the headphones on. Then he stood looking back at his son who was engaged in intercom crosstalk. *Ground/flight switch to Flight. Check. Set altimeter, the baro reading's one-zero-two-zero ... Altimeter set.* In the midst of this, Len removed his intercom mask, leaned across to Jeb and said, 'I always run through the checks on the intercom so the whole crew can hear. Good drill and good for morale. Everyone knows exactly what's happening.' He looked at Jeb significantly, then re-fastened his mask.

Been expecting you, old man. Was this being laid on? The thought went through Jeb's mind.

He listened to the intercom crosstalk between Len and the voice on the recorder which was presumably that of a flight engineer. He gathered that they were still on the ground and looked out of the perspex, half-expecting to see the silhouettes of other gigantic bombers taxiing around a perimeter circuit, the squat outlines of Nissen huts or a control tower. Instead, he could dimly make out Len's bed and bedside table.

But it was infectious, the engine racket, the sing-song intercom jabber. He wondered how Hengelow was being affected by it all. It must be stirring some memories. The man was still looking back through the bulkhead, watching Len's face with an expression of baffled impatience.

Magneto switches? Locked on. Brake pressure? Two-seven-five psi. Flaps? Fifteen degrees down. OK, rear gunner? OK, Skip. OK, mid-upper? OK, nav? and so on, as each member of the imaginary crew crackled back in the affirmative. When he asked *OK, bomb-aimer?* Jeb half expected Hengelow himself to reply, and indeed Len gave a momentary glance toward the bulkhead hole. But a recorded voice crackled its affirmative in the same moment that Hengelow looked away.

OK everyone, here we go. He pushed the four throttle levers forward in a steady motion as far as they could go and there came a tremendous surge of noise at the same time as the rpm indicators swung on their dials.

There was no doubt Len was very much in charge. The attention to detail was extraordinary. Spellbinding. Jeb forgot about the dimly visible bed in the corner. His imagination succumbed to the sound effects. It seemed to prompt sensations which in another part of his mind he knew could not be present, the bumpiness of the big aeroplane as it gathered speed along the runway and its tail lifted off the ground, the sudden smoothness as it lifted clear. He heard the tape represent the bump of the undercarriage as the wheels were raised into their cavities. There was intercom talk about pressures, fuel, indicated airspeed. From what was said, he was aware that they were making a wide circuit of their 'aerodrome' to gain height, then breaking off when the intercom voice called their altitude at 8000 feet. *Zero-six-six, Skipper. We should pass over Sherringham in three minutes and the assembly point in two hours and six minutes... Thank you, nav.* With all that before one's inner eye, who needed reality?

The flight seemed to settle down. It was clear from the

crosstalk that time was being telescoped; their five-hour flight was to take scarcely three-quarters of an hour. Hengelow had disappeared behind the bulkhead; Jeb could just see him sitting with his forehead resting on his knees, the headphones on, in an attitude of attention. Every so often the navigator would read off the altitude, advise if there were small course adjustments that needed to be made, and whether or not they were ahead or behind time. The throttle levers had been eased back following takeoff and Jeb had seen Len bringing the flaps up gradually in five-degree increments as well as making various adjustments to propeller pitch. The absorption! That was what was so astonishing; he was like a child so deep in the trance of his play he does not notice the calling parent or the school bell.

Passing over the assembly point now, Skip, alter course to one-one-two degrees... One-one-two, thank you nav. The sing-song was soothing; it reminded Jeb of the way someone might talk to a skittish horse. Idly he wondered what the target was.

And then he knew. Sickeningly he knew.

He squeezed halfway into the bomb-aimer's compartment, and sat on the step. Hengelow had not altered his position and did not look up when Jeb appeared. There were some maps tucked behind a bracket. Jeb took one out. It was a map of northern Europe with lines marked on it in pencil, out to a point in the North Sea, where had been written 'assembly point', then a south-easterly swing, crossing the coast just under the Danish border, another southerly swing, then a third, right across the heart of the city.

Hamburg.

He looked at the other map, which was a street plan of the city and he was able to recognise the thoroughfares, lakes, canals and docks where he and Mallory had ambled a few months previously. A cross in black ink, with a neatly written 'aiming point' was placed more or less where Jeb recalled the Rathaus and the St Petri church to have been. A dotted circle had also been marked in showing the planned bombing area. It encompassed St Pauli and part of Altona, possibly the very street where Elli and Ronya lived, though it was difficult to tell, for the map lacked detail. The route they would take over the city was drawn in.

Jeb looked up and saw Hengelow was watching him. It was clear from the expression on his face that he too knew what was intended, though there was no indication he had seen the maps. More mysterious was that he seemed to accept the fact. He could have stormed out. For perhaps a minute he regarded Jeb gravely, then he motioned to him to come close and said, in his ear. 'I'm going to choose to believe you had no part in hatching this scheme.'

For scheme, it began to appear, was what it was. Jeb shook his head in the negative. But he was aware of the meaning of what was happening. This was retaliation. Cunning, meticulously prepared retaliation. The son who had failed his O-Level exams had read the personality of his father accurately. The boy whose heart had broken when the flyer/hero deserted the family home all those years ago had chosen his moment to come back into the parent's presence. The twelve-year-old man, the thirty-five-year-old boy, had calculated finely that when brought into the presence of his son the older man's instinct would be to atone. To atone. For hadn't his whole life since the war been an atonement? Hadn't the need for atonement broken his son's heart?

The dicey bit, of course, had been to draw him into the web, this cavity of noise and systems. With nerve, timing, some luck, it appeared Len had done it. Now Hengelow sat listening, apparently resigned to hear out what had been prepared for him, as the intercom gave him their progress toward the target.

Yellow route marker visible ahead and slightly to starboard. Thank you, bomb-aimer. The patter continued. *Alter course to one-five-nine, Skip, seventeen minutes to target. One-five-nine, thank you, nav. Eleven minutes to target and on course. Thank you, nav, I can see the target now. Bit of flak about.* Suddenly the wall of the bedroom lit up as Len switched on the projector and the film. A moment later the slide projector behind Hengelow's head came on and the first of several aerial views was projected upon the screen under the perspex blister. Jeb watched Hengelow who in turn had shifted position to look

out of a small side-window at the film that was flickering
on the wall. The picture had been focussed so as to fit the
wall exactly. Little fires from incendiaries prickled the darkness, there were momentary flashes from anti-aircraft fire,
and the sudden but surprisingly slow convulsions of large
high-explosive bombs. The engines sustained their single
encompassing note, so uniform that it did indeed convey the
idea of a kind of silence in the intervals between the navigator
calling the time and course and the pilot's reply. *Eight minutes
and on course. Thank you, nav, stand by bomb-aimer. Standing by,
Skip*. The slide on the small screen changed and changed again.
Alter course to one-eight-zero, four minutes to target. Jeb saw Hengelow ease himself down so that he was poised over the blister.
It seemed so like the natural thing to do that the significance
of the move at first escaped Jeb. Then he saw. Hengelow
was going to participate! He momentarily inspected the bombsight to see if it was genuine, then squinted through it, and
took in his right hand a small trigger mechanism. *Three minutes
to target and on course . . . Thank you, nav, take over now, bomb-
aimer*. Jeb watched Hengelow closely as the intercom bomb-
aimer began reeling off his instructions. *Bomb doors open. Master
switch on. Bombs fused and selected*, each of which was repeated
by the pilot as the different procedures were accomplished.
Jeb could see Hengelow's lips moving. Was he praying, or
himself repeating the drill that came to his ears through the
headphones? The notion crossed Jeb's mind that the man was
accepting his role because he thought it was the only way
of bringing Len through the enactment. But the explanation
was not sufficient somehow. Hengelow's absorption in his
role was too complete, his acceptance too baffling, too
extraordinary.

*I can make out the red TIs now . . . Thirty seconds to target . . .
Left, left, left, steady, steady, right, steady, steady*. What Hengelow
might have been seeing as he looked through the bombsight
onto the screen which was now showing a slide with a
serpentine stretch of river and the haphazard oblongs of docks
in one corner, and a small white arrow placed in the middle
of what appeared to be a built-up area, Jeb could not guess.
He found himself crowded with thoughts on the older man's

behalf, anger at this mockery of the young men of Hengelow's generation, horror that the man had been inveigled into this grotesque charade where he was pretending to bomb a city where he had lived and was loved by so many. But the man was immobile over the bombsight, only his lips moving slightly, whether in prayer or a recitative of the intercom's rigmarole, Jeb couldn't hear. Then his thumb compressed the button on the trigger mechanism and held it down, and in this attitude he remained frozen.

Bombs gone. No hang-ups . . . bomb doors closed, came the voice of the intercom. *Thank you, bomb-aimer.* Hengelow did not move from his hunched position; he looked ridiculous in the shabby fawn raincoat, the headphones, Jeb only now noticed, too small for his large head. *Steer two-nine-two degrees, Skip. Thank you, nav, let's get the hell out of here.*

Jeb waited for Hengelow to move, wanting to say something, that the prank was ghastly, tactless, unjust. But he could think of no words that could govern the fearful import of what he had witnessed.

For he realised it was not about duping the man-of-peace into re-enacting a saturation bombing of a city where he had friends and a record of good works. The city was make-believe, a grid of streets on a screen. If Len didn't know that, Hengelow certainly did. Nor was this a prelude to any reconciliation, a case of 'Now I've served you out for deserting me so we're quits and can now be friends.' It was neither of these things. Rather, it was a demonstration that nothing had been forgiven, that the son was irreconcilable and would use the utmost of his cunning to inflict emotional pain upon the parent. Jeb felt numbed by the unspeakable cruelty of their relationship.

He climbed back into the main cockpit, unfolded the flight engineer's seat and sat down. It crossed his mind to put an end to it, to climb down and start pulling out power sockets, flinging open curtains. He looked at where Len was absorbed in 'flying' them back home. The projector had been switched off; but for the luminosity of the needles and numbers on the dials, they were in darkness. Occasionally the intercom jabber interrupted the even racket of the Merlins with course details, fuel reserves. Then it became evident that they had crossed the English coast and were making preparations to land *Superchargers to M ratio*... *Undercarriage*... *Flaps*... The tension had gone out of the crosstalk now. *Down she comes. Well done, fellows. First-class effort.* Jeb sat until Len had shut down the various systems. Then, with the aftersound of the engines still in his ears, he turned to Len.

'You bastard,' was all he could think of to say, 'you unspeakably cruel bastard.' Len patted his back companionably. 'Last op of the tour, old man,' he said, then sticking his head to the hatchway into the front he reiterated, 'Last op of the tour, we made it. Well done, everybody.' He made his way toward the ladder at the rear.

Silvery sealight flooded in. Eva was wrenching open the curtains and saying something about one of them having forgotten that he was boiling water on her stove. There was a kettle ruined; they had been very fortunate not to have started a fire. Len was looking at his feet, sullen, unyielding. Jeb felt caught out, as he had felt when Mother used to find him outside the limits on the Candleware Road,

The emergence of Hengelow from the fuselage took Eva by surprise. 'Bro, I had no idea. What *has* been going on?'

Her brother eased himself down the steps, not answering immediately. Then, as he passed her on the way to the door he gave her a sad smile. 'Hello, Sis. Lennie here has been showing me over his — creation.' He went out, not looking at either Len or Jeb.

5

Hengelow stayed until the late afternoon. He and Eva closed the door of her study and remained there. At one stage Eva came out to prepare some lunch for the two of them, and Jeb glimpsed Hengelow through the open door, folded into a chair, his long legs protruding from the fawn raincoat he seemed never to remove. He was wiping his face with a white handkerchief, carefully. He looked up.

Jeb had an impulse to go over and touch the man, to take his head in his hands, or place an arm around his shoulders, anything that would be an indication of the turbulent sympathy he felt for him at that moment. But he stood, withholding himself. Hengelow's voice, when it came, was more level, more composed than Jeb might have expected.

'I think the swimmer is not trying to be saved at all, old fellow. I think he's trying to drown the rescuer.'

'I led you into all this.'

The man didn't speak, but smiled bleakly and shook his head in the negative. Then Eva came back with a tray and the door closed on the two of them. Jeb wanted to say something more. But the brief glance Eva gave him as she returned with the tray made two things clear; he was not a Hengelow, and he was not of their generation. Their confab was none of his business. He went for a walk.

By the time he came back, Hengelow had gone. 'He thought it best,' Eva told him. She sighed, and added, 'He had planned to spend a few days here having a holiday. Apparently as a result of something you said to him.'

'Yes. I think I carry the can a bit.'

'It is quite needless for you to shoulder any blame for whatever occurred this morning. You were acting for the best.'

'He didn't tell you what happened?'

'No.' And when Jeb began to relate the incident she held up her hand and stopped him. 'This is between me and Leonard.'

She was waiting for him when he returned late from his shift at the petrol station. Jeb saw them both go into the study. They had not come out by the time he was asleep.

6

His return flight to Australia was in early August and in the two or three days remaining he avoided being alone with Len. It was not so much from repugnance for his tall half-brother as not knowing what to say to him.

In company with Eva he took one last walk across the sands. She requested that he find out from his mother what she would like done about the trust account.

'She won't want it. You'd be better off using it for yourself and Len.'

'Well, money is not as plentiful as it was. But it needs Lizzie's and Crispin's authority.' Jeb promised he would see his mother dealt with the matter.

'Will Len stay here with you?'

'I imagine. He trusts me. He has his big room upstairs.'

'How do you stand the noise?'

'Ear-plugs,' she said, like someone stating the obvious.

He planned to say goodbye to both Len and Eva on the front doorstep of her house, but Len insisted on walking with Jeb to the bus stop. His conversation was breezy, crass, a little wheedling. Certainly he was conscious that he had offended Jeb, though the latter suspected he had no idea why. Jeb's responses were monosyllabic. He wished the balding fellow would go away.

They stood waiting amid the roar of buses. Len said. 'You can say hello to our mother from me if you like.'

'Of course.'

He hesitated for a moment, then looked Jeb in the eye. 'You know, old fellow, I've often wondered why our mother didn't give you any more brothers and sisters. Haven't you?'

'I'm not your old fellow,' Jeb said tiredly. He looked Len quickly in the eye and saw what he thought was a gleam of triumph. His remark had hit home. He had seen his remark hit home.

Lizzie 1983

1

After Mother had clicked the car door gently shut, he turned the ignition in his Mazda, and drove away quickly. He wondered briefly how Merrin was fending at Peg's. She had offered to help with the clearing up, perhaps in mitigation of the strong words she and Peg had exchanged earlier in the evening, so Jeb had left her there while he took Mother home. Merrin had her own transport and would be able to get home by herself.

Did it make any difference, now that the conclusive bits of the story had tumbled out at last, accidentally almost, as a result of a family argument? It didn't seem to. He should have been upset. Perhaps he was. Not visibly though.

The dinner had been arranged by Aunt Peg because she thought Mother might need jollying up after the letter from Eva which had arrived a fortnight ago. She had insisted Jeb bring 'this Merrin-girl-of-yours' along, to introduce her to the family. He would have liked to evade the occasion. Not that he still held any grudge against Peg, though he found her condescension and what he called her 'knee-jerk opinions' insufferable at times. Merrin had strong views also and he foresaw the two would probably end up arguing.

The main reason for his reluctance was the feeling that what Peg insisted on calling 'the Family' might spoil this new élan in his life, which in common with his generation he was not game to call 'Love' and for which the phrase 'having a relationship' was too dreary. For it was exquisite, vagrant, all too recent and uncertain, this first-in-a-lifetime sense he had of 'having found someone', as Peg had promptly defined it. But he agreed to go. He had been taken up by her people, an old and extended Canberra family with roots in the Department of Trade and some complicated interest in a Manuka gallery. There were brothers exuding bonhomie whom he could rely on when he needed to borrow a trailer or a circular saw, forthright sisters with views on how things should be run. Merrin had known Rosie in primary school; the blond fellow was now selling computers on the Gold Coast — wealthy and still single, according to the grapevine.

He supposed Merrin would have to meet his relatives some time. He had told her very little about his family. She had met Mother once or twice briefly. The two of them had met at school — she was English staff, he was History.

Certainly Mother seemed to need cheering up. It was unforeseeable, really, her reaction to Eva's letter. The thing had been in her possession for a week before anyone else became aware of its contents. Then, one afternoon, Jeb had called on her after last lesson.

'By the way,' she had said, as he sat with a mug of tea in the lounge room, 'there's a letter from Len's Aunt Eva. Perhaps you should read it.'

It had contained the news about Hengelow. While he was reading, she had continued with the housework, pretending to be busy. She was as brisk and straight as she had always been, her eyes dark under unruly hair that was now steely in colour, as though scoured, her cheekbones a little more prominent, while her mouth gave the impression of having been pulled slightly awry. Aunt Peg had been urging her to have a studio photograph taken of herself.

'There's not one snap of you that does you justice, Lizzie dear.'

It was true, Jeb recognised. The pictures in the album showed her too much in the distance always, either turning toward others in the picture or rendered indistinct by the dazzle of sunlight. It was a shock to perceive how shadowy

a person his mother had always been, despite their proximity
to each other through the years.

As he turned to the last page of Eva's letter, Mother came
back into the room, and picked up a paper from the desk.

'I used to say to myself,' she began, not lifting her eyes
from the paper in her hand, 'that when it came to it, if
it lay in my power, I would refuse to bury him. I'd let some
council official put him into the ground in a cardboard box.'

In the instant before she turned her face to the window
so he should not see it, Jeb had seen the gleam of wetness
on her cheek. But her voice was level, steady. 'According
to the letter,' she continued, 'he seems to have had quite
a send-off in Hamburg.'

'Yes. People there liked him.' After Darmstadt and his
visit to England, Hengelow had eventually gone back to
Altona. Jeb had learned this five or six years ago when, out
of the blue, there had been a postcard from him on which
had been written, 'Greetings from Roni, Elli, Charlie,' nothing
more.

But it had been Mother's behaviour which had most startled
him. There was a sorrow being struggled against. He saw
the evidence of it straining under the hunch of her shoulders
and in the rigidity of her posture. After all this time! He
was numbed by the sense of all that subterranean life that
was being remembered and grieved for. And she had already
lived with the news for a week; what had her initial reaction
to the news been, he wondered.

'It's a long letter.'

'Yes,' then feeling he should supply more, he added, 'Eva's
very punctilious.'

'Oh, you don't need to remind me,' she replied immediately,
then sniffed. 'Charl used to tease her about it.'

'He was sixty-eight,' she said.

'Yes.'

'Pneumonia.'

'Eva says he had been weakened by other things . . .'

'He was found by the side of the road.'

'The autobahn,' he corrected, needlessly. She was torturing
herself. He could not have guessed that this was the way

she would react. He had wished she would stop it. She was affecting him.

'By the side of the road! Oh Charl!'

The 'Charl' was almost a wail, of sorrow, of protest, and Jeb feared she would break down. If she did he wouldn't know what to do, or even what to call her. But then she governed herself. He could tell by the set of her head and shoulders. She had always possessed such extraordinary self-control.

'Eva says that one of the *polizei* who found him knew who he was.'

For several minutes she stood with her back to him looking out of the window. Then she had said, 'Tell me all about him when you were there. And Eva too.'

She had always resisted his attempts to discuss his visits to Eva and Hengelow. So now he gave her an account of everything he could remember. And throughout his narrative she had not looked around at him so that he had to gauge her response by the times that her shoulders shook in convulsions of silent weeping and the times when she was calm, lifting her hand to her nose occasionally. After he had finished she had thanked him and stated that she would prefer to be left alone now. She was like a stranger he had happened upon.

2

In the week that elapsed between this event and Aunt Peg's dinner party, it crossed Jeb's mind that Mallory might like to know about Hengelow. If he didn't already. Jeb thought of telephoning, though somehow they were no longer on phone-call terms. Not that this amounted to anything acrimonious.

After his return from Europe Mallory had quit Canberra. The grapevine spoke of a succession of part-time tutoring jobs, and said that, apart from his students Mallory was practically a recluse. Once during the 1970s, Jeb had caught sight of Mallory's groomed figure hurrying in a lane behind the Manuka shops. Their exchange of 'Hey, stranger!' and 'Jim, I've kept on meaning...' betrayed entirely all their acquaintance could now hope to be. They stood, shifting feet, in a patch of sunlight. Mallory, Jeb learned, now had a year's contract tutoring European History at a Newcastle College of Advanced Education.

'Sounds precarious.'

'It suits me. I'm not ambitious.'

'They tell me the students these days are still reading Noddy.'

'*I'm* still reading Noddy! It's documentary evidence.'

Their banter flickered in this way, then died. Impossible to recapture that spontaneity, that elusive self-forgetfulness of their earlier relations. It had run away like water through the fingers. 'Someone told me you didn't see anyone these days,' he heard himself asking, and was told in reply that Big Ford was in Newcastle running a stained-glass studio, and that Mallory and he met for a drink occasionally, but that yes, he supposed he didn't seek people out. Then he had revealed, 'You'd know Roni and I exchange letters two or three times a year.'

'I'd no idea. Why?'

'Friendship. She — they were special.'

'*Besondere Freunde.* She told me she thought you were charitable.'

'Untrue,' he smiled. Cold air funnelled up the lane.

'If they were special why weren't you tempted to stay with them?' Jeb asked at last.

Mallory shook his head. 'I don't have the nous for sustaining social relationships, Jim. They're too — unruly. We found that out, didn't we. Letters allow things to go along at my pace.' He grinned, then looked away.

Jeb broke the silence. 'So you took off from Frankfurt because you were getting impatient with me . . .'

'With myself, impatient with myself.'

'All right, but how come you gave up the doctorate and came back to this — these precarious tutorships? You should be a professor.'

Mallory actually began to back away. 'Same reason, Jim. I saw in your bloke Charlie,' he looked at his highly polished shoes, 'the kind of person I would very much like to have been. All that inexhaustible good cheer and good will. But I knew perfectly well I was too — circumspect. The discrepancy made me unhappy about,' he smiled, 'the history of organised sports.'

'And not the fact that Roni was devoted to him?'

Mallory shrugged. 'I prefer being low-profile. Personal significance rather repels me.' He had to go.

'Shall we drop each other a line occasionally?'

'Why not!'

But they never had. And so now, with the news of Hengelow, Jeb decided in the end not to write, or telephone. Let him find out from Ronya, if he hadn't already,

Though Jeb decided he would mention it in his next letter to Roma. Still adorable Roma. Over the decade he had received a succession of postcards from her, written in her large, oddly childlike handwriting, featuring the words 'fabulous', 'gorgeous', 'terrific' with great frequency, and had written back to various poste restantes around the world. On gaining her pass degree in what she had called 'Mainly Other Studies' she had gone, first to Hong Kong where she had taught Berlitz English for a year, then to Mombasa and across Africa on her wits and with various companions. 'Tuareg Men!' was all one of her postcards had said. In Spain she had moved in with a civil servant many years her senior and with him had gone to the Algarve, Tangier, the Canary Islands. 'Fabulous, Cherub, you can have no idea!' she wrote in her headlong style, so warm, so inscrutable.

And it was true, he could have no idea. His own travels had been so timid in comparison to Roma's globetrotting. But he would tell her about Hengelow. She had urged on him the original adventure. And there was something about the two, widely spaced in age as they were, that made them kindred spirits.

3

Now, a week later, leaving Mother's after Peg's dinner party, he took the winding road over Scrivener Dam and through the Stromlo Pine Forest. Above him, between the trees, like a thoroughfare in space, he could see the tracering lights of cars on the new freeway as they sped south toward Weston Creek and Tuggeranong or north to Belconnen, those satellite towns that had sprung up in the past dozen years, enfilading the hills, reaching far into the dark with delicate tentacles of orange lights. Yes, at times, driving toward its outer reaches in the dark, say, or descending upon it at night in an aeroplane, it did look like a vast space-station, modular, disconnected from a planetary past.

He turned off at Black Mountain Peninsula, parked facing the lake, and sat watching the sharp little waves that broke and drained in rapid succession. He got out and walked along the stony beach, passing rubbish bins that overflowed with beercans and icecream papers. A plastic bag whisked past him, ballooning and collapsing, while the wind felt as though it were straight from the Antarctic; it niggled up his sleeves and down his neck, driving odd spots of cold rain against his face. If he looked one way, across the lake toward Yarralumla, he could see the blurry splashes of street lamps around the water-police station. When he turned round, the massive shawled hump of Black Mountain seemed to loom over and, at the same time, gather in the foreshores of the lake. A new arrival. Yes, things from the past surface in conversation and suddenly you no longer inhabit the place you thought you did, but another where the familiar tenets of your existence have been shifted about, like a room where the furniture has been rearranged.

A few yards from where he was standing the school bell and its disgusting contents had lain on its side on that last day of sixth form. To his right across the water the wind was driving in flurries through the reeds and bare willow trees on the islet where he had sat in the late afternoon sunlight with Mallory on that same day in 1967. How governable things had seemed then. History is the facts and how you see them, Mallory had told him on that occasion. He certainly had the facts now.

Yet some kinds of revelation, he reflected, were not so very startling; the furniture shifted but the room remained the same. It was as if such revelations focussed rather than created realisation. Out of the blue, what had remained for years unspoken came forward as the explanation you had always expected, intricate, yes, articulate and somehow fresh, but not immediately shocking.

Until you thought what kind of a life Mother must have been leading for all that time. Atrocious.

The wind tugged and buffeted. The roar of the traffic underlay the sough of the gusts, monotonous like the hum of some ambient generator with occasionally the howl of a siren or a high-pitched acceleration rising above it. Jeb returned to his car and sat. Twenty yards away a late-1960s Holden station wagon was parked, its doors opening and slamming.

'Aw Bre-ett! Jeez, you're a nerd! Let me back in!' In the light from the car's interior he could see a girl with tufty blonde and orange hair and a leather jacket decorated with chains and insignia. She had been locked out. In the back seat of the car were people pashing — there seemed to be more than two of them. 'It's freezing out here. Bre-ett!' The girl rattled the handle of the door and smacked the window.

He tried to recall who had started the argument at Peg's. Probably Peg. She had a way of declaring her position on things. Though what the point at issue had been was also not particularly clear. Tact versus sincerity? Humbug versus genuine feelings? Expression versus restraint? In any case it had been Merrin defending the 1970s against something Peg had called 'real values'.

4

So the argument defined itself with Merrin beginning sentences, 'Back in the seventies what people of your generation never realised was . . .' and Peg countering with 'If that's what you *really* think, I feel sorry for you, young lady,' while Uncle Neville nodded each time either of the two disputants declared anything, leaned back in his chair and punctuated the discussion with, 'There are always two sides to a question.'

Meanwhile Mother sat quietly, the abstraction on her face suggesting one who was listening to something other than the foreground noise. Then, in a pause she observed, almost as though to herself. 'Do you know, I sometimes think we spend so much time quarrelling about what we can't recover that we lose the opportunities for love that are right under our noses.' Jeb could not recall having heard Mother use the word 'love' before. It was not her kind of word and again he had the momentary impression that here was a stranger. She smiled, glanced quickly at both Peg and Merrin, then looked down at her lap. Her remark paralysed the dispute. They all sat, their eyes downcast. Peg collected the dessert plates with a clatter and scraping, and ushered everyone into the neighbouring room for coffee. Merrin went to sit next to Mother.

'You sounded just now as if you were thinking about someone in particular.' The younger woman regarded the older, voicing the question quietly, sensing some mystery. Merrin had that same directness Jeb had admired in Roma, though Merrin was more political.

Mother said *No, not really, except that . . .* She was sitting upright and on the edge of the easy chair, her hands on her lap, like someone intending to stop only a moment. Jeb found he had to observe her sidelong because Aunt Peg had sat herself down beside him and was claiming his attention. Jeb could not say what instinct it was that made him want to eavesdrop on that conversation between Merrin and his mother, his listening infuriatingly hampered by Aunt Peg broaching the subject which, Jeb realised later, was the reason she had invited him and Merrin to dinner.

There had been this woman — an American, Mother was saying at the same time Peg was admonishing him for not giving up enough of his time for his mother, *who I knew. She had come through a very difficult time in her life.*

'Of course the news about Charlie has been a bigger shock than she is prepared to admit.' Peg half whispered, putting her head forward in such a way as to place it in Jeb's focal path.

She had been married, very happily, and had a child, then —

'When was it you said you knew this woman?' Jeb interrupted across the room.

His mother looked at him steadily before replying; the light from a standard lamp was behind her, casting her face into shadow. 'When we were stationed at Gattisby.' She dropped her gaze and continued, *there had been the war...*

'Of course these things run very much deeper than you could possibly know,' Peg continued, scarcely noticing he had asked Mother the question. She is telling, Jeb realised. She is about to tell.

... came through unscathed — he had been an airman.

'All before you were born of course —'

... he declared that he intended to leave her and the child. He was bent on — well, let us call it some kind of religious life... atonement; because of some experience he'd had in the immediate aftermath of the war. There was now a prior claim on his life, he told her. He didn't have any right to a cosy family life any more.

'And Len was such a trial for Lizzie...'

... so, while everyone else was returning to families, having children, setting up home life again, my American friend...

'... hulking awkward fellow, even if he is your half-brother.'

... as this man prepared to detach himself from her and their child. She would always stress that she knew she was no different from anyone in that situation, hurt, baffled, initially not wanting to let him go...

'... him with his convictions, not that I want to dwell on them...'

... so she fought to keep the three of them together. Had it been a hankering after bachelordom or another woman there might have been...

'... be thankful he seems to have kept out of trouble for a while...'

... some finality. But this 'having no right to a cosy family life,' she held it to be so arbitrary, so bullish of him. He'd done nothing thousands of others hadn't — so far as she could discover. You see, she had not only been devoted to him in the way of husband and wife. She had seen in him a profoundly humane man, one in whom charitable impulses were quite instinctual. She was something of an idealist herself, and had formed the idea of them both doing something dedicated with their lives after the war. So how could he then forsake her and the child, particularly when she could see there had been no loss of love? He needed her more than ever; she could see that much...

'But we're looking to you, young man.' Aunt Peg wavered across his sight.'

... And, as I say, she described this terrible time to me, knowing full well it was a perfectly common predicament for people to find themselves in. She supposed she was taking it hard. Sometimes she wished he had been killed in the war, or that she had... He used to aggravate the separation by returning at odd times to see her or take the boy out; and the fact that she thought his departure had always been, well, whimsical, meant that she often had high hopes he would stay. She tried to get pregnant again ...

'It will be your job ...'

... it went on for a year or so, until it became, as these things do, a protracted, dreary, part-yearning, part-bitter heartache.

'You know what I'm alluding to, don't you?' Peg was patting his knee.

Then it became so that she simply wanted release. Release at any cost, from the weariness of it, the staleness of it ...

'I think you do know,' Peg was twinkling and still patting his knee.

'No,' Jeb supplied, 'as a matter of fact I don't.'

Then one day she found she was dispellng him. That was the word she used, 'dispelling'. This was more than simply a matter of accepting his departure, she explained to me. It was a case of watching herself cease to value that part of her life she had spent with him and the child ...

'Grandchildren,' Peg twinkled again, pronouncing the word *sotto voce*. She nodded toward Merrin.

This revaluation, she once told me, was a quite physiological thing. Her system, as she put it, was pushing him out ... Her vital interest in him, and all that she had planned to be with him — the life of dedication and so on — simply evaporated. It was like experiencing a return to strength after an illness ...

'Grandchildren,' Peg reiterated. 'She needs grandchildren.' Jeb nodded, looking at his feet, wishing she would shut up.

... only that she found her interest in the boy evaporated too. She was unable to say why. At ten years old he had begun to resemble his father rather too closely. She thought that maybe she had never found the child particularly attractive, his secretive ways, his endless prattle about mechanical things, a certain hangdog look he had at times.

She thought perhaps her interest in him had really been an expression of her devotion to the father. Whatever. This — not repugnance, but indifference toward the child was what she immediately recognised as the cost of her release, the sting in the tail, as she thought of it. She lost interest in her child. She ceased to value her own child...

'... to give her an interest in life.'

It turned her, she told me, into the most conscientious of mothers...

'And none of us are getting any younger.'

No longer being able to take an interest, she manufactured one. It was, she told me, a problem of stagecraft, learning the right words, the looks, the gestures; writing long, dutiful letters to the child at his school, organising camps, encouraging hobbies. Whenever he was present, she felt she was on stage...

'So the ball is very much in your court, young man.'

... until she became so adept that she might not have been able to tell the difference between her performance and what had once been the real thing...

'You understand what I am saying, don't you, James?'

Except that the child himself was old enough to tell the difference, and while she saw that he knew, then she knew that she was indifferent as to what happened to him...

'James?'

'Yes, all right! I'll bear it in mind. Let's drop the subject.' He looked steadily at Mother, who was looking at the floor. Merrin was saying that it was terrible and how could men get away with warping the emotional lives of women like that, and Mother replied that it was a case of one man and one woman, and there were no generalisations to be made.

'What happened to her, to this American woman?' Jeb's question was cruel, knowing, as he did, the answer.

'Oh, she had remarried by the time I knew her.'

5

He parked in her driveway and turned the ignition off. They sat in the after-engine silence for a time, not looking at each other.

'You always sounded so natural when you were talking to Len. Like any mother talking to her son.'

'You are confusing me with the American woman,' Mother

replied quietly. She made no move to get out of the car, but searched in her bag for cigarettes and lit one.

Jeb said, 'The American woman remarried and had another child.'

'Yes.'

'This second child grew up and, as an adult, went to stay with his half-brother for a time.'

'I believe so.'

'They didn't get on very well, and on the last day of his stay the half-brother asked him rather maliciously, why their mother had never given him any brothers or sisters.' He glanced at her quickly, then stared through the steering wheel at the dashboard with its faintly green luminous numerals.

'I'm sad to hear they did not get on well.'

'Not that the younger brother believed the slur that his mother's second husband was not his real father.'

'He was the real father.'

'But even so he did not know the answer to his half-brother's question.'

Mother averted her head to gaze from the side window, so that Jeb could only see its fuzzy outline. She let the cigarette burn without putting it to her lips.

'It may have been a problem of nostalgia,' she began. 'The American woman — on those occasions we used to sit and talk about this; sometimes used to complain how difficult it was to recover the exactness, the — exquisiteness of a time past when there were only words to do it with. She had come to England before the war, had met her first husband at a school ...'

'Yes, I — I mean, the younger brother already knows most of this.'

But Mother continued regardless. 'He was a foreign languages teacher at one of those boarding places which take boys between the ages of six and thirteen. She had come very much under his spell. His energy, that boundless, cheerful outpouring of himself, his extraordinary self-possession. But not just *his* spell. She was an American visiting England. The picturesqueness of the country, the welcome from other members of his family, charmed her utterly, and she found herself in the midst of an existence more vivid, more joyous, than anything she had experienced before. They married. The child came after a year, and the war a year after that.

'He might easily have been exempted from military service on account of his foreign languages. But this was the time of "chipping in" and "doing one's bit". (Don't those old phrases sound so odd now, comic and grotesque like gas masks and brown sticky tape on windows.)

'They had left the pretty little school in Kent at the outbreak of war and had lived in a house which later got swallowed up by London...'

'It was drabber, more pinched,' she continued, ignoring the interjection. 'He had a job translating foreign newspapers and came home each evening. She looked after the child. Through the blackout they used to talk about how, after the war, perhaps they might go somewhere and start a school, Fiji, Sierra Leone, Trinidad, the three of them together, living in a concrete shack with running water for only a few hours a day. It would be an adventure; at the same time they would be committing themselves to something really worthwhile for people. "Doing something worthwhile"; there's another of those phrases. For his part, he had a genius for energising the altruism in other people.

'Then he was accepted for aircrew and went off to Canada. She felt his enlistment was a kind of betrayal. Not that she said anything; he had, after all, only done what the times required. But the vague sense of injury niggled away during the year or so he was in Canada and, upon his return she insisted they put the child into a boarding school — although he was only four at the time — because she intended to become engaged in the war effort also.

'Oh she was perfectly aware, as she told me, that this was a form of retaliation. So the child went off to school and both his parents went off to war. She knew, as she told me, that her little family had simply fallen apart, but he persuaded her the pieces could be glued back together when peace came along. He was such a force.'

'That didn't happen.'

'No earth floors, no Sierra Leone. The doing of something worthwhile became dissipated in those pinched post-war conditions of snook and rationing and, following his departure, in loneliness. Besides, watching him, she had begun to wonder about this business of "the worthwhile".'

'So she remarried?'

'She blamed him for the fact she had ceased to take an interest in the child. Occasionally, the boy would look at her with appeal in his eyes, but it affected her like a boy looking out of a newspaper photograph. Yes, she remarried, a jolly fellow who had been put in her way. She might have had some ideas about a fresh start...'

'But she found, after a while, that she didn't care for him much either.'

Mother was silent for some moments before responding. Then she said, 'My American friend would never allow me to put words into her mouth. "Care for"? She used the word "detachment". She could see her second husband was a good man and a kind one, more homely, more sedate than her first. But he aroused no vital interest in her, not as she remembered her first having done in the intensity of their lives before the war. You can see what she meant by the problem being partly one of nostalgia.

'She began to wonder whether feeling was a thing that could be *aroused* at all. Whether all feelings were not manufactured, or learned and rehearsed.

'She became, she assured me, an effective wife and mother, though never by conviction. Something in the apparatus had stopped working, some irreplaceable part. You can see the strain her second husband must have been under, for one can't hide these things.'

'They danced well together, the American woman and her husband. Did you know that?'

'Efficiently,' she answered, and looked at the ash delicately poised on the end of her cigarette. 'They danced efficiently. It was, so my friend told me, the one opportunity for self-forgetfulness she was allowed to keep.'

'And their child?'

The furze shook ever so slightly as she spoke. 'Some things

came naturally — she used to worry he would run out on the road or wander away and get lost...'

'But...'

'But she was unable to say that she ever experienced... *attachment*. Perhaps no one does.'

If this were a film, Jeb thought, a son placed in these circumstances would have taken his mother by her shoulders and cried out *Not even me! Not even me!* But Jeb continued to gaze into the dashboard as though it were the instruments themselves that were yielding the information. No, he would not take her by the shoulders and shake her. He was not the demonstrative type, one characteristic he had inherited from her.

'Of course, my friend always tried to recover what she believed she had lost, that sense of spontaneous attachment which most people take for granted is a consequence of marrying and having children. She kept mementos of her first husband, not through some kind of hopeless wishfulness, but as talismans from the time when she thought she had been capable of genuine feeling.'

'Like a painting for instance?'

'That kind of thing.'

'But she never did become — less detached.'

The furze shook.

'That still doesn't answer the question why she had no more children.'

'It does. How could she?'

'Did the second husband want more children?'

'Of course. But she would not have it.'

'I still don't see...'

'Because she did not have the conviction they would matter.'

Mother might have been weeping. It was hard to tell. They remained in the silence she had made so potent, she gazing resolutely out of the Mazda's side window, Jeb gazing at the dashboard.

'And the American woman...?' he asked at length.

'A person I knew at Oldenrath.' She had opened the door and was getting out.

'Gattisby,' Jeb corrected gently. 'You said it was Gattisby.'

She had closed the car door quietly. Again he thought he ought to do something, jump out of the car, run over and hold her for a moment, let her understand that, despite what he had just learned about her relationship with him, it was the piteous nature of her life throughout those years he felt most keenly. But the occasion slipped away. He heard her front door close.

6

The girl and her jingling insignia had been re-admitted to the station wagon, from which odd sounds still issued. After five minutes, Jeb saw a fellow get out and lob several beer bottles, one after another, toward one of the bins. All missed, most shattered. Then he got back in and, with revs and fishtailing, the car drove away.

The war. Old WW2 as Mallory had referred to it. How far-reaching its after-shocks appeared to be. It was forty years, almost exactly, since the firestorming of Hamburg, and here was a woman, his stranger/mother, revealing one of the consequences of that awesome event. A tremor, forty years and thousands of miles away from the epicentre. He felt helpless in the face of her sense of loss. Having left her less than an hour ago, he now did not know how he could ever again simply turn up at her house — at what had once been their house. He was unable to imagine what he might say to her, what he might do in her presence, knowing as he did that his own existence had never been — what was her phrase? of 'vital interest' to her. Her honesty, her self-knowledge, was breathtaking, the meticulous facade she had maintained throughout the years heroic, hideous, pathetic.

Certainly he could not project himself into a future which dealt with her, could not foresee how carelessly a sort of healing might begin, as, carelessly, as inevitably, say, as the bark of a tree will gradually pucker protectively around the raw place of a lopped limb. He could not foresee, for instance, how within a few weeks, Merrin, for whom Mother will become a subject of loosely ideological respect and practical affection, will arrange for the three of them to repaint the interior of her house, how he, himself, will watch unobtrusively as consultations about colour schemes, furniture rearrangements between Mother and Merrin circumvent, simply circumvent, what he thought were the emotional minefields between mother and son. Nor could he have conjured a picture of the woman who will stand quietly behind Aunt Peg and Merrin's bustling relatives, unwilling to handle the wrinkled, livid thing in its flimsy cotton and oversized nappy, the plastic name-tag around its ankle like a tiny manacle, but who, once or twice, when people's attention is directed elsewhere, will reach an experimental hand into the hospital crib and touch the wispy tuft of hair, the tight-shut eyes. These things, which will come in their time and take their place in his understanding, emerging each with its degree of surprise and fitness, were inconceivable now as the short wavelets broke against the shore like the crunching of glass.

He backed the car and began the drive home. He would not stay with Merrin tonight. She would raise the topic of 'the American woman', making her own interpolations. He preferred to let what he had heard sort itself out in his own mind a little first. He returned to his own bedsitter behind the shops. As he parked in his carport he noticed someone had sprayed some new graffiti. Among the directions to halt woodchipping and go solar rather than nuclear, there was now a cryptic assertion in large, ill-formed letters that 'PROUT LIVES. PROUT REIGNS!' Whoever Prout was.

Len 1983

He sat high in the pilot's seat. All the gauges on the instrument panel were inert. The curtains were open and the window ajar to allow the warm evening air into his room. He could hear Aunty with a pair of secateurs snipping in the garden. She had told him she was seventy this year. Sometimes he did think she looked a bit stooped, her hair becoming more white than silvery. But Aunty wouldn't change. She would go on forever.

He had gone across to Germany with her, for the funeral of Crispin Hengelow who had once been his father. He hadn't seen the man for ten years or more, and then only briefly. Came in the morning, left in the afternoon, never came back. After Crispin Hengelow had departed, Aunty had made him go into her study, then looked at him very hard and said that she thought he had been very wicked. Wicked. There was an old word. It went right back.

There had been hundreds of people in the church in Altona. Hundreds. They had filled the inside to capacity and those that could not squeeze in had crowded around the entrance. He had seen a woman who looked as if her face had melted like wax — she was grin-weeping on the arm of a younger woman and was one of the people who were allowed to sit near the coffin, like himself. The younger woman had approached Aunty and said something in English and in

German 'We are all the family of Charlie, I think,' then a word glook-something-or-other, which Aunty said meant they thought they were very lucky. Well, if that's what they thought. It had nothing to do with him. They had taken the little jar of ashes onto a ferry and tipped them in the river. And that had been the end of that. He had been worried he would be upset, but he wasn't. It hadn't affected him at all.

Snip-snip from the garden. There were bands of colour on the horizon, like the bands of colour you sometimes found in stones after they had been polished. He got down and closed the window and the curtains, then returned to the pilot's seat. In the ten years since his half-brother from Australia had visited him, Len had completed both the navigator's and the wireless operator's compartments, fitting the different electronic aids, a genuine Marconi T1154/R1155, and the H2S indicator and receiver. But genuine old parts from Lancs or Lincolns were getting thin on the ground these days. A few weeks back he had acquired three shop mannequins and dressed them in overalls, mae wests and harness, and placed them, one at the navigator's table, one before the r/t set, and one lying on his belly in the bomb-aimer's blister. Now the tape had been fitted, as had the reel. It was to be Hamburg again. Maximum effort. He began flicking switches. The room resounded with the roar of the Merlin engines. Maximum effort. By the time he got back from this one, (if he got back from this one — there was always the chance of getting the chop) he realised, it would be dark outside. He had completed nearly twenty tours. Getting on for a record.

OK, rear-gunner? OK, skip. OK, mid-upper? OK, bomb-aimer? and he leaned slightly out of his seat to look down into the forward part of the aeroplane where in the glow from the slide projector he could see, silhouetted, the helmeted head of the mannequin.